THE BONES OF BENEVOLENCE

The Benevolence & Blood Series

The Bones of Benevolence

Lauren M. Leasure

To Steven — for taking care of me when I couldn't take
care of myself

And to my family — skip the prologue. Please. You know what?
Just text me and I'll tell you all the chapters to skip.

Stay in Touch

http://www.instagram.com/laurenmleasure
http://www.facebook.com/laurenmleasure

Receive special offers, giveaways, discounts, bonus content, and updates from the author by signing up for the newsletter at http://www.laurenmleasure.com

Content Warning

This book includes content that may be sensitive for some readers, including

- Profanity
- Violence and death
- Blood and gore
- Loss of family members
- Explicit sexual content
- Mental health and suicide
- Sexual violence
- Drugs and addiction
- Mental and emotional abuse

THE CONTINENT OF
ASTRAN

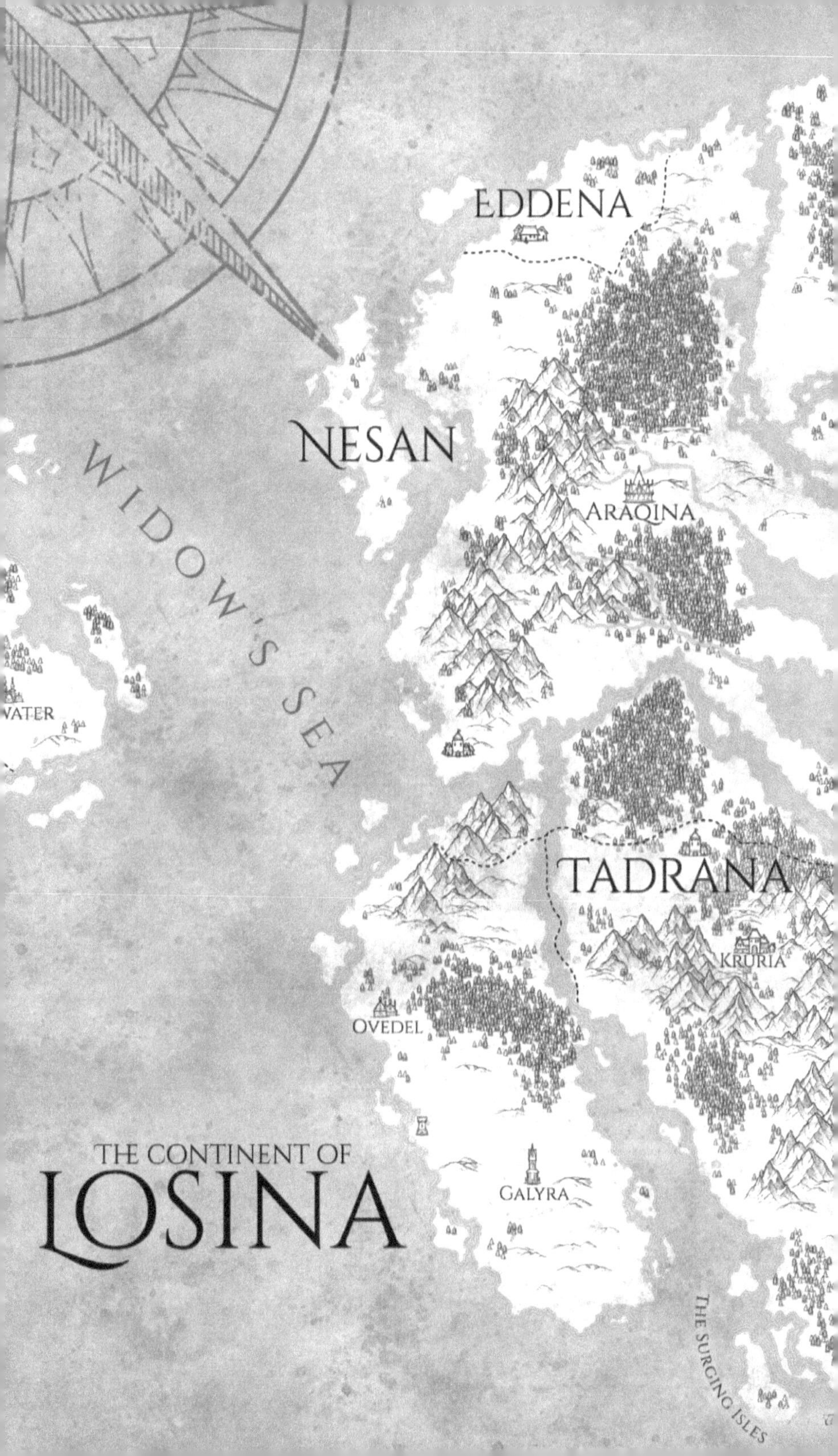

EDDENA
NESAN
ARAQINA
WIDOW'S SEA
TADRANA
KRURIA
...VATER
OVEDEL
GALYRA
THE CONTINENT OF
LOSINA
THE SURGING ISLES

The Benevolent Saints
Katia, Keeper of the Benevolent Saints
Tolar, Saint of Wealth
Onera, Saint of Miracles
Aanh, Saint of the Home
Soren, Saint of Heaven

The Blood Saints
Rhedros, Keeper of the Blood Saints
Faldyr, Saint of War
Liara, Saint of Hell
Idros, Saint of Storms
Noros, Saint of Pain
Cyen, Saint of Death

Pronunciation Guide

People

Petra – PETCH-ruh
Larka – LARK-uh
Evarius Castemont – ev-AIR-ee-us CAST-uh-mont
Calomyr – CAL-uh-mere
Miles – MY-uls
Bernadet – ber-nuh-DETT
Alvar – AHL-var
Solise – SOH-lees
Umbri – UHM-bree
Enella Augen – uh-NELL-uh AWG-in
Sentos Whitley – SEN-tows WIT-lee
Olion Summercut – OH-lee-awn SUH-mer-cut
Irabel – EE-ruh-bel
Sarek – SARE-ek
Wrena – REN-uh
Tyrak – TEE-rik
Kauvras – KOVE-ris
Ludovicus – lu-DOH-vuh-kiss
Raolin – ROWL-in
Balthazar – BAL-thuh-zar
Arturius – ar-TUR-ee-us
Anton – ANT-awn
Higgins – HIG-ins
Garit – GARE-it
Elin – EE-lin
Umfray – UM-fray
Belin – BAY-lin

Places

Eserene – ES-er-een
Aera – AYR-uh
Widoras – wid-DOR-is
Sidus – SIGH-dis
Prisma – PRIZ-muh
Ockhull – OCK-ul
Taitha – TAY-tha
Cabillia – cuh-BILL-ee-uh
Xomma – ZO-muh
Nesan – nuh-SAN
Eddena – eh-DEEN-uh
Malarrey – muh-LAR-ee
Tadrana – tuh-DRAH-nuh
Astran – AST-ran

Prologue

Four Years Ago

Fuck. I couldn't believe I was actually doing this.

"Is this the King's bedroom?" Her eyes were wide and sparkling under the light of the chandelier. All I could do was smile at her surprise. She had no idea this was my keep. She had no idea we were standing in my bedroom. "Calomyr, we cannot be here!"

"But we can," I answered, watching her eyes scan the room once again, completely unaware that the paintings on the walls were mine, the fine woven rugs were mine, the blades that hung above the fireplace... All mine.

"But what if–"

I kissed her, because every word she spoke pushed me one step further back from the edge, and I needed to jump. The cold reality of what I had to do was unavoidable, and my resolve was faltering. I couldn't lose my nerve. It had to be tonight.

"What if we just enjoy it?" I whispered, severing myself from her only far enough to see her bite down on her lip. Fuck. My cock stiffened at the sight of it, and I felt her go weak for a moment. I couldn't keep back the groan that formed in my throat. "You bite that lip, and it makes me want to—"

Focus.

I pulled her to me again, fighting to keep my mind on my task as I kissed her. But *fuck*, she was melting into me already. She smelled like sweet oranges and rosewater, and I could feel myself getting high on it. "I was tired of being quiet. I won't have to cover your mouth here," I breathed as I lifted her. My hands squeezed her ass and she wrapped her legs around me, a soft moan escaping her lips. Saints, I loved the noises she made for me, and I knew they wouldn't be stopping any time tonight. "The Keep is ours for the night."

"Cal, this is too much, this is—"

"Petra." My breath came too quickly and I fought for control. I didn't want to kill her any more now than I did when Castemont first suggested this plan, that I get close enough to the Daughter of Katia to kill her and keep her from burning the world at her hand. I closed my eyes, leaning my forehead against hers, and nodded to myself.

She may not be a queen, but tonight, she'd die as mine.

I fought with every ounce of strength I had to keep my will from being swallowed up by those autumn eyes as I pulled back to stare at her. "If you don't mind, I'm going to fuck you in the King's bed now."

She gasped, her want was almost tangible. I knew what those words would do to her. "As you wish." Her body heated against me and her hair fell around her shoulders as I laid her on the bed. Looking down at her, seeing her ready and willing, her eyes nervously looking around the room, afraid to be caught, the slight smile, the blush on her cheeks...

This. This is what I'd remember until my dying breath. Her, here, waiting for me.

It was time.

20

I fought to give her the smile she deserved as I stood above her, pulling my tunic over my head, using the split second the fabric covered my face to reinforce my will. And I'm glad I did, because when I looked down at her again, at the hunger that lined her face as she stared at me...

She could so easily be my undoing.

My belt and sword found the floor, but my eyes flicked to the bed for a tiny moment, reminding myself where the dagger was tucked under the mattress. It was a fight to keep my breathing even as dread rose in my chest. I leaned over her, my thumbs running up and down her neck as I stared down at her. "You are my Queen," I whispered, "and I'd like to treat you as such."

I knew that fire lurked somewhere deep within her, but in that moment, I thought to myself that just a look was enough to incinerate me right here, right now. Then she dropped her head to one side and pulled my thumb into her mouth, grazing her teeth across my skin. *Saints.* I let my eyes roll back in my head as I lost myself in the moment, pressing my thumb further into her mouth. Need throbbed through me as I trailed my thumb down her body, playing with the hem of her tunic as my other hand found its way to her waistband.

She pushed me away suddenly, and I froze for a second. Did she somehow know what I was going to do? But she drove me back to the bed and slung her tunic to the floor, her pants quickly following.

Petra stood over me in all her divinity, and I realized then that if she commanded it, I'd make sure all the stars in the sky bowed to her, along with every tree in every forest and every peak of every mountain if that's what she wanted.

But her command tonight was much simpler. "Off," she ordered, pointing to my pants. "Your Queen commands it."

I can't lose my nerve.

I did as I was bid then dropped to my knees before her. Panic settled into my body as I convinced myself to keep going. The feel of her skin on my hands, the taste of her in my mouth... I tried to commit it all to memory as I looked up at her, at the woman who, according to Castemont, would one day burn the world and everyone in it. She looked down at me like I was the answer to a lifelong prayer.

In the bedroom that she didn't know was mine, I imagined, for just a moment, that I didn't have to kill her. That'd we'd found each other in this life by accident, not by Castemont's design. I imagined, for just a moment, that she was truly my Queen, and I her King, as we made love high above the country we ruled together.

I was high on the thought of it, but shame quickly rushed in. All the color in the room turned gray as I clung to this final moment here, with her. "I could worship you forever," I whispered. I wasn't lying.

"Worship me later," she answered. "Your Queen would like to be fucked now."

For what was to be the last time, I did as she commanded. I grabbed her by the waist and tossed her to the bed like she was nothing. I couldn't look her in the eye any longer. I couldn't bear the thought of seeing her hurt. I flipped her on her belly and angled her hips up. "As you wish, my Queen." My voice was dangerously close to breaking as I quickly retrieved the dagger from beneath the mattress and placed it beside me. She couldn't see it, but it gleamed in the low light, relentlessly taunting me.

I was going to do it. I had to do it.

Her body opened like it was made for me as I thrust into her. My hands rested on her shoulders for a brief moment before I reached for the dagger, the blade shaking in my grip as I pointed the tip straight at her back, physical bliss and mental anguish running through me as I pounded into her.

"Scream for me," I ordered. Maybe if she screamed in pleasure, it would disguise the scream of pain that was coming for her. The scream of ultimate betrayal. "I want to hear you scream my name, Petra." *Louder. Please, for the love of the Saints, louder.*

22

"Calomyr," she moaned. It was like the name took the blade from my hand and drove it straight into my chest. Because it wasn't my name. She wasn't making love to me, she was making love to Calomyr.

Blade still aimed at her back, I willed myself to *fucking do it.*

No. I couldn't stab her in the back. If she was going to die as my Queen, she deserved the rightful dignity of the title. I pulled her to me, her head tipping back instantly, her eyes closed as I hooked one arm around her and aimed the dagger for her ribs. I reached my other hand between her legs, needing her to scream louder, needing her dying screams to sound something like ecstasy.

My mouth was pressed to her neck as I tried to keep myself from groaning, but it was no use. "Oh Saints." Her head fell forward and a part of me hoped she'd see the dagger, turn it on me, and end this all-consuming anguish. But her head quickly tipped back again as her body seized against me, completely unaware that her death was near and I was the one who would deliver it. My hand trembled and my knuckles were white as Petra pulled on every heartstring, gripping my soul between her delicate hands, threatening to break it in half.

She fit against me like the Saints had sewn us from the same cloth, carved us from the same stone, sculpted us from the same heartache. It was like they'd lit both of our fires with the same flame. But my flame was metaphorical. Petra's flame was real, and it would be the end of us all. She had to die.

I plunged the dagger inward–

And stopped short when she let out a whimper. The tiny, insignificant sound resounded through me. It grew louder and louder as it ricocheted off my last bit of will.

No.

I wouldn't do it. I couldn't do it. No part of me was capable, no matter how necessary it was.

I pulled back, just enough to toss the dagger to the ground, the *thud* muffled by the thick rug. It landed out of her line of sight as I grabbed her by the hips and turned her toward me.

Autumn eyes full of emotion met mine, and all the air left my body at the sight. I didn't care if she was prophesied to be the destruction of the world. Hell, I'd help her start the fire. "I want to look at you," I breathed. I hoped, in that moment, that my eyes could tell her everything I couldn't say. I hoped that she could figure out the truth that I was bound by blood against my will to keep hidden. I entered her again, watching her eyes widen as I pushed deeper, held tighter, fought harder.

I was done. I was out. I would march to Castemont and tell him I'd have no part of his plan any longer, consequences be damned. Petra would know the whole truth. As soon as it was safe to tell her, she'd know.

My lips brushed against her mouth as I leaned over her. "For as long as I live, I will remember this night." It was a promise that I intended to keep, knowing very well that Castemont may be the reason my life was cut short. But if it meant that she lived, then I'd gladly die tomorrow.

I unleashed on her, years of pent up resentment and self-control escaping through my movements as I drove into her again and again, feeling her tightening around me as she moved closer and closer to release.

She cried out, and it was the sweetest music I'd ever heard, enough to do me in. I reared back and clutched her waist with one hand while I pumped myself with the other. I wanted to scream out the truth, but it was her name that sounded instead. "Petra." Oh *Saints*, she stared into my eyes as we came together, her body writhing beneath me. "*Fuck*, Petra."

I would spend the rest of my life making her feel like this, no matter how long that life may be. If the prophecy was true then she didn't need my protection, but I knew in that moment I'd fall on my own blade if there was even a chance it would keep her out of Castemont's hands.

24

Her fingers caressed my cheeks as I stared, my soul laid bare for her. "Every day," I breathed, "I thank the Saints every day that they sent you to me."

PART I

Petra

Chapter 1

"Fuck you." I spat the words through gritted teeth, ready to incinerate the man who stood at the other end of my reach. The hot fury that coursed through every part of me was still foreign, but I let it grow, let it build into the firestorm I knew it could be. It hurt — *Saints* it hurt, like my body was being damned by Noros, Saint of Pain himself.

Seeing Lord Evarius Castemont's face further stoked the flames that were scorching me from within. His narrowed brown eyes, his nauseating smirk. "This is exactly where you're supposed to be, Petra," he replied nonchalantly, taking a step closer.

"Come any closer and I'll–"

"You'll what, dear?" His voice was thick with condescension.

I let myself explode, let Katia and Rhedros take control of me as I unleashed every ounce of my rage, every ounce of Benevolence and Blood as fire shot from my palms. The wind came next, punishing and ruthless, and Castemont's figure was obscured by the inferno. I let my head drop back in sweet relief knowing that somewhere among the flames that whipped and crackled, his dying screams were growing more anguished, more frantic, more–

A sudden pulse of energy pushed me back, my feet sliding against the gray stone floor of the Taithan throne room as adrenaline and confusion combined. The energy I expelled was hitting a wall, and that wall was growing, expanding, pushing harder and harder against me. Blue flames collided with mine, the force blowing me back even further as I leaned into it, desperately trying to keep my footing.

The light was near blinding as I tried to make out what was on the other side. Those blue flames grew higher, quickly overtaking mine as I felt the power inside me begin to waver and weaken. I opened my mouth to scream out for Katia or Rhedros — my mother and father — for any help against whatever this was, but the words died in my throat as my flames died too, snuffed out as if they were simply a candle in a hurricane.

I scrambled backward away from the blue flames, but it was no use — they wrapped around me, binding me in place like chains. But instead of burning heat, the flames pulsed with something icy. It was so cold that my body began to go numb, and soon my skin was cracking like ice on a pond.

What the fuck was happening?

The flames that subdued me remained as the rest of the room calmed again. Lord Castemont stepped forward, his hands clasped behind his back as he surveyed me with disdain.

"You were saying?" he hummed triumphantly, one brow raised and a crooked smile marking his face.

How?

I shot upright, my breath leaving my body in heaving gasps as my hands grappled for icy chains that weren't there. The room in the Taithan castle where I'd been dumped by Castemont materialized around me as I blinked wildly, trying to clear the fear from my head.

A nightmare. It had been a nightmare. It wasn't real. And yet, I was awakening to another nightmare entirely, and this one was real. Agonizingly real.

I glanced at the ceiling, finding nothing to center me in this new hell in which I found myself. Who was I now? I was no longer the poor girl from Inkwell. I was no longer the step-daughter of a powerful Eserenian lord. I was the prophesied Daughter of Katia, Keeper of the Benevolent Saints. I was the seemingly un-expected Daughter of Rhedros, Keeper of the Blood Saints. And I had no idea what any of it meant. I closed my eyes, hoping for the sweet oblivion of sleep to take me away from it all once more.

"Your Majesty," a rough whisper cleaved through the silence.

My head whirled around to see a gaunt face peering down at me. I scrambled backwards on the bed, away from the stranger, my defenses up. "Who the fuck are you?"

"I'm sorry to wake you," he whispered, his eyes wide. "My name is Tomkin. I don't have much time." His movements were shaky and nervous as he looked over his shoulder at the closed door. Only then did I notice the armor, the metal dark as liquid night against his sandy blonde hair and hazel eyes. A Cabillian soldier.

"Take this," he said, handing me a small canvas pouch before launching himself at the door, feet surprisingly silent despite his heavy boots. Hand on the doorknob, he quickly turned back to me, his voice just above a whisper. "You have friends in Taitha."

And he was gone.

Dawn was beginning to break, the dim silver tones casting shadows throughout the room as I sat dumbfounded, staring at the door. My heart still pounded against my ribcage, and I could feel raw exhaustion pressing down on me, heavy and demanding.

As I opened the small canvas bag, a candle the color of blood tumbled into my lap along with two small pieces of parchment. I squinted at the first one, which looked like a page torn from a book with a handwritten scribble at the top.

The Prophecy

FROM THE DEPTHS OF THE DEPTHS

OF A WALLED CITY'S SCUM

'NEATH THE HOLIEST MOON

THE PROMISED WILL COME

A DAUGHTER DIVINE

WITH BLOOD OF OLD CREED

AND THE WORLD WILL FORGET

THAT ON PAIN THE DEMONS FEED

I read through it three times, trying to make sense of the words printed on the page. *The Prophecy*. This is what the realm was waiting for? This is why the Board of Blood held Initiation? I peered down at the second piece of paper — a note.

> Daughter of Katia,
> You are safe in your room, guarded by those whose hearts beat only to protect you. You have an army at your disposal ready and willing to follow the Daughter of Katia. Cabillia is yours. Should you desire it, Lord Castemont and King Kauvras will be captured on your behalf. Light this candle and place it in the window come nightfall and your will shall be done.
> The prophecy was right....You and your power have arrived. We've been waiting a long time for you.

My stomach dropped as I folded the unsigned note between my fingers. My eyes shot to the narrow gap between the door and the ground where shadows marked the feet of the two guards standing just outside. *Holy shit.* My head spun as I frantically held onto the tiny sliver of hope that had come in the canvas bag.

But nightfall.

I had to wait until nightfall to light the candle, and by nightfall I'd be wed to Kauvras if he had his way. I'd be his *wife*. Nausea pooled in my gut as I gasped for breath. This was too much. This was far, far too much.

Devastation mixed with something sour as I thought of my mother, one of thousands of Vacants in Kauvras' army of leechthorn-addicted fiends, each one dead to the world and seen only as a disposable weapon. Solise's face popped into my thoughts next. I knew the healer's tiny form was huddled somewhere in the dungeons below the Taithan castle.

I tried to keep my mind from wandering further into the darkness, but I couldn't ignore it. Calomyr. Except Calomyr didn't even exist. He never had. He was King Belin Cal Myrin, the Invisible King of Widoras. He, too, sat somewhere in the dungeons, his memory in my head muddied by deceit and hurt.

I folded myself in half on the bed, squeezing my eyes shut against the blue flames that still danced in my head, staring at the shadow of boots outside my door.

Chapter 2

The only window in my room was barred, reminding me that while I may be sitting in a castle, it was nothing more than a royal prison. I stared through the beams of metal as the rising sun cast Taitha in shades of gold. Sounds drifted in — the rhythmic whoosh of brooms sweeping over cobblestone, the squeak of creaky windows being thrown open, the townspeople and their greetings of *good morning* and *lovely day* and *nice to see you*. My bottom lip had been chewed raw somewhere between all the worrying and at some point, I'd taken to gnawing on my finger-nails. The note that Tomkin had left lay on the bed next to the blood-red candle. I tried to take a deep breath, force the air into my lungs, but my chest felt too tight.

"Petra," a familiar, raspy voice breathed.

I turned, my eyes finding the metal ram's head mask that sat on Lieutenant Miles Landgrave's head as he slipped silently through the door. He'd been the one to drop me at Kauvras' feet. He'd been the one who'd wanted to trade me to the madman for answers about his past. My feet began moving back, my head shooting side to side, instinctively looking for something to protect myself against the man who'd seen to my downfall.

Miles threw his hands up in supplication. I slowed, unable to guess his intentions without seeing the face behind the mask. I *hated* not being able to read his expression, to look for the tiny cues a face would show. He inhaled sharply. "I'm not here to… Can we talk?"

My brows rose, looking the man up and down as I scoffed. "You want to *talk?* You deliver me to…this," I waved my hands at my glorified cell, "and you want to *talk?*"

He took a cautious step forward. "I didn't know," he whispered desperately.

I laughed, the sound harsh and dry. "You knew exactly what would happen when you delivered me to Kauvras. You *told* me as much, that you were going to trade me to get your *answers.*"

His broad shoulders rose and fell. I caught a quick glimpse of the angry, mottled scar under his chin as he tipped his head back in exasperation. "I–"

"Take your mask off," I demanded, my voice hard but barely above a whisper.

"Why?" he whispered.

"So I know who I'm talking to."

"I can't," he said, the words small.

"Take your *fucking* mask off. I want to see your face. There's no damned leechthorn around, so there's no reason to wear it." The thought of leechthorn turned my stomach, and I could almost taste the acrid smoke that had somehow hooked every other person who'd breathed it in…except for me.

"I can't." I swore I heard his jaw clench. Rage bloomed fast and hot in my chest.

I may not have known who I was, but I knew who I wasn't, and that was a person who was going to take any shit from Miles Landgrave. I stalked toward him, toward his massive frame that loomed over me. I could tell he felt small under my gaze even as

I looked up at him, that my stare burned into his skin. "Everything has been taken from me. Do you understand that? Everything I thought I knew... It's all been a lie." My teeth were gritted, the words searing my mouth as I spoke them. "I don't know who I am. I don't know what's going on. I don't know what's going to happen, and I don't want any of this. Now take your fucking mask off so I know who the fuck I'm talking to."

"I *can't*, Petra," he hissed.

My eyes didn't leave him as I remembered–

"Give me my dagger back," I demanded abruptly. He'd taken my dagger on the journey between the Onyx Pass and Taitha, the dagger that someone had left for me in my bathing room back in Eserene before Initiation. The words *THE MERCY OF KATIA* were inscribed on one side and *THE FURY OF RHEDROS* on the other. I had no idea who'd left it for me, or why they chose to do so. "I want it back. Now."

He shifted on his feet at the sudden change of subject. "I, uh..." He cleared his throat, but it did nothing to remedy the coarseness that always lined his voice. "I handed it over to Castemont."

My blood went cold in my veins. "You *what?*"

"It was before I knew... I'm sorry, Petra."

My teeth gnashed together as I stared. "You bastard. You absolute fucking bast–"

"Did you get my note?"

The mask of severity I had sculpted to my own face melted into genuine surprise at his words. I felt my nostrils flare as my eyes moved back and forth between the metal eye slits of the ram. "*You* sent the note?"

Sudden noise in the hall broke the fragile silence and Miles jumped back, head whirling to the door. One echoey voice rose above all the others. "I'd like to see my bride."

Kauvras.

Miles bolted, hurtling through the bathing room door within half a second as the scrape of the guards' boots sounded just out-

36

side. "Of course, your Majesty," one of them said, the door swinging open to reveal Kauvras' form in the doorway. The Rebel King of Cabillia. My captor.

Parts of him looked so much like his son. So much like Calomyr. *Belin.* The set of his shoulders, his steady gait. I had to remind myself not to freeze under Kauvras' sapphire stare.

"My beautiful Petra," he cooed, his face lighting with an almost boyish joy. It took everything in me not to look toward the bathing room door as he stepped toward me. "Did you sleep well?"

I stayed silent, wide eyed as he stared down at me. I debated telling him about the man hiding in the bathing room, debated using what little sway I may have had over my *betrothed* to have Miles thrown in the dungeon. But I kept my mouth shut, thinking only of the note, of the answers only Miles could have as Kauvras continued staring down at me with eyes of molten sapphire.

Somewhere in me, my fire smoldered. Should I let it flare and end Kauvras' life? It didn't sound like a bad idea. But something stopped me, something in the way he looked at me.

"Oh, darling, don't be shy," he crooned, reaching for my hands. "The Saints finally led you to me." I recoiled at his touch, my hands going limp in his grasp. "We'll have plenty of time to get to know each other." His eyes shone with something unstable, something unhinged and erratic, but there was something else there, though I couldn't figure out what. It made my skin crawl and sent a chill up my spine so shuddersome that I had to look away. "Breakfast will arrive for you soon," he continued, "and your gown soon after. The seamstresses worked on it all night."

That boyish joy stayed constant on his face. It almost made me feel sorry for him, almost as if that joy were innocence thrown like a threadbare blanket over something rotten and decaying. "Apologies for keeping you in this room. You don't seem to understand yet that you can't run from your fate. We'll be married before nightfall."

Shit. The candle. I prayed he didn't look behind me to where the only piece of my possible salvation lay on the bed, the pieces of parchment still folded next to it. *Shit shit shit.*

"Water," I blurted. "I'd like water. Please." *Just get out of here.*

He nodded. "Of course, my dear. I'll have some brought to you at once. And I will see you at the altar, my future queen." He sketched a bow, slipping through the doorway.

I was still frozen in place as one of the guards — unmasked — reached in to shut the door, but not before looking at me and giving me a curt nod.

The note had said that those who guarded my room were my...*protectors.* Was that nod supposed to mean something?

Silence settled as I rushed to stash the note and candle beneath the pillow. The masked Lieutenant stepped back into the room.

"I hadn't met him," he whispered, glancing warily toward the door. "Before yesterday, I'd never even seen him in person. I didn't know he was the Invisible King's father. And I didn't know that he was so..."

"Mad?" I whispered back, my own gaze not breaking from the door. "He's fucking *mad.* And you serve him. Blindly."

The ram turned to face me. "I'm sorry," he murmured, his voice grave. "I'm sorry I did this to you."

The apology bounced off me, the words meaningless in the face of their consequences. All I could do was stare at him. "Did you get your answers?" I whispered.

I had never wished for that stupid fucking mask to be gone more than this moment. He stared at me from behind the metal, something rippling off of him that I couldn't place. It was thick, weighted with words he hadn't said, and I knew he wouldn't.

"Go," I said flatly.

"Use the candle," he breathed, "even if it's..." He swallowed hard, the scar beneath his chin bobbing. "Even if it's in his chambers."

My stomach bottomed out at his words, bumps rising on my skin at the thought as he slipped out the door, leaving me in the sickening silence of reality.

◆ ◆ ◆

Three pieces of fruit. I'd make myself eat at least three pieces of fruit. I stared at the tray of breakfast that had been delivered to my room, trying to work up the nerve to bring the fork to my mouth. I fought down two strawberries and a chunk of melon, but let the eggs go cold. I stared at the mug of water, its surface rippling as I sat motionless.

Think, Petra. Miles told me I could put the candle in the window of Kauvras' room. But how the hell was I supposed to get it from my room to his without him seeing? I pushed away the plates in front of me, the fruit suddenly souring in my stomach as I considered what today would bring.

A knock on the door split my concentration and two small women entered, one on each end of a rolling rack, a massive garment bag hanging from the bar. "Your Majesty," one of them said, bowing her head. I snorted at the word, the sound startling the two women. "Your gown."

I didn't say anything as they shuffled in, throwing the room's wooden wardrobe open, hanging and unfurling the massive gown from its bag. I stared at the ruffles, at how similar it looked to the traditional Eserenian Initiation gown I had sewn for myself. I didn't know where it had been taken after I peeled the bloody, crusted fabric from my body yesterday, but I was glad it was gone.

Except for the fact that it was back in the form of an equally monstrous wedding gown.

The women smoothed the garment, the fabric splayed across the floor as they straightened the train. "Eserenian crystals, from your home," one of the women said quietly, pointing to the tiny stones affixed to the bodice. "Hand-sewn, your Majesty. Feel free to inspect them yourself. As closely as you wish." The two women quickly bowed their heads and left me staring as they slipped from the room. I stalked to the bed, pulling the thin pillow back to reveal where I'd hidden the candle and note.

We've been waiting a long time for you. I read the words over and over. Was I the only person in the entire fucking world who had never heard of the prophesied Daughter of Katia? And was nobody waiting for the Daughter of Rhedros? I tucked the note back under the pillow, starting for the gown hanging in the wardrobe, the gown that symbolized my fate.

In order to make it to nightfall, I'd have to marry Kauvras.

I ran my hands across the fabric, an overwhelming wave of longing crashing over me as I thought of Larka. The laugh my sister would have let out if she saw the gown... I could almost hear it. She'd make some joke about wiping her ass with the dress before suggesting we stuff it through the bars on the window and watch it fly to the street below. *Good fucking riddance*, she would have said.

I choked back a sob at the thought, letting my fingers trail over the intricate white lace that was sewn over silk. The sleeves ended in a delicate fringe, somehow elaborate and simple all at once. The crystals on the bodice glimmered softly in the light, reminiscent of the ghost of a life I'd once lived. My fingers caught on one that was slightly loose, and the crystal pinged to the floor, a tiny hole left behind and...

Something poked out. My eyes shot wide, peering instinctively back to the door before working the tiny *something* out of the slit in the fabric, tucked into the lining of the bodice.

It was a slip of rolled parchment. My hands grew clammy instantly, my stomach whooshing with hope and fear and desperation.

Under the dress. For the candle.

Before I knew it I was ducking to the ground, throwing layers of ruffled silk and tulle over my head, searching, searching, searching–

40

A thin elastic strap had been sewn inside the dress at the seam between the bodice and the skirts, just wide enough for the candle that lay under my pillow. It was so small I never would have noticed it was there.

A smile cracked across my lips, a quiet sob breaking with it as I climbed out from the ruffles, out into the idea that hope was here, even if it was as tiny as the strip of parchment in my hands.

◆ ◆ ◆

"You'll be retrieved in one hour's time," a monotone guard announced in my doorway. I didn't have the energy nor the heart to look back at him, to see if his face gave me clues as to his allegiance. I sat at the small vanity in my room, my unwashed caramel hair twisted into some semblance of something presentable. I'd found kohl in the drawer and ran it across my lashes, hoping it would help distract from the exhaustion that shadowed my eyes. At this point, I didn't think Onera, Saint of Miracles herself could've helped me.

I wished Solise were here now. More than my own mother, I wished Solise were here to talk to me, to tell me everything was going to be okay, to tell me I'd get out of here. As soon as I was retrieved from Kauvras' chambers, I'd send someone to get Solise from the dungeons. I breathed in as I repeated the plan to myself.

But she wasn't the only one imprisoned. My heart hammered in my chest at the thought of Cal. *No, Belin.* I felt the anguish in every bone of my body, felt its claws begging to pull me apart, consume me piece by piece. I pushed *Belin* from my mind and faced the mirror, finding hollow brown eyes staring back at me.

The diadem modeled after Katia's own sat on the vanity. The diadem that Castemont had given me. I clenched my jaw in anger at the irony, at the fucking *nerve* of the man. But I let the crown give me strength and willed the power of Katia to run through my body as I nestled it atop my head.

Exhaling, I stared at myself in the mirror again, the square set of my jaw, the smudges of purple beneath my eyes, the sharp nose that had never looked like Larka's for a reason I now knew — because I wasn't her sister by blood.

"Please," I whispered into the quiet, thinking that maybe Katia could hear me. I didn't know what I wanted, I just knew I needed someone.

Silence was the only answer.

I turned, the gown still hanging in the wardrobe. It was time. I unbuttoned and rebuttoned and pulled and tucked until it was fitted to my body, the gown hugging my figure perfectly. I reached for the veil that had been gently tucked onto the hanger and pinned it into my hair, throwing the tulle back from my face and repositioning the diadem. I avoided looking at myself in the mirror as I snatched the candle from under the pillow, hiking the ruffles of my skirts up to find the strap and pull it through.

A voice rang from the hallway, lilting and sick in its familiarity. I let my skirts fall as footsteps neared. The door clicked open to reveal Castemont in a pitch black surcoat stitched with the gold dragon of the Cabillian crest.

"What the fuck are you doing here?" I spat.

He laughed. He fucking *laughed* as he stalked toward me. "You look beautiful, Petra. Absolutely perfect."

"What are you doing here?" I repeated.

"I suppose, since your father is otherwise indisposed, I'll be the one giving you away." His tone edged on amusement.

My eyes narrowed, the anger growing even hotter in my chest. "My father isn't here because you *killed him*."

"I didn't kill your father."

"Rhedros is not my father."

He scoffed. "Rhedros *is* your father. Sarek Gaignory was no more your father than I am. Now we're going to be late. Come along."

I felt my face flush with fury at his words, hot vitriol bubbling in my mouth like boiling oil. "No."

42

"No?" he asked, a brow cocking atop a face still etched with humor. I stared, fists clenched at my sides as I steadied my feet on the ground. He sighed, an arm crossing across his chest, the other resting atop it while a hand held his cheek. "I'm not sure when you'll realize that you don't have a choice, Petra."

I seethed, my eyes flooding. "I never had a choice, did I?"

"You had the choice to cooperate and do as you were told, but you decided against that. So I'm afraid that privilege has been revoked."

"You never loved my mother, did you?" I knew the answer, but this tiny part of me clung to the hope that somewhere in him was something *good*. My hands trembled, white knuckled. My stare was hard and unforgiving as I surveyed the man in front of me. The man who had promised us the world. The man who had promised to protect my mother, the woman now expending all of her energy in search of leechthorn.

For a long moment he stared at me, his face unreadable. As much as I wanted to shrivel up and fade away, I refused to cower under his gaze. His lips pursed ever so slightly, as if words were fighting to be spoken. Finally, without a word, he reached for my wrist, but jumped back when he was met with the flames I'd let burn through my skin.

I knew I wasn't a person who would take shit from Miles Landgrave. And I sure as hell wasn't a person who would take shit from Evarius Castemont. The pain on his face, the way he cradled his now-blistered palm... Saints, it felt good. Flames still dancing across my fingers, I raised my hand, watching the glare in Castemont's eyes. I had little control over my powers, I knew that. But I also knew that meant I could level this side of the castle in a single breath. "I could kill you where you stand."

He straightened suddenly, his scorched hand flexing at his side. "You could. But you won't like the results."

I stepped forward. "You don't scare me."

"Maybe not," he replied in a mocking tone. "But if you kill me, you'll lose everyone you love. Kill me, and everyone in that dungeon dies. Everyone who, I imagine, must be patiently waiting for you to rescue them." He clicked his tongue and exhaled. "So go ahead, but if I don't return to the dungeons after your wedding, the guards have orders to execute all the prisoners."

"You're bluffing," I spat.

"I could be, but you won't risk it." He took a step toward the door and offered his good hand. "Now come along. We're going to be late."

Fuck. No, I wouldn't risk it. With the knowledge that the candle was tucked into my dress, I took his hand, nausea and anger intertwining into the desperate need for vengeance. As he led me through the door, I turned to look at the guards standing outside my room, each of them with a right fist over their chests, silently nodding as if to say, "We see you. We see you, Daughter of Katia."

Chapter 3

I wondered if Castemont had my dagger on him now. The sound of the bastard Lord's heavy boots hitting the stone floor echoed through the corridors as we took turn after turn. I wanted to drop my gaze, avoid everyone who stared, but I didn't. That's what I would have done in the past. Not anymore. I kept my eyes forward and tried to block out the soldiers and handmaidens and stewards who bowed. I didn't want to know how many snuck a fist over their chests, and I definitely didn't want to know how many didn't.

I began to recognize the antechamber outside the throne room when Castemont turned to hold both my hands, cringing when my fingers ran across his blistered palm. "Look at me," he said quietly, an attempt at fatherly love softening his voice. "Petra, darling, look at me." My face was set in stone, looking past him to the small window, to the light that poured into the dusty antechamber. The blue flames from my dreams burned in my head, the combination of both tremendous power and utter helplessness like a thorn in my side. "It's your wedding day. Smile."

My gaze flashed to him, his face blanching ever so slightly at whatever he saw in my eyes. "Do not tell me to smile. Do not tell me to do anything."

He ignored my command. "Cheer up. I'm delighted I get to witness your marriage."

"And I'll be delighted when I hear your dying screams as I burn you alive."

My words had no effect on him, his sickening smile still etched across his face. "You'll be married under the watch of the Saints, just like when I married your mother." He squeezed my hands, and it took everything in me not to pull his fingers backwards, not to claw at his face. "She's here, you know." I blinked, willing my eyes not to show the surprise I felt. "Your mother is in the throne room. She's waiting to watch her daughter get married."

Longing flooded through me, longing for the mother I'd never have again. Maybe it was longing for the mother I'd never had in the first place. But deep down, I knew her body may very well be sitting in that throne room, but the woman who raised me was gone. Long gone.

I needed to get through the wedding and then I could light the candle in the window. *I can do this.* Though the thought wasn't far from my mind that I was once again in a situation not because of my own actions, but because I had no other choice but to face the consequences of the actions of others.

A small handmaiden scurried into the chamber holding an oversized bouquet of ivory roses. She curtsied, thrusting the flowers in my direction. I took it begrudgingly, my grip crushing the delicate stems.

Castemont straightened, reaching over my shoulders to pull the veil over the diadem, letting the tulle fall over my face. I let him, grinding my teeth to keep from gouging his eyes out. "Just beautiful," he whispered, his hands clasped in front of him. "I believe it's time."

The Lord's shallow nod signaled the guards to open the doors, the throne room stretching before me like the maw of a wolfhound as they swung open. Hundreds of people were packed shoulder to shoulder, each of them rising and turning to face me. My stomach lurched as I swallowed back vomit. Kauvras stood at the end of the aisle, the gold stitching on his pitch black surcoat glinting in the dim light from the chandelier. His face erupted in childish glee once again as he met my eyes.

Not a lick of music, not a ruffle of fabric, not a breath could be heard. The smell of smoke suddenly hit my nose, and a crackling sound disrupted the silence. I looked down and realized — the bouquet I held was beginning to burn in my grasp. Fire licked its way from the stems to the petals as looks of shock and horror and awe surrounded me.

Castemont paused, his eyes fixed on the flaming bouquet. Smoldering petals fell to the floor around us, and I let the wind pick up to keep them from igniting my gown. He was unsure of what to do, I could tell. I tried to pull him along, because the sooner this wedding was over, the sooner I could light the candle. His feet stayed steady as he stared at the fire.

"I thought you were delighted to witness my wedding," I whispered, cocking a brow in challenge. His jaw flexed, nostrils flaring as he faced the altar and began walking once again.

My eyes fell on Kauvras, waiting expectantly for me, face alight as he watched his veiled bride approach him with fire in her hands. It raged now, the flames climbing as high as my chin, the pain my motivation to keep going. But I almost stopped in the middle of the aisle as I beheld who stood next to him. Wrapped in chains from neck to ankles was Calomyr — *Belin,* standing like a weathered statue next to his father. Another chain ran through his mouth as a gag, his sapphire and emerald eyes bloodshot and swollen and pleading. Dried blood crusted his face from a gash on his forehead. I was thankful for the veil as my eyes fell on the bruises that marred the bits of skin I could see. *Saints.* I wanted to run to him, to free him, to–

No, I told myself. *He lied to you. He's one of the reasons you're here. Let him rot.*

The petals and buds had all burned away, a smoldering trail left behind me as we neared the altar. Kauvras' smile deepened as he watched the last of the stems crumble to ash.

A priest wrapped in crimson robes waited with Kauvras. He opened his mouth, presumably to ask who gave this woman to this man, but whatever look he saw on my face caused the words to die in his throat. Castemont squeezed my arm almost painfully then wordlessly found his seat at the front of the crowd.

I couldn't lie to myself and say I felt strong. Not all the way to my core. The panic was there. The dread was there. The doubt, fear, apprehension... It was all there. But I *had* to do this for those I loved, and so I stood a little straighter, steeled my gut for what was to come.

Calomyr's eyes bored into me as Kauvras reached greedily for my blistered hands, and I fought the wince that rose from the pain. I turned my head to the mass of strangers before me, hundreds of people settled into velvet seats that must have been dragged in for the ceremony. My mother sat in the front row, her gaze empty and distant as Castemont grasped her thigh through the skirts of her navy satin gown, the familiar smug look on his face once again. Miles sat to Castemont's right, the Saints damned mask over his Saints damned face, white knuckled and still. The crowd was filled with Cabillian soldiers, some in armor and some in leathers, and from what I could see, some members of Cabillian royalty were tucked throughout.

With every curious, hollow, or steadfast gaze I met, I fought against instinct to look over at Calomyr.

The priest began speaking, holding the Book of Saints open, but not reading from it, as if it were just for show. "Ladies and gentlemen, the Daughter of Katia stands before the eyes of her

48

Holy Mother to join her soul with King Kauvras of Cabillia, Savior of the Realm." My stomach was churning with anger and anticipation. *Get through it and light the candle.* "This holy union will mark the beginning of a new age for the people of the realm. The age of Kauvras, Saint of New Beginnings."

Saint of New Beginnings? This had to be a fucking joke. Did he think he'd marry me and just...*ascend* to sainthood? Kauvras beamed at me, the sapphire in his eyes alight with excitement. I once again almost felt bad for him, for whatever inside of him had snapped, whatever had made him so *fucking* insane.

"With the power that flows through the veins of Petra, Daughter of Katia, Kauvras will lay ruin to this world, ushering in a new one free of all evil."

I had to stop my hands from shaking in anger, my feet from running in panic. *Lay ruin to this world?* So I was going to be used as a *weapon?*

"King Kauvras, Savior of the Realm, please lift the veil to reveal the face of your bride," the priest said. Kauvras was surprisingly gentle as he lifted his hands to my head, staring at the diadem as it was uncovered.

"Now please turn to face me," the priest continued. I surveyed the priest's face, his bland features offering no hint as to what he was thinking. Did he sympathize with Kauvras? Or had he too heard of my *explosion* and fallen to his knees as some of the soldiers had?

"King Kauvras, Savior of the Realm, will you swear to protect Petra and make use of her gifts to begin the world anew, free of all evil?" So, it seemed we wouldn't be taking the traditional wedding vows I'd been expecting.

"I will," he said, his voice thick with excitement, a smile plastered across his face.

"Petra, will you allow King Kauvras, Savior of the Realm, to utilize the gifts given to you by your mother Katia, Keeper of the Benevolent Saints, to begin this world anew?"

Silence crept in, heavy and uncomfortable. No, I had no intention of letting Kauvras utilize my gifts. I felt the crowd stir behind me, could have sworn I heard Castemont holding his breath. What were my choices here? Try to escape? Say no? I couldn't. I had no choice.

I'd never had a choice.

Just get through this and you can light the candle.

My words were strong, loud enough that every person in this damned hall heard me loud and clear. "I will."

"Then it is so. In the eyes of the Saints, I pronounce you husband and wife. King Kauvras, you may kiss your bride."

The blood hit my chest and face faster than I realized what was happening, spattering across my white gown as an arrow pierced the Rebel King's shoulder.

Chapter 4

The throne room erupted as Kauvras fell to his knees, grabbing at my skirts, blood trickling from the wound where the arrow protruded at an angle from his shoulder. Steel split the air as blades left their sheaths, chaos erupting across the throne room. The floor quickly went slick with blood as people sprinted for the doors to escape the sudden melee. My head whipped around to Castemont, the man hunched over my mother in some sick form of protection as he dragged her from the room.

I tried to turn to Calomyr but arms closed around me, dragging me back, all the while Kauvras clawed at me to stay upright as soldiers closed in around him.

The arms tightened around me and I thrashed against them, against the body that was suddenly pressed to mine. It was solid behind me, my attempts at escape proving pointless. "I'll get you out of here," a low voice rasped in my ear. Miles.

"Let me go!" I screamed, fighting against him, trying to find my flames.

He turned to me, his mask inches from my face. "I'll get you out of here." The words must have resonated with something in me because suddenly he was pulling me along and I wasn't resisting. He unsheathed his own blade, the sound ringing in my ears as he shoved me behind him. I could see him eyeing a door to the side of the dais crowded with people, his short but intentional steps taking us there inch by bloody inch around people fighting and screaming and dying.

Where did Calomyr go?

"Get her!" I heard Kauvras' voice shriek between the sounds of singing steel. "Get my bride!"

I tunneled into myself, trying to find any dregs of power, but I couldn't focus with the chaos unfolding around us. A man clad in the telltale black Cabillian armor rushed toward us, wild eyes on me like I was prey. "Hand her over!" he shouted, his sword raised high in the air. Miles met his blow easily, pushing the man back off the dais, but he didn't back down.

Miles' sword made contact again and again before the man finally crumpled to the ground. But then two more men came at us, their eyes even wilder, their faces even more menacing.

"Mind helping out, perhaps?" Miles snapped from under his mask.

"I'm fucking trying!"

One of the men broke past Miles, both hands on the hilt of his broadsword as he raised it above his head, closing in on me–

Come on, Petra. Do something.

I threw my hand out, a burst of fire and light colliding with his unmasked face. He dropped his sword as pained screams erupted from his chest. The second man was unfazed by my display of power as he continued swinging for Miles, something deranged in his movements.

"Unholy bitch," he spat, mouth full of yellowed teeth, his eyes on me but his sword aimed for the Lieutenant. Miles met him blow for blow as I tried once again to scrape together crumbs of my power. More and more men rushed toward us, some of them intercepted by other swords and arrows.

I managed one more shot of flame and sent the snarling man falling to the ground in pain just as his comrade had. A few men jumped back in fear at the sight of him clawing at his scorched face.

An arrow zipped past me, but I was too slow — it grazed my forehead, my blood spattering across my veil as the fabric stuck to the wound. I caught the eye of an unmasked soldier at the base of the dais, one arm waving wildly, the other swinging his broadsword. "Get her out of here!" he called to Miles over the din. His skin was almost as dark as his armor, his body moving between swords with a nimble grace that defied his lumbering frame. Against the stream of people still trying to leave the throne room, I saw dozens of soldiers pushing in, striking down their comrades as Miles moved me to the back of the massive hall.

"*Go!*" the man bellowed to Miles. "Get to the tunnels! We'll hold them off!" He disappeared into the chaos as Miles grabbed my wrist, cutting down men with apparent ease as we pushed through the crowd.

From all directions, arrows whizzed past my head as men rushed at us, war cries erupting from their throats as soldiers gutted soldiers. I couldn't tell who was who. Every man still standing bore black armor or fighting leathers, all of them branded with the gold dragon of the Cabillian crest.

We finally made it to the door as Miles stabbed the last man who stood in our way. A narrow, torchlit corridor opened before us, musty air hitting my nostrils as the door slammed behind us. "What the fuck is going on?" I demanded, the noise of the throne room still echoing off the stone walls. Miles was silent, his grip firm around my wrist as he pulled me behind him. "Tell me what the *fuck* is going on!"

"Shut up," he snapped, his pace quickening.

"Excuse me?"

He froze, whirling to me, stepping closer until his mask hovered inches from my face. I swallowed hard at the uncomfortable proximity. "Shut the fuck up," he breathed. "We're going somewhere safe."

Dumbfounded at his tone, I followed behind him. One turn, two, five, then ten until I lost track of what direction we were heading. "How the hell do you know where you're going?" I demanded as we wove through the corridors, only to be met with the Lieutenant's silence. The torches that had lined the walls were running out, and Miles grabbed the last one before the darkness swallowed us like a pit.

The sound of the chaos behind us faded but he slowed his pace only slightly. "These are escape tunnels," he murmured suddenly, the rasp in his voice sounding even more pronounced in the echoey corridors. "If I can remember how to get through, they'll take us all the way under the leechthorn fields and out to the mountains."

"The mountains?"

"If I can remember how to get there," he snapped.

We came upon a small alcove and he slowed, finally letting go of my wrist as he pulled a canteen from his belt and offered it to me. I pushed it aside. I wanted to ask him what the fuck was going on, but something stopped me. There was a nervous energy surrounding him, and it made the darkness around us even more unsettling.

"Someone shot an arrow at Kauvras," he murmured, his breath heaving from behind his mask.

"Thanks for the clarification," I quipped, my anger dripping with sarcasm. "Who?"

He didn't answer, instead craning his neck to look down the corridor behind us before shifting on his feet. "King Belin is safe," he said.

Sudden fury and longing and confusion pulsed with each heartbeat at the name. "Why would I care?" I snarked, fighting the edge in my voice that threatened to break me.

54

"He's safe. One of my men retrieved him and had him removed."

"One of your men?"

"I need you to stop asking so many questions."

He'd been apologetic back in my room in the castle, now he was being short with me. "What do you mean by one of your men?" I asked again, ignoring the bite in his tone.

He sniffed, rolling his head from side to side. "Since...yesterday, since the *incident*," he said, starting to pace, "there has been some...unrest." I cocked a brow. I could have told him that. "The Cabillian army is currently divided. I've... I've sort of become the leader of your supporters, so to speak."

I ground my teeth together. "Shouldn't *I* be the leader of *my* supporters?"

"You are. Technically." He stopped pacing. "In a sense. But you were locked away." Agitation marked his voice as he spoke, staring at me through the eyes of the ram. "But I was the only one who'd witnessed what happened at the Taithan castle firsthand. Not everyone knew exactly what happened, but everyone has now heard of your...*power*." He began pacing again, my eyes following him in the dim light of the torch. "It was a long night, Petra. A lot of rumors were flying around, and most of them still are. And now some people believe you are the Savior of the Realm. And others believe that Kauvras is, and that you were sent here for him to use your powers."

"So there are people that are supporting me blindly?" I shook my head. "Why?"

"If the prophesied Savior of the Realm shows up, they're going to have followers even if they plan to burn the world to the ground. Most of your followers act with blind faith, and that's enough for them."

I let my head drop against the stone and huffed a laugh. "Savior of the Realm."

"What?"

"Daughter of Katia, Savior of the Realm... So many titles. I can't keep up."

"Don't forget Blood of Old Creed and Child of Benevolence," he added. I cringed at the addition of two more titles to the list. "Castemont said the Bloodsingers are involved, so I bet they foresaw something."

Silence settled again as the blood curdled in my veins. Bloodsingers. *Ludovicus.* Castemont had said the Board of Blood was made up of Bloodsingers. I didn't even know what a Bloodsinger *was*, why they all looked the same and why they delighted in pain, but I knew for a Saints damned fact they were *evil.*

"I have a theory," Miles said quietly. I looked at him expectantly. "Normally when people talk about *the prophecy*, it's the part I gave you in the note. Not many people know that it doesn't end there but I didn't include that in the note." My brows raised. "I didn't want it to fall into the wrong hands."

"What's the rest?"

He took a deep breath and swallowed hard, the scar on his throat flexing. "*Her bloodline exposed by he who exacts pain, cursed to walk the realm when evil comes again.*"

I blinked, my brain running in circles trying to understand. What was he saying?

"I think it's saying your existence can only be uncovered, or confirmed, by *he who exacts pain*, which I believe is–"

"Noros, Saint of Pain." My ears were ringing as I shook my head. "You think that could be Castemont?"

"I know it sounds crazy."

It did sound crazy. But so did the ability to conjure fire and wind from nothing. So was the fact that I was the daughter of the Keepers. The idea that Castemont could be the authority over the infliction of pain and suffering? No, it wasn't crazy.

I bit the inside of my cheek, trying to come up with the words. "So what, he's *cursed* to live in a human body? How are we supposed to prove that?"

56

"I don't know, Petra," he snapped, his tone completely different now as he threw his hands up in exasperation. What the hell
was his problem? "Keep that to yourself," he spat, a finger pointed
at me. "There are enough rumors flying around. We don't need
people thinking Castemont could actually be Noros until we
know for certain."

"Do not point your finger at me," I snarled.

He dropped his hand, his knuckles flexing at his side. His
voice was a whisper. "I thought the arrow was headed for you."

The sudden admission caught me off guard, but I quickly re-
covered. "Without me, you wouldn't get those answers," I
sneered.

"Oh, I got my answers," he seethed back, stepping even closer
to me, the light reflecting off the tarnished metal of his mask. I
could feel the heat from his body as he stared, blood spattered
across the curved horns.

"And what? They weren't the answers you were hoping for?"

He was silent, but something glistening caught my eye and I
realized blood was trickling down his leather-clad arm. "You're
bleeding," I whispered.

His head fell to the side, raising his arm to look at the wound
on his bicep. It was bad — not life threatening, but the bleeding
was heavy enough to make me nervous. "It's fine," he said.

"Let me see," I commanded, plucking the veil spattered with
my own blood from where it sat behind the diadem on my head.

"It's not bad."

"Let me see," I repeated, more forcefully this time, my fury
flaring inside me. He turned, the movement begrudgingly slow,
the oozing blood catching the torchlight. "Don't think I care," I
muttered as I looped the veil around his arm. "I don't want to be
stuck down here when you lose consciousness." I tied off the fabric as he stared down the corridor.

An echo clanged from behind us, the sudden noise assaulting
the eerie silence. That was... That was the sound of steel. Footsteps
and steel.

Without another word, we were moving, my mind too full of renewed panic to think of anything else.

Chapter 5

The glow of white light cut through the darkness of the tunnel, contrasting the orange hues emitted from the torch. *Daylight.* I didn't know how long we'd been moving. An awkward, slow run was the only thing I could manage in my massive wedding gown. Only faint noises reached us from behind, the echoes of echoes. The tulle of the veil tied around Miles' arm should have been crimson by now with how heavy he'd been bleeding, and I eyed it as we continued toward the light.

"Stay here," he said flatly, barely stopping to hand me the torch as he rounded a corner.

"Are we in the mountains?"

He grunted in confirmation as he pulled his sword from its sheath. "I need to make sure you'll be safe here." He disappeared around the corner.

I tried to ignore the noises that still sounded from behind me, ignore the fact that they were the undeniable echoes of footsteps, that *someone* was coming, though they were still far away. The stone wall was cool against my back, but the blisters on my hand still ached and my head spun in every direction with questions.

Who shot the arrow at Kauvras? Did it kill him? Where was Castemont? Where was Calomyr — *Belin?* Where the fuck was Ludovicus? What answers had Miles been after? Where were we going and why? What would people expect from me? To be their ruler? I didn't know the first thing about leading people, let alone a realm.

The questions could've gone on forever.

I braced myself as footsteps approached from around the corner, Miles' imposing silhouette interrupting the daylight. "Every single soldier here is loyal to you, Petra."

My breath caught, and I wasn't sure if it was because of what he said or the way his voice wrapped around my name.

"This is the Oxblood Outpost. We're at the base of the Iron Rise." He started for the light, waiting for me to follow him. When he realized I wasn't, he turned back to see the confusion plastered on my face. "The Iron Rise is the highest peak of the Rhedrosian Mountain Range."

I fought to keep my eyes from widening at the name. "Rhedros," I said flatly, not a question nor a statement.

"His passage to Hell," Miles muttered, staring hard from behind that Saints damned mask. "What Castemont said," he mumbled quietly, stepping toward me. I panicked. Did he know what Castemont told me about my father? "Was it true? He said he pulled you from..." He trailed off for a moment as if he were considering speaking at all. "A shit hole?"

Okay. Not about Rhedros. "Yes."

"And he said your education was lacking."

My stare bored into the mask as I spat through my teeth. "Yes."

"My education was shit, too."

I didn't appreciate his pathetic attempt at whatever he was trying to do... Soothe me? Relate to me? This hot and cold was exhausting. "Okay, *and?*"

He took a small step back as if the venom of my words had stung him. "I only ask because it sounds like you've never even heard of the Rhedrosian Mountains."

"What reason would I have had to know they existed?"

"Because the Iron Rise is where Rhedros is said to enter and leave Hell. You know, the lore of the Saints." I looked at him with a raised brow. "You'll see." He started walking for the light. I fought the dread that rose in my gut, the urge to run.

The tunnel grew brighter as we took the last few steps, the world yawning open as we turned the corner. I blinked rapidly, the white-yellow light of what appeared to be the late afternoon sun stinging my eyes. There were a few small stairs up, and I ignored Miles' outstretched hand as I clumsily ascended them.

Figures began to take shape around me as I spun in place, trying to make sense of my surroundings. A few small structures stood on the patch of even ground, the dirt packed and solid. I could feel the mountain looming above me before I saw it, and even though the sun illuminated its side, what rippled off it was dark and heavy. Thin wisps of black smoke rose from the mountaintop in an angry column, as if the mountain itself burned low and slow from the inside.

"Petra," Miles' voice rasped.

I spun to see three dozen soldiers, all in the distinct black armor of Cabillia, all lowered to a knee, a fist across each of their chests. None wore masks, their words clear as they began to chant, "Daughter of Katia." Over and over and over again.

I continued turning, assessing these new surroundings, and that's when I saw it.

It looked like someone had simply taken a brush and painted a massive swath of violet across the ground at the foot of Taitha. The fields of leechthorn pulsed like they had their own heartbeat, moved in the breeze like the waters of Pellucid Harbor.

My eyes moved from the bottom of the small cliff we stood atop of, across the fields that had been obscured from view when we walked into the city yesterday. The soldiers behind me still chanted, the noise becoming a hum in the back of my mind. The fields were mesmerizing, so much so that I almost hadn't noticed what loomed above them.

Taitha was *burning*.

Massive plumes of thick black smoke barrelled to the sky — the same color that billowed from the Iron Rise. Crimson flames ate away at the towers of the castle. My heart lurched in my chest at the thought of Calomyr — Belin — still in there. Solise. Ma. And I realized that the men behind me, the men pledging their loyalty to me, probably had families within those burning walls too, and I was ultimately the reason it was on fire.

Emotions welled in my chest. "Get up," I snapped, taken aback by my own tone, overwhelmed with, well, everything. The soldiers didn't blink before rising, standing straight backed as the mountain that soared above them. "I'm sorry," I muttered, scrubbing my face with my hands. They were silent, patiently watching. Waiting.

Miles leaned in close to me. "They're waiting for you to say something."

I pinned him with my stare, the feelings brewing inside me close to boiling over, a confusing and terrifying mix of emotions. I was no longer flooded with conviction as I had been walking down the aisle. Now I felt small, the guilt pushing down on me making me feel even smaller. I took a step forward, closer to the men who were now loyal to *me*. "Um, hello," I said, far too quietly. *Get a fucking grip.* "Just Petra is fine. Please."

I did my best to avoid eye contact as I shifted from one foot to another, the stupid fucking wedding gown suddenly feeling like it was made entirely of lead. "I... I didn't know I was the Daughter of Katia. Not until yesterday. Never even knew that Katia had a daughter." I let out a choked laugh and rubbed my jaw, staring at the ground, the reality of the last few days, the last few *years* slamming into me full force. "I'm sorry," I whispered again. No one moved. "I'm sorry your city is burning because of me."

I heard the soft clank of armor and looked up to see one of the men stepping forward. His hand rested on the hilt of the sword at his side. This man was born to be a soldier, I could tell, something natural about the proud set of his shoulders. Dark stubble mottled his chin, the olive tone of his skin striking against the liquid night armor. He was handsome, with wide set shoulders and a strong, straight nose. He was probably only a few years older than me.

"Daughter of Katia, Lady Petra," he said, seemingly so uncomfortable using my name that he threw in a formal title for good measure. "My name is Lieutenant Otto Mason, Guardian of Oxblood Outpost. I, and the other soldiers who protect the Outpost, are loyal to you and you alone."

He fell silent, waiting for me to answer. I opened my mouth, unsure of what exactly to say. "*Okay*," I said sheepishly. Where the hell was the Petra who had threatened Castemont's life? Not here, that was for sure. "Thanks." Fucking Saints. "And please, just Petra."

"Whatever you need, we are at your disposal."

"I don't *need* anything." My chest began to heave as the weight of this seemingly forced title began to crush me, my ribs feeling like they were going to break again. "I don't want any of this. I don't want to be the Daughter of Katia, Blood of Old Creed, Child of Benevolence. I don't want to be the Savior of the Realm. I don't even know why the realm needs to be saved." My tone began to rise as I fought back the urge to shriek, to scream and rip my hair out and cry. "I want to go *home*."

The air in my chest felt thin as the soldiers stared at me. "I was born in the fucking *gutter of Eserene*. I was raised in a fucking cesspool. I watched my sister die. They told me my father committed suicide, but I *knew* he didn't. I fucking *knew*." I was screaming now, my face flushed as the tears spilled down my cheeks, the picture of finding Da's cloak in the cave digging its talons into my brain. The cloak Calomyr had planted. "And I was right, because Castemont fucking *killed him!* He killed my father so he could marry my mother to get to *me*." My arms were flailing, hysterics turning my vision red. "All because she isn't my mother at all, because my *real* mother is apparently the fucking Keeper of the Benevolent Saints who only *just* decided to show her fucking face!"

I hit the ground in a crumpled heap, the sobs ripping a canyon through me. I didn't care how many men stared. I didn't care what they thought. I didn't care that Miles stood over me. I just wanted to go home.

Leather-clad feet stopped just in front of me, and I peered up through teary eyes to see Otto, his brows knit together in...concern. That was concern I saw, and sympathy. A calloused hand reached down, the sunlight gleaming off the intricate gold detail on the black metal cuff at his wrist.

Wiping my eyes, I hesitantly reached for his hand and flinched as my blistered palm made contact. He pulled me up with ease given our similar heights, telling me a muscled body hid beneath the armor. "It's going to be okay," he whispered with a nod. I squeezed my eyes shut at his words. "It's all going to be okay."

Silence settled over the Outpost, the distant sounds of a burning city beginning to reach me, echoey clangs and crashes sounding too close for comfort. I didn't want to hear it, the screams, the sound of buildings burning, it reminded me of too much–

"*Petra*," Otto said, a faint smile on his lips at the use of my first name. "We're going to keep you safe, but something is about to happen." His gaze flicked behind me to where Miles stood near the entrance to the tunnel and nodded at whatever he saw.

I whirled around to Miles, seeing his familiar stance, hand on the hilt of his sword, mask glinting dully. "Whoever was behind us is almost here." His tone was flat. It was then that I realized the echoes I thought came from Taitha were coming from the tunnel.

Otto's hand gently pulled me away, but I dug my feet into the dirt, refusing to move. "Who?" I demanded.

"Could be Kauvras," Miles answered for him, too nonchalantly. "Or his men. Or it could be our men. *Your* men." He drew his sword, the sound of steel making the hairs on the back of my neck stand straight.

My eyes flew to Otto, but his face was the definition of calm. "We're going to keep you safe," he repeated intentionally. I wanted to tell him I could keep myself safe, but the thought of letting someone else do it for me... I nodded. He lifted his hand to the remaining soldiers who began to move, some unsheathing swords, some pulling bows from their backs, some moving toward a small cluster of rudimentary structures at the back of the camp.

"You need to hide."

Chapter 6

There was no time to react before a dozen soldiers surrounded me, the sun blotted out by their armor. "Hello again," a timid voice said, and I looked beside me to find a man with sandy blonde hair.

"Tomkin," I said, recognizing the face that had woken me from my sleep early this morning. He gave a small smile as he swung a rickety door open and led me into one of the dilapidated buildings at the Outpost, the other soldiers silently following.

There were rows of low cots across the dusty floor and a dozen or so crudely built wooden wardrobes, each pushed against a wall appearing to be made of stone and mud. "It's not the fanciest, but it keeps the rain out," he said with a smile as we walked to one of the wardrobes. "I'm sorry, your Majesty, but I'm afraid you're going to have to wait in here." He swung a creaking wardrobe open, the sound melting into the flurry of activity outside the building's thin walls.

"Just Petra," I repeated as I climbed between the hanging leathers without hesitation. It reeked of unwashed men, and I suppressed a gag as I gathered my skirts as best I could.

"I need you to stay silent. Don't come out. Don't move. Don't do anything until one of us comes to get you. Okay?" He was so soft spoken, a tiny bit of light in this hectic storm. I nodded, swallowing hard. He closed me in, and I was relieved to realize the doors were inlaid with some type of latticework. No one could see in, but I at least had enough light to see the outline of my blistered hand in front of my face.

I leaned my head back against the rough wood panel, my breaths shallow given the stench. But the sound of the building's door suddenly opening was just audible above the other noise. Heavy footsteps approached, and I tensed with anxiety. Whoever was in the tunnel wasn't here yet, were they? They said everyone here was loyal to me, but what if they weren't?

The wardrobe swung open to reveal a ram's head looking down at me.

"What are you doing?" I whispered harshly.

"Move your feet," he snapped, trying to climb in across from me. His tone was overly sharp as he shuffled into the wardrobe. "I realized that they saw me leave the throne room with you," he continued, his voice even more harsh. "If they see me here, they'll know you're here too. I've never been assigned to the Outpost." The vitriol that I felt from him was different than what I'd felt from him in the tunnels.

"Then take the Saints damned mask off. Then they won't know who you are."

"They will."

I furrowed my brows as I pulled my feet in, irritation brewing in my chest. "There are ten other buildings out here. Pick a different one," I bit out.

"If they find you, you'll need me to defend you." He swung his legs in, reaching forward and closing the door.

I scoffed, the reeking darkness closing in around us. "Are you forgetting the fact that I can shoot literal fucking flame and wind from my hands?"

"And how much control do you have over that?"

I opened my mouth, quickly closing it when I realized I wouldn't like my own answer. "Fucking prick," I muttered. "This is all your fault."

"I'm aware."

"You're a dick, you know." I hadn't really meant to say it out loud, but there it was.

"I'm aware."

I eyed the wound on his arm through the torn leather, the gash just visible in the low light. The veil I'd wrapped around it was gone, and the wound wasn't nearly as bad as it had looked. Blood had been gushing from it in the tunnels, and–

The noise in the camp quieted slightly, the sound of more swords ringing through the air. My chest began to burn, the familiar white hot feeling — my *power* — beginning to flare, my ribcage beginning to heat from the inside out.

"Archers at the ready!" a voice yelled. I held my breath. I think Miles held his too. "Aim!"

There was an eternity between each heartbeat, the air thick with fear and sweat.

"At ease!"

Miles let out a heavy breath. "What is it?" I whispered. "Who is it?"

"It's not Kauvras, and it's not his men. Stay here." He swung the door open and was gone within seconds.

I sat in stunned silence for only a moment before Tomkin rushed back in, his features relaxed in relief. "If the men who just arrived are to be believed," he said, extending a hand to help me from the wardrobe, "you're going to have quite the army."

◆ ◆ ◆

I felt dozens of pairs of eyes on me as I emerged. The energy was different — lighter, calmer, but there was still an air of obvious tension. Three men, only one of them masked, rested on bent knees, fists on their chests in a fashion I was growing rather sick of seeing. And of course, the chant.

"Daughter of Katia."

"Stop," I said firmly. "Please."

The three soldiers rose as Miles leaned in. "Don't tell them not to," he whispered harshly into my ear. "You need to inspire respect."

"I don't need to do *shit*," I spat back to him quietly, turning to the newcomers. He was right, but I didn't want him to be.

I recognized one man from the throne room, the man who'd told Miles to get me out, that he'd hold off Kauvras' men. He looked to be about twenty years older than me, his dark face rugged and war-weathered. But something about him was soft, and maybe that was because I had known from the moment he spoke to Miles in the throne room that he believed in me.

He stepped forward, the movement echoing extensive military training. "I am Commander Olion Summercut. My allegiance lies with you, Daughter of Katia."

I didn't correct him, instead clenching and unclenching my fists as the next man stepped forward. *You are the Daughter of Katia,* I thought to myself. *Stop resisting it.* This man was younger and looked more like the unranked soldiers that stood behind me. His dark brown hair was shorn close to his scalp, his eyes the same color. "I'm Sentos Whitley, and my allegiance lies with you, Daughter of Katia."

I nodded as the last man stepped forward, a tarnished silver wolf mask on his head. He was significantly shorter than the other two, probably three or four inches shorter than me. His build was slighter too, the armor seeming to swallow his body. He reached up to remove the mask, a curtain of black hair falling over thin shoulders, the slightly upturned eyes of a strikingly beautiful woman looking back at me.

"Shit," I whispered, my hand flying over my mouth at the flicker of my past tactless self.

She lowered her head slowly. "My name is Enella Augen, and my allegiance lies with you, Daughter of Katia." I stood in stunned silence. I had never seen a female soldier before, and I knew it was rude to stare, but I couldn't keep myself from gawking. She looked...like a fucking badass.

I stepped toward her, the Saints damned wedding gown dragging behind me, and surveyed her more closely. Her skin was a rich brown, a slight bump in the middle of her nose. She almost looked like Wrena. Same age, same thick dark hair, same warmth radiating from her. I swallowed back the painful memory of my friend as I thought of what to say.

"I'm sorry," I began. "I... I've never seen a female soldier before. Females weren't allowed in the Eserenian army."

"They're not allowed in the Cabillian army either," someone called from behind, their tone full of light humor, breaking the pressure that had settled over the Outpost. The corners of her lips quirked up as she fought back a smile.

"She's kicked more asses than you have and she'd easily kick yours," another person shouted, a chuckle moving through the crowd.

She held the mask in the crook of her arm. "*This* makes it easier to blend in." Even the way she spoke sounded like Wrena.

"Can I ask you something?"

"Anything, your Majesty," she answered.

"Just Petra," I said, and offered a smile. "Are you from Maplenook?" The sound of Wrena's home was ash on my tongue.

Her eyes widened slightly. "I am."

I sucked in a breath, something like dread and anticipation bubbling in my stomach. Before I spoke, I turned to Miles. "You can tell them all that they can go."

"You're dismissed," he called, and the men scattered about various tasks, Enella waiting patiently in front of me.

70

"I had a friend. One of my only friends, really. She was from Maplenook. Her name was Wrena." I looked down, a spark of shame flashing in my gut. "I never knew her surname." I held my breath. I didn't know what would be worse — if she knew Wrena or if she didn't.

Recognition flashed through her deep brown eyes at the name. "Wrena from Maplenook. She's my cousin. How did you–"

"She was one of my handmaidens. Back in Eserene."

Enella's lips thinned as she surveyed my face. "You said you *had* a friend..."

I looked to the ground again, working around what I needed to say. "She died. Not long ago." I couldn't look up at her. I couldn't look her in the face and tell her that her cousin died because of me. So I kept my head down, guilt sitting heavy in the back of my throat. "It was...my fault."

Enella took a deep breath. "She got out of Maplenook," she whispered, a slight smile on her lips.

"It wasn't under the best of circumstances," I replied quietly. "Her brother, Josef... He didn't make it out."

She nodded, a silent understanding between us. I was thankful I didn't have to tell her it was Kauvras' men that had raided Maplenook and killed her brother. Enella placed a hand on my shoulder, sympathy in her eyes. "We don't have to talk about it." She shifted her mask to rest beneath the other arm. "Have you eaten recently?"

Saints, I'd figured the Cabillian army was all brutality and malice. The people I'd met today were *kind*.

But come to think of it, I hadn't eaten anything since this morning. The sun was beginning to sink in the sky, and weariness hit me all of a sudden. "Come on." She began walking toward another stone building, a bit larger than the others. "There better be ale and bread in there," she shouted to the smattering of soldiers still in the small courtyard. "And someone get this girl some Saints damned clothes so she can get out of this fuckin' wedding gown. Hurry up, or I'll beat all of your asses!"

"Yes ma'am," Sentos Whitley shouted back with a grin.

"She's not lying," another soldier called, a chuckle following.

Sentos smirked. "Believe me, I know."

"Do you have a rank, Enella?" I asked.

"Call me Nell. And I'm not ranked. Just a soldier. Well, not *technically* a soldier, either." She opened the door for me, revealing what seemed to be a makeshift kitchen with some wooden countertops, a stone oven, and shelves of dishes. Just beyond lay a small mess hall with a few long, ramshackle wooden tables and chairs. "Like they said, women aren't allowed in the Cabillian army." She grabbed the pitcher of ale from the counter and filled two mugs, then tore two pieces of dry bread off a half-eaten loaf as I lowered myself to sit at a table. "But Whitley out there, he and I have been best friends since I moved to Taitha. And I'm not the only female in the military."

Whitley burst in, placing a stack of clothes on the table before me. "It's nothing too nice, but it's a hell of a lot better than *that,* your Majesty."

I winced at the title. "Thank you, Sentos." I said, offering a weak smile.

Laughter burst from Nell's lips. "Call him Whit. Whit the Piece of Shit if you're feeling formal," she jeered.

"Or Whit with the Big Di–"

"That doesn't even *rhyme,*" Nell sneered, interrupting him before the well meaning profanity could continue. Whit didn't seem to care.

"Thank you, Whit," I said with a smile.

"It's my pleasure. Anything you need, just ask. And I mean *anything.*" He winked at me, a smile on his face.

Nell rolled her eyes and scoffed. "Fuckin' Saints, Whit! Show the woman some damned respect! She's the Daughter of Katia, for fuck's sake." Her tone was light as my eyes darted back and forth between the two of them. The way she spoke reminded me of Larka in a way that didn't shoot pain through my chest, but instead made me smile.

72

Whit began to back towards the door. "Anything," he whispered again, the door swinging shut.

Nell plopped down in the chair across from me, handing me a mug and some bread as she tore into her own. "You can have him killed, you know," she shrugged. "I wouldn't argue too much." I laughed and grabbed the clothes, tucking myself into a corner to peel off the gown. "Sorry about him," she laughed. "Great guy. Shameless flirt, though."

"I can tell," I answered, carefully pulling the crimson candle from its strap inside the gown and placing it on the table next to the diadem.

Nell let out a breath, eyes moving between the diadem and the candle as I pulled on a pair of loose brown trousers and a fitted black tunic. Whit had even brought me a pair of brown leather boots. "I heard about the little candle plan," she muttered.

"Yeah, we didn't really make it far enough to use it." She continued eyeing it as I sat across from her once again. "Good plan, though," I added. Nell offered a lopsided smile as she looked at me. "How did you find yourself as a Cabillian soldier?"

She popped a piece of bread into her mouth, chewing thoughtfully before washing it down with ale. "Fever took my mother when I was young. I don't even remember her. My brother did, though. He was two years older. We were never very close, and my father drank. A lot. And he'd get angry." I felt the energy in the room sour a bit as she rehashed her past. "I think that's why I'm a good fighter. I was always at the other end of his fists."

I cringed, but her face remained neutral as she spoke. "Got pretty sick of it and knew I wanted to leave Maplenook. But it wasn't like I could beg. Everyone in Maplenook was poor. The one brothel in town had *some* form of morals and wouldn't hire anyone under sixteen. And Maplenook was so damned far from *everything.*"

"And Wrena?" I asked.

"Her father was my uncle, my mother's brother. I liked to spend time with her family. They were always kind, always laughing. But our fathers didn't get along, so our time together was always too short.

"I was fifteen when a textile merchant from Taitha came to town. I took it as my sign to leave. We rarely had merchants." I remembered Wrena telling me the same thing. "I begged Wrena to come with me, told her she needed to get out of Maplenook, that she was destined for bigger things. But she wanted to stay. She loved it there." Nell's expression briefly went distant and she absentmindedly chewed a piece of bread. "Anyway," she started again, righting herself and taking another swig of ale. "I bribed the textile merchant to take me with him when he went back to Taitha."

I didn't want to ask what she meant by that. She must have seen the question on my face though, because she put her bread down, a wicked smile curving across her face. "Yes, I *bribed* him. He wasn't half bad looking, so don't feel too bad for me. Didn't enjoy it much, though."

The cadence of her voice, the crudeness of her words reminded me so much of Larka, but this time the dark memories swept in. I swallowed back the thought, afraid that if I followed it I would end up spiraling into a dark pit I couldn't dig myself out of. "The merchant found me a job with a seamstress. She had a busy shop and I was responsible for keeping it clean, and in return I made a bit of coin and could sleep in the back. It wasn't much fun, but it kept me housed and fed. Whit came in one day, not too long after I'd moved here, to pick up a gown for his mother. Prissy bitch," she muttered. My eyes widened and she waved a hand at me. "Don't worry, he thinks the same thing. She's the living worst. The reason he joined the military was to get the hell away from her."

I laughed — actually *laughed*. In the middle of all the bloodshed and terror and uncertainty, I was laughing. It felt wrong. But it felt so, so good.

74

"He tried to make his move on me. Just like he does with every woman he lays eyes on. Didn't work, but we've been best friends ever since."

"What, you mean you didn't fall for his charming words?" I jeered.

Nell snorted. "He tried, believe me. And his words *were* charming. But even *Whit with the Big Dick* couldn't keep me from preferring women."

A laugh burst from my mouth. "Okay, makes sense. But have you..."

"Yeah, I've seen it." She grinned.

"And?" I mirrored her mischievous smile.

"I'll just say it's a good thing he's funny."

"Cheers to that," I chuckled, clanking our mugs together.

She took another long sip, her face turning contemplative. "I usually stay out here at the Outpost. I don't have a place in the barracks back in the city. Only went back because of all the commotion about the arrival of the Daughter of Katia." I hid my face, but she gave a smile. "And you? What's your story?"

"You want to know *my* story?"

"You're the daughter of a fuckin' Saint and can apparently shoot fire from your hands. Yes, I'd like to know your story."

Saints, Nell was refreshing. A normal person talking to me like I, too, was a normal person. So I took a deep breath and told her. About Inkwell, the soothsayer, Larka, and watching her die. About my father's murder and his cloak and the fire that took what little we had after that. About Solise and my mother and Castemont, the fucking bastard, and how I'd kill him with my bare hands if I had to. Wrena and Marita, the images of their bodies hanging outside the Eserenian throne room still fresh in my mind. Initiation and being kidnapped by Kauvras' men and the healing and Miles and the beasts of the Onyx Pass. Solise — dear, dear Solise. I told her of my explosion. The note. The wedding. And now *this*.

And I told her about Calomyr. What I learned yesterday, that he was the fucking *King of Widoras.* That he was in on it the whole time. That I was still in love with Calomyr, a man who didn't exist because he was really King Belin Cal Myrin. That his father was Kauvras. That I hadn't even really had the time to react properly.

I told her that I was *hollow.*

And Nell listened. Like her cousin Wrena had. She listened.

She blew a heavy breath from her mouth. "Well, shit." Her ale was long gone, and I pushed my mug her way when I saw her eyeing it.

"And I have no idea what's going to happen next," I breathed.

"I don't think anyone does. But you have a hell of a lot of support from what I've heard."

I cradled my face in my hands. "Yeah," I muttered, my words muffled against my palms. "That's what they're saying, isn't it?" My eyes found Nell's. I'd already told her my story. I might as well tell her about my current inner turmoil, too. "I don't know how to deal with all this."

"That's not surprising." She leaned back in her chair. "I don't think anyone would."

"I just..." I sighed, willing the building pressure within me to dissipate, if only slightly. "People believe in me. People who have never even met me are swearing their lives to me." I blinked hard, still trying to grasp the meaning of the words. "They don't know me. And I feel like...maybe I don't know myself either. I thought I did. I felt so powerful walking down the aisle, even with all the shit Castemont was holding over me. And before that, living in Inkwell, then in the castle. I knew who I was. But now..."

She pushed my mug of ale back to me. "You need this more than I do."

I took it from her and forced the bitter liquid down. Maybe it would help. Maybe not, but it was worth a try. I let out a deep breath, sinking a bit further into my gloom.

"I think I have a solution," Nell said, crossing her arms over her chest, an echo of a smile on her face. "Fake it."

I raised a brow. "Fake it? That's your suggestion?"

"Act like you know what you're doing. What other choice do you have?" She leaned forward, her elbows on the table and fingers laced under her chin. "Your followers are going to do whatever you say, anyway. Might as well put some conviction behind it, even if it's not real. And you never know, maybe you'll find yourself somewhere along the way."

I pursed my lips, trying to find a reason that wouldn't work. I nodded. "Okay."

"Don't worry," she said with a smile. "I won't tell anyone the truth."

I returned the smile, something different than flames glowing inside my chest. It was a feeling I hadn't felt in a long time. This stranger was becoming my friend.

The door swung open and Miles' figure loped in. Nell pushed her chair back and shuffled to her feet, standing at attention. "We have some things to discuss, Petra." His eyes looked to Nell. "Why are you at attention?"

I gave him a look of disdain. "She's a soldier, asshole."

"No she's not." Nell relaxed slightly, but kept her face stern. "I'm Lieutenant Miles Landgrave. I'm not sure where you fit into all of this, Augen, but keep your shit together and keep *her* protected. Got it?" His finger was pointed straight at me.

"Yes, Sir," she said evenly.

"Don't talk to her like that," I snapped at him, both of their faces swinging to me.

"Excuse me?" Miles snarled.

"Nobody here has to *protect* me. I didn't ask for this and she didn't either. None of these soldiers did. So *don't* fucking talk to her like that."

I'd have paid money to see the look on the face beneath the mask. His movements told me enough, the way he took a step back, his chest caving ever so slightly. Nell's eyes were wide and her lips were thin. I couldn't tell if she was simply being a good soldier or if she was holding back a laugh. "Sorry about him," I offered. She stayed silent, her face not betraying her truth. "Thank you for listening to me." My mouth turned up in a small smile. I had no idea how I could express my appreciation for the small reprieve of simply having a conversation.

Shoulders back, I faced Miles. I was going to act like I knew what I was doing. "Alright. Let's talk."

He stepped aside, gesturing toward the door, and I stormed out, the rush of adrenaline from yelling at him pulsing through me alongside my newfound pretend resolve. The low hum of a burning Taitha still hung in the air as the flames ate away at the city.

Miles led me to a newly erected tent. A massive table stood in the middle, a map sprawled across its rough, gouged surface.

I realized I'd never seen a map before.

An entire world unknown to me lay on that table, my eyes scanning over land masses and oceans, mountains and valleys, only a few which I'd heard of.

I lifted my gaze, and the grave, unmasked eyes of a dozen soldiers met mine. I felt like I'd been stripped naked. Their stares cut through to my bones, a thousand unspoken words on every face. *Act like you know what you're doing.*

"We need to prepare," Miles said from behind me, his gravelly voice low.

"For?"

The words slipped from under his mask, a hot iron to my chest. "War."

Chapter 7

My mouth went dry. *War*.

The other men in the tent stayed silent, their eyes moving expectantly to the ram's head mask next to me. "Commander Summercut brought news."

Summercut cleared his throat, his dark eyes stern as he looked at me. "By the time we left the throne room to come here, most of the fighting had cleared. Kauvras was retrieved by healers. He's going to live." I gave a small nod, swallowing hard at what that meant. "About half of the soldiers here in Taitha are loyal to you, and the other half to Kauvras. The problem is Kauvras' side has control of the Vacants." He paused, his lips pursed, poised to say something I knew wouldn't be good news. "There are roughly ten thousand Vacants in Taitha as of now."

The words hit my ears but made no sense in my brain. My mother was one of ten thousand. She was a *Vacant*. "Ten thousand..." I murmured under my breath.

"They're bringing in more everyday, from every major city on Astran, and he's had eyes on Losenia for a while as well."

Losenia. The continent across the sea. I knew absolutely nothing about it, aside from what little Wrena had told me. Allegedly, the whole reason Kauvras even started this sainthood bullshit was because of an issue with Nesan, Losenia's westernmost country. He told people that the previous Cabillian king — King Divos — was sleeping with the Nesanian Queen, and that she was calling the shots on trade with Cabillia. But Wrena said that she heard rumors of a Nesanian man stealing away the woman Kauvras loved.

Either way, bullshit.

A hundred questions came to mind, but they halted as a dozen pairs of eyes bored into me. Something hung in the air, something thick and uncomfortable that made it harder to breathe. "What?" I asked Summercut.

A fine sheen of sweat had formed on his brow. "In the chaos of it all..." He took a deep breath. "Castemont took four guards and...he escaped. With a large supply of leechthorn."

My brain went silent for a split second before my ears began to ring. He *escaped*? My hands balled into fists at my sides, the pain of my blisters ignored, anger coursing through every vein in my body. The *bastard*. I tried looking to Miles, to see if he'd come forward with his theory about Castemont's true identity, but he remained silent.

"My best guess is he's headed to Eserene." Summercut continued. "He's most likely making stops at any small village that Kauvras hasn't hit yet to build up his own army of Vacants."

I bit the inside of my cheek, fighting to keep the anger at bay. "Are there even enough people left to make an army?"

Summercut's head dipped into a slight nod. "Not as large an army as Kauvras', but with the protection of Eserene's walls..."

I stared at him blankly. "His own army. To fight...us." The Saint of Pain leading a military? My stomach turned.

Summercut's face was grave as he nodded. "Yes. And...King Belin is unaccounted for."

I spun to Miles. "I thought you said your men got him out of the throne room?"

"They did get him out of the throne room," Summercut answered.

"Out of the throne room to where? Where did they take him?"

Summercut pursed his lips. "They were given no orders past ensuring his safe exit from the throne room."

A tiny crumb of hope broke off the despair that hung like a cloud over my mind. I wanted so desperately to ask about him, hoped in the deepest parts of my being that he was okay. I hated that I had hope, hated that I wanted to hear that he was safe. I railed against it, but it pinned me down, that tiny crumb stronger than the despair it had come from.

Hope was always dangerous. Hope was weakness. Hope was vulnerability.

"So he's not in Taitha?" I asked, far too eagerly.

I felt Miles shift beside me as Summercut spoke. "Our fear is that Castemont took him."

My heart dropped and I let my head drop with it, my shoulders straining. Did the Invisible King go willingly? He must have. He was in on...*whatever* this was the whole time.

I tried to get a hold of every emotion that was bubbling up inside of me. My chest began to pound, heat rising quickly as my vision went red. I gulped in air, trying to quell the scorching heat, desperately needing to control it for fear I'd incinerate everyone in this tent.

And then I heard it. I heard *her*. "Petra," Katia's airy voice said. "Petra." I fought for breath, the tent suddenly feeling too small, smothering me. "Not yet."

I lowered my head, realizing the men had jumped back at the sight of my hands, the skin split and crackling like embers. "It burns," I whispered, a tear falling from my cheek to my hand and fizzling into steam.

"Listen to me," she said, her voice echoing through my head, calm and urgent all at once. "We'll need you soon. Not yet. Soon."

I imagined the flames winking out, the last embers of a fire fading into nothing. I felt my hands cool before a different burn set in, my skin going raw with more blisters. My eyes met Summercut's, and the voice that came from me was not mine — it was too stern, too weathered.

Nell's words echoed in my head again. I didn't know what I was doing, but I was damn sure going to make it look like I did.

"Let's prepare for war."

◆ ◆ ◆

Commanders and lieutenants and generals were introduced throughout the tent, their names leaving my mind as soon as I heard them. Calloused fingers pointed at different parts of the map, tracing lines from city to unfamiliar city, the names of them being thrown about faster than I could memorize them. Aera and Southridge and Redwater. I did my best to keep up.

I was able to pick out Eserene and the Onyxian Mountains. That was it. Not even any of the towns or villages near Eserene. I swallowed back the shame and frustration I felt at knowing so little as the soldiers rushed around me, arguing over the best routes and strategies.

"Castemont is most likely taking this route. These are small villages that Kauvras didn't bother with, meaning all of their citizens are ripe for the taking." Miles' finger moved through tiny dots on the map, from Taitha to Dry Gulch, through Carcalun and Sauveil and Millmouth before finally making it to Eserene.

"How many people would that be?" I asked, trying to keep my voice from betraying the panic I felt. "How many Vacants, if he uses the leechthorn?"

Summercut blew air through his lips. "Eight, maybe ten thousand total."

"And how many soldiers do we have?"

Summercut's eyes flashed to Miles before landing on me again. "There's no way to know for sure, but I'd say roughly three thousand."

Shit. That couldn't be good. I nodded and ran my eyes across the outlined route. "He'll have to go through the Onyx Pass," I whispered, images of bloodthirsty animals barrelling through my head. "Can he even survive that?"

"He's traveled the Pass before, multiple times," Miles answered gruffly. "He has guards, and he's well trained himself. As long as they stay on the path and there isn't another...*attack*, like when you traveled through, he has a good chance of making it, yes." My fist clenched on the table.

"It's true then?" A low voice rumbled from the crowd of men, coming from a burly general with a jagged scar on his cheek. "You really killed all those beasts?"

I pressed my lips together, giving a shallow nod. "I did."

"Holy shit," someone whispered. The tent stirred uncomfortably as the men continued staring at me.

"I saw her rip the spine from a wolfhound without even touching it," Miles declared. His voice raked nails down my back, my anger at him still sharp in my chest, still confused as to how he can be complimentary here in front of all these men and a complete dick to me when we were alone. "Three dozen beasts dead."

Summercut whistled, his eyes squinting with a hint of a smile, his head shaking in disbelief. "How did it feel?"

I opened my mouth to answer before I realized I had no idea what I'd say. "I... I don't know. I don't really remember. I was just focused on, you know, not dying." A laugh coursed through the small crowd of men.

"Remind me not to get on your bad side," someone said, coaxing another laugh from the group. I gave a slight smile.

"Believe me, it isn't a place you want to be," Miles grumbled under his breath, so low that I wasn't sure if anyone else heard it.

Now he's complaining about being on my bad side? What the fuck was his deal?

Summercut cleared his throat, once again looking to the map. "The issue here is time. I'm surprised they haven't sent a search party this way yet." His hand moved back to the map. "But the most important question remains. How do we get Petra to her rightful throne?"

"My *what*?" My head flew forward, a blistered palm splayed on the table.

"Your throne," he said, inclining his head. "As the Daughter of Katia, you have the most legitimate claim to the throne of Cabillia. To any throne in the world, really."

"I don't want–"

"You're not going to have a choice," Miles stated firmly. "Do you think that people are just going to let you fade back into obscurity now that they know who you are? Do you think that news of your arrival hasn't already traveled throughout the entire continent, maybe even beyond? You're the rightful queen."

Some part of me knew this was going to happen. I'd accepted the fact that some people were going to look to me as a leader once I found out my true heritage. But as a *queen*...

I squeezed my eyes shut and forced a deep breath into my lungs. I knew he was right. I could see it in the kneeling stances of the soldiers chanting. I could see it in the flashes of wonder that danced in the eyes of every soldier I'd spoken with. They believed in the Daughter of Katia beyond just her existence. They believed in her as a ruler. And the prophecy, the flames and wind that I was still trying to learn how to control... If they believed in all that, then by default, I supposed, they believed in me.

There wasn't much I could do to get around the fact that I was expected to rule — Cabillia, Astran, somewhere. In that moment, there was no other choice than to accept the role and everything it would require.

I had absolutely no idea how to be the queen the people needed. But I could fake it, just like Nell suggested. I gave a small nod before opening my eyes again, the room pulsing with salty resolve, most of it my own.

"Petra, you have the power to shape this world into something *good*," Summercut began. "Your intentions aren't evil like Kauvras."

Even though his intentions seemed to be, I wasn't sure Kauvras was actually evil. There was something in his eyes, something unhinged, unstable. The wild eyes, the outlandish words. Mad? Absolutely. But evil? Maybe not. Maybe just...unwell.

Castemont was evil incarnate.

"His supporters are just as maligned as he is," Miles explained. "They're not going to bow to you. And neither will the Vacants."

"I don't want them to."

"You're missing the point, Petra." The group collectively inhaled as Miles stepped even closer to me, the ram's face inches from mine. "They are what stand in the way of you and the Cabillian throne."

I chewed on my lip, my eyes wide as I thought. "The first step is eliminating them," Summercut said quietly.

What would a queen say in this situation? "A battle then. To kill as many of Kauvras' supporters as possible?"

"Kill, yes. Or sway their loyalty," Summercut answered. "But first..."

It hit me like a brick to the face. "But first, the Vacants."

He gave a grim nod. "We need to...deal with the Vacants. They won't care if you're Katia herself. They are loyal to leechthorn and nothing else."

I inhaled, trying to calm my erratic heartbeat in the tense stillness of the tent, the silence interrupted by the sounds of Taitha still burning across the fields of leechthorn. Deal with the Vacants? My mother?

I eyed Summercut. "What are you suggesting?"

Summercut shifted uncomfortably in place, looking to Miles. "Well... I think the best, most *humane* way–"

"You're going to kill them," Miles cut in, his breathing hard behind the mask. "You're going to put them out of their misery."

The shock was metallic in my throat as his words clanged through my skull. "What?" I demanded, brows raised.

"You're going to burn them. All of them," he answered curtly.

My blood instantly boiled as I pinned him with my stare. "Like hell I am! Are you insane?" I yelled, my blistered palms hitting the table as my gaze moved wildly about the room. "You want me to *kill* them? *Kill* my mother? You're out of your Saints damned mind if you think–"

"Petra!" Miles grabbed my shoulders, his grip so firm it bordered on pain. "They're already gone!" My breath was hissing through clenched teeth as I stared at my own convoluted reflection in the metal of the ram's head mask. I could feel his stare piercing through my skin. "They're already gone, Petra," he repeated, his words quieter, the edges softer, his broad palms still steadily gripping my shoulders.

My head turned to Summercut. His face was contorted with conflict, his eyes brimming with sorrow. He inhaled deeply. "It's the only way."

"I won't do it."

"You must," Summercut answered.

My head snapped back to Miles, his hands moving from my shoulders to my upper arms, thumbs moving back and forth across my skin. The touch felt *wrong,* like something that should comfort me but instead shot uneasiness through me. "I won't. And don't fucking touch me."

I shook myself free from his grasp, his hands falling unceremoniously to his sides as I shouldered my way out of the tent. I still felt his grip on my skin as I walked into the evening air.

"Your Majesty," I heard, turning to see Summercut had followed me. He stood before me, head lowered as soldiers moved around us. "Could I please have a word?"

I crossed my arms and nodded wordlessly.

"No one wants this," he said quietly. "This isn't how anyone wanted this to end."

"And how did you want it to end? What did you expect?"

He took a deep breath, eyes landing on the field of leechthorn that lay behind me. "I can't speak for everyone else, but I'd always hoped... I don't know, that there was some way to save them."

The fading daylight was a glint in his eyes, their color the same as the smoke that hung over Taitha. I let out a deep breath, the tension in my chest melting into empathy. "You really think the best option is to kill them?"

Summercut swallowed hard, the muscles in his jaw twinging. "I think it's the only option." His eyes fell distant again, on the city that continued to burn. "I don't say that lightly."

His features looked like they'd been chiseled from black marble, austere and intimidating as I believed a military commander should be. But his face was lined with grief and regret, the stark contrast between the severity of his features and the look etched into them punching a hole somewhere in my chest. Understanding poured in. "Kauvras took someone you love."

His lips were pursed as he looked at me and nodded. "My wife, Averyn, and our daughter, Miri." I heard him take a controlled inhale as if he were fighting back the urge to scream out in agony. "I wanted to provide for my family. I'd just joined the military when Kauvras discovered the effects of leechthorn. I didn't know what he was planning to do with it, of course. Before he set out on his conquest, he tested it on the poor of Taitha." I watched him chew the inside of his cheek, trying to maintain his composure. "I curse myself everyday for leaving them."

My chest caved in as he said their names, his tone rife with anguish. He was in mourning, even though they were still alive. "I'm sorry," I whispered.

"I am, too." He ran his tongue over his teeth. "Miri would be fifteen now, if she's still alive." I felt the ache in my gut as I looked at him, a physically painful, unrelenting throb. "I understand why you don't want to do this. I don't want you to, either, and none of the soldiers you see here want you to. They've lost family members, too. But, unfortunately," he continued, and I detected the slightest waver in his voice, "it's the only option."

I thought of Miles, if anyone he loved had fallen victim to leechthorn. And I thought of myself, of all the people I'd lost. Not to leechthorn, but to the dark cloud that seemed to follow me everywhere I went. This pain… It was enough proof for me that Castemont was indeed Noros, Saint of Pain. I couldn't let him win.

"Okay," I whispered. "I understand. I'll do it."

"This way, they can die with dignity," he murmured, and though he stood in front of me, I could tell he was far away, in another life, perhaps.

Chapter 8

Smoke billowed into the darkening sky as I watched the sea of leechthorn sway. The Outpost was abuzz with activity at my back.

No one had spoken to me since my conversation with Summercut, and I was glad they hadn't. His words hadn't left my head.

"Doing okay?" I heard a light voice chime from behind me.

I didn't respond as Nell lowered herself to sit next to me. She exhaled, popping the cork from a flask and taking a swig before offering it to me. I took as big a gulp as I could fit in my mouth, the burning liquid making my eyes water. It reminded me of the day I sat at the waterfront with Castemont. The day I told him that yes, he could marry my mother. Yes, we'd move to the castle.

What a Saints damned mistake.

"They're all talking about it, you know," she muttered. "The plan. That you're going to *eliminate* the Vacants."

My teeth instinctually ground together. I sat silently beside her.

"Petra, they're already gone. It would be a mercy to them."

"I know," I breathed, reaching for the flask again and taking another swig.

She cleared her throat. "So, Lieutenant Miles Landgrave," she stated, fictitious pomp in her tone as she changed the subject. "What's his deal? He seems like a dick."

"I can't get a read on him," I huffed. "One minute he's complimenting me and the next he's snapping at me." I swallowed back anger, tamping down the flames threatening to rise in my chest.

"He definitely cares for you, if that's what you're wondering."

I scoffed. "He handed me over to Kauvras so he could get *answers*." My eyes rolled in my head at the thought. "He doesn't care for me, Nell."

She let out a low hum. "I wouldn't be so sure about that. Though I guess I can't say for certain since I can't see the way he looks at you from behind that mask."

"I can guarantee he doesn't care about me. Any time he touches me…" I shuddered. "I don't know. It doesn't feel right."

"Huh."

I let Nell's words about his hidden face sit in my mind. "Why wouldn't he want to take off the mask?"

She grabbed the flask back from me, tipping it to her lips. "A lot of the guys who deal with the Vacants won't take their masks off for shit. My guess is because he's ashamed. Doesn't want people to see who he is because he can't face it. Either that or he's ugly."

A laugh escaped me, but silence quickly settled over the two of us again as smoke swirled through the night sky.

"Kauvras has preached about you for years," Nell said suddenly, a thumb running circles around the rim of her flask. "He promised us that the prophesied Daughter of Katia was coming. Told us he was going to use her to ascend to Sainthood to even the power between Benevolence and Blood." Her gaze was distant on the city. "He'd always say we were on the right side of history as his supporters."

"You support him?"

"Fuck no," she laughed. "But what was I going to do? Women aren't allowed in the military, but it was three meals a day and a roof to sleep under. So I snuck around a bit, made sure I looked the part, and did what I had to do to survive."

The words resonated with me instantly. I pushed the toe of my boot in the dirt, remembering everything I did in Inkwell to ensure my family survived. "And did you believe him? Did you believe the Daughter of Katia was coming?"

She smirked. "Never really thought about it, to be honest. Just figured he was another power hungry king. Didn't think much of his ramblings. Or that you'd actually show up." Her voice was somber but plastered with thin amusement, like she was trying to find the humor in the fact that everything she knew had changed within a matter of hours. "I always thought he was just mad."

I inhaled, working through the meaning of her words. "Do you know why Kauvras is the way he is?" I asked. "Why he started all of this?"

"You want to know if the rumors are true, huh? If the Saints actually spoke to him." A mischievous smile danced on her lips.

"I know nothing, Nell. I want to know *everything*." She took yet another gulp of liquor. Saints, this girl could drink.

"He's never admitted it. But this lot can't hold gossip in for shit. The story goes, *supposedly*," she began, dramatic emphasis on the word, "Kauvras had fallen in love with a lowborn woman in Taitha. This was back when he was still just a loud-ass rebel rising up against the previous king, King Divos. But Kauvras didn't court her long before he left her for his cause. But he was heartbroken, and so was she." She wiped her mouth with the back of her hand. "A Nesanian trader showed up and fell in love with her.

Apparently she forgot all about Kauvras and fell in love with the trader, too. That's all I know."

"Nothing about a Nesanian queen sleeping with King Divos?" I asked, recounting Wrena's words.

"Not that I know of. Wouldn't discount it, though."

I exhaled, trying to fit the pieces together. "Do you think the woman that Kauvras left was Belin's mother?"

She pursed her lips and shook her head. "No idea. But, the Nesanian trader had supposedly gone back home after Kauvras threatened not only his life, but the life of the woman he'd once loved as well."

"Kauvras loved the woman but threatened her life?" Cal told me his mother had been murdered... Had it been Kauvras?

She smirked. "Love's fuckin' crazy sometimes."

"Do you know her name?"

"I don't. I don't know if anyone outside of Kauvras' inner circle does. Don't know if she's still in Taitha. She could be dead."

I laid back, not feeling any better than when we started this conversation.

"Listen, Petra, I know this is a lot. But we're going to get you to that throne," Nell said, her voice full of conviction.

"I just–"

A hoarse shriek cleaved the air and bodies hit the ground as men rushed out of the tunnel and into the Outpost. I shot to my feet and scrambled back, the sound of screaming steel piercing my ears as soldiers collided with soldiers.

"There she is!" one of the men bellowed, slitting the throat of a leather-clad soldier and letting him drop before stalking toward me, a lion's head mask glinting in the torchlight.

My blood went icy as Nell's hand wrapped around my arm, yanking me back. And then I realized–

They were all wearing masks. Every soldier who came from the tunnel was wearing a mask.

The men at the Outpost began to fight, but the ambush was too sudden. Within seconds, men — *my* men — were being

92

plowed down, flint pulled from bags, pipes held to screaming lips. "*No!*" I screamed, pulling against Nell's surprisingly solid grip. "*No, no, no!*" Tomkin was on the ground, a masked man at his shoulders and another at his feet as he coughed and heaved and fought. More masked soldiers spilled from the tunnels, carrying the too-familiar chains with manacles. Still the man in the lion's mask stalked toward me.

I let the familiar rage build within my ribcage, burrowing deep into myself to the depths of my newfound powers. It could end with the Outpost being swallowed by an inferno, but I had to do something.

"Petra!" Nell screamed as she unsheathed her own sword. "Come *on!*"

I couldn't run. I had to save them, save these people who had shown me such kindness, who *believed in me*. I continued digging, trying to gather anything and everything that resembled fire and light and fury in my soul. If I could just conjure up enough to get one small spark, one tiny flame–

Suddenly a tall body was in front of me, ram's horns curving over his heaving shoulders. Miles' sword was drawn, blood already dripping down the hilt as he came face to face with the man in the lion mask. But the lion wasn't alone anymore — four other masked men let bodies drop to the dirt before joining their comrade, blades ready.

"Whit!" Nell roared the same moment I saw him, a wicked gash dripping from his cheek as he pulled his blade from a bloodied chest. Nell's call had garnered the attention of the others and they closed in around us, Summercut finding his place next to Miles.

"Hand her over," the lion growled.

"And *you* are?" Miles answered, his raspy voice more authoritative than I'd ever heard it.

"I am Commander Magnus Stone, here on behalf of King Kauvras to collect his bride. *Hand her over.*"

"I don't think I will." His voice was taunting now.

Stone's feet dug into the dirt. "I am your Commander and you will do as I say. She is the property of King Kauvras by law." His voice was thick with pent up ferocity, but it was nothing compared to what was brewing inside me.

"Is she though? I was at the wedding. I didn't see a kiss."

"Last chance," Stone growled.

Miles laughed. He *laughed*. The kind that came from deep in his belly. "I don't think so."

The commander took a step forward, his figure all the more menacing, all the more unpredictable with his features hidden. Miles didn't flinch. "Do you think you can protect her from me?" Commander Stone asked, his voice full of malice.

"Oh, she doesn't need my protection." Funny, that's not what he implied earlier when he asked if I knew how to control my powers or jumped in the wardrobe with me in the event I needed to be *defended*. It added fury to my fire.

Nell angled her head back just slightly, her eyes remaining on the conflict in front of us. "Get ready," she whispered.

For what exactly, I didn't know, but my fingers began to burn as I felt my rage simmer beneath my skin, itching to be released.

"Hand her over," Stone demanded again.

Miles' voice was a teasing whisper that sent chills up my spine. "Come and get her."

Kauvras' men charged, war cries erupting from behind their masks as Miles and his men suddenly hit the ground. "*Now!*" Nell screamed, diving out of the way.

I understood.

My hands flew up in front of my face, my skin splitting as flames flew from my palms. The scream that ripped through my throat could have rattled Hell as I let the burn consume me, streams of fire crashing into the metal mask on the commander's face. *Holy shit.* It took only seconds for the mask to glow red, molten metal dripping from the lion's maw as Commander Stone hit the ground, clawing at his face before his entire head erupted in a burst of fire, the wind whipping at the flames.

And still I burned. But this felt different than my eruption in the throne room. This fire burned lower but hotter, brighter, *stronger*. Instead of feeling as though my bones would break, the fire wrapped around them, fortified them with a web of flame. As I watched the lion's movements grow slower and the flames grow bigger, it felt...*good*.

The other masked men had fallen back, shielding their faces as I turned my fury on them. Gold went red and melted as the smell of burning skin hit me. Everything in me smoldered, my eyes, my mouth, my *soul*. I savored it, let it overtake me.

I waited for Katia's voice, waited for her to tell me to lay my flames down, to which I'd tell her to kindly fuck off. But the voice I began to hear wasn't hers...

"Burn them," it whispered, the voice resounding through my body as my lips curved into a wicked smile in recognition. I'd never heard this voice before, but I knew exactly who it belonged to. "Burn them to *ash*," it hissed.

Rhedros.

I obliged, plucking the fleeing masked men from their escape one by one and letting them suffer, delighting in their pain, their anguish, their–

It was Nell's voice I heard this time. "Petra!"

Shit.

Reality suddenly slammed into me, my vision dotted with red as I dropped my hands, the sound of crackling embers surrounding me. "We need to *go*," she urged.

"They won't be the last ones," Miles heaved as he and the other men pushed themselves up from the ground.

My eyes shot to the tunnel as echoed yells hit my ears. The quick movement made my skull pound, and I swayed on my feet, suddenly hyper-aware of the exhaustion that slammed into me. This didn't feel good anymore. Nell's hand shot to one shoulder while Miles went for the other. "Petra, we have to go *now*," Nell pressed.

"Incoming," Summercut called to the Outpost before turning to me. "*Go!* We'll hold the Outpost as long as we can!"

I understood what they were saying but I couldn't move. Every inch of me simultaneously burned and felt like it was made of stone. I managed a weak nod as they pulled me through the Outpost and between the buildings to the boulders that made up the steep incline of the mountain.

"Whit!" Nell screamed, the man already sprinting to join us. "Come on!"

"Yes ma'am," he answered, falling into stride beside her as she and Miles continued to pull me along.

I wanted to tell them to stop, to tell them that it *hurt*. But I couldn't do anything but stumble along, missing every other step, my head still swimming.

"You're going to be okay," Miles breathed before he heaved himself up a boulder, reaching down for me. The pain of my blistered hands shot lightning down my arms. I let out a choked cry. "Just hang in there a little bit longer."

But I was still burning, the warmth calling to me, urging me to slip into its embrace.

Chapter 9

"There is nothing I want more in this eternal existence than to spend it by your side. But we're only in this place because of something sinister. It cannot stay this way, my love."

I heard a muffled sob, as if the person it came from was trying to hold it in. "He's going to go after her." Katia.

I opened my eyes only to be greeted with a vast empty darkness that pinned me down.

"We can't be sure it's him." Rhedros' voice was softer now, no longer a seething hiss like it had been at the Outpost.

I heard Katia's breathing quicken and I tried to turn my head to look for her. Nothing. Where were they? Where was I? "I know it is."

"Then I'll find him and destroy him."

"Hello?" I whispered, my voice hoarse and scratchy in my throat.

Katia and Rhedros both gasped, the sound echoing through the darkness that surrounded me.

"She's waking up." That was neither Katia nor Rhedros' voice. The words were far away, dampened and distant like I was underwater and someone was whispering from the surface.

"Fucking Saints, Whit! Would you give her some space?" Nell. That was Nell. But where were Katia and Rhedros? I opened my mouth, trying to say the words, but all that came out was air.

Cloudy daylight suddenly set my eyes watering as three silhouetted forms crouched above me. I blinked furiously, my eyelids gritty, my mouth dry as the Keepers of the Saints slipped away. My hands lifted in front of my face, knowing I'd find no blisters where there should be dozens.

"Petra?" The ram's head took shape above me, the metal glinting in the gray light as Miles stared down at me. "Petra? Can you hear me?"

The tone of his voice, the softness behind it... Irritation set in, and I wanted to rip that damned mask off his head now more than ever. My head dropped to the side, and I realized I was on the bank of a small pond, the surface rippling in more than one place, as if someone had just been skipping rocks. I was thirsty, I realized. So fucking thirsty. "Water," I croaked.

In an instant Nell had a waterskin to my lips, her dark eyes surveying my face. "You're a fuckin' badass, you know that?" Nell laughed.

I smacked my lips, my tongue feeling odd in my mouth. "I'm learning that," I muttered, earning a soft laugh from Nell. "What happened?"

"You melted some faces, we fled, and you passed out," Whit explained. "You've been sleeping for two days."

Shit. "Where are we?"

"Half a day's hike into the Rhedrosian Mountains," Miles answered, gesturing to the dense forest and mountain slopes that loomed above us. A small fire burned next to the pond, a rabbit roasting over it on a makeshift spit. "As far as we could carry you before we needed to rest. We wanted you to sleep." I noticed his hand was on my shoulder, thumb stroking small circles, the feeling once again unsettling. As if he felt my attention on the gesture, he pulled his hand away, placing it on the hilt of his sword.

"We're a few days' hike from Aera. We'll need to gather more supplies." I remembered them mentioning Aera in the tent, a small town to the north of Taitha and the Rhedrosian Mountains.

"They're going to come after us, no?" I asked, trying to prop myself up on my elbows.

The three soldiers looked at one another. "They should have already come after us, yes," Nell answered. "We can only assume Summercut and the rest were able to hold them off, but we can't assume they aren't on our trail. Kauvras will figure out you escaped sooner or later."

I nodded, letting my body drop back to the ground. The three soldiers looked expectantly at me. "You all followed me out here?"

Nell's eyes narrowed. "Of course we did. We believe in you. We're going to follow you wherever you lead us."

"Like shadows," Whit added with a grin. "Well, shadows with swords."

"Shadows with swords?" Nell scoffed. "That's not intimidating at all. We're like...a penumbra. *The Penumbra.*"

Whit raised a brow. "What does that even mean?"

"A better word for shadow. We'll be your Penumbra. Me, Whit, and Landgrave."

"Do not rope me into this," Miles growled.

"Too late, bud," Nell quipped. "You're a part of the Penumbra."

I smiled back at her. "The Penumbra... I like it."

"You can't say it too much or else it'll start to sound like it's not a real word," Whit jeered.

I swore I could feel Miles roll his eyes from behind his mask.

My eyes landed back on Nell. "I'm assuming you have a plan."

"You assumed correctly," Nell said, moving to sit next to me. "My idea, of course, no thanks to these idiots."

Miles immediately straightened. "I am your Lieutenant and–"

"Except you're not," Nell quipped, all the formality I'd seen her show Miles back at the Outpost completely disappeared. "I'm not a soldier, remember? You said so yourself." She looked at me and gave me a wink. Miles stayed still, staring at the not-soldier from behind his mask. "Saints, I'd love to pull that mask off you and see the bloody look on your face. Lucky for you, I do have *some* respect."

I decided then that I really, *really* liked Nell.

"Alright," Nell started again. "We need to get to Aera. Since you're the only one in plainclothes, Petra, you'll take a few coins and go into town to buy us all cloaks. Landgrave, Whit, and I will hang back. Don't really want to draw attention to our armor over there. Aera has a Cabillian military presence, but not much. We'd stick out, and we don't need people asking questions."

"What about the damned mask?" I asked, gesturing to Miles.

"I'll keep the mask on under the hood of the cloak."

I blinked, dumbfounded at his resolve to keep his fucking face hidden. "Are you kidding me? What is so wrong with your face that you won't show it?"

"The mask stays on."

I raised my brows at him as Nell leaned in and whispered, "*Definitely* ugly."

Whit cleared his throat. "Once we have cloaks, Nell and I will get food. You and Lieutenant Landgrave will go to the blacksmith."

My eyes squinted in question. "You need a weapon," Miles offered.

"Why would I need a weapon?" I asked incredulously. "I kind of...*am* a weapon."

"You can't control it," Miles said matter-of-factly. "Until you learn to control it, you're going to learn to defend yourself with a sword too."

I wrinkled my nose at the thought. "Why don't I practice *controlling it* now?"

"Look around, Petra. This entire forest could go up in flames with one wrong move. Dry wood and fire? Not a good idea." I knew that all too well, a lesson Castemont decided to teach me in Inkwell when he set my home ablaze. But I didn't like the fact that Miles was right. "You won't be able to learn much between now and when we get back to Taitha, but I'll teach you the basics of sword fighting so you have options other than burning the whole city down."

"Again," Whit added.

Nell rose and began dismantling our makeshift campsite, descending into an argument with Whit as to which of them had more kills back in the throne room.

"Are you going to be able to walk?" Miles asked quietly as he stood.

I sat up. My joints were a bit stiff, but nothing that would keep me from walking. "I'll be fine." I stretched my neck, wincing at the tightness of my muscles as I pushed myself to stand, ignoring the hand he'd outstretched for me.

"We can get to Aera in two days if we hustle," he said. I gave a nod, Whit and Nell's bickering fading into the background as I followed behind them. "Until then…" Miles looked around before finding a broken branch about the length of my arm, testing the weight in his grip, then tossing it to me. I fumbled to catch it, but with the haze of unconsciousness still hanging over me, it landed on the ground with an inelegant *thud.*

"What the hell am I supposed to do with this?" I asked as I grabbed the branch from the ground.

"That's your sword until we can get you a real one."

"I'm not carrying this–"

"That's your sword until we can get you a real one," he repeated, his tone sharper.

I opened my mouth to fight but Nell's voice caught my attention. "Let's *go*," she called back to us. "Teach and walk! Teach and walk!"

Branch in hand, I trudged forward, keenly aware of Miles' looming presence beside me. "First lesson," he started, unsheathing his own sword, the noise garnering a glance from Whit and Nell as we caught up with them. "Balance."

I all but rolled my eyes. "Really? Can't you just teach me to swing a damned sword?"

"No. Every soldier learns balance first. It's non-negotiable. It'll be a little more difficult since we're walking, but get the hang of it now and by the time we get some real steel in your hands you'll be better for it." He held his hand in front of him and rested the end of the hilt on his flattened palm. Even as he walked through the blanket of dead leaves and twigs, the sword didn't waver in the slightest. "Your turn."

I huffed against his command but obliged. I *should* learn to defend myself with something less...chaotic than the fury that burned within me. Palm out, I rested the splintered edge of the branch in my hand.

Thud.

"Again," Miles commanded evenly.

I reset. Over and over and over, I propped the branch up only for it to tip within seconds. Each time it landed on the ground, I felt my rage burn hotter. The hours passed, the branch never stilling for more than a few seconds, all the while Miles watched silently, patiently, expectantly.

◆ ◆ ◆

Two days of hiking. Two days of balancing a damned branch on my palm. Two days, and all I managed to do was hit the five-second mark...once.

102

It was late afternoon when we heard the braying of horses — the first sign we were nearing civilization. "We're close," Miles said, his voice rough with agitation.

"Kauvras didn't raid Aera?" I asked, wondering if I'd find only the remnants of a city when we arrived.

"Not yet. If he attacks Aera, it compromises Taitha's trade route on the Hudna River. It's on his list, though," Miles explained flatly. "Remember the plan?"

Indistinct voices began to sound as we crested a hill to find a small city laying in the crook of a rushing river. Aera. I looked nervously out over the collection of buildings. There was no castle like in Taitha or Eserene, just rows of structures on narrow streets. "I'm going to buy cloaks," I answered.

Miles dug a few coins from a pocket on his side and placed them in my hand. "And then you come right back. Got it?"

I raised a brow at the tone of his voice but decided it wasn't worth fighting over. The prospect of spending a few minutes by myself was actually quite enticing. "Yep."

"We'll be right here," Nell added.

I gave a short wave over my shoulder and trekked down the hill toward the city. I wondered if the people of Aera knew about the Daughter of Katia, if they'd heard what happened in Taitha.

As I neared the city, the familiar smell of filth assaulted my nose, and I let a smile quirk my lips as Inkwell rushed into my memory. Aera was markedly nicer than Inkwell had been, but I recognized the same stalwart, hard working people, the same rundown cottages, the same sounds of carts and horses and haggling.

For a moment, I let myself pretend I was walking to see Caroline, the only seamstress in Inkwell. I let the shadows of the cottages feel like the shadows of Eserene's city walls lumbering above me. I was going to see Caroline and then go to the market to buy half-rotted potatoes for my family, not cloaks for three strangers.

For a moment I was *home.*

But the accent that began to filter into my ears was not Ink-wellian, and the color of the dirt in the street was too red. The boots people wore were sewn in a different style with different stitching. The people seemed too friendly. The sunlight was different.

I was different. I wasn't the same person I'd been in Inkwell. I'd been penniless and hungry. I'd been a thief. And now I was... Now I was expected to be a queen. Of what, exactly, I didn't know. But I was going to be a queen.

Focus, Petra, I told myself. Cloaks. I needed cloaks. My eyes scanned the signs on the shops that lined the streets as I neared what seemed to be the middle of town until I found one that seemed suitable, *Rosalinde's Clothing and Textiles.* The sweet feel of solitude crept into my bones as I pushed the rickety door open. A small woman greeted me from behind a dusty counter, the lines in her face deep set, her eyes sunken in.

This simple, mundane task of buying a cloak... I let myself enjoy it, cherish the solace of doing something so ordinary. Hangers ground against wooden racks as I let my hands run across the fabric, as if these very hands weren't responsible for taking the lives of so many men and women already. As if they wouldn't soon be responsible for eliminating ten thousand Vacants, possibly more.

I was mad at Miles for even suggesting it, even if it was the right thing to do. *Saints,* he pissed me off. But it was the discomfort that his touch brought me that was front and center in my mind. It truly did feel almost familiar, like something I'd felt from someone before, just...different. It was wrong, unsettling. I tried to swallow back the uneasiness, but still it sat like a lump in my throat.

Anxious thoughts brewed in my head as I piled my cloaks on the counter, thoughts about Miles and the Vacants and the prophecy I'd found myself a part of. Before long, everyone would know who I was. Everyone would know I was the Daughter of Katia. I took a deep breath, one of my last as *just Petra.* But out

104

of the grimy shop window, something caught my eye — the sign on the shop just across the street.

The Empty Mirror: Purveyors of Blood Magic and Dark Thaumaturgy.

"Excuse me," I asked the shop worker as I handed her a few coins. I felt silly even asking her, but I couldn't ignore the draw of The Empty Mirror. "What exactly is that shop there?"

She squinted her eyes through the window and her lips contorted in a twisted frown. "Unholy, that's what it is," she croaked, a few gnarled yellow teeth poking through her gums. "An affront to this city and an affront to the Saints."

"But what exactly *is* it?" I pushed.

She sniffed, the mildness she'd exuded suddenly turning much more hostile as she surveyed my face. "You not from here?"

I offered a smile, hoping to soften the vitriol that now hung in the air. "Oh, born and raised here, ma'am," I offered, surprised the lie rolled off my tongue so easily. "My Ma would never tell me anything about it whenever we'd pass by, and well, I'm just curious." I did my best to sound as innocent as possible.

Her milky eyes remained on me as she stared through narrow lids that drooped with age, her jaw grinding back and forth. "A Bloodsinger."

I fought to keep my face straight as my heart stumbled over its next beat. Suddenly aware of the shopkeeper's gaze burning into my face, I blinked hard. "Oh," I answered quietly. "How...horrific."

"No place for a young lady such as yourself," she added, her tone suddenly softer, presumably because of my reaction. "Hoping now that the Daughter of Katia has arrived, the likes of 'em will be destroyed."

My jaw clenched like an iron vice at her words. Heat rose in my cheeks. "Yes," I said sheepishly. "Hopefully." I offered the old woman a nervous smile, reaching for the folded cloaks on the counter. "Well, thank you, ma'am."

"You get home safe," she called after me.

The door slammed behind me as I whisked away from Rosalinde's and away from the Empty Mirror, stomach churning and mind spinning as I returned to Miles, Nell, and Whit.

A Bloodsinger. A fucking Bloodsinger. I stopped mid-stride. What if they had answers? What if they knew more about the Board of Blood or Castemont's plans? I was going to have to convince Miles to let me go in.

No. Miles didn't have to *let* me do anything. I didn't need his permission. I didn't need anyone's permission.

I turned on my heel, hearty resolve pulsing through every vein, and marched right back to the Empty Mirror, praying to every Saint that the shopkeeper of Rosalinde's didn't see me slip through the painted black door.

A smell like burning metal knocked me back, circling my head with an unpleasant heaviness. The only light in the small room came from the burning candles that sat on every flat surface, the flickering illuminating the smoky air. Black and gold furniture lined the room, the elegant design odd in a place that was reminiscent of a dungeon. Various doorways were scattered across the walls, heavy wooden doors standing guard of whatever was behind them. An eeriness crept into my chest at the stillness of the room.

"Hello," a spindly voice said, and I jumped at the sudden noise in the silence, whirling to see a wisp of a man standing in one of the doorways.

I cleared my throat as I stared into the smoke, but it was too thick to discern any of his features. "Hello," I offered weakly.

"How may I be of assistance today?"

I blinked at his words, at the sound of such a mundane question while I stood in the presence of someone who was familiar with pure evil. "What... Can you tell me what it is you can assist me with?"

The man stepped toward me, his face suddenly clear enough to see, and I froze. Because the man staring back at me looked identical to Ludovicus.

Chapter 10

"Is something wrong, dear?" the man asked, his words slithering down my spine. He smoothed his hands over his pitch black suit, almost as if he were self-conscious, his silvery-gray eyes shimmering in the low light. They weren't as unnatural a color as the members of the Board of Blood, but it did nothing to stop the fear from lighting up my veins.

I realized my mouth had been hanging open. "I'm sorry, it's just that you look..." I tried to make sense of it in my head, at the prospect of more men like the ones who tortured me so freely in Eserene's throne room. All of them had died that day — all except Ludovicus. He was somewhere beneath the castle of Taitha. Hopefully he'd burned along with it. "You look very familiar." I clenched my jaw, every nerve in my body on high alert.

"I'd think so," he answered with a smile, taking a step toward me. I instinctively took a step back, clinging harder to the folded cloaks in my arms.

The man raised his hands in supplication. "Apologies, dear. I didn't mean to frighten you." His voice had grown even softer, even more spindly. "My name is Alvar, and I am the Bloodsinger of Aera."

I nodded, my eyes never leaving his sickeningly familiar face. I shouldn't have come here. I should have returned to the group like I was supposed to. But what if… "I'm—" I caught myself. "My name is Larka."

"Very nice to meet you, Larka," he said with a smile. "You're interested in the services I provide?"

I weighed my words carefully. "I'm… I'm just wondering what exactly those services are."

"You haven't heard of blood magic?" he asked, a single thin brow raised.

"I…" I swallowed hard. "I've heard of it. I just…don't know what it is exactly."

He nodded, his lips pursed as he extended a hand to the tufted velvet settee. I ignored the offer and instead lowered myself to the claw-footed chair across from him, eyeing the leisurely way he sat, the long, pointed nails that had clawed through my nightmares.

"You don't know what blood magic is," he repeated back to me, as if it weren't a question but a thought spoken aloud. I gave a slight shake of my head, and his brows furrowed as he assessed me. His stare suddenly felt deeper, more invasive now. Hands steepled beneath his chin, his face was contemplative. "Where are you from, dear?"

Should I tell him the truth? I supposed I should. If anything went wrong I could always just set his building on fire. Right?

"Eserene."

He nodded, sitting back once again. "As I thought. Blood magic, and therefore Bloodsingers, are forbidden in Eserene. They have been since the War of Kings ended over one hundred and twenty years ago. Eserenian residents must travel to Blindbarrow in order to see a Bloodsinger, which most people forgo out of fear of the Onyx Pass." He cocked his head and pursed his lips. "So tell me, dear Larka, how can it be that I look so familiar to you?"

My eyes narrowed as I contemplated his question. Would he know Ludovicus and the Board of Blood? Did he know that his *brothers* had tortured the young women of Eserene's royalty for years? He looked at me with eyes I expected to be laced with malice but...weren't. His gaze was inquisitive, curious in a way that I hadn't seen among the members of the Board of Blood.

"I'm not quite sure why you look familiar," I answered apprehensively.

"I ask this because we Bloodsingers tend to have some...*similarities* between us. We tend to be recognizable. As do our patrons...in some cases." My mind grappled for the meaning of his words. "Using blood magic comes at a cost. Each favor granted, each answer given comes at the cost of beauty."

The cost of *beauty*?

He must have seen the confusion on my face, because his mouth turned up in a smile that was nothing short of wicked. The sight was too familiar, too unsettling, and I recoiled. "With a small sacrifice, blood magic can do almost anything, grant almost any wish."

My eyes widened at the prospect of this, at the prospect of bringing back everyone I'd lost, at returning to my normal life. My heart rose in my chest as I thought–

All wickedness melted from his features. "It cannot revive those already dead," he said flatly, as if he'd recited the words a thousand times before, and my heart returned to its normal broken state. "It also cannot change events of the past." My gaze dropped from his face at the slight defeat I felt. "It can, however, give you any answer you could possibly be looking for. It can also give glimpses into the future. And lastly, blood magic can influence the actions of others. All you need is a sacrifice of human blood. A simple finger prick is enough. We need just a drop."

I blinked hard as I tried to make sense of what he was telling me. My mouth opened and closed, trying to form around words I couldn't find.

"It is an enticing thing, is it not? To think that the world is much more malleable than you once believed? The bones that hold up this world can so easily be broken," he murmured, "so long as you know where to strike." One skeletal ankle crossed over the other and he smiled again, though his wispy, eerie voice was almost tinged with regret. "But, like I said," he started again, his voice somber, "it comes at a cost."

I shifted uncomfortably in my seat. I didn't know what he was implying.

"I was not always a man with such distasteful features, dear Larka." I stared at the man. His skin was disconcertingly pale. His features were too sharp, too angular to be human. His limbs were long and almost skeletal. But his eyes — there was a softness about them, a kindness in the way he watched me watch him. His eyes seemed...human.

He offered another smile with paper-thin lips. "I was once a dock worker who could command the attention of anyone with my looks alone." His gaze traveled elsewhere, to a distant past. "But the appeal of blood magic was strong, as it tends to be, and I became a regular patron of a Bloodsinger in a tiny town on Roughwater Island," he said with a sigh.

"It started small. There was a captain of a merchant ship that would often dock at the port, and he had a daughter." His eyes were still in some far off place, further softening at the memory. I recognized that look – had seen it in Wrena's eyes when she told me about the man she'd loved and lost. "She was the most beautiful creature I'd ever seen. I never knew why she traveled with her father. Maybe it was her father's attempt to keep her away from no-good men like me." He laughed, and it was dry and hollow, laced with a sadness I knew too well. "I started asking the Bloodsinger for small favors. I just wanted her to look at me at first, to see me. Then I wanted the Bloodsinger to tell me her wants, her fears, what made her happy... I asked for just a simple conversation with her."

His finger began to tap against his knee. "It happens slowly. My skin went pale at first, then my brown hair went black as night." He ran a bony hand through the oily strands that sat on his shoulders. "Before long, even my voice lost its luster. Too much of a good thing, as they say, but I wanted her to fall in love with me."

"And did it work?" I asked, rapt with attention.

Another sad smile showed across his face. "We enjoyed many walks along the coast together, many nights sitting on the dock talking and telling stories. She never once asked about my changing appearance, though her father had been wary. But I'll never know if she'd fallen in love with me as I had with her. She left with her father for Tadrana and the ship never returned. It was assumed..." I nodded as he trailed off, the bitter smell of loss hanging in the smoky air.

And though this man looked so similar to the ones who'd ripped me to shreds, broken my bones and tried to sever the soul from my body, my heart ached for him as he remembered. "I knew blood magic couldn't bring back the dead. And yet, I tried. Every day I visited the town's Bloodsinger, every day I sacrificed the life coursing through my body for a chance to see her again until I ran out of beauty to give. Eventually, before I went too far, I decided to become a Bloodsinger myself and learned the art of blood magic."

Every answer. Every single answer for every question that my entire life had raised... It all sat before me in the form of this man. I could ask him if Noros came to the realm disguised as an Eserenian lord. "Do you..." I started, unsure of where I wanted the conversation to go. "Do people visit you often?"

He sighed, his face breaking into a close-lipped smile that didn't meet his eyes. "No, they don't. Blood magic is... Well, it's frowned upon. Even I can understand why. I do try to dissuade my patrons from unnecessary favors."

I stared at him through narrowed eyes. "You look down on your own profession?"

"It's very easy to fall victim to the draw of it all. I myself am living proof of that. And the public doesn't look at us very kindly. I understand that, as well. Given my appearance, this is my place in society. I've come to accept it."

Two sides of my mind were at war as I looked at the man. "So if I've met someone who looks just like you..."

"It doesn't necessarily mean they're a Bloodsinger," he offered, the hiss of his voice contradicting the kind nature of his words. "But typically, when someone has elicited the services of a Bloodsinger often enough to look as I do, they usually can't find employment elsewhere and choose to practice blood magic themselves."

My brain was running laps around itself as it desperately grasped for something, anything that could give me a hold on what he was saying. "The Board of Blood," I blurted before I realized I was talking. "Are they Bloodsingers?"

Alvar cocked his head, his brows furrowing over his silver eyes. "I don't believe I've heard of a Board of Blood."

My heartrate quickened. "Garit, Higgins, Balthazar, Anton, Arturius, Raolin," I rattled off, "and... Ludovicus."

"I'm afraid I'm unfamiliar with the names, though there have been talks amongst my brothers of schemes to find the long-awaited Daughter of Katia, and some Bloodsingers have predicted she'd be born in Eserene. Bloodsingers, however, are strictly prohibited from taking part in such schemes, though I wonder if you came across some nefarious patrons." His tone was more annoyed with the prospect than concerned.

The words I'd wanted to say lodged in my throat as my chest tightened. So the members of the Board of Blood may not have been Bloodsingers, is that what he was saying? Was he saying that they were regular people — *evil* people — who had enlisted the services of Bloodsingers and lost everything that made them look human?

And they were looking for me?

"Are you okay, Miss Larka?" Alvar asked, leaning forward, concern on his face.

I stared at him, bile surging from my stomach along with the one question I needed answered, the one thing I needed him to confirm. My words came out in a hoarse whisper. "So Bloodsingers don't harm people?"

He sat back, his eyes wide. "Saints, no. Though we practice a form of magic that most of society considers unsavory, we still have a strict set of laws we must abide by, set by the Sanguilite. One of those laws is that we cause no direct physical harm to another being. Did someone…"

If he'd finished his sentence, I hadn't heard it as realization hit me like a cannonball to the ribs. The little I thought I knew about the Board of Blood had gone out the window, thrown by Alvar's words.

The Board was not made up of Bloodsingers. Bloodsingers weren't malicious. The Board of Blood was made up of people who'd been ensnared by the allure of blood magic.

I shot up from the chair, clutching the cloaks for dear life as if they could keep my brain from thrashing inside my skull. Alvar stood slowly, smoothing his hands down his chest as he stared at me with concern. "Thank you," I blurted, "for your time."

"Of course, Miss Larka. You're always welcome."

With nothing more than a parting nod, I left Alvar and The Empty Mirror with a pounding heart and head, both so heavy I could have collapsed in the street.

Chapter 11

"What the hell took you so long?" Miles demanded as I approached the group waiting at the top of the hill. "You've been gone an hour."

"I couldn't find a shop with cloaks," I offered weakly, hoping he wouldn't see through the lie.

Nell eyed me but said nothing. "Lieutenant Sunshine over here hasn't stopped pacing since you left."

I passed the cloaks to my waiting companions, folding my own over my shoulders after Miles all but snatched his from my grip. "I'm on edge," he snarled under his breath, the words clipped as he pulled his hood up over the ram's head.

"You're *really* going to leave the mask on?" I asked him, brows raised. "You look ridiculous."

"Let's move before we lose daylight."

I rolled my eyes at him. He did look ridiculous, like some kind of reaper, the twisted metal ram's horns protruding from beneath his hood. "Whitley, Augen," he commanded, pointing to Nell and Whit, "find food, water, and supplies. The plan is to travel back to Aera, but we need to be prepared in case a detour is necessary." They nodded, setting off toward the city. "You," he said to me, "with me."

"Yes, Sir," I muttered, following as he began to descend the hill. I was sure he shot me an irritated glance from behind the mask.

"Meet back here in an hour," he called out.

◆ ◆ ◆

My mind was mush as I tried to make sense of what Alvar told me. I didn't want to think anymore. I blindly followed Miles as we wove through the streets of Aera.

"There's a smith up ahead. Keep your mouth shut and let me do the talking. Got it?" His tone was harsh, so harsh that something in me finally snapped.

"What is your problem?"

He continued walking, each of his steps intentional. "What?" he asked flippantly.

"Do you feel guilty for what you did to me or not?"

He stopped in the middle of the red dirt street, spinning to face me. His stare held me in place for a long moment before he finally spoke. "Yes, I feel guilty, Petra."

I mulled over his words, the clipped tone, the square set of his shoulders. "You're awfully rude to me despite that guilt. Then you turn around and complain about being on my bad side. And then you're complimenting me and my powers in front of a tent full of soldiers. Next, you're snapping when I ask any sort of question. I'm sick of this back and forth. Which is it?"

I felt his gaze burn into my skin as he took a step closer to me. The knotted scar flexed from where it peeked out below his mask, his face now hovering inches from mine. His stare was intense, even though there was a layer of metal that separated his eyes from mine.

"You're infuriating."

116

I scoffed, one brow shooting up. "*I'm* infuriating?"

"Yes, Petra, you're infuriating. I was supposed to hand you over to Kauvras."

It took everything in me to keep my voice quiet as I spat through gritted teeth. "Are you fucking kidding me? How does that make me infuriating?" I looked around, making sure no one was looking at us. "And let me remind you, you did hand me over to Kauvras."

An agitated sigh sounded from beneath his mask, the tense energy rippling off of him. "And now I'm doing everything I can to undo that mistake. I always assumed the Daughter of Katia would *want* to burn the world down, and I didn't care. Why should I care? The world's given me nothing. Might as well burn it all down." I heard him swallow hard as he shifted on his feet, the hollow ram's eyes pinning me in place. "I don't know you. You don't know me. But seeing you in that throne room, watching you realize your entire life was a lie, watching you lose everything, and knowing it was ultimately *my* fault?" His breathing quickened as his voice rose, distress evident in every word he spoke. "I can't do that to you, Petra, because I know how that feels. So apologies for my attitude toward you. I...don't know how to cope with what I've done."

For a moment, I just stared at the man in front of me, his truth ricocheting off the inside of my head. "You know how it feels," I repeated back to him, "to realize your entire life is a lie? To lose everything?" I spoke more to myself than to him as I realized what he was saying and a wave of understanding washed through me. "Your answers..." I whispered. "They weren't what you thought they'd be."

He was quiet for a moment, the silence settling softly between us. "I thought that knowing the truth would help me, maybe heal me in some way. But it left me with more questions." His head dropped.

"You lost everything?"

I took his silence as confirmation. The citizens of Aera moved around us, completely oblivious to the revelations taking place on the city's dusty street.

"What? Your family?"

"I never had a family.

"A woman?"

He looked away quickly, his throat working.

I nodded, pushing my own roiling feelings down, knowing the feel of the gaping hole that hung open and bleeding inside his chest. "A woman."

He exhaled, his head shaking slightly. "She's..." His voice trailed off, his shoulders tensing and relaxing. "Her name was Cielle."

"Well I hope that one day you can get more answers about her." I knew that wasn't all there was. I knew there was something beyond Cielle. "And about whatever else you're looking for."

His fists opened and closed as he turned back to me. His voice was so low, so gravelly that it blended in with the footsteps of the people that passed by. "I'm sorry I used you as a bargaining chip." The apology rang through me, his voice heavy-laden with a sincerity that caused a deep ache to form in my ribs.

I'd never considered myself a particularly moral person. I can't say I wouldn't have done the same thing had I been in his shoes. "You were doing what you thought was right. You were doing what you thought you needed to do," I murmured, loud enough for only him to hear it.

"Yes," he answered, the word so thick with heartache and regret that I felt it in the deepest parts of my soul, the feeling sickeningly familiar. I knew what it felt like to do what I thought was the right thing — giving Castemont my blessing to marry my mother — only for it to turn into the most grave mistake I'd ever made. "Don't think I'm asking for your forgiveness." He shook his head slightly, something brewing behind the mask. "I don't deserve your forgiveness."

A sigh left my lungs, and with it something dark, replaced by a foreign lightness that commanded my attention. "Maybe not," I offered. "But you deserve to forgive yourself."

The air between us was charged, with what, I couldn't tell. Lieutenant Miles Landgrave wasn't untrustworthy. He wasn't my enemy.

Intentions made us human. They were what separated us from the Castemonts of the world. Mistakes, misjudgments, misunderstandings... They were all a part of being alive and breathing.

And I supposed, so was the ability to forgive.

We stood in the bustling street, the dust hanging in the air the same way it did in Inkwell. But there was one difference — the feeling in my gut. Life had been hard, and there had always been a hunger deep within me. A hunger for sustenance, of course, but also a hunger for safety, for security, for stability. And though my world was in turmoil, it seemed the hunger was gone, replaced instead by the honey-thick warmth of something else. My hand raised of its own volition, reaching to rest against the cold surface of the ram's cheek as I stared into the dark, depthless eyes.

Who was behind that mask? Could I forgive him? No. I wasn't there yet. I wasn't sure I'd ever get there. But it didn't need to stop me from finding something good in the midst of all the bad.

I raised a brow. "You're still going to teach me to fight, right?"

His shoulders relaxed as he let out a huff of a laugh and stepped back, the tension gone all at once. "Of course I will." I couldn't see him smiling, but I felt it from behind the mask. "Let's get you a real weapon," he said, holding a hand out in the direction of the smith. "But please do keep your mouth shut, and let me do the talking."

"Glad to see you're still an asshole," I muttered, fighting a smile.

"And you're still infuriating."

◆ ◆ ◆

We exited the smith's shop into the dusky light of evening, a thin, unadorned sword hanging in a sheath at my hip. It felt strange on my side, bobbing with each step I took, the weight reminding me of all I had to do and learn and conquer.

I walked wordlessly beside Miles, an ease radiating from him I hadn't felt before. But as comfortable as it should have felt, I still had that unsettled feeling – eerily familiar, like I should feel content in this companionable silence but just...wasn't. And there was still an undeniable awkwardness of unanswered questions that stalked us as we made our way back to the others.

"I'd like to stop here," Miles said suddenly, pointing to a sign hanging above the street.

"Oh, Yuri's Bookshop?" I responded, taken aback as I read the sign. I'd never been to a bookshop. There had to have been at least one in Eserene, but it sure as hell hadn't been in Inkwell. Most Inkwellians didn't even know how to read — my family had been outliers in that regard. "Okay."

"I've always loved bookshops," Miles murmured, his voice so low I could barely hear it. "Pick something out if you'd like. We'll make Whit carry it on the trail."

Amber candlelight illuminated shelves upon shelves of books, the smell of ink and parchment capturing all of my senses. "Good evening," a middle-aged man called, almost completely hidden by the mountain of books piled on his desk. The man's face blanched when he noted the metal mask covering Miles' face.

The Lieutenant gave him a gruff greeting and the man relaxed slightly, though his eyes remained warily on us. Miles didn't turn to me as he disappeared into the shelves. "I'll be just a minute."

Rows upon rows of books filled the small space, the stacks towering high above us. There were ladders and step stools scattered throughout, propped against shelves where hundreds of books lay out of reach. I let my eyes scan through the countless

120

volumes, overwhelmed and at ease all at once. I didn't *want* any book in particular, but I supposed this could be my chance to learn something, anything about the world I knew so little about.

"Excuse me," I asked the man behind the counter as he looked up from the multiple books he had sprawled in front of him. "I'm looking for something about the Saints."

"Any particular Saint?" he replied, pushing a pair of thin spectacles up his nose as he stepped away from his desk. His salt and pepper hair glowed orange in the low light.

"Oh, um..." Katia? Rhedros? Noros? "All of them, if you have something like that."

"Tall order," he replied. I almost backed away, embarrassment flooding through me. *He thinks you're an idiot.* "Check row number four. Three quarters of the way down you'll see a shelf labeled *Saints*."

"Thank you," I said quietly, escaping into the solace of the stacks. I ran my finger down the spines of the neatly arranged books and let myself relish the calm ambience of the shop.

There were books upon books of every Saint, Benevolent and Blood, their powers and what they ruled over. I'd hoped to find something on the Daughter of Katia, but a thick, leatherbound book caught my attention; *The Complete Lore of the Saints: Legends, Myths, & Truths.* It was beautiful — gold filigree on a smooth, dark leather spine.

"Find something?" Miles' low, raspy voice broke the silence. I jumped, spinning to find his mask peeking through the shelves of the stack behind me.

"You know, the whole *friendly Miles* thing is kind of weird," I said as I pulled the book from its place, running my hand across the cover. "I think I prefer the blunt and angry Miles."

"He's still here, don't worry. But it's impossible to be angry in a bookshop," he said almost absentmindedly as he rounded the stack. "*The Complete Lore of the Saints?*"

"I think I should try to learn something," I answered. I thought about asking him what he knew about the other half of my parentage – no one had so much as mentioned Rhedros besides Castemont, but I held back.

"There's probably some good information in there about Noros," he murmured. "Maybe we can make a connection to Castemont."

I nodded, swallowing hard at the prospect of what lay ahead. Alvar's words came back to me, that he could give us answers, even an answer as to whether or not Castemont was Noros. But I knew deep down it was him. I forced air into my lungs, willing the dread out of my gut. "What'd you find?"

He held up a small novel, *The Lost Son*. "I used to really love to read," he said quietly, flipping through the pages. "I'd like to start again. And considering everything I know has changed, I figured I'd try to hold on to this part of my past."

I stared at the metal mask that was now less of a threatening presence to me. "Who are you, Miles Landgrave?"

He laughed, a sound that echoed off the stacks and through the whole shop, straight into my bones. "I'm slowly learning." He pushed past me to the counter, handing the man a small stack of coins and bidding him farewell.

"Thanks for this," I said quietly as we exited, the book clutched to my chest. No one had ever bought me a book before, and something about it made me feel...happy.

"Least I could do, considering."

"You're right. Least you could do."

Chapter 12

"Bag of honey apples, three loaves of bread, a waterskin each, and some kind of cheese that the shopkeeper talked Whit into buying," Nell said as she laid out their provisions at the top of the hill.

"He said it'd never spoil," Whit offered.

"It's at least two and a half days back to Taitha," Miles started. "Whitley, Augen, when we near the city, you two will go ahead to assess the state of it, then report back. We'll come up with a plan then." The two soldiers nodded as I turned to the forest that yawned open before us. The last light of day coated Aera in a rich gold, but the forest beyond was already dim beneath its canopy. Something about the darkness tonight was especially unsettling.

"What do you say we find a pub and fill our bellies before we leave? Nell asked, her eyes looking beyond us to the streets at the bottom of the hill.

"No. We're leaving now," Miles answered firmly.

"I wouldn't mind a hot meal," I chimed in, looking at Miles expectantly. "Before the world goes to shit. I'd like one more meal that doesn't come from a rucksack."

I could tell he was reverting to his usual irritated state, but I didn't care. "We leave the second we're done."

◆ ◆ ◆

All traces of friendly Miles were gone, replaced firmly by Lieutenant Miles. I tried not to stare at the way he awkwardly lifted his mask to shove a spoonful of rabbit stew into his mouth. Whit and Nell were either unbothered or ignoring it completely.

I was on edge, a pit in my stomach opening for a reason I couldn't discern. For a moment, I wished we'd left when we'd planned to. The darkness of the forest may have been unnerving, but the amount of people here was even more so.

We ate silently in a corner of the pub beneath the only inn in Aera, the rough and burly patrons barely pausing to look at us. Raucous laughter shook the walls as mugs of beer clanked together, the sound of fists on tables an irritating metronome to the tension that had returned to my shoulders.

"Ten silver she ain't the real Daughter of Katia," a man bellowed from a table near us, his words slurring as beer sloshed over the rim of his mug. I sat a bit straighter and felt Nell and Whit do the same, Miles' masked stare on me as we listened.

"Ten silver she *is* the Daughter of Katia," someone answered even louder.

"Oy," the innkeeper yelled as she polished a glass behind the bar, a ratty apron hanging over a well-fed body. "No arguin' 'neath this roof! The Daughter o' Katia's returned and I won't hear nothin' sayin' otherwise. 'Tis an unholy act to deny it."

My stomach began to churn. "Nothin' unholy!" the first man howled with a laugh and a belch, shakily standing on drunken legs. He was massive — broad shoulders and an unruly auburn beard that reached halfway down his chest, his face pock-marked

124

and oily. "She's the holiest person alive. Ain't nothin' unholy 'bout it." He took another sip of his beer, a smile revealing angled yellow teeth. "But I'd do some unholy things to 'er."

Miles' knuckles went white as half the bar roared with cheers and laughter. Nell shifted uncomfortably. I did my best to keep my face straight as I took stock of the patrons. A good amount wore grim expressions, unamused by the burly man's words.

"You don't e'en know what she looks like, mate," someone yelled out from across the room.

The man tipped his mug to his mouth, swallowing down the rest of his drink, the foamy liquid spilling out the sides and dripping through his beard. He wiped the back of his hand across his mouth and slammed the mug down on the table, a wicked smile across his face. "Don't matter what she looks like. If they're claimin' she's a Saint's daughter, that means she's got a Saint's cunt!"

Miles shot to his feet, Whit behind him in an instant, their chairs clattering to the floor as the man spun to face them. Miles' sword was pulled so quickly from its sheath I was surprised that sparks hadn't flown.

Silence blanketed the pub. The man's eyes roved up and down Miles' figure, landing on the point of his sword. They were about the same height, but the man had to be twice Miles' weight. The Lieutenant was all lean muscle and agile limbs. This man was a fucking tree trunk.

The man took slow, drunken steps toward the Lieutenant until the point of the sword dug into his unadorned leather-clad chest. My breath hitched as I surveyed the room for exits, for any escape route. I felt tension radiating from Nell beside me, the heat doing nothing to help my anxiety.

Years of de-escalating all the fights that Larka had started... That was one thing. Drunken giants were another.

"Look at this, boys," the man growled. "We got ourselves a masked Cabillian soldier right 'ere. One of Kauvras' *sheep*, wi' the mask to prove it." The man pointed to the horns that curved around Miles' face as his mouth turned up in a nauseating snarl. A few of the other pub patrons grumbled with low laughter.

"Back the fuck off," Miles seethed, the authority in his voice ringing through the room.

"Gettin' pretty up 'n' arms 'bout the Daughter of Katia," he slurred. "Is she one of these fine ladies 'ere? 'Ave we been blessed with 'er holy presence?"

With the sword still pointed against his chest, the man turned his attention toward me. I froze under his stare, the sword at my hip begging to be pulled but my dismal skill level demanding I didn't. A low buzz of fury took shape in my chest, the heat beginning to build.

This was about to be very, very bad.

"Bit plain of a pair for either to be a Saints' daughter," he remarked, a half smile revealing his yellow teeth.

And then Miles did something I never would have guessed he'd do — he turned to me. With the tip of his sword still against the large man's chest, he turned to me.

My eyes narrowed on him momentarily as I realized he was waiting for *me*, for my command. I thought the pub had been still before, but an even deeper stillness creeped across the room as the patrons watched the exchange.

It hit me cold and hard — I could tell Miles to kill this man and he would, without question. I could tell him to back off and he would, without question. I'd experienced a flood of power in the Taithan throne room when I realized the truth of my bloodline, but I'd never in my life had power like *this*.

My eyes left the Lieutenant and landed on the bearded man. I could see confusion cross his pock-marked face as he realized that Miles was waiting on my command. I saw his mind begin to turn in on itself as it flipped through the reasons a masked Cabillian soldier would be taking orders from a woman.

The man clenched his jaw and snorted out a laugh that didn't reach his eyes, his shoulders straightening. "You gonna have 'im, kill me, sweetheart?" He sucked his teeth, his eyes roving over my body, lingering too long. "Go ahead, give the order."

Something overcame me then, something much bigger and more wicked than myself. I pushed my stool back and stood, stalking toward him. His size was much more daunting now that I stood directly before him, but still I stared at him, unafraid. With the crook of my finger, I ushered him closer. The man smirked and bent down, my lips moving to his ear as I placed a hand on his cheek.

"You're going to wish he'd been the one to kill you."

Fire erupted from my palm, his scraggly beard instantly catching as his skin quickly began to bubble beneath my hand. A few of his friends shot to their feet, blades unsheathed, only to jump back as the man fell to the floor screaming, clawing uselessly at his face. The fire spread quickly, and soon his entire head was engulfed in flames. The heat of satisfaction burned hot in my chest as the smell of burning flesh hit my nose.

What coursed through me was an angry, tumultuous storm of hatred and rage and the sudden need to prove myself. The feeling wasn't foreign — I recognized it as the same sweet fury that had overcome me at Oxblood Outpost. I let it take control again, its gray talons sinking deep into my flesh as I watched the man writhe and screech in agony.

Rhedros was here, and with him all his rage.

Within moments the man's screams died, his limbs going still as the fire ate away at his body. The only sound was the crackling of flames in the otherwise silent pub. I grabbed a mug of ale from a nearby table and doused the fire, letting the last of the foam drip and sizzle into steam.

The atmosphere had gone still once again as the last of the smoke dissipated, but something charged seemed to crash through the space, invisible lightning striking me and stoking my fire. Mouths hung agape and eyes were stuck wide across the room when I finally tore my stare away from the dead man.

Nell and Whit's heads were both bowed, fists across their chests. I turned to Miles, his sword hanging in his hand as he raised the other fist to his chest. But I could tell he was staring at me. I let it bolster me as I took a step forward. I didn't feel unsure like I did before I learned the truth of my parentage. I didn't feel angry at the hand I'd been dealt. I felt like the queen I needed to be.

"I am Petra, Daughter of Katia," I declared, my voice solid and unwavering. "The blood of the Saints runs through my veins. Despite what you may have heard, I bow to no man. I serve no King. And though I may be seen as a weapon, I am the only one who can wield it.

"The truth is, things in this world are changing. While I may not have all the answers, what I do know is I will fight for the good of the realm. Whatever the Rebel King has told you, whatever he says my purpose is," I let the stares of strangers soak into my skin, let their awe and disbelief reinforce me, "it's all a lie. There will come a time soon where you are forced to choose between me and your King. Choose wisely."

My words echoed silently through the pub as I turned to my companions — my *Penumbra* — and nodded, promptly heading toward the exit.

A thin, gangly man with an eye patch intercepted me, his hair stringy and body visibly unwashed. He was silent, the stare from his remaining eye intense and uncomfortable. But he dropped to a knee in the now-familiar stance — head bowed, fist across his chest. "Daughter of Katia."

One by one, the patrons of the pub dropped to the ground. And instead of shying away from the proclamation like I'd been doing for days, I pushed my shoulders back, stood as tall as I could, and let them chant.

"Daughter of Katia. Daughter of Katia. Daughter of Katia."

People from the street had begun to gather at the door as I continued to walk, Miles, Nell, and Whit close behind. The words were a drum beat in my head, the animal within me growing wilder, more restless as power soaked into my bones.

The street became more crowded by the second, some people on bended knee, others simply curious, watching, waiting. Stepping into the mild night air, feeling dozens of eyes on me, I let the feeling overtake me, let my blood — the blood of the Saints — push me forward.

"Is it her?" a woman's voice yelled from the crowd.

"I don't believe it," someone else yelled.

I turned to Miles, his gilded stare sending something through me that caused my blood to pound harder through my veins.

"Show them," I heard Katia whisper in my ear.

"Show them who you are." Rhedros.

On a dusty, torchlit street in a foreign town, I listened. I let my head fall back, let my arms raise as the wind picked up and my palms ignited. But this time the wind wasn't whipping and the flames weren't angry; the air was strong and steady, rippling through the cloaks of the gathering bystanders. The flames were tamer, dancing toward the sky like seagrass in an ocean current. No blisters bubbled on my palms, no pain racked my body. It felt sweet and it felt *right*, like *this* was what these powers were meant to do.

I was vaguely aware of the crowd as every single person dropped to their knees. Someone wept with joy, a few people chanted in prayer, and I continued to burn. With a deep breath I pulled my flames back, urged the wind to die down, and let the world flood back in, content in this body, content in this role.

But my head hit the dirt road like a stone as a blade sunk deep into my chest.

Chapter 13

"This is a fucking nightmare. The moment we're out of here, I'm going to–"

"Stop fussing."

"She could have died and you're going to tell me to stop fussing?" Rhedros' voice echoed through the darkness.

"Watch your temper, Rhedros," Katia replied. "She was never going to die."

He clicked his tongue. I was back in that in-between, the void where I saw nothing but an endless expanse of black, no bodies to the voices that echoed around me. But there was another voice this time, a low, muffled droning of words I couldn't distinguish.

"This is what we've been trying to avoid," Rhedros snarled.

I tried to move my head, tried to sit up, but my body didn't respond. I was completely numb. I'd hit the dirt and looked down to see a dagger protruding from my chest, but after that...nothing.

"We knew this was going to happen."

Rhedros grunted in frustration. "I just thought we had more time."

I pulled on the tether that held my consciousness to this bodiless nothing as I tried to form words.

"We need her," Rhedros murmured. "We can't do this without her."

"Can't do what?" I managed to whisper, my voice scratchy.

"I *knew* it was her," Katia answered suddenly, her voice hollow with disbelief. The droning noise continued. It almost had the cadence of someone speaking.

I tried to pick my head up but was once again greeted with the feeling of numbness. "It's me."

"How is she hearing us, Rhedros? How is she speaking to us?" Katia asked, her voice frantic.

"I don't..." Rhedros replied, trailing off.

"Where are we?"

The darkness faded away as a dusty, wood paneled room materialized around me, my eyes opening involuntarily upon the waking world.

"During Katia's time as the Keeper of the Blood Saints, she conjured up an army of beasts controlled solely by her." It was the same low noise that I'd heard in the darkness, much clearer now. "Kelpies guarded the sea and soulhags guarded the land. Most notable, however, were her five drivas, the earliest ancestors of dragons and fearsome guardians of the skies."

I let my head drop to the side to see half a ram's head mask peeking out from behind *The Complete Lore of the Saints*, its leather glowing orange in the firelight that burned in the hearth.

It was Miles' voice that had somehow echoed its way into the in-between. "Like dragons, Katia's drivas were winged and scaled with rows of razor-sharp teeth and the ability to breathe fire. That is, however, where their similarities end."

I blinked as I watched him, the way the book was propped up in his lap, his nicked and scarred hands wrapped tenderly around its covers. Warmth rushed through me and a weak smile crossed my face at the sight of the formidable Lieutenant perched in a rickety wooden chair.

"The average driva was three times the size of the average dragon, with a wingspan the width of two warships placed end to end, and teeth the length of a man's arm. Her largest driva, Adorex, was–"

"Reading me a bedtime story?"

"*Shit*," he spat when he lowered the book to see me staring back at him. "You're awake."

"How long this time?" I asked quietly, still disoriented.

"Just a few hours. It's past midnight now."

I propped myself up on my elbows, realizing I was in a small cot, body covered with a coarse blanket. As I pulled it back, I looked down to see my entire torso wound in bandages, a bloom of dried, crusted blood in the middle. I should have been in agony, but there was no pain beyond the soreness of sleeping in a bed that was unfamiliar to me. "Someone stabbed me?"

He gently closed the book and placed it in his lap. "Yes. Well, someone threw a blade."

I let myself fall back into the pillow. "Kauvras' men?"

"Kauvras' men," he confirmed. I took a deep breath. "Apparently they weren't actually trying to kill you. Just maim you enough to immobilize you."

"How considerate of them," I muttered, scrubbing my face with my hands, not a blister to be seen. "So how did we get...*here*? And where is here?"

"Eat first," he said, leaning to the small bedside table to pick up a tray of stew and bread before placing it gingerly in front of me.

"Just answer the Saints damned question."

"Eat your Saints damned food," he quipped back, his voice playful but still edged with authority.

I begrudgingly took a bite of bread before realizing how hungry I was and grabbing for the same rabbit stew we'd eaten earlier

132

in the night. Miles sat back as I ate, his position far too nonchalant to be talking about an attempt on my life.

"About thirty of Kauvras' men had been tracking us," he started. "Not surprising. They found you pretty easily once they arrived." He let out a gruff laugh.

I considered his words, thoughtfully chewing on the stew. "And where are Kauvras' men now?"

"You've got a lot of friends in Aera, Oh Holy One," he replied. "I'll just say that after you went down, the townspeople wanted to keep your fire burning, figuratively and literally."

My eyes widened as I took in what he meant, and I suppressed a triumphant smile at the thought of Kauvras' men burning before I looked down at my chest again. "And I'm guessing you did...this?" I asked, pointing to the bandages wound around my otherwise bare chest, trying not to let my embarrassment show.

He sat forward in the flimsy chair, the wood creaking beneath his weight. His mask glowed dull in the low firelight, his hands hanging between his knees. "I have more respect for you than to undress you without your permission."

My cheeks burned, a charged silence suddenly expanding between us. That same uncomfortable feeling flooded my veins beneath his stare.

"Oh," I answered quietly, shoving a spoonful of stew in my mouth in an attempt to distract myself from the awkwardness.

"The innkeeper dressed your wounds," he added, looking away. "Helmina was more than happy to assist the Daughter of Katia."

Relief flooded through me but quickly dissipated when I thought of our companions. "Nell and Whit?"

"They questioned Kauvras' men...*briefly*," he started. "Enella Augen is a hell of a soldier. Better than half of my men, I'll give her that. Didn't take long for her to get answers out of them and then let the townspeople take over." He sat back again, his posture relaxing. "Once they knew the path was clear, they set off for Taitha again. Got a head start to see what's going on in the city."

I sank deeper into the thin mattress, but a restlessness settled over me. I didn't want to be in this room any longer. I wanted to get back to Taitha, get back to Solise and my mother and sort through this fucking *mess*. "Can we leave now?"

"Now? It's the middle of the night."

"I know. I just want to get back."

"Sleep, Petra," Miles said flatly.

"I'm not tired." Which wasn't entirely the truth. In fact, there wasn't a lick of truth behind the words at all. I was exhausted to my very bones.

"Can I ask you something?" The question was sudden, the energy of the room quickly changing. His voice was sober.

"Okay."

He sat back in his seat, his shoulders squared and rigid as he took a deep breath. "How did you know King Belin?"

His words hit my ears but didn't make sense for a moment. I wasn't sure what question I'd been expecting, but it sure as hell hadn't been that.

And I had no idea how to answer him.

My mouth bobbed open and shut a few times as I sifted through my mind, trying to find the words I needed. Miles sat motionless, waiting as my head began to shake. "I didn't know King Belin. I knew who he was pretending to be."

"And who was that?"

I pursed my lips, my eyes closing at the thought of the man I'd so desperately loved, the man who didn't exist. "He told me his name was Calomyr. Cal," I breathed. "He told me he was a Royal Guard. He told me about his entire life, about his mother and his brother and how they died and how he always wished to meet his father. And all of it was a lie." I shook my head against the thought, hopelessly trying to keep the floodgates intact. "He told me he loved me," I whispered more to myself than to Miles.

"And you believed him?"

I stared at the Lieutenant and shrugged slightly, brows turned up. "I didn't have a reason not to."

"And you loved him." Not a question but a confirmation. A hot knife in my fucking chest.

Tears flooded my eyes and I did my best to blink them away. I was sick of tears, sick of crying. "I loved Calomyr, yes," I choked out through a stiff jaw. "But Calomyr was never real."

Miles watched me with a preternatural stillness as I tried to pull myself together. But the thought of the elaborate lie I'd been fed made my skin crawl, made my chest tighten.

"And what about Castemont?" he asked quietly.

The sadness dissipated, quickly steaming into hot anger. I took a deep breath, my throat feeling acidic at the sound of his name, the tears quickly clearing from my eyes as I began to see red. "He's the one behind all of it. He's the reason I'm here. The fucking Saint of Pain. I'll tell you, he's lived up to that title."

"I think..." Miles started, leaning forward in his chair. "I think he's the reason I'm here, too."

I stared at him with confusion, the words hanging heavy in the air between us. My voice went hoarse, croaking out only in a whisper. "What?"

His throat worked beneath the mask. "I think I'm a part of his plan. Well, I think I *was* a part of his plan."

My head shook in disbelief, my hair falling around my bare shoulders as I sat straighter. "*How?*"

He took a tentative breath. "I'm still trying to figure that out myself."

Goosebumps rose across my skin despite the fire that crackled in the hearth. Sparks flew into the chimney, the reflection of the flames dancing in the dull metal of the ram's face. "Who are you?" I whispered.

Miles sat back, expelling a deep breath as he nodded. He slowly reached for his mask, a fist gripping each metal horn as the gnarled scar beneath his chin peeked out. *Holy shit–*

The door burst open.

"Oh, goodness!" the woman I recognized as the innkeeper — Helmina — chimed as she closed the door behind her. Miles and I both jumped at the sudden intrusion, my eyes still glued to the mask that had been *so close* to coming off. "Wasn't expectin' to see ye awake, yer Majesty." She lowered herself into a clumsy curtsy.

I cleared my throat, offering her a small smile. "Thank you for dressing my wound."

"Tis my honor," she replied, reaching into the pocket of her apron and pulling out another roll of bandages. "Just wanted to check on how ye were healin'. Lieutenant Landgrave here said ye'd heal yourself, but I didn't know how long it'd take ye."

I ran my hand over the bandages, the dried blood rough beneath my fingers. I knew that nothing beyond a small red mark remained of the wound that would've been fatal to anyone else. "I think I'm okay. Thank you, Miss Helmina."

She smiled in return. "I've washed yer clothes, though I don't think ye'll be gettin' much use out of a shirt wi' a hole in it." She gave a hearty chuckle as she looked toward the chair near the fire. "There's a fresh one there, yer Majesty."

"Thank you, and I'm sorry about the man downstairs. The one I...killed."

Her shoulders bounced with the laugh that erupted. "That was Aysik. Ye did us all a favor by riddin' us of 'im. Nasty bugger." I fought back a smile, but her easy going nature was most welcome in a time where everything was uncertain. "Please, if I can be of any assistance, don't be hesitatin' to ask. Stay as long as ye like, yer Majesty, and ye too, Lieutenant." She bowed her head, crossing a fist across her chest. "Tis truly an honor, Daughter of Katia."

As she left, a stiff silence fell over Miles and me once again, but exhaustion was threatening to pull me under.

"Sleep, Petra," Miles ordered.

"Take the mask off."

He leaned forward. "Sleep, Petra."

I rolled my eyes. "Where will you sleep?" I asked lazily, letting my cheek hit the pillow.

He opened his hands, gesturing to the chair he was perched on. "Right here."

Even though I could control flame and wind, even though I was far more dangerous than the Lieutenant who sat before me, knowing that he was watching over me instilled a sense of peace in me I didn't know I needed.

"You..." *Shit.* I wasn't actually going to say it, was I? "You can join me, if you'd like."

I fucking said it.

He straightened, clearing his throat. "Oh, it's... It's okay. I'll be okay here."

Disappointment and relief at his answer were a heady mix in my chest. Mostly relief, I thought. "Okay. Please take the mask off," I tried one more time, my words slower than I'd anticipated, eyes drooping.

"Maybe tomorrow." But something in his voice told me that probably wouldn't happen.

"Then read to me again."

He crossed an ankle over a knee as he picked up the book. "You better listen. I'll be quizzing you tomorrow."

I didn't even make it through the chapter's title before sleep closed in.

Chapter 14

"Tell me everything I need to know about Katia." Miles and I had walked in silence for long enough, the woods so repetitive around us that I had no idea how the man knew where he was going. We left Aera yesterday, and it'd been nothing but trees and rocks and sticks. I needed something to break up the monotony.

"Okay," he answered, his voice rugged, and I could tell he was Lieutenant Miles once again. "Only if you work on your balance."

I scoffed, but unsheathed my sword and nestled the delicate grip in my palm. It was a lot easier to balance a blade than it was a tree limb.

"The Forgotten Saints burned the Old World down, and placed Rhedros in the New World."

"The Forgotten Saints," I remarked, sorting through the little I knew, trying to remember if I'd ever heard of them.

"They were here first," Miles explained. "The Forgotten Saints were the ones who ruled before the Benevolent and Blood Saints. Rhedros was placed in the New World as a force of good.

But Malosym created a child out of hatred and ash and managed to slip her through to the New World. That was Katia."

I stopped in my tracks, my blade falling to the ground, my brows furrowed. "*What*? So you mean Rhedros was the Keeper of the Benevolent Saints, and–"

"Yes," he affirmed without turning to me. "Katia was the Keeper of the Blood Saints."

I grappled with this piece of information. "How did–"

"No one knows. But at some point, they switched places." Still Miles walked, unbothered by the fact that I was completely dumbfounded. "And Malosym, the one who built Katia from nothing, was the leader of the Occulti, a demon horde that over-ran the Old World. That's the reason the Forgotten Saints had to burn the Old World. There were just too many of them."

My mind reeled as I stepped over stones and logs, trying to keep my footing while my brain was focused everywhere else but my feet. "I didn't know that," I said quietly.

We walked in silence, and it could have been for a minute or an hour as I grappled with this new information. Miles' voice startled me when it suddenly broke through my rampant thoughts. "Any idea who your father is?" he asked, his voice no-ticeably apprehensive.

I opened my mouth but hesitated when I realized I didn't know what to say. Should I tell him? Maybe he'd know some-thing, some piece of lore or legend that could help me make sense of it all. But no one had ever mentioned the Daughter of Rhedros. "No."

"Huh." He held a branch back for me as we shuffled through a dense patch of brush.

"What you were reading back at the inn in Aera," I started, "about Katia's creatures."

He let loose a laugh. "Kelpies, soulhags, and drivas."

"Katia controls them?"

"According to the lore of the Saints."

"You don't think I could..."

He came to a stop, turning to face me. "Do you?"

I stared up at him, trying to remember what he'd read to me. I'd heard stories of Katia's charges, how a herd of kelpies stopped Faldyr, Saint of War, from wiping out the entire world with a massive tidal wave. Soulhags inhabited the underground in tunnels beneath our feet, with bodies made of stone and hair made of cobwebs. And I'd been told a few stories of Katia's drivas and their massive talons and snapping teeth and their ability to kill with a single fiery roar.

"No," I answered flatly. "Those are legends. Not the truth."

"The Daughter of Katia was a legend, too," he replied, turning around to resume our journey. I let the thought sit with me, but logic took over before long. I could understand a world where the Saints governed, but a world of kelpies, soulhags, drivas… That was impossible.

"Where does Noros fit into all this lore?" I asked.

Miles was silent for a moment. "I'm not sure. But apparently he's the only one who can positively identify the Daughter of Katia. *When evil comes again.*"

I placed my sword in my palm, trying to balance as I walked, but it fell to the ground once again. "And you think you were a piece of his plan?" I asked.

Miles sighed. "Like I said, I'm still trying to figure that out myself."

"Maybe I can help you sort it out."

He shook his head, the ram's horns catching the late-morning sunlight that filtered through the dense canopy. "I think it's probably more complicated than either of us realize." He paused his walking and turned to me. "Keep balancing."

I rolled my eyes but obliged. "And when am I actually going to get to swing this sword?"

Miles suddenly whipped around, unsheathing his sword quicker than lightning. But before he could knock my blade from my hand, I had my own hilt in my grip and my sword in front of my face. He froze, his head cocked in surprise at my speed, blades fixed in front of us. I was surprised at myself too, but I didn't let it show.

"Okay, Holy One. Not bad." He relaxed, looking me up and down. "Let me show you a basic swing."

We fell into a routine — balance, fight, balance, fight. I wasn't able to balance the blade for too long, but I was quicker on my feet than I'd thought I'd be, and much less clumsy. Maybe it was a Saints-given thing. I took satisfaction every time I blocked a swing, enough that the blows Miles landed stung a little less than they would have otherwise.

But with every swing, every dodge and every turn, it felt as if the teeth of a driva gnawed at the back of my mind, begging the question — what the hell was the Saint of Pain doing here?

◆ ◆ ◆

I finished up the last of the small chunk of dried rabbit that Helmina sent along with us. The mid-afternoon sun was blinding where it filtered through the trees. I wiped my hands on my trousers, standing to face Miles. "I'm ready."

He nodded, swiftly packing up the rest of our food and taking a position across from me. "You sure?"

"Absolutely."

Miles lunged, his sword meeting mine with a metallic peal that bounced off the trees. He had bone-crushing strength, but I had speed, so much so that I easily took a step back and parried as his sword sailed through the air. I was set to dodge it until my foot caught in a small divot and I had to flail to keep myself upright.

"Good," he said quietly from under his mask. "Remember, balance."

Without so much as a nod I moved to strike, catching him off-guard and sending him stumbling backward.

"Remember," I taunted, "balance."

I swore steam billowed from the ram's nostrils as he righted himself, his head nodding as he chuckled. "Alright," he muttered, "let's go."

And the dance began. This was different from our past practice; before, we'd kept moving, kept walking, but now we stayed in the clearing, circling each other like two predators. I knew he was letting me land the few blows I did, but I let myself get lost in the rhythm of clanking swords and heaving breaths. Every swing of my blade bolstered me, reminded me that I might have a fighting chance outside my divine powers.

Miles' movements were much more fluid than mine, a type of grace I could tell had come from years of practice and training. Each step was measured, each dodge was an intentional reaction practiced hundreds of times over. And though my slim blade was laughably smaller than Miles', I was impressed at my ability to counteract his strength.

Our swords ground together and we both stepped back, surveying each other, daring the other to make a move. "Impressed?" I asked, out of breath but antagonistic.

"Don't get cocky," he warned, his low, raspy voice taking on an edge of authority.

"But are you impressed?" I prodded.

"Not yet."

His movements were quicker than I could follow, and in three razor-sharp steps he'd struck the blade from my grip and backed me against a tree, his broad palm wrapped around my throat, pinning me in place.

All I could do was stare at him in shock, his thumb and fingers on the sides of my neck with just enough pressure to make my vision go spotty. He smelled like oakmoss and the forest just after it rained, and I was frozen in shock at the position he'd manage to trap me in. His chest heaved, mere inches from my own with every breath, my heart pounding so hard I knew he could feel it in my throat, beating against his hand. My jaw flexed as he stared at me from behind his mask.

"Fight me," he breathed.

I struggled to get a word out as an air of panic set in. This man was a trained soldier, a weapon in his own right, and every moment spent within his grip reminded me of that.

"Try to get away," he panted, and his voice had changed. There was the familiar authority of a lieutenant commanding his soldier, but somewhere behind it was the sour taste of worry, of desperation. "Fight me, Petra. Show me that you can protect yourself."

I was frozen. I should be fighting him, but all I could do was stare back and forth between the tiny slits in his mask, searching through the darkness for a glimpse of the human eyes it hid, desperate to know who he was. I told myself to summon my flames, to fight him, told myself to obey him just this once, but I couldn't. The familiar feeling flooded through me again. Why did Miles make me feel this sort of push and pull?

He leaned in, the ram's forehead pressing against mine. "You know you've wanted to kill me since our trip through the Onyx Pass. You shy away at my touch. You're disgusted by me. So go ahead, Petra. What's stopping you?"

My hands flew to where he held me, clawing uselessly at his wrist. I thrust my knee forward but he blocked it with his own, easily holding my legs to the tree trunk, the impact causing me to wince in pain. I threw my body from side to side, harnessing every bit of physical might I had, but his hold on me didn't so much as budge. He had me in an iron grip, and my only way out would be to tap into my well of power.

As if he knew what I was thinking, he nodded. "Do it. Find your fire," he snarled through gritted teeth as I fought. "Dammit, Petra, show me you can do it!" He was pleading, begging, his voice pained. I summoned that fury, let my blood run hot until it boiled, let the light expand within my chest–

Oxygen suddenly rushed into my lungs as his grip loosened and he fell. My body erupted into a scream as Miles landed face down in the dirt with an arrow in his back, his mask tumbling away from his head, a thick mane of shaggy obsidian hair falling around him like a halo.

No.

He groaned in pain as I dropped to my knees beside him, my hands grabbing at his arm as sunlight caught the stream of ruby red spilling from his wound. "Miles!" I screamed, bile rising in my throat. "Miles, please!"

Someone shot him. With that realization I whipped my head from side to side, searching the trees for the source of the arrow as the sobs tore from my chest, my body instinctively moving to protect him. "Who's there?" I called, my voice laden with ire, unafraid of the fact that I could be shot with an arrow at any moment. "Who the *fuck* is out there?"

I spun toward the sound of hooves as a mounted horse walked slowly toward us, a figure silhouetted by the sun. I could just make out a bow slung over their back.

Miles moaned into the earth again and I silently thanked the Saints he was still alive as I scrambled to my feet, forgoing my thin blade in favor of his broadsword. I allowed the fury that had been building inside me to smolder. With no effort, fire traveled up the pommel of the broadsword, igniting across the blade like wildfire as I stalked toward the rider. My control was slipping away, and I knew one wrong move would set the forest ablaze. But still I marched, flaming sword in hand. Whoever shot Miles was going to burn at the end of it.

"Petra," a voice called from horseback. My heart stopped — or maybe it started beating so quickly I could no longer feel it. My blood went from boiling to freezing as the sword's flames were extinguished in an instant.

He dismounted, his own sword drawn as his molten gemstone eyes traveled from me to Miles' crumpled form. The broadsword fell from my grasp, still smoking, and I stared at him, words turning to ash on my tongue. The bruises had faded slightly since I'd seen him standing next to his father, but the gash on his forehead was still angry and jagged.

Calomyr — *Belin* — took a hesitant step toward me. And all at once those gemstone eyes held me in place. "Are you okay?"

PART II

Calomyr

Chapter 15

Four Years Ago

Fuck her if you have to. That's what Castemont said. The words echoed through my mind. When I held Petra as she lay limp in the street in the pouring rain, unconscious and barely breathing after Castemont ordered her house be set ablaze... I knew if I continued to see her, I was going to lose my nerve. I'd given in and fucking kissed her. I couldn't lie to myself and say it had been a part of the plan. I kissed her because I wanted to. I shouldn't have, but I did. And it was going to make it so much harder to do what I needed to do.

So I holed myself up in the King's Keep for a week and tried to straighten out my mind. I wasn't in this for love. I was in this to save the realm. My feelings for her couldn't be stronger than my commitment to the plan.

Petra's delicate hand was wrapped in mine as I led her over the ledges and ridges of the cliff face. What radiated from her was heated anticipation, and it infected me like a damned fever that my body couldn't fight. She gave my hand a squeeze, and the movement was so subtle, so insignificant, that I may not have even noticed it if it'd been anyone else. But it was *her*, so it almost derailed me completely. I was teetering on the edge of surrender.

Fuck her if you have to.

There was a difference between what Castemont told me to do and what I was about to do. I didn't *have* to do this. I could have carried on with Castemont's plan without doing this. But I wanted to do this, and I'd been a fucking fool to think I didn't want to take her to the cave and ravage every inch of her fucking body.

But the dark cloud that was the incessant truth followed me everywhere I went. My want couldn't exist on its own, because I couldn't exist in Petra's world without Castemont. I was the King. Untouchable. Invisible. Our paths wouldn't have crossed — *couldn't* have crossed — if Castemont hadn't designed the map.

Did this all-consuming desire I had for her come from that fact? Did I only want her because she was the one person in the entire realm that I couldn't have? Anyone else. I could have anyone else, but it was Petra, and it'd been Petra from the moment I met her.

It's just sex. I repeated it to myself over and over. *It's just sex.* Feelings didn't have to be involved. Feelings *weren't* involved. Maybe I was close to losing my nerve, but I had the control and discipline to keep it.

Right?

She had no idea these thoughts ran unrestrained through my mind as she followed behind me. Her eyes were hooded, her bottom lip pulled between her teeth every time I looked back at her. *Fuck.* There was absolutely no way she didn't know what that look was doing to me, what those autumn eyes were telling me without a word. She had to know.

The dagger was tucked into my boot. And if it worked out, she'd soon be in her most vulnerable position, pinned beneath me in the throes of ecstasy as I moved inside her. I could kill her and be done with it.

Fuck her if you have to.

Maybe I wouldn't kill her this time. But I wouldn't let myself enjoy this. I absolutely couldn't. But she could. That was going to be a part of the plan, I decided. I was going to make sure she enjoyed it, and I'd end her life another time.

Fuck her if you have to.

I all but threw her into the cave and finally let myself do what I'd wanted to do since the moment I first saw her at Cindregala. My hands roved over her hips and I pinned her to the cave wall as she writhed with need. She moved against me like the Saints made her body to fit mine. *They didn't*, I reminded myself. I hooked her legs around my waist and ground into her, closing my eyes. I was afraid that if I looked at her, I'd crumble.

This means nothing to you. This is a part of the plan. It's just sex.

But I couldn't help it. I had to look into her eyes. I needed to see the anticipation that was there because of me. I pulled back, instantly knowing I'd made the best decision and worst mistake of my life, because what I saw in her gaze… If she wanted to burn the world to the ground, I'd light the match for her. All she had to do was give me that look.

It's just sex. Focus, Cal.

I needed to move, because if I kept her pinned to this wall, the cave would collapse around us. A change of scenery was what I needed to help me focus. I laid her in the middle of the cave and stood over her, trying to get a fucking hold of myself now that she wasn't pressed against me. *Just make her come and be done with it.*

She took in my bare chest as I undressed, the look in her eyes fucking *feral*. She was drinking me in, and it took everything in me not to let her swallow me whole.

I can do this.

Her eyes suddenly softened as I leaned over her. It almost looked like a flash of sorrow as she watched me with haunted eyes, and a bolt of concern shot through my core. "Are you okay?" I asked her, unable to help myself. "With this?"

She grabbed me with such ferocity that I knew my back would bear the marks of her fingernails for days. I'd wear them as a badge of honor. Her hands moved to her tunic as she wrung it from her body. I pulled back and let myself stare at her bare chest.

I was going to fucking *devour* her.

No, I wasn't. I couldn't.

But I had no control over myself when the words slipped out of my mouth. "Absolutely perfect."

A moment. I could let myself get lost for just a moment. A moment wouldn't hurt. It was a part of the plan.

I took her hard and fast as the lights began to dance across the cave. I tasted every fucking inch of her and watched her unravel beneath me. I told her to come for me and she obeyed. She obeyed *beautifully*.

And as I watched her eyes roll back in her head and felt her nails rake across my back, I wished with every part of me that I hadn't agreed to Castemont's fucking plan. I wished that she and I could just *be*.

I wished that I'd never set eyes upon him.

Chapter 16

Thirteen Years Ago

"You don't get your eyes from your mother." A finely dressed lord stepped in front of me and peered curiously between me and Aunt Berna. We stood to the side of the bustling market at Bellenau Square. His hands were clasped leisurely behind his back, but the tall guard next to him was stern in his posture.

"I'm not their mother," Aunt Berna answered, a brow cocked.

"Ah, I should have known you were their sister." The Lord chuckled and gestured to me and Tobyas. Aunt Berna let out a giggle that I'd never heard from her before as she batted her lashes.

What's going on?

"So *do* you get your eyes from your mother?" he pressed.

I was used to the look of awe on strangers' faces when they saw my eyes. Aunt Berna said they looked like gemstones that'd melted in the sun. I didn't mind the looks too much when I was younger, but I was fourteen now. Far too old for strangers to ogle at me.

My aunt set her fruit-filled basket down on the shopkeeper's counter and nodded to him while he counted up her purchase. "Go ahead," she said gently with a hand on my back, "tell him."

"The blue is from my father," I replied to the seemingly kind stranger, but an uneasy feeling settled over me. "The green is from my mother."

"And where might they be?" he asked with a raised brow, his brown eyes darting beyond us to the crowded market. His tone was light, as if he were just striking up a simple conversation, but he was actually being rather nosy.

I cleared my throat as Tobyas fidgeted next to me. "My mother is with the Saints. My father... I'm not sure where he is." Aunt Berna jabbed an elbow into my ribs. "*My Lord.*"

"My sincerest apologies for your loss," the Lord answered, bowing his head. He sounded sincere, but something about him...didn't feel right. "Did you inherit anything else from your father? Your height, perhaps?"

I narrowed my eyes at the man. I was tall, yes. But I couldn't remember if my mother had been tall, and I had no idea how tall my father was. But why did he want to know? "I'm not sure, my Lord."

"And how old are you, young man?"

"I just turned fourteen."

He turned quickly to the guard beside him before looking back at me. "Fourteen and this tall already? You could be a Royal Guard one day."

I didn't want to smile at the man who made me so uncomfortable, but I couldn't help it. I'd wanted more than anything to be a part of the Royal Guard since Tobyas and I had arrived in Eserene five years ago. "Thank you, my Lord."

"I want to be a Royal Guard!" Tobyas whined.

Lord Castemont let out a hearty laugh. "I'm sure you'll be just as tall as..."

154

"Belin Cal Myrin," I offered, "but I just go by Cal. And this is Tobyas Vic Myrin. He goes by Tobyas."

The Lord's eyes widened. "Your names are very unique."

"Our Mama said she could never decide on a name, so she gave us each two, a real name and a nickname."

Tobyas piped up. "Even though I don't use mine."

He was met with a nod. "And your surname is unique as well."

"Yes," I responded, trying not to narrow my eyes at his words. "It was our mother's middle name, though I'm not sure why she chose it for our surname. We like having a piece of her with us now that she's gone."

"Make sure you remember it, because I'm going to be the head of the Royal Guard one day," Tobyas chimed.

The Lord laughed, his eyes crinkling at the sides. "Well, Tobyas, I'm sure you'll be just as tall as Cal one day, and you can be in the Royal Guard as well."

My little brother beamed. "Bet I'll be taller than you," he teased, punching my arm.

"And *your* eyes," he said abruptly to Tobyas, staring into the pools of midnight black, "they're neither your father's nor your mother's?"

Aunt Berna leaned in and spoke quietly, but I still heard what she said. "They have different fathers."

"I see," the Lord answered, looking intently at my aunt. "I must apologize for my impoliteness, my Lady. You are?"

She lowered into a curtsy. "Bernadet Carrowin, my Lord. Their caretaker. They call me Aunt Berna. I took them in when..." She tried to hide her mouth from us with her small hand, but it was no use. "They're from Taitha."

I was surprised she'd given up that information. King Umfray wasn't fond of outsiders, and she'd just told a Low Royal that's exactly what we were.

"And your husband?" he asked, his eyes stuck to her.

"I'm unwed, my Lord." Was that a smile she was trying to hide?

The Lord cocked his head and reached for her hand, bending to press his lips to her knuckles. I watched a blush creep across her face. "My Lady."

"Ew," Tobyas scoffed.

Aunt Berna spun on him. "Tobyas!"

"That's quite all right, Miss Carrowin," the Lord said. "I didn't mean to offend the boy, it's just rare to find someone of such beauty and generosity in Eserene."

I fought to keep my eyes from rolling as Aunt Berna let out a delicate laugh. Was she really going to fall for this?

"My name is Lord Evarius Castemont. This is Tyrak, my personal guard." Tyrak gave a slight nod, his face blank and rugged, black hair and olive skin swallowing the sunlight. "A pleasure to meet the three of you."

Aunt Berna's blush rose again as she lowered herself into a curtsy. "You as well, Lord Castemont."

His eyes roved over mine again, his gaze intense. I felt Tyrak's eyes linger on me for a moment as well, his face still expressionless. I didn't flinch beneath their stares, reminding myself to be brave like Mama used to tell me to be. She'd always told me to be brave, kind, and honest. I thought I was doing a pretty good job.

With a nod, the Lord and his guard rejoined the rest of the market patrons. I stared as the crowd parted for them like sharks moving through a school of fish.

◆ ◆ ◆

"Come *on* Cal," Tobyas whined as we walked over the cobblestone streets of Prisma, Eserene's wealthiest district. "We're going to miss it!" The shadow of the castle loomed overhead as we made our way to the cliffs, wooden swords in tow.

"We'll get there," I answered, nodding at people as we passed. Tobyas' wooden sword cleaved the air as he bounced around the street slaying invisible monsters.

156

Even though I didn't particularly like him, ever since Lord Castemont had suggested I could be a Royal Guard one day, I decided I was going to act the part. That meant I had to march, not run, to the Cliffs of Malarrey.

The Lord had come by our house a few days after we met him in the market. How he knew where we lived, I wasn't sure, but he brought a bouquet of flowers for Aunt Berna and two wooden swords for me and Tobyas. I was too old to play with a wooden sword, but it felt kind of powerful to have it strapped to my side. Almost like a real guard.

"Watch it!" an old man barked as Tobyas barely missed the man's arm with an unruly swing. Tobyas didn't skip a beat, continuing to swing and dodge enemies that weren't there without so much as an apology.

"Look!" Tobyas suddenly called, pointing his sword to the castle looming overhead. At the very top of the highest turret, a figure stood on a balcony, looking out over the city. "King Umfray! He's right there!"

The man was too far away to tell if it really was the King of Widoras, but Tobyas began frantically waving his arms trying to catch the person's attention as we continued walking. I wondered if the King was still in mourning. It'd been a year since his son passed. They told us he'd caught a fever, but the rumor was that he'd actually been drunk and fell into the harbor. Some even said he'd been pushed.

I'd only ever seen the King from afar, during parades or when he addressed the city from a balcony on holidays. Aunt Berna said he was a good king, but I didn't know if that was true. Sure, we were more than fine in Prisma, but every district wasn't like that. Aunt Berna told us we were never allowed to go to Inkwell because it was full of people that were so poor and hungry that they'd attack us for the coin in our pockets. But we were poor and hungry when we lived with Mama, and we never attacked anyone.

If I were ever King of Widoras, the people of Inkwell would be the first I'd help.

I glanced back at the man on the balcony, but he'd disappeared.

We rounded the corner of Maple Avenue to the waterfront of Pellucid Harbor. I liked living in a city on the water. Growing up in Taitha, I'd always felt a little suffocated. But in Eserene, the horizon over the sea went on forever. I couldn't see the Onyxian Mountains from within the city walls, but I knew they were there, watching over the sea like King Umfray supposedly watched over his people.

The cliffs drew nearer as Tobyas continued to swing his sword. "I want to go back to the Onyx Pass so I can kill a bonehog," he called over his shoulder as he thrust his wooden blade forward.

I shuddered at the thought. We'd spent four nights camping in the Pass on our journey from Taitha to Dry Gulch to Eserene after Mama was killed. The guide that escorted us told us we'd be okay as long as we stayed with the group. We made it through unscathed, but the screams and snarls of the beasts still rang through my mind like they'd been howling just for me.

"You were too little to remember the Onyx Pass, Tobyas. Besides, you couldn't kill a bonehog," I answered as we began to ascend the hill to the top of the cliffs.

"I could kill any of the beasts in the Onyx Pass."

I rolled my eyes. Tobyas was twelve now, but he still acted like a child sometimes, something that other boys his age had already grown out of. He loved his books — devoured them like his favorite pastries. And he loved playing soldier, even more so now that he had a wooden sword. He often frayed my nerves, but I didn't mind it, especially because I'd been forced to grow up so quickly. He could be a kid for a little longer.

"Do you know how big a bonehog is?" I prodded.

"Doesn't matter how big it is. Just gotta know where to stab it." He swiped his sword through the air as he ran up the incline, overshooting and almost catching himself in the leg.

"You're going to hurt yourself," I called.

"Am not," he answered, just in time for him to overdo his follow-through and strike himself across the arm. "Shit," he hissed.

"Hey!" I barked.

"Aunt Berna isn't around!"

"Doesn't matter."

"Who cares–"

"What does Aunt Berna say?"

Tobyas' arms dropped to his sides as he let out a sigh, dropping his head back in exasperation. "If you're not smart enough to say something without swearing, you're not smart enough."

"That's right."

He rolled his eyes as we reached the top of the cliffs. Tobyas plopped to the ground and hung his feet over the side. "Well in my opinion, smart people say *fuck*."

And he slid over the edge.

Even though the drop was short, I still got nervous every time I saw him disappear. Aunt Berna had taught us a lot, but she'd never taught us how to swim. I tried to keep my pace slow and deliberate like a Royal Guard would, but I couldn't help but scramble to the cliff's edge to make sure he'd actually landed on the thin strip of rock a few feet down.

"Let's *go*," he called over his shoulder. I let a tiny sigh of relief escape when my eyes found him. I lowered myself over the edge to land behind him as he began making his way across the face of the cliff. "We're going to miss the lights if you don't hurry the *fuck* up."

"You can't just throw the F-word into any sentence and call it good."

He began swinging his sword again, landing each imaginary strike with the F-word. We rounded the cliff, getting closer and closer to our secret hiding spot. Tobyas' face moved toward the sun every few seconds as he sped up, watching it inch closer to the center of the sky.

We reached the cave as the first lights began to flash, when the sun bounced off the waves to reflect off the crystals that made up the cave's ceiling. They grew brighter and brighter until every surface of the cave shimmered with dancing lights. I sat down on the rock toward the deadend of the cave, leaning my head back to let the lights swarm me like fireflies. Tobyas stood in place, his head moving back and forth, back and forth.

A dull spot in the sea of brilliance caught my eye. In my peripheral I saw a tiny row boat floating in the sea's waves. I almost ignored it, but...it seemed to be heading into the harbor from the sea beyond the breakwall. Row boats usually took captains and their crew from the shore to their ships anchored in the harbor. To see a boat rowing from the open sea into the harbor...

Suddenly, the lights disappeared and the cave was dim once again. "I think the lights were better last time." Tobyas said abruptly, disappointment lacing his voice.

My vision snapped back to where he stood, his face still glued to the ceiling of the cave. "Not everything can be perfect all the time," I told him.

"That's stupid." He kicked the ground.

I inhaled, letting out a laugh at his response. "Such is life, Tobyas."

Chapter 17

"I'm the daughter of a lord," Aunt Berna said, daintily dabbing the corner of her mouth with a napkin. She'd pulled the *good napkins* from the cupboard when Lord Evarius Castemont told us he'd like to have dinner with us. He'd invited us to his residence in the castle, but Aunt Berna insisted he and Tyrak come to our home for dinner so she could make her famous braised beef.

I didn't know how it could be famous when the only one who ever talked about it was her.

Tyrak had opted to stand guard outside the front door. I wished I could join him after about five minutes of driveling conversation. Aunt Berna had flitted about the kitchen all day, fussing over every detail and sending Tobyas and me to the market more than once. She wanted everything to be *just so*. That's what she'd told us over and over all day.

I'd never seen her like this, and I wasn't sure I liked it.

"Lord Carrowin... I'm afraid I don't know the name," Lord Castemont replied before placing a forkful of beef in his mouth.

"He lived in Anicole," Tobyas piped as he pushed steamed carrots around his plate.

"Anicole? How does the daughter of an Anicolian lord find herself living in Eserene?"

Was she batting her lashes *again*?

"My father was Lord Hans Carrowin, born to a long line of Anicolian noblemen. Both my parents had passed, and I was set to marry the truly wretched son of a baron." She shuddered slightly. "But with no parents left alive, I had no one to hold me accountable." A coy smile lit her face. "I took the family fortune, arranged an escort, and decided to start my life in Eserene."

Lord Castemont's eyes widened. "A woman who takes initiative." He leaned back slightly and surveyed her petite features, her blue eyes and sandy blonde hair. "How refreshing."

"Thank you, my Lord," she answered, bowing her head. Tobyas shot me a look of disgust, but I made sure to keep my face straight.

Aunt Berna was pretty. I knew that. Men looked at her everywhere we went, even some women. But no one who approached her ever seemed good enough for her. To be honest, I didn't know why she took us in. She could've married someone and had children of her own, but she chose us instead. She was strict and always made sure we used our manners, but she had fun with us, too. She'd always told us she hoped we'd have an uncle one day, but that she had to make sure he was perfect for our family.

I was absolutely sure that Lord Castemont was *not* that person.

But still, she blushed and giggled as he spoke, blooming in his gaze like a rose in her perfectly tended garden. I picked at my braised beef, the taste of it souring in my mouth as I stewed over the fact that she cooked it for *him*.

"I'm not a native of Eserene, either," Lord Castemont said, dabbing his mouth with a napkin. "My father was a merchant from Taitha."

"Taitha?" Tobyas blurted. "So you've traveled the Onyx Pass, too?"

Lord Castemont took a sip of wine. "What if I told you I've traveled the Pass dozens of times?" My brother's eyes widened. "Mostly to Blindbarrow, but a few other diplomatic trips to other cities and countries. As long as you're experienced with a sword, you can make it through the Pass just fine."

Tobyas stared at him in disbelief. "Whoa."

"Taitha," Aunt Berna cut in. "How did you end up in Eserene then?"

The Lord smiled fondly. "My father was the favored spice merchant of the late Cabillian King Divos. The King actually helped me earn the position of squire to a young Nesanian prince who was studying in Taitha. But when I was seventeen, my father passed at sea." His eyes turned reverent.

"Oh, my deepest apologies," Aunt Berna crooned.

"Thank you, Bernadet," he answered with a sad smile. "He was a great man, and King Divos ensured I was well taken care of after his passing. But I had no desire to stay in Taitha." His face flashed with a hint of sorrow. "Too many memories had been soured after I lost my father. So the King arranged a squire position for me in Eserene, and luckily enough I befriended King Umfray. He granted me lordship upon my twenty-first birthday and assigned Tyrak as my personal guard."

Aunt Berna diligently listened to every word that came from the Lord's mouth. I tried to shoot Tobyas a glance, but even he was wrapped up in Lord Castemont's story.

"Sometimes it just takes being in the right place at the right time. Isn't that right, Cal?" he laughed.

Why was he singling me out? I did my best to muster a smile. "Yes, my Lord."

"Forgive me for asking, but you never married?" Aunt Berna asked, fingers laced beneath her chin.

"Since I was not born in the country of Widoras, I was not required to enter the marriage market at any point." Aunt Berna seemed to deflate a bit at his answer, and I watched as the Lord noticed. "But it's never been out of the realm of possibilities." She blushed — *ugh* — and nodded. He smiled with crinkled eyes and looked back to his plate. "Dinner was lovely. Let me help you clear the table," Lord Castemont chimed as he folded his napkin.

"That is very kind, my Lord," Aunt Berna answered in a melodic voice I'd never heard before.

"Just Evarius."

My gaze shot down as I tried to hide the scoff on my face. Tobyas wasn't so smooth as I was, and a choked laugh escaped his throat.

"Tobyas Vic Myrin," Aunt Berna said sternly. "Manners."

My brother fidgeted in his seat. "Sorry."

"Off with you two," Aunt Berna commanded, shooing us away with a hand. "You're excused." The disciplinary tone wasn't reflecting on her face anymore as she looked back to Lord Castemont and smiled.

"Don't go far, boys," the Lord called. "I'd like to show you both something as soon as I'm done helping your lovely aunt clean up. And remember, I brought dessert." I felt Tobyas perk up next to me as we shuffled toward the staircase.

Aunt Berna's house was beautiful, with hand-stitched upholstery and shiny marble floors. It was what I'd always imagined the inside of the castle in Taitha to look like, probably the Eserenian castle too. There were a bit too many soft pinks and creams for my liking, but Aunt Berna was proud of her home. We learned very quickly after arriving in Eserene that we didn't touch the painted pottery, we didn't sit on the settee with dirty clothes, and we always took our muddy boots off before we entered the house.

Tobyas usually did all three of those things anyway.

He and I each had our own rooms at the top of the stairs, each bigger than our entire hut back in Taitha. Both rooms had soaring windows that looked out over the small courtyard in front of the house and the cobblestone street beyond.

164

"What do you think of Lord Castemont?" I asked Tobyas as we settled on the bench that sat before the window in my room.

He didn't take his eyes off the street. "It's obvious he's wearing a wig," he answered.

"What?"

"The man," he said, pointing absentmindedly out the window to a plump, middle-aged gentleman wrapped in a fine surcoat despite the uncomfortable summer heat. One of our favorite things to do was to make up stories about the Prismanian passersby, and I could see the wheels turning in Tobyas' mind. "He's wearing a wig. He lost his hair because he's stressed out that his wife is spending all of his money."

I let out a laugh at the mop of hair that sat atop the man's head. "And his only hope is to marry off his son to the daughter of some rich sucker for the dowry."

Tobyas snorted, peering down the street, looking for his next victim.

I cleared my throat. "Really, though. What do you think of Lord Castemont?"

"He brings us gifts. And he's been through the Onyx Pass a lot, which is pretty interesting," Tobyas murmured with a shrug, his eyes narrowing on a woman with a thick fringe of feathers around the collar of her frock.

"But aside from that. Do you think he likes Aunt Berna?"

He shrugged again. "Everyone likes Aunt Berna. She's a very likable person."

"Don't be a smartass."

Tobyas' brows raised at the swear I'd used, but then face crinkled as he considered what I said. "He compliments her a lot."

"So you think he likes her?"

"Yuck," Tobyas spat.

"Tobyas."

He let out a dramatic sigh. "I don't know, *maybe*," he answered, his response entirely unhelpful. His eyes remained on the street as he pointed to the woman with the feathered collar. "That woman is *rich*."

I narrowed my eyes in the woman's direction. "How do you know?"

"Those are ciakoo feathers. Do you know how rare a ciakoo is?"

"No."

He shimmied off the bench, disappearing through the doorway for only a moment before returning with a monstrous book, *The Fauna of Astran.* "Look," he urged, placing the book in my lap and pointing at a page.

There was a sketch of a ciakoo mid-flight, its outstretched wings as pitch black as the rest of its body. "Its feathers look black until you see them in the light. Then they're blue and violet and green," he explained, climbing back into the seat next to me. Tobyas leaned over the book, his finger trailing beneath the words on the page. "Ciakoos are very rare on the continent of Astran. The bird is said to be a good omen. Overhunting by people in pursuit of good fortune has reduced the ciakoo's numbers dr...dra–"

"Drastically," I offered.

"I would've gotten it!" Tobyas whined. I knew he would have. He always did. Even though we learned later than most, Tobyas and I were good at reading. Aunt Berna had made sure of it. I didn't like to read very much, but Tobyas burned through books like wildfire. Fables, geography, history, the lore of the Saints... He loved it all. Aunt Berna was always bringing home new books for him to read. His room was like a library.

Tobyas turned his eyes back to the page. "The lore of the Saints says that the ciakoo is actually Rhedros, Keeper of the Blood Saints, taking the form of a bird to search the land for his great lost love." Tobyas wrinkled his nose.

"His great lost love?"

He let out a heave of a sigh, gathering the book into his arms before slipping through the doorway again. A moment later, he reappeared with another massive book cradled to his chest. *The Complete Lore of the Saints: Legends, Myths, & Truths.*

The book fell open and he pawed through the pages. I had no idea how he remembered what information was in what book, but I stared as he flipped to the exact page he was searching for. *The Great Lost Love of Rhedros.*

Tobyas let his finger hit the page. "It is said that the reason behind the fury of Rhedros is the loss of his life's greatest love. Rhedros was born to two of the Forgotten Saints and was placed in this realm as a force of good."

I narrowed my eyes. Rhedros was the Keeper of all things evil — death, storms, Hell, war, and pain. It made no sense that he would be good.

Tobyas let out another heavy sigh at my confused expression, as if my ignorance greatly inconvenienced him. "If you actually read it, you'd understand." He gripped the book and shook it for emphasis.

"Give me a summary."

He rolled his eyes before flipping to a section closer to the front of the book. "The Forgotten Saints were the world's first governing force. They ruled over everything the way the Benevolent and Blood Saints do now. All forces in the Old World were balanced, but when the Occulti grew too numerous, the Forgotten Saints were forced to burn the Old World to ash to start anew, themselves included, but not before planting a seed of good in the New World.

"They placed a child called Rhedros among the ruins of the Old World, hoping to set the New World on a path to righteousness. Rhedros matured and began making plans for more forces of good, but he quickly sensed that a balance remained in the world that could only be caused by an evil pr...propor...proportionate to his benevolence." I felt Tobyas' satisfaction through my daze. "He quickly found that forces of evil had slipped past the defenses of the Forgotten Saints to leave a child born of fury and hatred, a child called Katia."

"The Occulti? What's that? And Katia was evil? So why–"

"I don't know, Cal." His eyes flipped back to the page as he gave a shrug.

"There's nothing in there that explains why?"

Tobyas slammed the book closed. "Read it and find out."

I huffed in frustration, but I wanted to know more. "Can I borrow the book?"

"Under one condition."

"You want my dessert."

I was met by a cheeky grin. "You saw he brought chocolate pastries. My favorite."

I let out a sigh. "You can have one bite."

"Two."

"Deal. And normal-sized bites, not giant bites." He plopped the book in my lap, the weight daunting but promising.

With impeccable timing, Aunt Berna shouted from downstairs. "Boys!"

We padded down the stairs to see Lord Castemont standing with our wooden swords in hand, Tyrak at his side. "Who wants to learn how to wield a sword?"

Chapter 18

"A clean slice is the goal," Castemont said, Tyrak's sword in his hand as we stood in the small garden behind our house. Aunt Berna had fire lamps installed a few years ago so Tobyas and I could play into the night, and the shadowy light made the Lord and his guard look even more imposing. "But before you can make that slice, you have much to learn."

"How much could there be to learn about swinging a sword?" Tobyas asked.

In two quick movements, Lord Castemont lunged forward and swung, knocking the wooden sword from my brother's hand. Tobyas' face flushed with embarrassment. "No fair," he muttered, bending down awkwardly for his sword.

"*Much* to learn," Lord Castemont repeated, passing the sword back to Tyrak. It looked much more natural in the guard's grip with his calloused hands and clean-cut leathers. "Tyrak here has volunteered to give you lessons, should you be interested."

The guard nodded his head. "I believe you have the potential to join the Royal Guard one day," he said, his tone rugged. His olive skin glowed dimly in the light of the lamps, his eyes and hair as dark as the shadows that danced around the garden. "You just need a bit of training." Though he spoke to both of us, his eyes were glued on me.

"Cal has the height," Aunt Berna called from where she sat on a bench in the garden. Lord Castemont moved to join her, taking a seat a bit too close to her for my liking. "And I'm sure Tobyas will, too, in a few years," she tacked on as if it were an afterthought.

Tyrak gave a slight nod. He bent his knees, the hilt of his sword still in his grip as he surveyed me. "What is the most important thing to know about fighting?"

"Stab the other guy," Tobyas chirped.

Tyrak's eyes crinkled with the hint of a smile. "That is important, yes." He began walking a circle around the two of us. "Balance," he explained, "is the most important thing to remember about fighting. Balance can be the difference between standing and falling, between winning and losing, between living and dying. Keep your balance, and you may keep your life, even if you lose the fight."

He moved closer to me, and though I was used to feeling eyes on me, his stare felt different. It felt thick with unspoken words, and the slight furrow to his brow ruined his mask of composure.

Halting in front of me, he suddenly threw his sword in the air, the pommel landing perfectly in the palm of his hand, the blade standing straight up. "When you can hold the blade to the sky in the palm of your hand without it wavering, then you will be ready."

Tobyas wasted no time, his tongue stuck out as he concentrated on standing his wooden sword straight up. It quickly clattered to the gravel. "That's impossible," he called seconds later.

"You see me do it with your own two eyes and tell me it's impossible?" Tyrak's voice was laced with amusement.

My brother grumbled under his breath as he tried again, Tyrak's eyes refocusing on me. He cocked a dark brow expectantly. I swallowed, quickly standing my sword in my palm. It didn't take long for it to join Tobyas' on the ground.

"Good," Tyrak stated, nodding his head. "But you can do better."

My first reaction was to flinch at the bluntness of his words, but he was right. I could do better. Retrieving my faux blade, I tried and tried, meeting the same ending each time.

The fire lamps had begun to burn low and Tobyas had long since given up, but still I tried. I managed to get it to stand perfectly straight a few times but would have to shuffle my feet to keep it from tipping over. Every time it landed on the gravel I'd get a little more frustrated.

I wondered if my father knew how to wield a sword, wherever he was now. I bet he could. So I was going to learn, too.

"It's late, Cal," Aunt Berna's voice cut through my concentration. I realized that at some point Tobyas had curled up on the bench, his head resting in her lap as he dozed.

"Let me try one more time," I begged. She gave a small nod as she yawned and I propped the sword up on my hand. Balance. I was doing it, I was—

Out of the corner of my eye, I noticed Lord Castemont place his hand on Aunt Berna's back as he leaned over to whisper in her ear, and the sword once again hit the gravel.

"I'm impressed," Tyrak said. "You've made more progress in one night than I see other trainees make in weeks."

I wanted so badly to appreciate his words, but half my attention remained on the garden bench. "Thank you, Sir."

"I'll be back tomorrow for another lesson."

Lord Castemont approached me, a hand extended. I met his grasp, sure to give a firm handshake like Aunt Berna had taught me. "Keep at it and you'll be in the Royal Guard in no time. Thank you for dinner, Bernadet." I cringed as he used her first name so informally. "It was an absolute pleasure."

"The pleasure is all mine," she crooned, dipping her head in the way that was becoming nauseatingly familiar. I fought to keep from rolling my eyes.

"Midday tomorrow?"

"That would be lovely," she answered. "I'll have tea ready."

The Lord gave a beaming smile as he bowed his head and moved to the gate that led to the street. "Goodnight."

I waved a hand. "Goodnight, my Lord."

◆ ◆ ◆

The city had long since gone to sleep, but a candle burned next to my bed as I flipped through Tobyas' book. Aunt Berna taught us numbers and history and manners, but she hadn't taught us much about the Saints. Something intrigued me about the fact that Rhedros had been born good. A section titled *The Forgotten Saints* sat open in front of me. My lips moved silently as I read the words in my head.

"In the Old World, the Forgotten Saints were the ultimate authority. Humans feared their power and begged for their blessings and mercy, much like they do of today's Benevolent and Blood Saints. Little is known of the Forgotten Saints, either because few stories made it through the burning of the Old World or simply because they were more elusive than the Benevolent and Blood Saints, but it is known that the Forgotten Saints were a unified force, unlike today's Saints." A drawing of nine ambiguous silhouettes graced the bottom of the page, crowns of all heights and shapes upon their heads.

"The scourge of the Old World was the Occulti, a horde of demons that could take the shape of man or beast. The horde was led by the Malosym, Breaker of Wills and Ravager of Souls. Malosym was the eternal nemesis of the Forgotten Saints, but since the Saints could not die by any hand but their own or that of a human, Malosym was never able to succeed in eliminating their influence. Instead, he commanded the Occulti to lay ruin to everything built by the Forgotten Saints.

"Under Malosym's reign, the demons of the Occulti could possess a living being or create new life, and their ability to do both knew no bounds. The Occulti thrived on chaos and anguish, and cared for little beyond spreading evil far and wide." A faded picture was nestled beside the text, a black cloud hovering over a city with buildings lying in ruin. "They tortured, maimed, and killed, feeding and gaining strength on the pained and dying screams of innocents as they destroyed cities."

I wrinkled my face at the thought. "The sole vulnerability of the Occulti was each other. The horde was interdependent. When pain was caused to one member of the horde, pain was caused to all. When one demon perished, its brethren seemed to grieve and work to avenge its death. In turn, their mourning period furthered their devastating destruction.

"Malosym could only be killed by Holy Flames, commanded by the Forgotten Saints. When the Occulti grew too numerous to be controlled by the Forgotten Saints, the Forgotten Saints had no choice but to set the Old World ablaze, killing Malosym and his horde."

I fought back the rising discomfort and flipped through the pages of the book, but a title caught my attention: *The Daughter of Katia.*

"Seers say that a child will one day be born to Katia, Keeper of the Benevolent Saints, a daughter with the same blood that pumps through the Heart of the Eleven. She will be the Savior of the Realm, keeping it from falling to darker forces. It is presumed that the father of the child will be either Tolar, Saint of Wealth or Soren, Saint of Heaven, the only two male Benevolent Saints, though this is not known for certain."

"It is also unknown whether the Daughter of Katia will be able to access the wells of power of the other Benevolent Saints or the Blood Saints who originally called Katia their Keeper. When the child will be born unto Katia remains unknown, but it will coincide at some point when Noros, Saint of Pain, is cursed to walk the realm." A robed, full-figured woman with blurry features stood tall on the page, the crown atop her head like a beacon in the night. Her hands were outstretched, palms to the sky, the perfect picture of holiness. I'd never guess she'd been born the Keeper of the Blood Saints.

My eyes began to droop, heavy with exhaustion under the impending dawn. I hadn't meant to stay up so late. I wanted to be well-rested for my next lesson with Tyrak. I tried to flip through more pages, the promises of stories of Katia's beasts and Rhedros' fury beckoning me, but sleep won the battle.

◆ ◆ ◆

I rubbed my eyes against the scorching Eserenian summer sun. Tyrak's shadowy figure stood before me, his eyes on my face. Lord Castemont had joined Aunt Berna and Tobyas inside to prepare afternoon tea, though chances were Tobyas was talking the Lord out of any sweets he may have brought.

"You didn't sleep much last night," Tyrak stated matter-of-factly. He held his broadsword in one hand, my wooden sword in the other.

"How do you know?"

A corner of his mouth lifted in a smirk, his dark eyes crinkling. "Balance is the first thing you learn. Then you must learn to read your opponent, assess them for vulnerabilities."

I raised a brow, unsure what he was getting at.

Tyrak tapped my left knee with his blade. "You stood straight as an arrow during your lesson last night. Today, you lean to one side." He tapped the back of my shoulders next. "And you slouch."

I quickly straightened, pulling my shoulders back and squaring my jaw. Tyrak chuckled under his breath, extending my wooden sword to me. "Balance." The straightforward order had me lifting my weapon immediately.

It didn't take long for it to land on the ground with a dull thud. "Again," Tyrak ordered, the clipped tone of his voice different from last night's lesson.

I took a deep breath, narrowing my eyes as I focused on the palm of my hand. *I can do this.* Once again, the sword quickly overturned and clattered to the gravel. "Again," Tyrak's voice sounded.

A frustrated grumble escaped my chest. Suddenly the tip of Tyrak's blade was beneath my chin, propping my face to look at him. My eyes flew wide with a flash of fear. "None of that nonsense." His blade left my chin, but his eyes kept me pinned in place before they quickly flashed toward the house. "When Castemont suggested I train you and your brother, I had no choice but to agree. I serve him and do as he bids. Did I think the potential was there? Maybe so, but most likely not. Now, I knew you possessed the height, but I did not foresee you possessing the skill. A very, very pleasant surprise."

"I can't even balance a damned wooden sword."

He let out a chuckle. "It will not be easy, but I truly believe you have the skill to serve in the Royal Guard."

I furrowed my brow. Every member of the Royal Guard had silver-streaked hair and lines on their faces. The position was earned after years and years of service in the Eserenian army, and only the best of the best ascended the ranks.

I ran my hands over the dull wooden sword. "The Royal Guard is a long way away for me."

Tyrak stepped closer. His gaze was intense, almost uncomfortably so. "Lord Castemont is a very well-connected man. I make no promises, but if you keep up with training, I'd bet he could get you into the Guard as soon as you reach eighteen years."

My head spun as I stepped back. The Royal Guard? *In four years?* Images of clean cut leathers and expertly smithed helmets flashed through my head as I imagined myself marching with the Guard, serving a member of Low Royalty in the castle. Maybe even High Royalty someday. Maybe even the *King*.

"If you can commit to putting in the work, I will commit to training you. Not the obligatory training regimen I'd planned on Castemont's order," he said, his head nodding in the direction of the house where the Lord was doing Saints knew what, "but a regimen meant to forge a warrior."

"Yes," I blurted without thinking. "Yes, I'll commit to that."

Tyrak's face was etched with approval and pride as he nodded, stepping back once again. That approval and pride felt like it was glowing inside my chest. "Balance," he commanded.

I lined the sword up, my gut steeled with resolve. I'd just found some semblance of balance when Tobyas' voice sounded from the house and my blade tumbled to the ground.

"The Lord and his guard have to go," he called.

Tyrak momentarily lowered his brows before straightening again and giving me a terse nod. "Tomorrow," he said, and I nodded back the way I thought a Royal Guard might nod.

Lord Castemont stepped out of the house, Aunt Berna behind him. "I'm terribly sorry to cut your lesson short," the Lord offered. "I'd completely forgotten about my trip to Inkwell."

"A trip to Inkwell?" I asked. A strange kind of excitement rose in my gut at the idea of visiting the slums of Eserene.

He nodded. "A few other lords and I travel to Inkwell every so often to offer bread, clothing, and coin to the neediest of residents."

"Can I come?"

"Absolutely not," Aunt Berna cut in.

"But–"

"Ah!" I could tell by the look on her face that she wasn't budging. "It's far too dangerous for a young boy."

I was fourteen. Not a *young boy*. But I bit my tongue as I watched Lord Castemont. "I must agree with your aunt, Cal. It's far too dangerous." I tried to hide my disappointment as he turned to Tyrak and nodded.

The guard cleared his throat. "I'll get you there at once, my Lord." He turned to Aunt Berna. "My Lady," he said, lowering his head as they headed for the gate.

"Goodbye!" Tobyas called cheerfully.

"Farewell for now," the Lord answered, smiling at Aunt Berna's dainty wave.

Tobyas ventured into the garden to pick up my wooden sword. "Let's go to the cliffs!"

Chapter 19

A few years ago, Tobyas was playing soldier with a tree branch instead of a wooden sword. I saw the disaster coming from a mile away and screamed after him to stop swinging so recklessly, but did he? Of course not. He tripped over his own foot and his branch went flying straight into a vendor's display of fruits. Melons, sweet oranges, and honey apples went rolling in every direction.

Tobyas sprinted away, of course, afraid of being scolded. "I'm so sorry," I said to the woman who owned the cart, immediately shuffling through the street trying to collect the fruit and clean up Tobyas' mess. "He's just a kid. He got a bit carried away." But she didn't hear a word I said and sprung straight into a tongue lashing that was rather disproportionate to the crime. I understood why she was angry, though. Selling fruit was how she made her money.

Today, he swung his wooden sword twice as erratically. "Watch where you're swinging Tobyas," I called after him as he swung his wooden sword through the air far too close to unsuspecting Eserenians…again. "Better not repeat the tree branch incident."

"I'm going to be a Royal Guard too, you know," Tobyas said, completely ignoring me. His dark eyes glinted in the sun the same way his black hair did as we walked through Prisma on our way to the Cliffs of Malarrey.

"You have to train," I replied.

He scoffed. "That's just boring. I already know how to swing a sword. You're the one who needs training." Without thinking, I pulled my own wooden sword from its sheath at my hip and lunged for him, knocking his sword from his grip.

"Hey!" he cried, his face going red with embarrassment as I let a satisfied grin plaster mine. He wasted no time retrieving his sword before winging it through the air to land flat across my back.

My spine arched against the strike. Tobyas quickly realized his mistake and took off in a dead sprint, sword flailing, people staring as he screamed. I let my legs take me, the eight inches of height I had on him meaning my strides were longer and I was faster. Much faster.

He rounded the corner to the waterfront, his overly-dramatic screams attracting attention from everyone within earshot. Just as he reached the grassy lawn of the waterfront, his sword slipped too low, his foot catching behind it. He went tumbling head over heels, flying through the air, landing on his back with a mighty thud.

The laughter came from deep in my belly as he sat up, rubbing his head, completely bewildered. "Idiot," I muttered when I finally caught my breath.

"Shut up," he answered, brushing himself off and returning his wooden sword to its sheath. "Come on."

We sparred with the swords as we moved up the hill to the cliffs, the rhythmic clanking of wood on wood like a drumbeat to the perfect day.

◆ ◆ ◆

"Look," I called to Tobyas, pointing to a deposit of crystal that jutted out from the cliff face.

His eyes widened. "I wonder if they glint like the ones in the cave."

We'd missed the cave's midday lights, but weren't too disappointed since we found a path we'd never taken before. "Be careful," I added, eyeing the ledge that was uncomfortably thin and the waves that crashed below it.

"Yeah, yeah," he sneered. "Think we could climb up to that ledge?" He used his sword to point to a ridge of rock a bit further down the cliff face. "I can see the footholds all the way from here."

I squinted at the cluster of rocks. "Let's find out." We plodded along the ledge, tiny pebbles falling loose beneath our feet and disappearing in the deep blue water below. I loved days like this — the sun was boiling, but it lit the harbor like stained glass in a cathedral.

"Faster!" Tobyas yelled at me. "That footwork needs improving if you want to join the Guard."

I kept my pace steady. "Shut up!"

"Bet you won't make the Guard at eighteen."

I stopped in my tracks and turned to him, a shit-eating grin on his face. "You don't think I can do it?"

"A silver piece says you can't."

I narrowed my eyes. "It's a bet."

He gave me the hardest handshake he could manage, sure to look me straight in the eye like Aunt Berna had taught us. "It's a bet."

I scoffed, smirking as I came upon the footholds. "This looks sturdy enough," I mumbled, surveying the short climb to the ledge.

"Can you just hurry up?" Tobyas said, tapping his foot.

180

"I'm sorry for making sure it's safe enough for you, King To-byas," I answered sarcastically, gripping the rocks and securing my fingers before hoisting myself up to the first foothold. "I should just let you fall and die, right?"

"I wouldn't die."

"You can't swim."

Tobyas answered with a dramatic sigh, crossing his arms impatiently.

I tested the feel of my weight on the bit of rock. Satisfied it was secure, I curled my fingers around the ridge and pulled myself up on my elbows, shimmying the rest of my body up.

"The ledge is wide and it looks like it goes pretty far in both directions," I shouted. I turned back to look up the cliff face, tufts of grass growing over the side of the plateau. "I think I can reach the top of the cliff from here!" If I could get my hands over the edge, I could easily scramble to the top. "Watch!"

I jumped and caught the ledge, and my feet found tiny toeholds, helping me awkwardly climb the rest of the way.

It was the westernmost part of the cliff, a spot we'd never been before because of the rocky pits and outcroppings that separated it from the main cliffs. The path Tobyas had found seemed to be the only way here. I threw my hands in the air triumphantly, delighting in the pitiful sulk on his face.

"Hey!" Tobyas cried. "How'd you get all the way up there?"

"I'm tall!" I boasted.

"No fair."

"You'll be up here in a few years."

Tobyas moved to take the first foothold as I turned to look at the plateau around me again. "I'm going to see if there are any other paths around here!"

"Yeah, whatever. Enjoy the view!" he answered, his voice thick with bad attitude.

The entirety of Eserene was visible in the distance, framed by the massive columns of rock jutting up from the cliffs. An idea flashed through my mind — there could be another crystal cave on this side of the cliffs. Tobyas would be pissed if there was a crystal cave only I could reach. The look on his face would be priceless.

I ran to the far edge, carefully looking over the lip down the sheer cliff face. No signs of a cave, but I did see an inlet we hadn't yet explored and a rough ledge that looked like it could take us to it, and—

A clipped scream split the air in two, the sound so out of place among the crashing waves that it took me a moment to realize where it came from.

Tobyas.

My legs couldn't carry me fast enough to the edge, the air closing in around me as I skidded to a halt. "Tobyas!" His name ripped from my throat like the edge of a knife. Where was he? All the rocks looked the same, all the ledges looked the same—

"TOBYAS!" My voice broke as I frantically whipped my head back and forth, my eyes desperately searching the cliff face for any sign of him.

Where is he where is he where is he?

Then I saw it. A cloud of crimson in the water, quickly swallowed by the waves that crashed over the rocks far below. *Too far below.*

"No!" I jumped down to the ledge and slid over the steep incline, my eyes glued to the waves, my ears straining for his voice. "Tobyas!"

I bent down to unlace my boots, ripping at the leather. I had minutes, maybe seconds. He couldn't swim. *I* couldn't swim, but I was going to swim. I *had* to swim.

"I'm coming, Tobyas! I'm coming!" It was a far jump. I just had to make sure to land past the jagged rocks, then I could climb over them and try to find him.

The waves picked up then, the sun suddenly smothered by a mass of gray clouds that had formed, blotting out the clear blue sky. Thunder crashed out of nowhere as the waves pounded the

182

cliff face harder, rough white water tumbling in with force I'd never seen before.

I stepped back, took a deep breath, and leaped off the ledge—

A monstrous wave collided with me, higher than I'd ever seen in the harbor. It slammed me back against the cliff face, leaving me in the exact place I'd leapt from. I shook the impact from my head and leaped again, determined to get to Tobyas, but another wave pinned me to the rock. I gasped for breath when the wave pulled back, only for the saltwater to crash over me again, as if Idros, Saint of Storms himself, was holding me in place.

The rain started then, heavy and unforgiving between the waves that assaulted me. "Tobyas! Please!" The rain pelted against my skin so hard it was almost painful, but all I could think about was getting to Tobyas. I scanned the harbor for a boat, for anyone that could help, but I saw no one through the sheets of punishing rain.

Lightning spiderwebbed across the sky, illuminating the craggy rocks that lay beneath the water's rough white surface for a split second. They were angry serrated knives pointed and ready to kill.

My eyes stung and the thunder rattled my skull like Idros was bludgeoning my head with his mighty fist. All I could do was scream out for my brother. Over and over, between the waves, the lightning, and the rain, I screamed. Helpless. Hopeless.

As a wave rushed back, I sprang forward, once again launching myself through the air, plunging to the water below.

The sheer force of the wave sent stars circling through my vision as my head slammed into the cliff. The water didn't pull back this time, the current so powerful that I was completely paralyzed. My lungs began to burn before long. But the wave didn't let up.

My mouth flew open on instinct and I choked on the force of the seawater that entered my lungs. *Please,* I thought. *Please, someone, anyone. Get my brother.*

As the edges of my vision clouded over and darkened, my mind clawed with desperation for a way out. But there was no way out. There was only saltwater and muffled screams as I was swallowed by complete darkness.

◆ ◆ ◆

Briny water scorched my raw throat as it came back up, my abdomen clenching as I heaved. I was hot, and my entire body convulsed under the brutal sun as I remembered.

Tobyas.

I clambered to the edge of the cliff, staring down the sheer drop to the pulsing waves below, the depths the color of lapis lazuli. Endless. Empty.

No. No no no no no.

I could have pushed harder against the water to get to him. I should have. It couldn't happen like this. *This isn't happening. This can't be happening.*

I had to get home. I had to get to Aunt Berna. I had to get to–

Castemont. Lord Castemont would have access to a boat. He could send someone out on the water to search for him. Maybe Tobyas was stuck on a rock somewhere. Maybe he fell but the giant waves pushed him against the cliff like they did to me. He had to be waiting for me somewhere.

I lowered myself down to the ledge and started for the city. My entire body ached as I pushed my legs faster, my bare feet scrambling over the thinner parts of the cliff as quickly as I could, careening down the hill and winding through the manicured streets of Prisma.

"Cal?" My feet pounded to a stop on the cobblestones as I whipped around to see Lord Castemont and Tyrak. "We were just headed back to see your aunt, what–"

"Tobyas!" I choked, gasping for air. "He's in the harbor! I need a boat!"

Castemont looked at Tyrak then back to me, his eyes wide but brows furrowed. "What are you—"

I grabbed his shoulders, unconcerned about the informality or the fact that Tyrak could cut me down for touching the Lord. "Tobyas is out there!" I yelled, pulling the man back toward the waterfront, my lungs burning.

"Take him," Lord Castemont ordered Tyrak.

"My Lord—"

"I can make it three blocks unguarded. I'll get Bernadet, you get Cal to the docks. Johan should be there. Commandeer his vessel if you have to. Go!"

The Lord took off down the street while Tyrak and I sprinted for the waterfront. "There's a fisherman," Tyrak pushed out as he sprinted beside me, matching me stride for stride. "He'll take us out to look for him. What happened?"

I pushed my legs harder, hoping Tobyas could sense I was coming for him. "We were climbing," I gasped, my chest on fire. "He's out there waiting for me."

Tyrak was wordless beside me, only the sound of his heavy breath giving me hope as we neared the docks.

"Johan!" Tyrak shouted, a hand in the air as we approached. "Johan! Your boat!"

A red-faced, gruff looking man was repairing a fishing net on the dock, my bare feet and Tyrak's boots pounding on the wooden planks. His boat was small, with dirty rolled up canvas sails crowding the deck, but anything would do at this point. "Tyrak? What—"

"My brother's out there!" The man surveyed me as I stood before him, his shock at my eyes and height all the more irritating as time pressed in on me.

Tyrak hadn't slowed, instead leaping directly on the boat and reaching for the mooring ropes.

"Aye! What do you—"

"We have permission from Lord Evarius Castemont to commandeer your vessel," Tyrak offered quickly as he unwound the last rope. I hopped into the boat, my eyes moving between the folded canvas sails and the cliffs that awaited us.

"Then it's 'yers for as long as ye need it."

"Do you know how to sail?" I asked Tyrak, my voice desperate.

"Well enough. Hold tight." He dropped the canvas, and I had no idea how he did it, but he caught the seemingly nonexistent wind, steering us right for the cliffs.

"I don't know what happened." I chewed a fingernail, scanning the water. "He just fell."

Tyrak stayed silent as he zipped around the deck. "Point me in the right direction."

The cliffs grew closer, my desperation turning leaden in my chest. "Tobyas!" I screamed. Over and over I screamed his name, fighting the impending break in my voice. "Tobyas! Can you hear me?!"

"Where did he fall from?" Tyrak asked, his voice stern.

"The cliffs to the west. We'd never been there before. The waves were huge."

The guard was quiet, brows furrowed as I furiously searched the rocks, trying to get a look into every crag, dip, and pit.

"Tobyas!" I kept screaming.

Tyrak joined in, his voice quickly going hoarse as he called for my little brother. "Tobyas!"

The only answer was the sound of our own cavernous echoes and the waves pounding the desolate cliffs. I choked back sobs, each one growing harder every time I called his name only to be met with silence.

"That's where he fell from!" I yelled, a finger pointed to the ledge. Then I saw it — the cliff didn't meet the harbor, hanging over the water and leaving a small gap. I could just make out a few chunks of rock that were easily wide enough for Tobyas to crawl on. "Look!"

"Okay, hold on," Tyrak answered. I held the side of the boat in a white-knuckle grip, leaning over as far as I could as Tyrak steered us toward the overhang.

"Tobyas!" I yelled, my voice renewed with hope. He was in there. He had to be in there. But as we neared, I saw the waves swell to wash over the rocks, closing the short distance between the water and the cliff, flooding out any chance of my brother waiting for me.

"No," I whispered.

"Cal, I'm–"

"NO!" I bellowed, my salt-raw throat protesting. I was going to find him. He was waiting for me. I threw myself over the edge of the boat, hoping I'd find him under the surface, clinging to life.

The second I hit the water I sank like a stone, my movements in an attempt to swim completely ineffective. I kicked my legs out and clawed through the water, but the surface grew farther and farther above me as my head felt like it would implode. I opened my mouth to scream but only a stream of bubbles came out before seawater rushed in. My eyes were wild as they moved from the surface to the depths below me, no sign of Tobyas anywhere. I was going to die, and I was never going to find him. He would be waiting for me forever.

Chapter 20

I was far too old to sit in my Mama's lap, but I knew it made her happy. We sat in the rickety rocking chair while Tobyas pushed marbles across the packed dirt floor.

"Will you tell me about my father?" I asked, hoping she finally would.

She smiled the small smile I always loved, the one that made her green eyes squint just a little bit. "Your father is a great man. He had to leave to keep us safe."

I couldn't believe it... She was actually telling me something. I held my breath, afraid that if I spoke too soon, she'd stop, but I had to ask. "But wouldn't we be safer if he were here to protect us?"

"Not necessarily, my love." Mama rested her cheek on my head. "Your father is fighting for peace, but not everyone wants the kind of peace he does."

I furrowed my brows. "So someone wants to hurt us?"

She planted a kiss on my cheek, and I leaned against her chest, listening to the *thump thump thump* of her heart. It was too fast. "They don't know we exist, darling. Your father knew it was better that way. He is very brave, and very kind, and always honest, just like you." I smiled against her chest. "You must always be brave, kind, and honest, okay?"

"Okay. Did he love me?"

She let out a breath and looked at me for a moment. I thought maybe she was remembering something because of the look in her eyes. "Your father didn't even know you were growing in my belly before he had to go. But if he met you, I know he'd love you very, very much."

"Tell me about my father!" Tobyas chimed in, quickly climbing onto Mama's other knee.

"Your father," she started, her voice warm, "was a master marksman. He was a prince from Nesan."

"Why did he leave?"

"Your father wanted to stay here with us, but he had to go back home to Nesan."

Tobyas gave a toothy grin. "*My* father was a prince!" he taunted.

I didn't care that my father wasn't a prince. I still wanted to meet him. Mama told me that I'd know him if I saw him because my eyes were a mix of his and hers.

"Belin?"

"Yes, Mama?"

"Belin, wake up."

"Mama?"

"Belin."

That wasn't Mama talking. Only my Mama called me Belin. That was...

"Belin."

I felt a hand on my cheek, a cool palm against my clammy skin, and the blue sky materialized above me. I felt like my body was carved from ice that was on fire, like I weighed as much as a boulder but could float away at any second.

I folded myself in half as I coughed, retching up seawater once again. My eyes were bleary and stinging as I realized I was laying on wooden planks, and I pushed myself up on my elbows. *The dock.* I felt a hand on my back as I expelled more of the ocean that had entered my lungs.

"Tobyas," I choked, neither a question nor a statement.

"I'm so sorry, son," the man's voice answered. I looked up to see Tyrak crouched over me, his leathers sopping wet, water dripping down his face from his hair.

I heard the sound of pounding on the dock, turning my head to see two blurry figures sprinting toward me.

"Cal!" Aunt Berna cried, her skirts bundled in her fists as she skidded to a stop, bending down to hold me to her chest. She sobbed into my shoulder, and I was thankful the sound of her wails masked the sound of my own.

"I'm sorry," I whispered in her ear between sobs. "I couldn't save him." My heart felt like glass that had been smashed with a hammer. I didn't know how this much pain could be in my body. *It was my fault.*

"He…" Tyrak started, his own face marred with sorrow. "He jumped in to try to find him."

Aunt Berna's choked howls reverberated through me, lighting up every muscle I hadn't pushed hard enough, every piece of me that I could have put into saving Tobyas but didn't. I should have been watching him. I shouldn't have climbed to the top of the cliff and left him alone.

The guilt was going to swallow me, and I was going to let it.

◆ ◆ ◆

Losing Mama hurt. It hurt my entire body. But it didn't hurt now like it used to. It had taken a while to get into the rhythm of our new life in Eserene, but once I did, laughing with Tobyas became easy again. Before long, I stopped thinking of the image of Mama's head split on the floor every single day. It only came up sometimes, only on the bad days. I'd done just as she'd told me to do. I'd been brave and I'd been kind and I'd been honest.

But losing Tobyas...

There was no color. The world was gray where it had been bright. It was muffled where it had been teeming with sound. I couldn't do this without him. We'd always been together. Losing him meant... Losing him meant losing me.

His wooden sword washed up on the waterfront a few days later. Lord Castemont and Tyrak found it when they were on a walk. They brought it home to me, Lord Castemont's somber face contorted with as much of a smile as he could muster, but I couldn't look at it. I told him to get rid of it. I didn't want the reminder because...

We never found Tobyas.

My aunt's movements were slow around the house. She always made sure I was fed and clean, but conversation was rarely made beyond that. We weren't her children, but she'd raised us for the last five years. She'd poured her energy into making sure we were educated and sheltered and *happy*. And we were.

But now the house felt empty. I felt empty. And I know she did too.

Aunt Berna wiped the countertops, her face blank. "Let me," Lord Castemont said sympathetically, taking the rag from her hand and guiding her to the settee. "You should rest."

I sat unmoving in one of the plush cream colored chairs, my cheek against my fist, watching as the Lord tidied the kitchen. He'd been by each day to make sure we were doing okay. And even though we never found Tobyas, Lord Castemont had purchased a plot in the city's cemetery with his name carved across a stone. It was a shady spot beneath flowering trees, far too quiet and peaceful for the tornado that was Tobyas.

Aunt Berna collapsed into a puddle of tears when Lord Castemont led us to the plot, and he held her against him and let her cry. Tyrak's hand rested on my shoulder as I clenched my jaw as hard as I could. They'd seen me cry so much already. I couldn't cry again. It took all my effort to choke it back, to look at his name etched in stone and not crumble completely.

TOBYAS VIC MYRIN
RESTING IN THE ARMS OF THE SAINTS

I wished the inscription specified that it was the Benevolent Saints. Either way, he shouldn't be in the arms of the Saints at all. He should be right *here*, reading his books and traversing the cliffs and stealing my desserts. But he was somewhere at the bottom of the sea because I didn't save him.

◆ ◆ ◆

"Up for training today?" Tyrak asked lightly, craning his head around the corner of the living room.

I lifted my eyes to him, lids heavy and half-closed, managing a small shake of my head. It had been a month, and I'd only managed to leave the house once. To see Tobyas' empty gravesite.

The guard walked into the room, cutting a commanding figure with his hand on his sword, his boots clunking against the marble floors. Lord Castemont had coaxed Aunt Berna into sitting on the front porch for tea. He'd asked me to join, but I didn't. I couldn't. Not when it was my fault my brother was dead.

"Come on. Give me an excuse to get away from the lovebirds," he jeered, trying to inject humor into his voice.

"I don't want to train."

He crouched down, meeting me at eye level. "How about we work on balance? Hmm?"

His voice was kind, and I realized then that I liked him a lot better than I liked his lord. He just seemed more...genuine. Lord

Castemont was nice, and I had no reason not to like him. And I suppose I did like him now. I just liked Tyrak more.

But I didn't want to work on balance. I didn't want to see a wooden sword.

I took a deep breath and shook my head. "No, thank you."

"How about this," he offered, standing up and pulling his sword from its sheath at his hip, the sound of ringing steel bouncing off Aunt Berna's pristine walls and floors. "If you come outside and try to balance, you can do it using my sword."

My brows lifted. A real sword? An actual sword used by an actual Royal Guard?

He gauged my expression, a small smile on his face. "You're going to be in the Royal Guard in four years anyway, right? Might as well get used to using a real sword."

Bet you won't make the Guard in four years. The words were so clear in my head that I had to remind myself Tobyas wasn't sitting right next to me. I took a deep breath, trying to let the hurt float away like wisps of smoke in the air.

"Okay."

◆ ◆ ◆

The sun felt foreign to my eyes after spending the past weeks inside.

"Ready?" I nodded, pushing my unruly hair back from my face. "First we balance, then we cut that hair," he said with a sly smile, and handed me his sword.

It was much heavier than I thought it'd be. I didn't know how I could swing it without falling over, even with my height. I guess Tyrak was right, balance was important. The silver hilt was adorned with filigree, and three small rubies were set just below the guard. I turned it in my grip, noticing some of the filigree had been worn away by Tyrak's hand. I tested its weight again, adjusting my stance to account for it.

And damn if it didn't feel amazing in my grip.

Tyrak worked to suppress another smile. At what, I didn't know, but I pushed everything from my mind to focus on the steel in my hand. "Begin."

I set up the pommel, standing the gleaming blade straight up, the edge staring at me tauntingly as it caught the sun. I breathed out, letting my palm mold to the rounded end, letting it center me, letting it...

The blade stood straight. Not a tremble, not a wobble. I didn't dare breathe as my eyes traveled up the steel that pointed to the sky, the sound of my heart like a metronome to keep me steady. I felt Tyrak's stare on me, felt the disbelief rippling off him. I let it bolster me further and clenched my jaw as I fought the smile that threatened to break my composure.

I was doing it. I was doing it. *I was doing it.*

Footsteps on gravel broke my concentration as Tyrak stepped forward and grabbed the hilt. I blinked at him, at the face that was plastered with awe.

"I haven't seen a single person master this challenge quicker than three weeks," he breathed. "And that's with a wooden sword. You just..." His eyes widened as he continued to survey me. "You just balanced a broadsword. You've had what, two training sessions before this? Before..." His voice trailed off as he broke my gaze. I swallowed back the emptiness.

"Thank you," I muttered, kicking the gravel.

"Mark my words. You'll be a Royal Guard at eighteen."

Bet you won't make the Guard at eighteen.

Tobyas' words shot through me, ricocheting off my bones and pulsing beneath my skin. They resonated with Tyrak's words, melding and meshing together until clarity blew the fog of grief from my mind.

I knew what I had to do. I knew what my little brother would have wanted me to do.

I was going to prove Tobyas wrong.

194

Chapter 21

"What are you reading?" Aunt Berna asked quietly as she placed a mug of tea in front of me before returning to her task of salting strips of beef.

"A book about the creatures Katia controls. Did you know that the lore of the Saints says that her largest driva, Adorex, was more than three times the size of a dragon? And had three times as many teeth and talons the size of a broadsword?"

"I didn't know that." She let out a small laugh. "But it sounds like I'd much rather meet a dragon than a driva."

"Well considering dragons have been extinct for thousands of years and drivas don't exist, I don't think you'll have to make the choice." This was the longest conversation we'd had since Tobyas. I'd asked Aunt Berna to bring me books from his room each day. I couldn't go in there yet, but reading made me feel like he was here. I could hear him reading every word with me.

"I think drivas do exist," Berna said absentmindedly. "In the Saints' realm."

I scoffed. "They've found the bones of dragons, but never the bones of drivas." There was no way they were real. Besides, I wasn't even sure the Benevolent Saints were real anymore.

We sat in an uncomfortable silence for a moment as she continued working. I could feel her dredging up the nerve to speak, as if she had to prepare for what she was about to say. "Seems you've taken a liking to Tyrak."

I didn't look up from the book. "I suppose so," I answered, turning a page.

"He says your training is going well."

"It is."

Her voice was still quiet when she answered, but it was laced with something like pride. "My boy is going to be a Royal Guard."

My eyes shut at her words. I was steadfast in my ambition; I knew what I wanted and how to get it, but it was still painful to think of the reason I was pushing so hard.

"Maybe," I muttered in response. I kicked my feet out under the table, all my muscles aching from the few weeks of hard training Tyrak had put me through. He had me lifting stones and pulling wooden carts, doing sprints and learning basic swordsmanship. He was teaching me how to read people — how to sense what they were thinking and feeling from their face and body language, and how to anticipate their next move. It was grueling, but the sweat and grit kept me distracted from what hurt the most.

Some days, when the training was over and the house was painfully quiet, I'd run. Through the city, past the waterfront, up the hills and to the cliffs, I'd push my legs past their limits, gasping in the salty air as I sprinted. I'd cover every inch of the cliffs I could get to, working on quickening my footwork on the thinner parts of the ledges, just like Tobyas had told me to do. I'd stop in the cave only to add push-ups or squats, pretending my little brother sat on the rock as the crystallized lights danced over me. "Come on," he would have said. "That's really *all* you can do?"

I let his ghost taunt me and push me. With every step I took on the cliffs, I let my eyes wander, just a little bit, just in case he was out there somewhere.

Sometimes, in the back of my mind, I wished that the ledge would give way. I wished that my foot would land wrong, or I'd misjudge a step. An accident. I wished for an accident.

Cracking my knuckles against the table, I blinked hard to push the thoughts away and resumed reading.

"And what do you think of Lord Castemont?" Aunt Berna asked abruptly, her tone nonchalant, eyes still intent on the salted meat.

I'd known this question was coming, had seen the way she looked at him. It was like he was the sun in her sky, like he was the moon and the stars too. And he looked at her like she held up the sky completely.

I heaved in a great sigh, preparing for the conversation I didn't want to have. "Why do you ask?" I took a sip of the tea.

"No reason." A lie. A very obvious lie. "It's just that we've been spending a lot of time together, and he said he'd like to officially enter a courtship, but–"

"*What?*" I spat, choking on the tea as I sat up straight. I hadn't been expecting *this*. A courtship was only entered with one goal in mind: marriage.

"What?" she repeated back to me.

"He wants to *marry* you?"

She wiped her hands on a rag and placed her fists on her hips. "Is it so hard to believe a handsome lord wants to marry me?"

"No, Aunt Berna, it's just..." I placed my elbows on the table, scrubbing my face with my palms. "He's a *lord*. And I understand that you're well-regarded in Prisma and the rest of Eserene, but we're not royal. How could he court you?"

She turned away, face hidden as she began packing the strips of meat in rolled paper. "That's the thing. He *can't* court me. A marriage between a royal and a commoner can't just...*happen*. It has to be approved. He said it could take years."

"What–" I cut myself off, sure that if I continued I was going to say something I'd regret. I stared at the back of her head as she worked, measuring my next words. The house was silent for a long moment. "I... I don't really know if I like him."

She spun to me. "Why not?"

"I mean, I guess I like him. I just... He's nice, Aunt Berna. He is. He just gives me a bad feeling," I explained, trying to keep my tone mild.

"Well that *bad feeling* is the reason you could be a Royal Guard at eighteen," she snapped defensively, a finger pointing sharply at me.

"I know that, and I appreciate it," I answered. "I can't help it, though."

"Are you jealous?"

I gawked at her. "Jealous?"

"You and Tobyas had me to yourselves since the day you arrived in Eserene. Does it upset you that I'm spending time with someone else?"

"Aunt Berna, no." I rubbed my chin with my palm, uncomfortable at the accusation in her stare. "I'm...*happy* that you're happy. I just don't ever want him to hurt you. But I'm always kind to him, right? Always."

She let out a breath, her shoulders sagging, face softening slightly. "You *are* always kind to him. That's one of my favorite things about you. You're kind even to the people who you feel don't deserve it."

Of course I was. It was a promise I told my mother I'd keep. She told me the world wouldn't always be kind to me, but I could be kind to the world. The world was *not* being very kind to me right now, and some days it was hard to be kind to the world.

"Do you feel he deserves kindness?" My words were small as I surveyed her face.

She gave a soft smile. "I do. He's a good man, Cal. I just wish he could simply court me instead of stringing me along," she said sadly, slowly returning to packing the salted meat into paper. She

198

paused as I watched her cock her head in thought. "Promise me something." She turned to me again, a fragility to her expression I'd never seen before.

"Okay."

"Promise me, that when the time comes, you won't string someone along. You'll be intentional in your actions when pursuing someone, rules and laws be damned. Can you promise me that?"

"What do you mean?"

"I mean that when you meet someone one day and find yourself with feelings for them, you won't make them wait around for you."

I gulped, surveying the look on her face. It seemed an easy enough promise to make. Members of the Royal Guard couldn't marry, anyway. I'd never have the opportunity to *string someone along* as she'd said.

"Of course. I promise."

She smiled, walking from the counter to plant a kiss on my head. "I love you," she said against my hair before pulling back to look at me. "I'm proud of you. I'm proud of the man you're becoming. I'm proud of the big brother you were and always will be."

I closed my eyes. I hoped I could prove her right one day, that I could be a good man. As she cleaned up the countertop and I blankly stared at a page about how kelpies rose from the sea, I thought of all the ways I'd prove Tobyas wrong — and prove Aunt Berna right.

Chapter 22

Eleven Years Ago

I looked over my shoulder, sure that someone was going to catch me and drag me to Aunt Berna for a tongue lashing. But no one stared at another person in a brown cloak walking through the district of Sidus on an early winter morning.

She always told me to stay away, that where I was headed was dangerous, that people were attacked in the streets for the cloak off their back or the coin in their pockets. But two and a half years of training with Tyrak had given me the skills I needed to survive a quick walk through the poorest district in Eserene. I was strong, tall, and easily able to defend myself should I need to. Tyrak had begun to train me to use a dagger, so I had some idea how to use the blade tucked into my boot.

The streets began to grow noticeably more destitute as I walked, the rough cobblestones looser and fewer as packed dirt streets took over. A fine dust hung in the air despite the dirty snow that lined the streets, and even as I held my sleeve to my nose, I felt it cling to the insides of my nostrils and stick to my throat. Houses got smaller and more dilapidated. People looked more haggard. Even the accent of the people changed. Prisma's words were soft and rounded. The people here spoke in jagged, rough accents, their voices louder and hoarse with dust.

Inkwell.

I didn't know what I was doing here. Didn't really have a plan. Maybe I wanted to see if it was like where we lived in Taitha, if the people were just as poor.

They weren't. They were much, much poorer.

Huddled figures littered the streets, gangly people doing their best to shelter from the early winter cold under threadbare cloaks. There was so much *noise*. People yelled. Coughed. Begged. Rickety carts bumped through the streets. Rats skittered underfoot. Loose shutters blew in the frigid wind. Even in the cold air, the stench was overwhelming, and I shivered at the thought of what it would smell like when the snows melted and the sun was beating down.

Lord Castemont had told me a little about Inkwell. He led a small group of Low Royals to bring handouts of bread and meat for the neediest people in the district every so often. I'd always admired that. It wasn't a task given to him by King Umfray. It was something he did because he wanted to help those who needed it most.

He'd been good to us, always there to lend a hand, always there to comfort Aunt Berna on the days she missed Tobyas the most. Those days were growing fewer and further between each day, but the Lord didn't leave. He'd keep her company while I trained with Tyrak, which, these days, was almost constant. So I supposed I was coming around to the Lord. I guess.

He still hadn't gained the approval to court my Aunt Berna, even after two years of petitioning the High Royal Court. It's not like it made a difference, though — the two of them acted as nauseatingly in love as if they were in an official courtship. It was just a part of life by now, a part I had unfortunately grown used to.

What I hadn't gotten used to was the fact that no one so much as looked my way as I entered Inkwell. Gaunt faces trudged by as I turned onto Gormill Road, the main road in the district. The anonymity was actually kind of nice. I was so used to being gawked at by strangers that saw me. First for my height. Then for the unusual color of my eyes when they got a closer look. But in Inkwell, no one batted an eye at the cloaked giant walking down Gormill Road. Everybody was focused on something more important. Survival.

Between the shops and homes that made up one side of the road and the city wall that made up the other, the air felt lighter. Far less imposing than it had on the side streets. Gray daylight shone on the people walking through. Old women clutched wicker baskets. Men hauled crab traps and fishing poles on tired backs. Small children tugged on their mothers' cloaks.

No one tried to rob me. No one threatened to hurt me. No one did any of the things Aunt Berna said they would do if I ever set foot in Inkwell.

They were all just people. People trying to make it through. Put food on the table. Keep their families warm and sheltered. Aunt Berna had been wrong. The people of Inkwell weren't dangerous. They were *human*.

King Umfray had to do something about this. How could he sleep soundly, high in his keep, knowing he had subjects that were forced to live like this? That he had subjects forced to die like this? I was going to raise the issue to Lord Castemont.

A wail split the air. "Please!" I whipped my head around, but I seemed to be the only person disturbed by the cry. I turned to where it was coming from, tried to listen for the voice again. "Please!" I heard. It was a woman's voice, frantic and pained. "Please!" Still, no one on the street so much as flinched.

I turned off of Gormill Road, following the sound of the woman's cries, acutely aware of the dagger stashed in my boot. More cries came from more voices, a mix of pain and pleading

202

and...pleasure? But above all other cries, I could hear her. "Please! *Please!*"

Bumps raised on my skin as I beheld a derelict structure standing over the seedy side street. A crowd of visibly dirty men milled around outside. *The Painted Empress.*

Oh, a brothel.

I'd heard of the Painted Empress. It was always spoken about in hushed tones, as if the very name of the establishment was poison on the tongue. Now that I was staring at the building, I think I understood why.

I crouched to the ground, leaning against a building on the other side of the street, trying to match my position to the ten other people around me hunkering down from the punishing cold. My eyes were fixed on the men outside the brothel, my ears listening for the woman's cries. "*Please!*"

Not one of them flinched at the sound of her voice. A few of them passed around a bottle, taking turns swigging from it and belching loudly. Every few seconds they'd erupt in laughter. The sound grated on my nerves like metal on stone. It was the kind of laugh that only followed a crude joke. A joke that would bring a blush to the face of anyone with a lick of conscience.

A constant stream of men flowed in and out the door, and it wasn't just Inkwellians. There were people dressed in everything from dirty, patched clothing to Prismanian finery. I narrowed my eyes, looking to see if I recognized any of the Prismanian men, all the while listening for the woman's cries. They'd seemed to stop. Nausea hit my gut, sour and heavy as I watched. I didn't know what I was looking for. Didn't know what I was hoping to—

Lord Castemont suddenly emerged from the front door, hands straightening the lapels of his coat, Tyrak close behind him.

Mother*fucker.*

I was frozen as I watched him raise a hand to the men outside the brothel, all of them giving a nod or wave in farewell. The

Lord and his guard descended the steps, turning up the street, heading out of Inkwell.

The dagger was already in my hand and I was moving before I knew it, the heat in my chest so intense that I wondered whether it was possible for a human to catch fire. With each step that brought me closer to him, the flames grew. The rage was all-consuming and unfamiliar.

In one fluid motion I had him pinned to a rotting wooden building, his coat fisted in my grasp, dagger aimed at his chest. Tyrak's own blade was drawn in a split second, the soldier in him emerging as his sword quickly found itself resting against my throat.

"What the *fuck* do you think you're doing, Castemont?" I screamed in his face.

He raised his hands in front of him in defense. "Cal, what are you doing here?" he asked, bewildered. I saw red as I stared into his eyes, my teeth gritted. "I should ask you the same damned question."

"Release him, Cal," Tyrak urged quietly, and I knew that for my sake, he was tamping down the protective instincts he had for his Lord. He was ignoring the oath he'd taken to protect him. If I were someone else, *anyone* else, my throat would be slit. I would have been a feast for the rats the moment I laid a hand on him.

"I'm not a patron of the Painted Empress," Castemont blurted, and though the fear in his voice seemed genuine, I didn't believe him.

"Bullshit," I seethed, nostrils flaring, and my grip grew tighter on his coat, the force with which I pinned him increasing. I was stronger than him — much, much stronger than him, and I watched his face blanche as that very fact dawned on him. I could kill him where he stood, and he knew it.

"Release. Him. Cal," Tyrak repeated, his voice more authoritative, his blade shifting against my neck to remind me it was there. "Let him explain."

"It's quite alright, Tyrak," Castemont sputtered. "It would make sense that the boy would be angry, given what it looks like."

"It *looks* like you're being unfaithful to my aunt." My words were clipped, my vision spotty with rage.

"It's a part of my outreach," he stammered. "The other lords are too proud to enter the brothel to help the women inside. It's a task I undertake on my own."

My eyes moved to Tyrak, his face hard set and jaw locked as his gaze met mine. His expression didn't change as I stared at him, his dark eyes unreadable as they always were when he took on the role of guard.

"Tell him, Tyrak," Castemont urged.

Tyrak continued to stare at me, his chin dipping in an almost imperceptible nod. "The other lords will not accompany him."

I turned back to Castemont, his panicked eyes meeting mine. I inhaled, my jaw squeezed so tightly shut that I thought my molars would crack. I released my grip on him, lowering the dagger to my side and taking a step back. Tyrak's sword found its sheath and he, too, stepped back. The Lord visibly relaxed, but I hadn't. Not internally.

Humor entered Lord Castemont's eyes and his face broke into a smile as he slapped a hand against my arm. "A mix-up!" he joked.

I wasn't laughing.

"Does my Aunt Berna know you're here?" I asked, my chest still heaving, the rage taking its time leaving my body.

"She does," he answered with a nod. "She's aware that I visit the Painted Empress on occasion with food and coin for the women."

"And you're not a patron," I repeated back to him.

He let out a boisterous laugh. "Saints, no."

I nodded, quickly leaning down to replace my dagger, but my eyes caught on something like tiny rubies on leather. "Is that blood on your boots?"

Castemont looked down, flexing his foot, the fine leather creaking in the cold air. "There are some rather, I'll say, *violent* patrons that we run into from time to time."

I stared at him, my brows furrowed. "I heard a woman from outside," I murmured, trying not to wince. Her voice was clear in my mind. "She was pleading."

Tyrak's expression didn't change, but his eyes darted in the direction of the brothel. Lord Castemont's lips thinned, his eyes closing momentarily. "We have little say in the matter of what is...*allowed* at the Painted Empress, and some patrons..." His brown eyes found mine, the sorrow that lined them almost palpable. "They have desires that can only be acted upon within the confines of an establishment such as this."

I knew enough about sex to know that it wasn't always what Aunt Berna had told me — between two people that were in love, and preferably married. I knew it was often outside those bounds. But what I'd heard coming from inside, the anguish in that woman's voice...

"Did you help her?"

Lord Castemont inhaled thoughtfully, as if measuring his words to shield me from the horrors behind that shoddy door. "She was given coin, yes."

Tyrak's expression still hadn't changed. It did little to calm the storm that churned within me, the all-too familiar discomfort toward Castemont rearing its ugly head.

The Lord shot a hand out, clapping a palm against my bicep, a cheery smile on his face. "Why don't you join us for a drink?"

"I'm sixteen, my Lord," I answered, returning to the normal formality of our relationship. I'd come so close, *so close* to driving my dagger through his chest. A part of me still wanted to.

"And I'm a very well-connected man," he answered, his arm wrapping around my shoulders as he led me up the street, Tyrak close behind. "You're going to try the best mead in Eserene."

◆ ◆ ◆

'Tis said a lass, a bonny lass, with hair of golden yellow
With perky tits, an ample ass, ne'er said yes to a fellow
To find the truth, come early June, I walked down to the tavern
I drank my fill and paid my tab and asked if I could have 'er

The bonny lass was no' impressed wi' the ring upon my finger
'O she told me to leave her be, and that I needn't linger
So one spring eve, I took my leave, left my wife for the tavern
Instead I hoped the bonny lass would fin'ly let me have 'er

I look around and up and down, I search the drunken faces
Looking for my bonny lass, fin'ly in her good graces
The barkeep said she'd shock me dead 'cause much to my alarm
Who'd 'a thought that I'd've seen my wife upon her arm

The pub erupted in laughter and applause, mugs clanking together as their contents sloshed over the sides. Even Tyrak broke the façade of a Royal Guard to smile when the song ended.

The three of us sat at a table with uneven legs in the middle of a dusty Sidus pub, Lord Castemont steadily sipping mead as Tyrak eyed the tavern's patrons. Even though it was early in the day, the place was filled to the brim with drunkards, mostly men with shaggy facial hair and dirt under their fingernails.

I still felt a bit uncomfortable. Out of place. Lord Castemont set a mug of mead in front of me a half hour ago. I'd taken one obligatory sip. The liquid was bitter. Unpleasant. I couldn't bring myself to drink more no matter how much he eyed me. All I could hear above the din of chanted songs and raucous laughter was the woman in the brothel.

Please!

Another song started up, the mood in the pub shifting from celebratory and carefree to somber and deliberate.

"Do you know the story of the Daughter of Katia?" Lord Castemont asked suddenly, his eyes pensive as he watched the tavern's patrons.

"I do," I answered flatly, my eyes following his to the crowd. The entirety of the pub seemed to sway like ocean waves on a calm day.

Tyrak shifted uncomfortably in his seat, and I tried to keep my eyes from darting to him. He saw something. Sensed something.

208

Lord Castemont took a sip of mead and leaned in. "She's coming," he whispered, the words barely audible above the drunken chanting. "*Soon.*"

I furrowed my brows at him. "How do you know that?"

One side of his mouth turned up in a sly smile. "Just a feeling," he answered, his words slow and almost slurred. He wasn't drunk, was he? I'd seen him down a few mugs of ale, but he'd seemed just fine before now.

"Just a feeling?" I repeated back to him. He gave a knowing smile in return. "The prophecy is that she'll come to be the Savior of the Realm, yes?" I asked, and Castemont nodded, excitement in his eyes. "Do you believe the realm needs saving now?"

"I believe the realm may need the Daughter of Katia soon," the Lord answered, something in his eyes that I didn't recognize. "Do you know the only one who can positively identify the Daughter of Katia?"

I shook my head. "I don't."

"Noros, Saint of Pain. Others can take a guess at her identity, but he's the only one who will know for sure."

My eyes narrowed on him as he swayed with the rest of the tavern. "So if you think the Daughter of Katia is coming soon, then you think Noros is, too?"

He leaned in, a knowing smile on his face. "I think he's already here."

I opened my mouth to question him, but he slammed his mead down and joined in singing with the rest of the tavern.

The day that she comes
Out 'a walled city's slum
We'll all witness somethin' quite holy
So pray that she's good
When she's born from the blood
And delivers the world from its folly

Oh, oh, the ebb and the flow
The fire and the wind and the water
The world it may turn and the world it may burn,
At the hand of Katia's daughter

"Why is your mug still full?" he demanded, his voice taking on the bellowing authority of a lord once again.

The foamy amber liquid clung to the sides of the mug. "I don't really like the taste, my Lord."

"The taste isn't the reason you drink it," he chuckled. "Now, drink!" he commanded.

I pursed my lips. "I'd rather talk to you about the people in Inkwell, if we can do more to–"

"Drink!" he yelled again, a sly smile on his face. "Your Lord commands it."

My eyes turned to Tyrak, hoping he'd tell Castemont that I had to train later today, so I shouldn't be drinking. But he simply nodded once.

Tipping the mug to my mouth, I did my best to take a few sips. I couldn't help but gag at the taste.

Lord Castemont let out a hearty laugh as he watched me. "Keep going, Cal." He turned to the barkeep, a hand waving her down. "Mindra! Two more, please!"

"My Lord, I–"

"*Drink.*"

I did as I was commanded.

Oh, oh, the ebb and the flow
The fire and the wind and the water
The world it may turn and the world it may burn,
At the hand of Katia's daughter

◆ ◆ ◆

210

"I'm going to do you a favor." I think it was Lord Castemont talking to me. It had to be. It wasn't Tyrak. Who else would it be? "I'll distract your Aunt Berna. You slip past her, go to your room, and sleep it off. I won't tell her you're drunk."

I started laughing. My whole body shook. My insides were warm. I guess my insides were always warm, but I just felt it now. I threw my arm around Lord Castemont. "I like mead," I whispered to him. "I'm whispering so no one knows I'm drunk."

"I think they already know, son," he answered, returning my laugh.

"How in the world would anyone know I'm drunk?"

"You're walking sideways, Cal."

Oh shit. I *was* walking sideways, which made me laugh even more. He was funny. This was funny. I was funny.

We were walking by buildings, somewhere... Prisma? It was Prisma. "Hello, Prisma!" I bellowed. "I like mead!"

"Cal, you need to be quiet," the Lord said in a hushed tone, though I think he was holding back a laugh. "People are staring."

My body felt so loose and so warm, my limbs felt like they were made of butter. Biscuits and butter — that's what I wanted. Aunt Berna's biscuits that she only made on holidays, and fresh butter.

"Hey, when we get home, can you ask Aunt Berna to make me some–"

One moment I was looking down at Castemont, the next Castemont was looking down at me. It seemed, actually, that I was...on the ground.

"Shit," Tyrak murmured. "Stay still, Cal."

I stared at the sky and then there were people there. A dozen people were staring down at me, and they all had their hands over their mouths.

"Find a healer," I heard Tyrak say to someone. A healer? "Now!"

"Look at me, Cal," Castemont said suddenly, his face looking worried. "Keep your eyes on me. Don't look down."

"Why–"

I looked down. I looked down, and I shouldn't have. The mead turned to acid in my gut, the warmth in my body fading quickly as I saw the bone protruding from my shin. My head was propped up on the curb, and it began to throb just as my senses caught up with the pain. Maybe Castemont was right. Maybe the Saint of Pain was here.

"My training." It was all I could think about. I'd fucked up, and I'd fucked up *bad*.

"It needs to be set immediately," Castemont said, his face hovering above the break.

A small old woman appeared. The healer began sorting through a bag as my vision started to get hazy. My teeth gnashed together as people shuffled around me. Words of dismay and pity filtered through the fog.

"I'm going to give you something for the pain before I set the break," the healer said, her voice soft.

"He can't have arri root," Lord Castemont murmured to the healer. "He's been drinking."

The healer's lips thinned. "We can wait until he sobers up, but the longer he goes without setting the bone, the higher his risk for infection."

I felt pretty damned sober right now, but I knew what she was saying. I pulled every bit of intestinal fortitude from my core that I could muster. "Do it," I spat. "Just do it and be done with it."

I didn't watch as her hands gingerly reached for my leg. "On the count of three. Ready?"

No.

"One, two, three."

Chapter 23

"Drunk?!" Aunt Berna's voice was almost shrill. "What the hell were you thinking, Cal?"

My broken leg was propped up on a kitchen chair that Lord Castemont had dragged into the living room. I was silent. I had nothing to say. I hadn't wanted to drink. I only did it because I'd been ordered to. Now my head pounded along with my tightly wrapped leg.

"I don't know," I murmured, more to myself than to her. I didn't. I could've ignored him.

Aunt Berna paced back and forth across the room, her face beet red with anger. Lord Castemont leaned forward in his chair. "It's a normal part of growing up, Berna."

"Don't you even think of speaking," she snapped at him. "You let him get drunk. And in a *Sidus* pub? Might as well have taken him to Inkwell."

Our eyes met momentarily. *Don't say anything.* He looked back to Aunt Berna with an apologetic expression. "If I may," he tested. Her brows raised, but she let him continue. "Once he started, I couldn't stop him. I intended to bring him home and let him sleep it off, but then he fell."

I still didn't know how I fell. I couldn't remember. I was walking with Lord Castemont and Tyrak and suddenly I was on the ground with a bone sticking out of my shin. The thought made me queasy, and my entire leg throbbed.

"You think this is how a Royal Guard acts?" Aunt Berna yelled. "Do you see Tyrak getting drunk and breaking his bones in the streets?" Her hand flew out, pointing at Tyrak. "Is this how you act, Tyrak?"

He stood silently at the back of the room, dark eyes shadowed and glued to me. Out of the corner of my vision, I saw Lord Castemont turn to him. Tyrak's eyes met his for only a moment before they were back on me. "No. It's not."

The disappointment in his voice... It gutted me. I blinked hard, wanting to hide my face. My shame. My stupid fucking broken leg.

"I ought to ban you from training," Aunt Berna seethed. I straightened, fear rushing through me. "In fact, I think I will."

"No," I breathed, my eyes wide. I tried to sit up straighter, but my leg shot pain through my body in protest. "Please."

"Berna, darling," Lord Castemont crooned. Something about the words derailed her anger, and the façade slipped just enough that her face softened. "It was a mistake. I think the pain of his broken leg is punishment enough."

Her eyes landed back on me. I knew her mind was running in circles, thinking about how to handle the fact that her boy had fucked up so badly. "Will he even be able to train again?"

My jaw clenched. Dread pooled in every part of me at the prospect as I watched Tyrak think. "It's a bad break. He could end up with a limp. It will be difficult." We hung on his next words. I think all of us were terrified of what he'd say. "But I think it can be done."

"That's *if* I allow it," Aunt Berna cut in. Her eyes flicked to Lord Castemont. "Don't you have somewhere to be?"

"Goodness," he huffed, quickly rising. "My next appointment to petition the High Royal Court for our courtship." He smoothed his surcoat, nodding to Tyrak and leaning in to kiss Aunt Berna on the cheek. "I believe we're getting close to earning their approval."

I always thought it was odd that Lord Castemont attended these meetings alone. Shouldn't the members of the High Royal Court want to meet the woman he's petitioning to marry?

"You'll be lucky if I go through with it, considering this happened under your watch."

"I'll be lucky either way, having known you," he crooned, flashing her a smile. I knew she was trying to stay mad, but she had to hide the blush that crept into her cheeks. "Farewell."

An awkward silence blanketed the room as the door closed behind them. I stared down at my leg and nausea bubbled up once again.

Aunt Berna sighed and lowered herself into a chair. She pinched the bridge of her nose before her blue eyes met mine. "I just don't know what got into you, Cal."

My teeth clenched around the truth. I fought with myself whether I should keep it in or tell her. Then I remembered Mama's words, to be brave, kind, and honest. I guess it was time for honesty. "He ordered me to drink."

She lifted her face. "Who did?"

"Lord Castemont."

She was silent for a moment. Her eyes narrowed into slits as she pursed her lips. "You expect me to believe that?"

I opened my mouth but no words came out at first. "That's the truth, Aunt Berna. He ordered me to drink."

"And Tyrak, your *trainer*, just stood by and let it happen?" I'd never seen her so angry. Not even when Tobyas tracked mud all over her hand-woven rug from Kruria. And she'd been *angry*.

"Yes."

She sat back and crossed her arms, tapping her toe on the ground. "And how did you end up in a Sidus pub with Lord Castemont and Tyrak?"

Shit. "I was on a run," I blurted without thinking. "For training."

"A run through Sidus."

"Yes, through Sidus. And I ran into Lord Castemont and Tyrak leaving Inkwell. They were going to the pub and…I asked if I could join." The lie burned my tongue as I spoke it. I wasn't being honest anymore.

Her toe suddenly stopped tapping. "They were leaving Inkwell?"

"Yes."

Aunt Berna's expression went blank at my answer. But she suddenly blinked hard, snapping out of whatever thought had been behind her neutral face. A heavy sigh escaped her nostrils and she shook her head. "Lord Castemont did not force you to drink. You're lying because you don't like him."

Shock bolted through me. "That's not true, Aunt Berna, I do like–"

"I'm disappointed, Cal."

My words tangled in my mouth at the look on her face. I couldn't fight her on this. She was going to believe him over me. That fact made my chest feel hollow, because even if I wasn't telling the whole truth, he *had* ordered me to drink. I looked at my hands folded in my lap. "I'm sorry."

She took a deep inhale and it felt like her stare would burn a hole in my skin. The pain in my leg was excruciating, and I felt like maybe I deserved it for disappointing her. The minutes felt like hours as I sat in my shame. But her face softened suddenly and she reached for my hand. "I know things have been difficult since Tobyas died," she said. The words hurt just as much as the day he'd fallen. "I'm proud of the work you've put in. Are you going to drink again?"

"No, never."

216

"You have a bad break, Cal. Just like Tyrak said, you could walk with a limp forever and be ineligible for the Guard." My chest heated with fear. She stared down at my leg. I tried to keep my eyes from looking back down again but I couldn't. Even if I hadn't looked at it, I knew just how bad it was. "But if anyone can come back from something like this, it's you."

I sat forward slightly, a tiny sliver of hope flickering like a candle in a dark room. "So I can train again?"

"Once you're healed, you can train again. As long as you promise me never to drink again."

My face split into the biggest smile it possibly could. "Thank you, Aunt Berna. I promise." I tried to lean forward to hug her, but the pain from my leg stopped me in my tracks.

She closed the distance so I didn't have to, folding me in her arms before pulling away with a stern look on her face once again. "But one more slip up like this, and you're done," she warned.

I nodded. "I won't slip up. I promise. I'm going to make the Guard at eighteen, just like I planned."

She stood and bit the inside of her cheek as she stared down at me. "We'll see."

Chapter 24

Nine Years Ago

"We stand here today as you swear in as members of the Royal Guard, Protectors of the Realm, and Guardians of the Royalty of Widoras."

My heart pounded like a war drum in my ears. It reverberated through my chest as I waited on bended knee on the dais of the Eserenian throne room. I felt the eyes of Aunt Berna, Tyrak, and Lord Castemont on me as King Umfray's croaking voice echoed off the marble floors and carved columns.

"Your training and skill have proven you fit to uphold the sanctity of the Eserenian Royal Court," he continued. The soldier next to me shifted uncomfortably. I knew some of the others weren't thrilled that an eighteen year old was joining the Guard. These men had served in the Eserenian army for years. Only eight other soldiers were being inducted today, all eight of which were thoroughly gray around the ears.

All eight of which I assumed didn't like me.

I let their dismay roll off my back and stared at the floor. It was a fight to keep my eyes from moving to the King. I'd never been this close to him. I wanted to see if he truly was as old as he sounded.

"Now you will take the lifelong vow of the Royal Guard. Please rise."

Not only was I the youngest of the men, but I was also the tallest and arguably the most agile. The others received years of training, but no amount of training could return a man to the former spryness of young adulthood.

"Will the sponsors please join their inductees?"

Lord Castemont rose from his place in the audience, straightening his finely made surcoat and striding easily to the dais with the other sponsors. His face glowed with pride, and I fought back the smile that threatened my neutral expression. I was so grateful for the man — for his kindness and belief in me. I didn't know why I ever doubted him.

Sometimes people are kind simply because they are kind people.

I caught Aunt Berna's stare behind him, her cheeks rosy and eyes watery and crinkled with the largest grin I'd ever seen. Lord Castemont still hadn't had the courtship approved by the Royal Court, but they still spent all their time together. I watched her gaze travel from me to him and back again. Tyrak sat next to her, his familiar stoic grace a steady presence in the buzzing room. He was one hell of a trainer. I hated him a lot of days. But still I thanked the Saints I had him.

"Sponsors, please collect your swords and stand before your inductees," King Umfray declared. The sponsors crowded around a rack and retrieved the sword that would be granted to their inductee.

Lord Castemont settled in front of me and I blinked at the blade that rested in his palms. Three rubies caught the light of the chandelier, the same three rubies I'd marveled at for years now. Tyrak's broadsword rested in Lord Castemont's palms, that prideful joy still radiating from him. My eyes flicked to where Tyrak sat in the crowd. There was a slight smile on his face as he nodded at me. He was giving me his sword. I swallowed hard, the honor causing a lump to form in my throat. All I could manage to give him was a shallow nod in thanks.

Lord Castemont placed a hand on my shoulder. "You did it," he whispered to me. "Not that I ever doubted you." I fought to keep my face neutral, but I wanted so badly to smile.

King Umfray moved to stand in front of the inductee next to me, instructing him to take his vows.

"Thank you," I whispered to Lord Castemont.

"I know talent when I see it," he answered with a nod. "Are you ready?"

I nodded back as King Umfray prattled off the vows and the soldier kneeling before him agreed. My eyes moved from Castemont to Tyrak to my aunt, and I let myself bask in the pride that marked each of their faces as the King finished up and moved to settle before me.

My breath caught as I beheld him. *His eyes...* They were molten sapphire. Not quite as vibrant as the blue of my own, but noticeably similar. He *was* old, but the shape of his face... Under the sagging of age, I could tell it looked familiar. Was it the same as mine?

Was... Was King Umfray my father?

His gaze roved over my face, a flash of recognition passing his features when he noticed my eyes. His mouth bobbed open as he stared.

I stayed silent. My brows knit together as my mind careened through space, trying to add up everything I knew. It didn't make sense.

"Belin Cal Myrin?" he finally asked me, voice hoarse and eyes still wide.

"Yes, your Majesty," I answered with a whisper.

"My, my," Lord Castemont interjected, voice heavy with disbelief. King Umfray's stare stayed locked on my own. "You two... You look just alike. Why haven't I noticed it before?"

I could feel the eyes of every person in the throne room on us, murmurs rippling through the room, our own words so quiet there was no way anyone could hear them. "You're the eighteen year old, yes?" he asked.

"Yes, your Majesty."

"And you were born in Taitha?" he questioned, brows furrowing.

"Yes, your Majesty."

He surveyed me further, his gaze burning even more brightly against my skin. "Is your father..." he murmured.

"He's a bastard," Lord Castemont cut in. "Never knew his father."

The King's brows furrowed as he thought. "You don't think..." he murmured as he turned to Lord Castemont. "He couldn't be–"

"No, my King," Lord Castemont answered before the King could finish. "It would be impossible."

I clenched my jaw, afraid that I was staring at the man who gave me life. "Forgive me, your Majesty, but I must ask–"

"I'm not your father, boy," he said abruptly, though not unkindly. "I stayed loyal to my wife, Saints rest her soul."

Lord Castemont shifted. "Saints rest her soul. Though many kings have bastard-born sons, your Majesty."

The King's gaze snapped to the Lord, a sparse white brow rising. "I stayed loyal to my wife," he repeated. There was a bite to his words now. "How dare you suggest otherwise." The pooling gleam in his eye, the hurt on his face... King Umfray was telling the truth. He wasn't my father.

I didn't know how to feel.

"Of course, your Majesty. My sincerest apologies," Lord Castemont answered, lowering his head.

The King nodded, turning his attention back to me. "How peculiar." His stare lingered for a moment longer before his face returned to its neutral expression, that of a king. Resolve showed in every one of his features. "Are you ready to take your vows?"

My brain cleared instantly at his question, at the moment that was the culmination of the last four years. "Yes, your Majesty."

"Please kneel," he commanded, and I lowered myself to the ground, pushing back the apprehension and questions that surged within me.

I was here. I did it. I made it to the Royal Guard at eighteen. I felt the eyes of Aunt Berna and Tyrak on me from the audience, the pride beaming off of them like ripples on the surface of a pond. But I couldn't help but feel the absence of another set of eyes who should've been here, too.

"Will you solemnly swear to dedicate your life to the service of the Royal Court of Widoras, giving your body and soul for its protection and preservation?"

"I will.'"

"Will you place the Royalty of Eserene above the love of another, forgoing marriage and family in favor of a life of service?"

"I will."

"Will you uphold the sanctity of the Court, its traditions and rituals, until you take your last breath?"

"I will."

"And will you die for your King should it be necessary?"

"I will." My heartbeat was thunder in my ears.

"Please raise your head." I stared at the man, his eyes still searching mine as he stepped aside. Lord Castemont now stood before me, Tyrak's sword balanced across his palms before placing it in my own. His eyes — were those tears?

King Umfray cleared his throat. "Welcome to the Royal Guard."

◆ ◆ ◆

I lowered myself to the rain-soaked ground, hanging my arms over my knees. I was more than happy to abandon the raucous roar of the banquet hall in exchange for the solace of lapping waves at the bottom of the cliffs. A low fog hung over the harbor. My hair was just long enough that pieces stuck to my forehead even though the rain had seceded to nothing but mist. The silver piece in my hand had long grown damp as I turned it over and over in my palm, surveying the waves as they swelled and died.

"He's not my father," I said into the ether. I knew it wouldn't respond. But a part of me hoped it would. "I believe him. He's not. But you wouldn't believe how similar we look." Heavy clouds hung in the skies, threatening to unleash a downpour once again.

I pushed myself to stand and took a cautious step forward, toeing the edge of the cliff as I clamped my teeth. My feet sloshed in my boots and anguish rose in my chest. I wouldn't cry. Not again, so I did my best to blink the tears back. "I did it, Tobyas," I whispered, the wind and the waves all that would hear. "I did it. I made the Royal Guard at eighteen." Looking across the water, never straight down, I huffed a laugh as I ran my hand across my jaw, images of our last day threatening to invade my mind. And I let them.

The wind tugged at the hair still plastered to my forehead. I breathed into the vast empty and flicked the silver piece off my thumb, watching as the waves swallowed it. "Told you so."

Chapter 25

Six Years Ago

"I don't want you to panic when you see her," Lord Castemont stated. We'd ridden through the Onyx Pass and were finally coming out of the thick of the forest into the outskirts of Blindbarrow. "Umbri has...taken her blood sacrifices a bit too far."

I was more nervous to see the Bloodsinger in Eserene's neighboring town than I had been to camp in the Onyx Pass. I knew about the monsters that lurked in the forests of the Onyx Pass. I knew where to strike, how to maim, how to kill.

But I knew little about Bloodsingers. They practiced blood magic and were strictly forbidden within the walls of Eserene. Each sacrifice was made at the cost of vanity, so they all seemed to have the same sinister features. And they sacrificed to the Darkness Beyond, some force that was not of this realm. That was all I knew. The only reason I was here was because Lord Castemont told me he had something he wanted me to see. I turned to Tyrak, but his face gave no clues as to what he was thinking.

224

"Do you know what happens when a Bloodsinger pushes past the limits set by their authority, the Sanguilite?" Lord Castemont asked. I pursed my lips in thought but came up with nothing. "After their skin pales and their bodies waste away and they no longer look anything like themselves, the Darkness Beyond goes for their souls."

I narrowed my eyes. "What does that mean?"

"It means the Darkness Beyond takes what makes them human. Compassion, humility, mercy, empathy. It all goes to the wayside if they get too greedy." A chill crept up my spine at his words. It was almost as if he were referring to something demonic, something beyond the evil in this realm. "Most Bloodsingers haven't gone so far. Most sacrifice only their looks and retain their human qualities. They help people make small sacrifices and urge them to exercise self control in their desires. That is the Sanguilite's command." He turned to me with grave eyes, a warning behind the look. "But not every one of them does."

"So Bloodsingers are just regular people who sacrificed to the Darkness Beyond and decided to help other people do the same? Why wouldn't they keep other people from partaking in something so vile altogether?"

He nodded. "Unfortunately, when they look the way they do, that is the only role society deems fit for them. So the cycle continues."

"And when they go too far, they turn into monsters."

"Precisely. Completely merciless."

I stared, keeping the question behind my lips until I couldn't hold it back any longer. "The Bloodsinger we're seeing, Umbri... She's gone too far?"

The Lord squared his jaw. "Yes, Cal. She has." His tone was even, but it didn't stop the eerie feeling from creeping into my gut.

"How come your appearance hasn't changed with your blood sacrifices?"

"Like I said, Umbri doesn't follow the rules. But she is the only Bloodsinger even remotely nearby. So we have no choice."

I kept my mouth shut but I couldn't shut my mind up. There was a choice. There was always a choice.

◆ ◆ ◆

"Welcome," the small, wispy woman said, her voice hollow and haunting.

"Umbri," Lord Castemont greeted. His voice was far too cheerful for the darkness that surrounded us in the tiny shop. Tyrak had been all too happy to wait outside, and I thought I heard him praying to the Benevolent Saints under his breath as we left him on the street. Acrid smoke hung in the air. My nose and throat stung with every breath I took. "A pleasure to see you again."

The Bloodsinger bowed her head slightly, her thin, oily black hair falling against cheekbones that were too pronounced. Her eyes were an unnatural shade of ruby. I tried not to stare, but I couldn't help it. She looked like she'd crawled from the deepest pit of Hell, her fingers so bony that it looked like they'd snap with a gust of wind. "The pleasure is all mine, Lord Castemont."

Though I towered above both the Lord and the Bloodsinger, I felt like the smallest person in the room. I squared my shoulders, pushed my jaw forward, and reminded myself of my position and skill.

"This is Belin Cal Myrin, an esteemed member of the Royal Guard," the Lord declared. I made no effort to extend my hand, instead opting to take on Tyrak's usual greeting of a slight nod.

"So young for the Royal Guard," Umbri remarked, emotionless.

Lord Castemont gave a small laugh, turning to me with a familiar look of pride. "He's been in the Guard for three years already. A bit shorter in the tooth than most of the Guard, but an exceptional soldier all the same."

I dipped my chin in another shallow nod, my eyes glued to the Bloodsinger. My gut turned as she stared back.

Lord Castemont turned back to Umrbi. "I've brought him along to show him your craft. He's from Eserene, so he's rather unfamiliar with blood magic."

I wanted to correct him, tell him I did know what blood magic was because technically, I wasn't from Eserene. I kept quiet, though, instead further surveying the room. Multiple doors stood closed around the perimeter. The brick walls looked like they were covered in soot.

"A first-timer," Umbri remarked. I said nothing as the woman's eyes bored into me, her irises the color of freshly spilled blood. "Come along." The gaunt woman heaved one of the doors open, ushering us through to a windowless room where the darkness quickly swallowed us.

Panic seeped into my bones, my heart thundering as the darkness grew thicker, more formidable. It was my duty to protect Lord Castemont, and I didn't feel I could do that here. "My Lord," I leaned in and whispered through the pitch black. "I think we should leave."

"Nonsense, Cal," the Lord answered, his tone light and completely unbothered.

"Lord Castemont, I must insist, I–"

"Shh. Watch."

Tiny flames sparked as dozens of candles came to life at once. The small room was all at once illuminated in shadows that flickered and danced. Lord Castemont's smiling face was cast in the orange light as he watched. The ivory candles were lined up, perfectly uniform on the stone floor against the back wall of the room. Sitting on a small wooden altar was a single candle that rose high above the rest, its column blacker than the darkness that had surrounded us moments ago. It seemed to swallow all the light around it, soaking it up as if light were its life force. The Bloodsinger's shadow stretched across the walls like a reaper closing in on its victim. But there was nothing else in the room

— only us, the candles, and the creeping feeling that our lives were in danger.

"Lord Evarius Castemont of Eserene," Umbri started. Her voice sent a chill through me like metal on stone as she stood before the altar. "Is it true that you come once again to seek the blessings of the Darkness Beyond?"

"It is," the Lord answered flatly, as if the eeriness of our surroundings had no effect on him.

"A blood sacrifice is required to proceed."

I swallowed hard. My eyes were wide as the Lord stepped forward, reaching into his coat and producing a small vial. He pulled the cork out as Umbri stepped aside, the flame of the black candle suddenly burning brighter than the others, an unsettling red glow radiating from its center. My eyes flashed back and forth between Lord Castemont and the Bloodsinger, their expressions leaving me even more unsettled, more panicked–

"*Timu en sangu verinia hostinhah,*" Umbri chanted as Lord Castemont stood before the altar, holding the vial upright over the flame. "*Nia nhah shisweh nia nilzha, agyun, kepitaa, sarehka, az styaa.*"

Something evil lurked here, and Umbri's words summoned it.

The Bloodsinger gave a small nod and Lord Castemont slowly tipped the vial, letting a single drop of blood escape and fall to the flame. It let out an angry hiss, its light banking then growing brighter, larger, the shadows around the room moving more erratically.

"*Hostinhah!*" Umbri yelled to the empty room with a voice that was now noticeably more sinister. "*Disim!*"

An ear-splitting screech clawed at my ears. It pulsed and throbbed as the taste of blood rose in my throat. I slammed my hands over my ears as hundreds of tiny shadows crawled up the walls, pouring out of the flame on the altar. It was the opposite of the lights in the cave — malevolent, destructive energy coursed through the room with the shadows that were now moving from wall to wall like a swarm of angry insects. My bones were vibrating with the screech that hadn't let up.

My whole body began to ache, and before long that ache turned into searing pain, every inch of my skin burning as if I laid alight on a pyre. I opened my mouth to scream but it felt like a fist was wrapped around my throat, choking the noise back down.

"*Krevok!*" Umbri commanded, and the shadows halted, the scream in the room dying down to a faint whistle. All the pain left my body as if that's exactly what Umbri had commanded it to do. "*Vrel nia sangu minu ke sraa.*"

The Bloodsinger gave a small nod to Lord Castemont, who quietly cleared his throat.

"Please show the young guard, Belin Cal Myrin, the future I'm proposing to him."

What?

All at once the screech resumed and the shadows began to move again. This time they grew until they cast the entire room in complete darkness once again. The candles snuffed out with a hiss as the pitch black settled around me. "Lord Castemont?" I called frantically.

No answer. My breath caught as I blinked against the black.

"We're going to be late to the meeting with the Royal Treasury."

A room materialized around me, and I squinted hard against the sudden bright light. I was in...a room. A massive, opulently furnished room, with a desk made of carved white stone that matched the floors. Art hung from every wall in intricate gold frames, and the ceiling was painted to match. A large, overstuffed settee sat opposite two equally overstuffed chairs, a low marble table in the middle with a pitcher and wine goblets neatly arranged.

"Cal, did you hear me? We're going to be late." I whirled to see Aunt Berna standing toward the back of the room near a soaring window. The sun was so bright I could barely make out a large body of water behind her as my eyes adjusted. Her face flashed with concern as I stared at her, dumbfounded. "Are you well, dear?"

My feet started moving before I could stop them. The view from the window became clearer as I neared it. *Eserene.* The harbor stretched to the horizon as the districts of the city lay before me. I was...

I was in the castle.

I spun to Aunt Berna, grabbing her by the arms. "Where are we?"

"What?" she asked, her face plastered with confusion and concern.

"Where are we?" I shouted again, shaking her.

"What do you... We're in your keep." Her eyes were wider than I'd ever see them as she stared at me.

My arms dropped to my sides and I blinked as I tried to figure out what the fuck was going on. *How am I–*

The door suddenly swung open, and an exquisitely-dressed Lord Castemont strolled in with a bundle of papers in his arms. "Your Majesty," he said cheerfully as he bowed his head. "I have the reports you requested."

Your Majesty? I stepped back, my hand instinctively going to my sword at my hip but finding nothing there. I wasn't wearing my leathers anymore. I was in a white surcoat embroidered with gold, nicer than anything I'd ever owned. My eyes caught on Lord Castemont, a sly grin on his face.

"What happened?" I demanded, my tone sharp.

He raised a brow, a look of satisfaction on his face before turning to Aunt Berna. "Berna, dear, would you be so kind as to give us a few moments alone?"

Aunt Berna's face was still the picture of pure confusion as she gave a small nod and leaned in to plant a kiss on the Lord's cheek. She looked at me for one more moment, her eyes searching mine, before quietly shuffling out of the room.

230

"Have a seat," the Lord offered as he sat down on the over-stuffed settee in the center of the room.

I was dazed as I lowered myself onto one of the chairs. "How? We were in Blindbarrow."

"You're the King of Widoras, Cal. Well, I suppose I should say King Belin," he said as if he were simply stating a fact.

"*How?*" I demanded.

"It won't take much convincing for King Umfray to make you his heir. He'll be so happy to learn his second cousin sired more than his share of bastards."

I perked up for a moment. "So my father is King Umfray's second cousin?"

"No. You have no blood relation to the King. But the resemblance is strong enough to be more than believable. And he was so happy to have an heir that he didn't care that your claim to the throne wasn't legitimate."

My heart was erratic in my chest at what he was implying. "So King Umfray is dead."

"In this time, yes. The red delirium took him to his grave."

I squinted my eyes at him, trying to put the pieces of this puzzle together. "In this time." It wasn't a question. It was fucking shock. "How do you know all this?"

Half his mouth turned up in a smile. "This isn't my first time here. I've seen it all, Cal." He sat back in his chair. "Think of all this as a little preview of what could be."

This wasn't real. It couldn't be. I ran my hands down the front of my surcoat. It felt real. I leaned forward, bringing the pitcher of wine to my nose and inhaling. It smelled real. Could it be?

"But how did you know–" Then I realized. "The Bloodsinger."

A knowing smile crossed his face. "The Bloodsinger," he repeated back in confirmation. "I learned this with the help of Umbri. I just wanted you to see it firsthand."

I collapsed back in the chair, my breaths coming in unsteady gasps. "I'm the King of Widoras."

"You are. And you're using your position for good." I raised a brow at him. "Poverty in Widoras is the lowest it's ever been. The citizens of Eserene are thrilled with your reign. Even the people of Inkwell have enough to eat. All thanks to you."

My eyes squinted. I let myself entertain the hallucination for a moment. "Really?"

"See for yourself," he offered as he spread the pages he'd been holding across the small table before us. There were ten sheets of parchment with numbers and figures that my brain couldn't focus on before he pulled them away again. "Your people are fed, housed, and happy. The country's economy is the best it's ever been. The people *love* you."

I sat back. I knew I looked like a fucking wide-eyed idiot, but I was trying to sort through how the hell this could all be real. Blood magic could show me the future? This was all because of a single drop of blood?

"You will have to follow my plan to get here," he said suddenly. He leaned forward slightly in his chair as if he were trying to get a better look at my face, as if he could read my thoughts.

I stared at him. His expression was relaxed, like we were having a simple conversation on Aunt Berna's porch. He was completely unconcerned.

"You need to kill the Daughter of Katia."

My eyes flew wide as I stared at the man. "You want me to *kill* the Savior of the Realm?"

"But that's the thing. She won't be the Savior of the Realm. She will burn the realm to the ground, and everyone along with it, including Inkwell and your Aunt Berna and you, Cal. I saw it myself with the help of Umbri." His eyes fell distant. For a split second, I thought I saw a flash of fear cross his face. "One life for the good of many."

"So the books are wrong? The prophecy is wrong?"

"I'm afraid so, your Highness."

My mouth hung open as I tried to wrap my head around what he was saying. "How the hell are we supposed to find her?"

232

He smirked. "I already have. She's here, living in Inkwell."

I pursed my lips. I didn't know what to think. He'd *seen* it. He'd sacrificed to the Bloodsinger and seen the world burn at the hands of the Daughter of Katia. And she was here.

"I truly believe that you and I can save the realm *together*," he added quietly, his face thoughtful. "I want to see you on the throne, Cal. It's your throne, and I want to see you as King Belin. You have the ability to keep the realm from burning, and lead the people of Widoras into a newer, brighter future as their ruler."

A familiar uneasy feeling settled in my gut, the feeling I got when I first met Lord Castemont years ago. Like something was wrong, but I couldn't place what it was. His eyes were on me. I could feel him watching me as I sorted through the reasons I had not to trust him.

But there were…none. That was the thing with Lord Castemont — everything was always just a bit too good to be true, but it always ended up coming to fruition.

"And how do you propose I kill her? Approach her in the street and slit her throat?"

He tipped his head back and laughed. "It'll be a bit more complicated than that, I'm afraid, but you may be able to have some fun in the process." I eyed him. His tone was too nonchalant. "She's close to your age. Classic Inkwell trash, but not entirely unattractive from what my spies have seen from afar." I clenched my fists at the disrespect, but kept quiet. "So you romance her. Show her a good time. She'll be excited at the prospect of marrying the King, so you do everything you can to make her think that she could be your queen. Get close to her. Fuck her if you have to. Then kill her."

I cringed at the crassness of his words. "I can't do that, my Lord. You know I can't."

He leaned forward again. The look on his face was so intense I couldn't break away from his stare. "You must. If you want to keep the world from burning, you must. I've always believed in you, haven't I?" he breathed into the silence as he leaned in even closer to me. "The moment I met you, I knew you were destined to be great. The Royal Guard at eighteen, the youngest in the history of the entire continent of Astran. And now a king." He gave a small smile. "I always knew you had it in you. And I know you can do this, too."

The Lord reached for a wine goblet and drank deeply as he watched me. If I could become King, if I could make a difference...

I couldn't believe I was considering his proposal.

One life for the good of many. I could help the people that so desperately needed it.

I opened my mouth to speak, but it took far more effort than I thought it would. "Get close to her and kill her?"

"Yes. She has some family members that may...*compromise* the mission, but I've got a handle on that. And as soon as you are officially crowned King of Widoras, your work can begin."

And always be brave. My mother's words echoed through my mind. Was it brave to push aside kindness and honesty for the greater good? Did betraying my morals, Mama's morals, make me brave?

Always be kind. But how could killing someone be kind? Was it kind to take one life if it meant that every other life could be saved?

Always be honest. I'd have to lie to her to get close to her. I'd have to pretend to be interested in pursuing her, when it wasn't so.

For the good of the realm.

I stared at the man who had become like a father to me. Who *had* always believed in me. Who'd given me every tool I needed to meet every goal I'd ever set.

The world around us began to grow darker, colder, the low screech of blood magic assaulting my ears again as the room in the castle turned to ash. The shadows returned and the candles

234

of the Bloodsinger's room flickered to life again. Umbri's figure came into focus, standing in the same place she'd been before.

"I'll do it," I said flatly, my mind far more silent than I was comfortable with.

Lord Castemont stepped forward. "Excellent. And Cal," he added, "don't tell your aunt."

I nodded. I knew she wouldn't even remotely approve of this. And though the smile on his face was warm, my insides had gone as cold as the marble floors of the castle that awaited me.

Chapter 26

"Don't you have a cousin who fathered more than a few bastards?" Lord Castemont asked, an ankle crossed over a knee as he leaned leisurely back into the navy velvet chair. His hand was wrapped around a goblet of wine, his easy going demeanor doing nothing to calm my nerves.

Though the furniture was different, we sat in the same room the Bloodsinger had shown us. I sat straight as an arrow. I was afraid to touch or say or do anything wrong in front of the King. I was used to being around Low Royalty — Lord Castemont and his peers were never too formal, never required much of me beyond my basic guard duties. I was terrified I was going to compromise this phase of Castemont's plan by fucking up some obscure rule of etiquette.

That, and the fact that I was going against every instinct in me by lying to the King. *I was going to lie to the fucking* King. I'd been so terrified, in fact, I hadn't even been able to introduce myself. Lord Castemont had to do it.

Old King Umfray rubbed at his chin. A thin layer of white stubble dotted his sagging jaw. "A second cousin, actually. Javor. Oddly enough, he's a priest." He let out a chuckle and took a sip of his wine then cleared his throat as he thought. "I believe he lives in Araqina now. Leads the cathedral there." Araqina, the Holy City, where it's said the Saints first began to build the human realm. "I've no idea how or why he'd have been in Taitha."

Lord Castemont thrummed his fingers on the upholstered arms of the chair. "I'd say that's the most plausible explanation. The two of you are *clearly* related."

I leaned forward and wrapped my hand around my wine goblet, trying to dispel the anxiety that had me in a chokehold. I didn't take a sip, and I saw King Umfray take notice. "Not a drinker, lad?"

"No, your Majesty."

He cocked his head. "Not even after a long day of guard duty?"

"Cal had a mishap a few years back," Lord Castemont interjected in a light tone. I sucked my teeth, trying to quell the frustration I still held toward that day. I swore my leg pulsed with phantom pain. "He's chosen to abstain. He knows his limits, a very kingly quality. Another sign he must be related to you, your Majesty."

He was laying it on a bit thick. It had to be obvious to the King what we were trying to do. I shifted uncomfortably in my seat, the shame of being dishonest making me sweat. I had grown used to my leathers and armor in the time I'd been in the Royal Guard, but Lord Castemont had fitted me in a surcoat and trousers for today's meeting. They felt foreign on my body, and though they were custom made, I still felt that one wrong move would pop every stitch. I was suffocating.

The King's eyes assessed me the same way they had been since we sat down. As if he were trying to make sense of a situation that made no sense at all. "I suppose so." His tone was incredulous, his gaze narrow as he thought.

Guilt and fear rose in me. He was going to figure us out. He was going to pick up on the lie. He was going to see right through the plan and have us thrown out of the city. Maybe even beheaded.

But I forced myself to play the part. I let myself pretend that this was the moment I dreamed of my entire life, that I was finding out who my father was.

My voice was apprehensive when I spoke, and I had to fight to keep it from wavering. "You think your second cousin Javor could be my father?"

The King inhaled deeply, his wrinkled face contemplative. "Your features *are* strikingly similar. And your eyes..." He turned to Lord Castemont. "And you don't think he could be—"

"No," the Lord cut in. "He has no children."

He? Who was *he?* I opened my mouth to ask but caught myself, afraid to derail the plan. "So you and I are distant cousins?" I suggested, surprised I didn't stumble over any of the words.

The King let out a laugh that quickly devolved into a raspy cough, raising his thin, wrinkled hand to his mouth to take a gulp of wine. That'd be the red delirium setting in. He'd soon begin bleeding from the inside and drown in his own blood quickly after. "Yes. Second cousins, once removed I believe." I nodded and tapped into the story my mother had told me about my father. If I was going to be lying in order to steal the throne, I may as well tell some truth. "My mother..." I started, clearing my throat. "She told me he left her to fight for his cause, that he was worried for her safety because people didn't believe in his mission. He didn't even know she was pregnant."

Lord Castemont tensed, and I knew it was because I had divulged unnecessary information. I ignored him, though, and King Umfray cocked his head in thought. "That sounds like—"

"Javor," Lord Castemont cut in quickly, some kind of look in his eyes as he quickly glanced at the King. Uncertainty swept over me as I watched a tension form between the two men.

"Tell the boy," King Umfray croaked, irritation suddenly lacing his voice.

Lord Castemont shifted in his seat slightly as I watched him. "You're aware of Kauvras' uprising in Cabillia, yes?"

"Of course, my Lord," I answered, my eyes narrowing.

"Kauvras is King Umfray's younger brother."

"Much younger. And I was questioning whether you could be Kauvras' son," the King added.

I nodded, swallowing hard as I turned to Lord Castemont. "And you don't think that's a possibility?"

"I don't, given it is well known that Kauvras is impotent."

The King sniffed, nodding slightly as he considered. "A fall on a fence post as a child," he murmured with a wince. "I remember the scream." He sighed, a wrinkled finger tapping his tired face. "Javor does seem like the most likely candidate."

Lord Castemont hummed in agreement, looking expectantly between me and the King, but the King's eyes were hard set on me. "Belin Cal Myrin."

I had to play it cool and pretend like my insides weren't crumpling under the weight of anxiety. "Yes, your Majesty?" I finally asked when my skin began to crawl.

A sly smile split his face in two at my question. "You're my heir."

It worked. It fucking worked. This had been the goal all along, but the shock that rang through me was cold and metallic. I didn't have to act shocked like we planned. I *was* shocked. It happened so quickly and took such little convincing. "Your heir?" The words came out in only a whisper.

His eyes crinkled as he looked at me, something like pride in his stare. "You're my heir, Belin Cal Myrin."

Lord Castemont leaned forward. "You're the next King of Widoras."

I shook my head, the surprise on my face genuine. "But–"

"I had one son, Saints rest his soul," the King stated. "No other family member of mine is worthy of the title." His words were bitter.

I somehow straightened even more in my chair as my head still shook in honest disbelief. It was all beginning to close in on me, the fact that I was going to be King of Widoras, the fact that it was a lie that would put me on the throne. "Your Majesty, thank you kindly, but there are far more worthy men. Lord Castemont would be a better choice."

The Lord's face shot to me, surprise etching every feature. But I knew it was a mask over a face that was screaming, *That's not the plan!*

"Lord Castemont is not of my blood. And though I agree he would make a fine king, I prefer to keep the title in the family's bloodline."

I ignored Lord Castemont as I stood quickly, my head swimming and my vision almost fuzzy. This was happening. I was going to rule.

"Please," King Umfray said, "have a seat. Maybe you could try a bit of wine."

I ignored his offer as my knees locked and panic rose in me at the prospect of ruling. Nowhere in my mind had I actually expected this to work. The walls began to press in and nausea hit my gut like a suckerpunch. I suddenly felt like I was sinking beneath the surface of Pellucid Harbor once again.

"Your Majesty," I started, "I cannot accept this position." I suddenly felt like cursing Lord Castemont for dropping this weight on my shoulders. "I'm a bastard, and I was born in Cabillia. I was born to be a soldier, not a king."

"Exactly why you'll make a fantastic one."

I stared at the man, his eyes almost as vibrant as mine, dulled only slightly by age. I grasped for clarity in the muddy water of my mind, tried to make sense of all that was happening and how quickly everything was changing.

A deep breath in. If I did this, I could make a difference. *For the good of the realm.* "Okay." I nodded, pursing my lips as I tried to figure out how I could make this work for me. "But I have conditions."

Lord Castemont tensed in the corner of my eye, and the old King smiled as the corners of his eyes creased with deep wrinkles. "The art of negotiation is a necessary skill for a king to possess."

"I'm afraid these conditions are non-negotiable."

His smile only deepened as he beamed with pride. "Go on."

I swallowed hard. "I will stay a member of the Royal Guard until it's time to ascend the throne."

The smile was gone instantly, replaced by shock. "May I ask why?"

"Cal's dream as a young child arriving in Eserene was to be a part of the Royal Guard," Castemont answered for me, his tone edged with an almost imperceptible air of irritation.

The King looked to me and I nodded. "It's very important to me."

His face turned thoughtful. "As...noble as it is to want to live a life of service, it's far too dangerous for a royal heir to serve."

"That's the second condition. I want complete anonymity." Silence descended over the room. I was met with the narrowed eyes of the King. I didn't even want to look over at Lord Castemont. "I don't want to lose the freedoms I have now. I want to be able to walk through the city unguarded for as long as I live. I can be a better King that way."

His mouth bobbed open as he tried to find a rebuttal. "Your subjects will want to know who their king is."

"Then I'll have to do so well that they forget to care about what I look like." I looked to Lord Castemont, his gaze intent on Umfray. The Lord was thinking about something, I could tell. Something was going on behind his eyes.

The King nodded slowly, a shaky hand resting on his cheek. "It will be difficult to accommodate such a request."

"Non-negotiable."

He nodded slowly and let out a deep breath. "Very well."

I lowered my head in thanks. I'd made it work for me. I was doing what Lord Castemont wanted me to, but I was going to ensure I could still do what I wanted. I was going to remain Cal, *and* I was going to be King of Widoras.

◆ ◆ ◆

"Are you out of your Saints damned mind?" Lord Castemont whispered the moment we were out of earshot. Tyrak stood nearby, quietly observing. "*Anonymity?*"

I narrowed my eyes and tried to think of a response that would be adequately respectful. I chose to keep my mouth shut.

"That wasn't the plan, Cal," he spat through gritted teeth. "You were supposed to use your position as King to woo the Daughter of Katia. Now what the hell are you going to do?"

I scoffed. "Do you think I'm incapable of seducing a woman as myself?" My voice was louder than I'd anticipated. "Do you think I need a crown to do that?"

"Do not raise your voice at me. I am your Lord."

"And I will soon be your King."

It was something beyond fury that flashed in his eyes. Dark. Fearsome. And it was gone as soon as I saw it. The scar on my leg flared with pain as I stared him down, disdain rising within me, same as the day I saw Castemont walk out of the Painted Empress in Inkwell.

Castemont stood taller suddenly, stretching his neck and inhaling deeply, as if to set himself right again. He nodded, straightening his cuffs. "Yes, you will be. Isn't that right, Tyrak?"

Tyrak's face betrayed nothing as he gave a terse nod. "Yes, my Lord."

Castemont faced me again, a forced smile on his face. "I apologize for my temper. I wasn't expecting you to suggest anonymity. We will work around it."

242

And though I was set to be King of Widoras, I had a feeling that the power of the position would never truly be mine.

Chapter 27
Five Years Ago

"A lot of beautiful pieces here," my aunt remarked. She stood beside Lord Castemont, his hand on her lower back as they peered over the case of jewelry that had been left to me by King Umfray. Rings and belts and pendants, all solid gold and crusted with obscenely large gems, all waiting expectantly in my dressing room. "Some of these are fit for a queen." I could tell she was trying to make it come across as an absentminded observation, but I knew it was anything but that. I braced myself for the question I knew would come next. "When *do* you think you'll find yourself a queen, Cal?"

I knew she was aching inside. She and Lord Castemont had been together for eight years now, and it still wasn't yet officially recognized by the Court. He'd attended monthly appointments with some amalgamate of High Royal leaders, a board or convocation that the king was apparently not a part of. Every month,

244

they denied his request. "I think they're close to approving our courtship," he'd say every Saints damned time, and she'd try to hide the disappointment from showing. She'd gotten worse at it over the years. It was eating away at her.

"Haven't really thought about it," I replied, straightening the hem of my unassuming surcoat that would go beneath the ridiculous ceremonial cape. It hung in the wardrobe behind me, haunting me like a ghost as I looked in the mirror. Without the cape, no one would know I was on my way to being crowned the King of Widoras. I was still uneasy about the entire situation, about the lies we'd told to get here.

"Well you're not going to find your queen in the brothels."

My eyes flew wide. "How do you know—"

"Cal, you smell like a different type of perfume multiple times a week. You know I'm not stupid." My ears heated with embarrassment and I looked away. "You're not stupid either. You know you're not going to find her at Amalthea's Desire or the Silken Vixen."

Humiliation washed over me, but at least she didn't know about—

"Or the Rider's Bathhouse."

Shit. I righted myself and tried not to shrink under her gaze.

"I'm not there to look for a queen," I grumbled. When I was sworn into the Royal Guard, I'd taken an oath to forgo a partner and family and remain unwed my entire life. Though it wasn't expressly forbidden, I stayed away from the brothels out of respect for the position. But I wasn't a member of the Royal Guard anymore, not really. I knew that the search for a queen would commence soon after my coronation, so when King Umfray passed and I was *technically* released from my duty to prepare for my ascension to the throne, I took the opportunity and ran with it. For all intents and purposes, I was still acting as a Royal Guard...except for the brothels.

The truth was that I had met some beautiful, interesting, and truly captivating women. The sex was phenomenal, but I was always sure to ask them about *them* — where they were from, if they had any family nearby, what they liked to do when they weren't working. It always caught them off guard at first, but it usually didn't take long for them to open up.

"I'm sure he'll find a queen soon enough," Lord Castemont offered. I had to fight an eye roll. I wouldn't have been surprised if he had a few women in mind already.

"Why do I have to wear all the ceremonial garb?" I asked, trying to change the subject. "It's just going to be a few of us there."

Aunt Berna turned to me, a soft smile on her face. "Let me see my boy as King of Widoras just once." Her hand grazed my cheek and pride radiated from the touch. But the smile quickly faded and her hand dropped as she turned back to the case of jewelry, peering at the baubles that rested on velvet. "I don't know when you'll be dressed like this again considering you want to live in the shadows like a common rat. How are you supposed to find a queen if the women you meet don't even know you're King?"

I sighed at the passive-aggressive comment. "I want to be able to come and go as I please. You know this."

She nodded, her back still to me. "You want to be able to go to Rider's Bathhouse."

"You know that's not the reason."

"Well maybe it's one reason," she muttered.

This eye roll, I didn't hide. "Aunt Berna."

"I know, I know," she laughed. "It just seems like more trouble than it's worth."

I sighed. "If a king takes a planned trip to the slums of a city, what's going to happen?" I asked her. She turned to me and cocked her head. "It'll be announced. It'll be curated and planned down to the number of shits the horses pulling my carriage will take. I'm not going to get an accurate picture of the people there."

"I suppose so."

"Or if I send someone in my place, I'll get a secondhand account of it. I'd get a watered down version of the truth. But if I walk into Inkwell as no more than a normal Eserenian resident, from say, Sidus, no one is going to think twice. I'll see the real, raw truth of the state of Widoras. I can be a better king if they don't know I'm a king at all. I'll be able to better help my people."

Aunt Berna took a deep breath and nodded her head. "You're going to be a good king, Cal, no matter what. Your mother would be so proud." My eyes misted over at her words, even more so when I realized what was coming next. "Tobyas, too."

I dropped my head, blinking hard. "Yeah, he would be proud, wouldn't he?" I nodded to myself. "Bet he'd have plenty to say about that gaudy cape, and he'd say it with a shit-eating grin on his face, too."

She smiled again, her blue eyes alight in the glow of the chandelier. "I can hear him now," she laughed, sorrow behind the sound. "*That's stupid,*" she sneered in a mock-Tobyas tone. I couldn't help but laugh, too, because she was right. "And don't think I missed that swear in there. If you're not smart enough to say something without swearing..."

"You're not smart enough," I mumbled. "Yeah."

Lord Castemont stepped forward, looking at me in the mirror. "King Belin Cal Myrin," he mused with a prideful smile on his face.

"Not just yet," Aunt Berna said playfully, finding her place next to her Lord. He wrapped his arm around her waist and pulled her toward him to plant a kiss on the top of her head. "He still has to get through his coronation."

"The arrangements have been made?" I asked.

Lord Castemont nodded. "All corridors from here to the throne room have been blocked off. Only the necessary people know what is going on today. The rest of the Royal Court has been made aware of your need for anonymity." I didn't hear the contempt in his voice, but I knew it was there.

I nodded. "And the priest is waiting?"

"Yes, with the crown and scepter. We'll have a private meal in your keep afterwards."

I inhaled and took one final look in the mirror as just Cal. "Okay. I'm ready."

◆ ◆ ◆

"I'm proud of you. You know that, right?" Lord Castemont said, his voice low as he walked alongside me to the throne room. "I'm so very proud."

I bowed my head. "Thank you, my Lord."

"And we're on track with the mission."

My stomach turned at the mention of it. Every time I'd managed to push it just far enough out of my brain to forget about it for just one moment of peace, it came crashing back in. I'd taken Castemont's word that this needed to be done, that the Daughter of Katia needed to die. I just hated that I had to be the one to do it.

"You know, this anonymity thing may actually work better than my original idea," he murmured, his voice low.

I exhaled. I was sick of talking about the plan. I was sick of thinking about the plan. I was sick of being a part of this stupid fucking plan. But I answered anyway, because I knew he wouldn't drop it. "Yeah?"

"A member of the Royal Guard is much more approachable than a king. She'll probably be faster to relax and let her defenses down."

"Probably," I answered absentmindedly.

"Definitely. I'm sorry I doubted you. It'll move the plan along much quicker." I didn't answer, keeping my eyes ahead. "There's something I need to tell you, Cal," he said suddenly. There was concern in his tone, and the way he looked at me mirrored that.

"What?"

He peered back to where Aunt Berna walked with Tyrak behind us. "There is no way for me to officially court your aunt."

248

The words settled between us. His eyes stayed on me, as if he were watching for my reaction as we walked through the barricaded corridors. To be honest, I wasn't sure what my reaction was. But I feigned shock and sorrow like I knew I should. "Why not?"

"The law clearly states that royalty cannot marry outside their ranks."

"Am I not able to override that as King?"

"Unfortunately the laws are set. I can petition the court all I want, but they will never budge, even if you intervene."

I knew I could fight the law, but I wasn't sure I wanted to. I could easily go to the library and pore over tomes to find some kind of loophole. It would be worth Aunt Berna's happiness. Uneasiness settled over me as we walked, and I forced myself to play the part I felt I should. "What did she say when you told her?"

"I haven't had the heart to tell her yet. I just can't stand to be the one to make her upset."

Of course he hadn't told her, which meant I had to. I was the one who was going to be the bad guy. Lord Castemont was putting me in the position to explain to Aunt Berna that she couldn't marry the love of her life.

The doors to the throne room were propped open already. My eyes flashed over the carved marble columns, settling on the two depicting Noros. The first was the Blood Saint on his knees, back to the viewer with fingers flexed in the dirt as if the Saint of Pain was in pain himself. He was outside Katia's palace, the entirety of the structure covered with vining flowers. His great ruby encrusted sword, Aegrabane, was strewn on the ground beside him. The second column was a carving of the Saint sitting upon his throne, his facial features too nondescript to tell what he looked like. Blood cascaded down the arms of the throne to a pool on the floor. He was pain incarnate, and he looked the part.

The priest stood smiling on the dais, the Book of Saints in his wrinkled hands. The crown and scepter waited on a velvet pillow that sat on an altar just beside the throne. And the throne... I'd seen it a thousand times while in the Royal Guard as court was held, but seeing it now was another thing entirely. It was a massive mahogany monstrosity detailed in gold. The sight of it made me wildly uncomfortable, but I had no choice but to keep walking.

Today, I'd be crowned King of Widoras. But what made me even more nervous was the fact that I was going to have to break my Aunt Berna's heart.

◆ ◆ ◆

"To King Belin Cal Myrin," Lord Castemont said, his goblet raised high in the air. His brown eyes glinted in the chandelier's light. There was far too much food for the four of us, and I gnashed my teeth together to keep from complaining. Half of this could have gone to someone who needed it, and we'd still have more than enough.

"To King Belin Cal Myrin," Aunt Berna answered, clinking her goblet with Tyrak's and the Lord's. "Long may he reign. Though I wish he'd reign in something other than leathers."

I rolled my eyes. I'd changed almost immediately from the ceremonial attire to my leathers. They were far more comfortable. Besides, I'd looked fucking ridiculous.

"Did you see the look on the priest's face?" Lord Castemont started as he cut into a slice of roast duck. Tyrak shifted in his seat, quietly picking at the sliced carrots on his plate as he eyed the Lord. "He couldn't believe he was one of the only people who'd ever meet the Invisible King."

"The Invisible King?" Aunt Berna questioned.

"That's what they're calling him." Lord Castemont gave a sly smile. "There's an air of mystery about him, and the people are intrigued."

I nodded. "The Invisible King. I like it. Looks like I'll be able to stay anonymous."

"Which means there will be less of a scene when your Aunt Berna and I are wed. You'll be able to enjoy the day with us without a spectacle."

Motherfucker. Really? He was going to make me break it to her now? I looked at the half-eaten pheasant on my plate, my anger toward Lord Castemont rising at a fever pitch. "Yes," I answered with a smile. "It'll be much easier. I'm looking forward to it."

Aunt Berna's face lit up. "I never even thought of that. You're right."

Lord Castemont's face went blank, but I could see the fury peeking out from behind his eyes. "I'll keep petitioning the Court until they give me a definite answer."

"You do that," I answered with a sarcastic smile. Tyrak's eyes were glued to me in warning. Whether he was warning me out of protection for his Lord or for my own sake, I couldn't tell.

"I will," Lord Castemont answered. "The meetings have been going well."

"I'm sure they have. For years now."

Aunt Berna placed her fork down on her plate, all traces of joy gone from her face. "I don't know what's going on here, but you two need to cut it out."

Three pairs of eyes landed on her. "What are you talking about, dear?"

"This bizarre power struggle. The snide comments, the passive-aggressive remarks. It's been going on since he was sixteen," she explained, her voice even but stern. That was the Aunt Berna I knew, not the doe-eyed puddle that fawned over Castemont. The Aunt Berna I knew called people out on their bullshit, like this, and she was finally calling him out on his. "I don't know if it's because you're envious of Cal's position as King," she pointed to Castemont before pointing to me, "or if *you're* envious of our relationship. But you both need to stop."

My ears heated with embarrassment and outrage, and I took a sip of water to try to combat it before I spoke, but Lord Castemont beat me to it. "No envy here, darling," he offered. "I simply want to guide Cal to be the best man he can be."

"He can do that on his own. He's already one of the best men I know."

A strained silence settled over the room. But I could tell Aunt Berna didn't feel the tension. She stared Lord Castemont down, unflinching in her intensity.

"Really, Bernadet? After all we've shared? After everything I've done, this is how you speak to me?"

"No one asked you to do those things, and I'll speak to you how I wish. You are not courting me, and you are not my husband. You have no authority over me."

Lord Castemont sat back in his chair, inclining his chin as he looked across the table at my aunt. It was meant to look leisurely, but it was purely antagonistic. He knew that. The problem was...so did she. "You're a very strong woman, Bernadet. I've always admired that about you."

"No," she answered, folding her napkin and placing it on the table as she shook her head. "You're not complimenting your way out of this one, Evarius. Especially not with a backhanded one like that."

"That's not my intention."

She narrowed her eyes and leaned in. "Isn't it, though?" Her voice was nothing above a whisper. "I think I'll retire for the evening." She stood, smoothing her skirts. Lord Castemont rose too, but she shot a hand out. "Alone."

My eyes followed her as she marched out of the dining room, her steps echoing down the corridor. "What the hell, Cal?" Lord Castemont spat.

I inhaled, staring hard at the Lord. "That was your doing." My eyes flashed to the corridor as the last of her echoed steps faded away.

"She won't leave me, if that's what you're thinking."

“I wouldn’t be so sure about that.”
“Believe me. She won’t.”

Chapter 28
Four Years Ago

Things between Aunt Berna and Lord Castemont were never the same after that night. But he'd been right, she hadn't left him. I kept my mouth shut on the matter. I didn't need to be involved. And to be honest, I was looking forward to the day the plan was carried out, because then I could keep my distance from Caste-mont.

It'd been two years since I agreed to go along with his plan. One year since King Umfray passed and I ascended the throne. And six months since Castemont and I worked out the logistics of this very day. He'd introduced me to the dozens of spies he'd employed over the years to watch the Daughter of Katia from afar. Of course, they were none the wiser to my identity.

"You have eyes on her?" he asked under his breath. We stood in the cordoned off area of the waterfront reserved only for royals. The morning of Cindregala was in full swing with a harbor full of ships and all of Eserene watching them.

I answered with a nod, watching the same head of thick brown hair moving through the crowd that I'd been watching from afar all morning. That Castemont had eyes on for years.

The Daughter of Katia.

"And you're absolutely positive it's her?" I asked.

"I have it on good authority."

I know he did. He'd had spies watching her for years at this point.

This was it. My feet started moving. I dodged the stares of festival-goers as I neared her. Her eyes were glued to the harbor as she trailed behind two women — a full-cheeked brunette and a lithe blonde who Castemont told me was her sister.

I sped up, planning to catch her attention like I caught everyone else's. Everyone else was always staring at me. She'd be no different. Hands in my pockets, I strode by her, making sure that I was in her full view. But she simply let me pass, her eyes transfixed on the harbor before her.

Damn.

I looped back around, intent on catching her eye. This time I cut directly in front of her, between her sister and her friend. Still, her gaze didn't stray from the harbor for even a moment. I was completely invisible to her, something I would typically be happy about.

A challenge, then. I could rise to it.

Marching behind her, I purposely nudged her hard enough to get her attention — too hard, *fuck*, because now she was on the ground. *Good fucking job, Cal, knock over the Daughter of Katia.*

She was embarrassed as she straightened herself out on the ground, her gaze low and hidden. This was perfect, actually. The perfect way in. The handsome stranger who helped her up. My hand shot out, and then she looked up at me.

Her eyes were the middle of autumn. The last warm day of the year, when it's been cold for a week now, but you walk out in the morning to the surprise of mild air amid the changing trees and fallen leaves. And you know that tomorrow it'll be cold again, and the sun will take on its dull winter hue. But for today, *just for today*, it's warm again. That's what I saw in her eyes.

Shit.

I couldn't tell if it was shock from the fall or my eyes on her, but she stared back. There was the attention I'd been expecting. But for a moment, I couldn't move, couldn't think of what to say. I finally shot a hand out to her, an apology in my mouth but stuck on my tongue. "Are you okay?" It was all I could think to ask.

She reached out, the feel of her hand in mine a contradiction in and of itself. Small but hardened. Delicate but prophesied to be the destruction of all that exists. "I'm fine." She stood taller than I thought she would, and she dusted her hands on her cloak as she collected herself. "Thank you."

I blinked hard, trying to keep my wits about me. But something about her was throwing me off. How could *this* be the person destined to burn the world to ash? This tall, brown-eyed peasant in a torn cloak was going to bring the world to its knees?

Get close to her, then kill her.

"Try to be more careful."

"Mhm," she hummed. I had her attention now. She was melting under my stare, just like I hoped she would, but–

As if she pulled a mask off, she snapped out of it, her jaw squaring for a split second as she turned back to her sister and friend. "Enjoy Cindregala."

"Wait." I grabbed her shoulder, and her eyes found mine again. I drank her in, *Saints*, I lapped up every second I remained in her view. *You have to kill her in the end*, I reminded myself. But I let myself study her face, her strong, straight nose, the curve of her lips, and those damned autumn eyes. "What's your name?"

"I have to go. My sister is leaving." She turned away, out of the gentle grip I had on her shoulder. "Thanks again."

256

Back into the crowd she went, leaving me...*wanting*.

◆ ◆ ◆

Castemont's study was silent. My mind was anything but.

I could still see Autumn Eyes frozen in fear as she watched the flaming ship headed straight for the seawall, straight for her sister. I'd lunged to help tow the rope in, to help in her efforts to save the sailors desperately trying to flee the path of a fiery death, but Castemont placed a hand on my shoulder. "Her sister would need to be *dealt with* anyway, and maybe we'll be lucky enough that it'll take out the Daughter of Katia, too," he murmured in my ear. "Let nature take its course."

So I stood and watched. I stood and watched the flaming ship. I stood and watched a dozen men die that I could have saved if I helped. I stood and watched as her sister's leg was tangled in the rope, and as the rope was pulled into the churning harbor by the sinking debris of the ship.

But I couldn't stand and watch as Autumn Eyes finally started moving toward her sister. She finally took off in a dead sprint toward the impending explosion, and so did I. It was far too late though, and she froze for a moment when a flaming plank of wood speared her sister through the throat as she was pulled into the harbor at the exact moment the ship collided with the seawall.

Now, Lord Castemont sat behind his massive mahogany desk. I was across from him in a brocade-upholstered chair. He clutched a wine goblet, staring me down in the silence.

"This could all be over right now. But you saved her."

I swallowed hard, my eyes set on his. "I wasn't going to let her die like that."

He placed his hands flat on his desk, a fragile calm laid over the quiet rage that I knew was behind his eyes. "That is exactly how she should have died. An accident. That accident was divine intervention. That accident was the Saints keeping your hands clean. This entire thing would have been handled for us had you just let her die."

She'd been blown back by the explosion, but flaming debris continued to fall to the earth. She was sitting dazed in the midst of it all, with a massive gash on her face and blood spattered across her clothing. Somehow she stood up again and immediately began stumbling back toward the epicenter of the explosion. I didn't think, I just grabbed her by the arm and yanked her back, my eyes glued to the sky as chunks of wood and metal rained down. She fought like hell against me, screaming *Larka* the entire time, until I finally turned her around, holding her face in a firm grasp as I screamed. "Go! You need to get out of here! She's dead! *She's dead!*"

Her eyes rolled back, the wound on her forehead jagged and oozing as she collapsed. "I've got you," I whispered to her as I hauled her away, just far enough out of the melee that I knew her family would find her laying limp and bleeding. "You're okay."

Lord Castemont stared hard at me, and I stared right back. "It's your blade in her back now."

"I'm aware," I answered flatly. "Just like we planned."

"Like you planned what?" I spun to see Aunt Berna standing in the doorway of the study, her expression unreasonable as she stared at me. "*Your blade in her back?* What's going on?"

I looked back to the Lord, his face betraying the tiniest sliver of shock. "Bernadet, I–"

"What's going on?" she repeated, her eyes hard on me.

"It's just an expression," Lord Castemont offered with a smile, feigning nonchalance.

She stared at me with a mix of sternness and pleading in her petite features. I inhaled, the weight of the world pressing in on my chest. "I have to kill the Daughter of Katia."

A thin brow raised as she made sense of my words, jutting her chin forward. "You have to do what?"

Lord Castemont's face was laced with disappointment, sucking his teeth as he shook his head before he turned to Aunt Berna and offered her a smile. "Why don't you have a seat?"

Aunt Berna didn't move. She didn't move when Lord Castemont asked her to sit again. She didn't move as I told her the plan, and why we had to do it.

When I'd explained the last of it and the room fell quiet again, she finally shifted on her feet, her face melting into concern. "Evarius…" The uncertainty in her voice was tangible. "You want him to *murder* her?"

Lord Castemont's face softened as if we weren't talking about ending a life. "I know it's morbid. But if she's not taken care of—"

"*Taken care of?* Call it what it is, Evarius," she snapped. "You want her murdered."

The Lord pursed his lips and closed his eyes against her words. "It's not as simple as that."

"You're using *my boy* to do *your* dirty work, and I'm not going to stand for it."

I cleared my throat, righting myself. "I'm capable of making my own decisions, Aunt Berna, and I've chosen to follow Lord Castemont's plan."

Aunt Berna laughed, a sickening sound that bounced off the marble. She peered at me from behind her lashes with one brow raised. "You believe a Saints-forsaken *Bloodsinger* that the Daughter of Katia is not only here, but that she plans to burn the world to the ground? You believe that the only way forward is to murder an innocent woman?" She shook her head, blinking hard. "Saints, she's barely more than a girl!"

My eyes narrowed on her as I sorted through the reasons in my mind, but I couldn't escape the familiar feeling of dread. "Do you think I want to take her life, Aunt Berna?"

"No, I don't. I think, despite the passive-aggressive shit between the two of you, you're so far up Castemont's ass that you'll do whatever he says regardless of how insane it is." Her voice was still even and measured, but I could tell that a furious heat was rising within her. "Aren't *you* supposed to be the King of Widoras?"

Lord Castemont stood suddenly. "How dare you speak to your King that way."

Aunt Berna stepped forward, staring at him from across the desk, her tiny frame dwarfed by the man who was supposed to love her. Her stare was hard and her stance steady. "How dare you involve him in something so vile."

"Stand down, Castemont," I commanded, but the Lord didn't budge. His face had gone distant, a manic heat pulsing from him as his eyes bored down on my aunt, his fists clenched and knuckles white. "*Stand down, Castemont,*" I repeated. "That's an order from your King."

His lip twitched slightly before he relaxed and straightened the hem of his surcoat. Dropping back to his chair, he gave a shallow nod. "Yes, your Majesty," he murmured quietly.

Aunt Berna had yet to relax, her nostrils still flaring, her face still contorted with disdain. I stood and stepped in front of her to block her from Castemont's view.

She softened before me, her familiar maternal energy returning as she reached a hand toward my cheek. I lowered my face to meet her and savored the feeling, basked in the glow that was her love for me.

"This is something I need to do," I whispered to her, my eyes closed.

She didn't answer, but when I opened my eyes, the look on her face almost gutted me. It wasn't disappointment — it was far, far worse. She looked at me with *pity*.

How would Autumn Eyes look at me the moment I drove the dagger into her chest? Maybe she'd be angry that I stopped her pursuit to burn the world. Maybe it would be confusion I saw, dazed at the fact that I'd known about her plan all along. But what I saw in my mind, the look that was on her face when I imagined the moment...

Hurt. Gut-wrenching, soul-crushing hurt lined the features I'd already memorized, like the wound I would open between her ribs would be nothing compared to what I would do to her heart. How could I imagine this when I'd spoken to her only once? I could see it so clearly — her brows would furrow, her mouth would fall open and she'd look to her chest to see a dagger protruding and my hand around its grip. Would she fall to the ground at my feet? Would she rip the dagger from her chest and toss it to the side and clutch at the wound, trying to contain the Saints' blood that pulsed through her?

I hoped that with her last breath she'd turn the dagger on me. Because a world where I was the reason those eyes were forever closed... That was not a world I wanted to live in.

"I have to do this," I repeated to Aunt Berna, though the words I spoke were for me. *One life for the good of many.*

Aunt Berna's lips thinned and her stare lingered for a moment before she turned away, her skirts swishing across the marble as she marched for the door.

My gaze turned to Castemont, his face hard-set with resolve. His mouth opened to speak, but I threw a hand up. I didn't want to hear his voice, didn't want to look at his face a second longer.

"I'm going," I said quietly, my voice flat and emotionless. But cold, endless anguish rushed through me with every beat of my heart.

Chapter 29

I figured I could kill two birds with one stone with my first trip to Inkwell as the King of Widoras. I could check in on its residents, see where I could start trying to help, and I could monitor the Daughter of Katia. And I could make sure she healed okay after the explosion at Cindregala.

So... Three birds with one stone.

I told myself I didn't care if the wound on her forehead healed. She was going to die anyway. But it had been bad. There would no doubt be a scar left behind.

Castemont told me I'd probably see his spies lingering around Inkwell, and he wasn't lying. I recognized a dozen of the men he'd introduced me to as he explained *the plan*, and these motherfuckers were *bold*. When I passed Copper Street, the street where Autumn Eyes lived, I could see one of them standing right outside her house, making no attempt to hide the fact that he was staring directly in her front window.

I was in plainclothes, and it actually felt kind of good to be out of my leathers. I had a pouch of coin to hand out to anyone who may need it. And shit, every person I passed needed it. I prayed to every Saint that I wouldn't hear that woman's pleading screams again. I kept my head down, the hood of my cloak covering my face as I traversed the rough dirt streets of Inkwell.

"Me first," a snarled man's voice sounded from behind me.

I almost didn't look over, but then I heard it. "Please." Her voice was quiet and weak. It wasn't the same voice I'd heard coming from the Painted Empress, I could tell. But nonetheless, it was a woman begging. "Please, no."

"You took 'er first last time," another man answered. I turned my head to see the backs of two men standing side by side, just a few feet from the side of a dilapidated, vacant wooden cottage. "It's my turn."

"Please, just let me go." I couldn't see her, but I could tell she was trapped between the two men and the building. Shit.

I was moving, assessing the situation as I approached. Two men, each about six inches shorter than me. Slim. Wouldn't be a fight. That is, if they decided to be stupid and provoke me. "May I be of assistance, Miss?" I asked, peering over the heads of the two men to see the woman. She was a petite redhead, so thin she looked sickly. Her eyes were hollow. I knew she had no fight left in her. This wasn't her first interaction with these men.

"She's ours," the first man answered. Looked like he was choosing to be stupid. *Saints*, he looked like shit. Smelled like it too, with hair so greasy I couldn't tell if its true color was brown or blond. His crooked nose had been broken, maybe more than once. I could tell I wouldn't mind breaking it again.

"She's *mine*," the second man answered, and he didn't look any better. A massive scar ran from the left side of his forehead across to his right cheek. His lips were chapped and bleeding, and the teeth behind them were rotted.

I looked past them again, to the woman cowering before them. "May I be of assistance, Miss?" I repeated.

"Back the fuck off, mate," the first man growled, staring up at me, completely unafraid. "We had 'er first, and we'll have 'er again before you get yer turn."

I raised a brow, dumbfounded at the audacity. "Yeah? Is that what she wants? Because it seems to me that's not the case."

"Doesn't matter what she wants," the second man answered.

"What do you want, Miss? Would you like to lie with these men?"

She was silent, her ocher eyes the size of the moon as she quivered, just managing to shake her head. "No."

"Doesn't seem like she's interested, gentlemen. Time to go."

The first man approached me, puffing his chest as he stared up at me. *Fucking stupid.* "Doesn't matter what she wants," he said, repeating his friend's words. "I want 'er, so I'm gonna have 'er."

He spun back toward her, but I grabbed him by the shoulder. "No, you won't."

"Who are you to tell me what I can and can't have?"

My mouth turned up in a close-lipped smile. "I can't tell you that. But she can. And she's saying you can't have her."

I felt the cold metallic tip of a dagger pierce through my tunic, and looked down to see just that. The idiot had pulled his blade on me and genuinely thought it would end well for him.

"You sure you want to do that?" I asked, glancing down to the dagger once again before my eyes found his. They were bloodshot, his ruddy brown irises dull and dead.

"Absolutely, mate. No one takes what's ours."

"*Mine,*" the other man cut in.

I leaned in. "She's not yours, *mate,*" I whispered.

As if my words had snapped something in him, he thrust his blade forward. I was faster, though — so much faster, and it was nothing for me to knock the blade from his hand and wrap my arm around his neck, lifting his feet off the ground and squeezing just tight enough to make him choke.

His friend panicked for a moment, his eyes wide as he fumbled for his own blade in a sheath at his hip.

264

"Nice try," I laughed, my grip tightening on his neck for a moment before releasing him. His feet scrambled to keep him upright as he gasped for air. "You won't touch her again. Understand? As a matter of fact, you won't touch any other woman unless they explicitly ask you to, which, judging by your breath alone, will never happen."

He righted himself, swallowing hard as I watched feral anger flash in his eyes. He charged me — the dumbass fucking charged me, and before I knew it my hands were on the sides of his head, and I was wrenching with all my strength.

The man crumpled to the ground in a heap, eyes open, neck bent back at an angle I knew wasn't good. Oh shit. *Oh shit.* I'd fucking killed him.

The woman let out a horrified scream at the sight as her hand flew to her mouth. The man's friend jumped back. His face flashed from shock to disbelief to anger as he stared at me. "You've bloody *killed him!*" I fought to keep my breath even. I hadn't meant to kill him. "Constable!" he screamed. "Constable!"

No one in Inkwell even turned to look at the scene, as if assault and dead bodies in the street were commonplace. Even though I knew the constable wasn't coming, I had no desire to stick around. I leaned toward the woman, her face still shock-stricken. "Go," I whispered, taking the pouch of coins from my pocket and slipping it into her hand. She was frozen in fear. "Miss." Her eyes finally met mine, wild and terrified. "Take this and go. Out of Inkwell." It was more than enough to buy her a new life in another district, hopefully far away from the scum that still screamed out for the constable.

"You'll be dragged before the King and beheaded for murder," he snarled, saliva spewing from his mouth.

I let out a dry laugh. "I'm sure I will be."

"Yer goin' straight to Hell, mate," he spat.

"I'll be sure to save you a seat."

The man dropped to the ground over his friend, the grief seeming to hit him all at once. I tried not to let any guilt creep in as I turned to the woman who was still clutching the bag of coins in her hand. I gave her a quick nod, and it appeared she understood. She tucked the pouch into her cloak and bolted.

Good.

I walked away from the scene, thrill and guilt coursing through me. Even though his blood hadn't spilled, I still felt it drip from my hands. I needed to get out of Inkwell. This had gotten too real. I'd find Autumn Eyes another day. *Don't call her that,* I thought to myself. *Don't name an animal you intend to slaughter.* Around the corner, back to–

Shit. I'd collided with someone, and they were on the ground. "Watch where the *fuck* you're going," they spat, gathering themselves. They looked up, and it was...

It was her. Autumn Eyes. *The Daughter of Katia,* I corrected myself.

"You," she whispered, ire in her voice.

It made me smile for some reason. I couldn't fight it, but I was frozen like that, completely arrested by her stare. What was I supposed to say to her? "Didn't I tell you to be more careful?"

She stared at me unblinking for a moment, her eyes somewhere far away. Then she scrambled to right herself. I realized I hadn't offered her my hand. *What the fuck, Cal?* She was walking away, and I needed to stop her. I remembered the gash on her forehead. "Are you okay?"

Autumn Eyes spun to me. "What?"

I scanned her face again, looking for any sign of the scar that should have been there. "Are you okay?" I asked. "Were you hurt that day? In the explosion? In the stampede?" I knew the truth. I'd seen it with my own eyes. The wound had dripped down her face.

She stared at me like I had three eyes before looking me up and down. Her face contorted into angry disgust. "What's your fucking game?"

Shit. Did she suspect something already? Did she know I was after the Daughter of Katia? "I don't..." I stammered. She smelled like sweet citrus, and I had to keep myself from moving closer to

266

her. "There is no game. I just want to know if you're okay." That wasn't a lie. "You had a pretty nasty gash on your forehead." Also not a lie, even though it was nowhere to be found.

Her eyes stayed on me for what could have been an eternity. I relished it, the honey and chestnut and umber of her eyes keeping me locked in place.

"I'm fine, thank you," she said flatly and spun on her heel, immediately scurrying away from me.

"Wait!" I called with absolutely zero idea what I would say. Autumn Eyes turned back to me, her face unreadable. There was something about her, I didn't know what. Something about her gripped me by the throat and kept me staring. I thought of what to say and chose the first thing that came to mind. "What's your name?"

She raised a brow and continued staring. I could tell she wanted to ignore me, leave me on the dusty road, but I prayed to every Saint that she wouldn't. "Petra."

Petra. It meant *rock.* And shit if I wasn't stuck between a rock and a hard place. I realized she was waiting for my name in response. *Fuck.* We hadn't thought about this. What was I supposed to say? *Hi, I'm Belin Cal Myrin. But don't worry. I'm not* that *Belin Cal Myrin.*

"Calomyr," I spat out with a hand on my chest. That was believable, right? Bellsin would be my last name if she asked. Calomyr Bellsin. Thankfully, she didn't ask. "Do try to be more careful, Petra."

She spun on her heel and threw a hand in the air. "Watch where you're going, *Calomyr*." I let out a laugh, because I couldn't help it.

But I was afraid that I was fucked.

Chapter 30

I pushed through the front door to find an empty hearth, the house silent and almost pitch black. Something hung in the air, but it was nowhere near as noticeable as what was missing. The kitchen sat eerily empty, the only light coming from the fire lamps on the street, the house cast in shadow. No pots on the stove, no vegetables or meats on the cutting board, nothing to suggest my Aunt Berna was near.

Something was wrong.

"Aunt Berna?" I called. There was an unmistakable panic in my voice that I didn't try to conceal. "Aunt Berna?"

"Cal." It was a sound so quiet that had I not been listening for it I would have dismissed it as the wind.

My steps were urgent as I neared the ornate rug in the living room to see the shadow of a limp figure sprawled over the settee.

"Cal."

I fumbled in the dim light for the matches on the mantle, my hands shaking as I lit the first candle my hands could grab. The flickering orange light fell on my aunt, her petite limbs splayed out in a manner that sent nausea roiling through me.

My knees hit the ground, my hand frantically grabbing hers only to be met with skin so cold that it felt like I was holding the hand of Cyen, Saint of Death. "Aunt Berna," I breathed. Disbelief — I was in disbelief that the languid body in front of me was my vibrant, fiery aunt.

But deep within me, I knew what I was staring at. It was death, slowly creeping forward on his stallion, eyes locked firmly on his target. Inevitable. Inescapable.

Her lips parted, her breaths shallow as she tried to speak. "M-my Cal."

Tears flooded my vision and I did my best to blink them away. I had to keep the floodgates intact. "I'm here." I pulled her hand closer and leaned in. "I'm here. You're going to be okay."

She was not going to be okay.

Her lips contorted into something that looked like her familiar smile, an echo of an echo of the woman she was. She was fighting for consciousness. "N-no," she answered, her voice weak. "I'm n-not going to b-be okay." Every word was a battle. The pain and labor that came with each breath was a stake through my chest.

"What happened?" The truth, it seemed, was an unwelcome companion riding beside Cyen, making no attempt to hide itself.

She swallowed, her brows furrowing over closed eyes, her lashes brushing sallow cheeks. "Castemont. P-poison in my t-tea."

Silence overtook me first. The kind of silence that's so vast your ears start to ring. But then the rage came for my mind, body, and soul as his name rang through my skull. My teeth gnashed together, and it took everything within me not to clench my fist around her delicate hand as I stared at my aunt, the woman who'd given us *everything* only for that bastard to take it away.

But the rage dissolved the longer I looked at her. In the candlelight I could see foam at the corners of her mouth. Her lips were thin and gray. Her skin was pale and almost lifeless. I let the tears fall then in the face of the truth, uncontrollable and wild. She tried to smile again, and I did my best to return it as I stared down at the woman who'd loved us so, so well.

"Y-you were the..." She heaved in an arduous breath, the sound sending more tears from my eyes. "The greatest j-joy of m-my life. You a-and your brother. My boys."

I brought the back of her hand to my lips, selfishly using it to hide the devastation that I knew she could see in my face.

"I-I'm going to s-see Tobyas," she whispered, her eyes closing briefly.

"No."

"And..." Another strenuous breath shook her. "If I-I'm lucky, I'll m-meet your mother, too."

I bit the inside of my cheek as hard as I could. "No." It was all I could say. "*No.*"

She exhaled, the sound so drawn out that I knew her last breath was near. "It's okay, Cal. You're go-going t-to be okay."

"He's dead. Do you hear me? He's fucking dead the moment I get my hands on him," I said through gritted teeth.

One corner of her mouth turned up almost imperceptibly but quickly dropped. "Y-you won't do it."

"Have no doubt that I will kill him."

"No. You w-won't kill her."

I froze. She was talking about the Daughter of Katia. She saw right through me.

"Br..."

I exhaled as much anger as I could and tried to soften my grip on her hand. "It's okay, Aunt Berna," I breathed, though each word sounded almost as labored as hers. "It's okay, you don't have to say anything." I fought the shaking sobs that threatened to overtake my body.

"Brave." I could feel her hand try to squeeze mine as she spoke. "Br-brave, kind...and honest. L-like your Mama t-told you."

270

I had no choice then but to surrender to the pain. Her words carved my heart straight from my chest and clutched it with bare hands, still beating and bloody. The last bit of strength she'd been using to grip my hand slipped away as her fingers went limp and her eyes fell on a realm far past this one.

My head dropped back, the sob that came over me so powerful, so guttural that not a sound left my body as it racked through me, ravaging every corner of my soul. And I wished, for one selfish moment, that I could slip away with her, that I could leave behind this city and my reign and the agony that the Saints had dealt me in this life. I'd *finally* be with Tobyas and my mother again. Aunt Berna, too. And maybe, if Castemont succeeded in his plan, I'd see Autumn Eyes as well.

But I knew I couldn't leave this realm while *he* still walked it, while *he* still breathed the ocean air that Aunt Berna could no longer. And I knew what I had to do.

I was going to kill Lord Evarius Castemont.

Chapter 31

My eyes were focused only on my next step as I marched. None of the lords or barons bowed as I passed, because they had no idea the King was making his way through the castle in pursuit of one of their own. Grief had melded with acrimony and it pulsed through my every vein. It grew larger and more violent with each step that brought me closer to Castemont.

I stalked through the corridors of the Low Royal castle, turning the corner to find Tyrak exactly where I knew he'd be. It was a fight to get enough air in my lungs to appear just calm enough on the surface so as not to trigger Tyrak's internal alarm bells. "You deserve a drink, old man." I forced a tight smile. "I need to talk with Lord Castemont. Go on down to the pub."

The guard's façade broke, a sly smile breaking across his rugged face. "Twist my arm." He clapped a hand on my bicep as he left his post, seemingly all too happy to leave his Lord unguarded.

"Tell them to put it on the King's tab."

The moment he rounded the corner, I pushed through the doors of Castemont Hall.

Silence greeted me as I entered the foyer, almost the same silence that I'd walked into at my aunt's house. But I could tell that not all was still.

He was here.

"Tyrak?" the Lord called.

I made no attempt to conceal my echoing footsteps as I stalked through the cavernous hall toward his study, turning the corner to find the motherfucker perched at his massive mahogany desk, scrolls and papers strewn across its surface.

"Cal? What–"

I lunged, my hand closing around his throat as I leaned over the desk, completely dwarfing him as I pulled him to his feet. He sputtered, wide-eyed as he stared at me in surprise.

"*Why?*" I spat through a tight jaw.

He answered only with garbled choking sounds, his hands clawing uselessly at my grip. I pulled him over the desk by his throat, papers fluttering to the ground as I dragged his body across.

His eyes began to bulge from his head, and I knew I could kill him in one swift move. But before I sent him straight to the fires of Hell that waited beneath the Iron Rise, I wanted to know *why*. I loosened my grip enough for the air to rush back into his lungs.

"Tell me," I demanded. My voice was low and controlled, and I relished the fear it brought to his features.

He was gasping, trying to pull in as much air as he could while my palm still compressed his airway. "She...was...only...getting in the way."

I threw him clear across the room and watched as his body slammed into the dark wood walls. He landed on the marble floor, his head cracking against the stone, choked whimpers leaving his crushed airway as he tried to speak. "Th-this...is bigger than her, Cal." He pushed himself to stand, straightening himself as he pushed his shoulders back with a wince. "It's bigger than us."

I was moving before I knew it, the bastard pinned to the wall beneath my arm in an instant, my sword pointed to his chest. "You *killed* her," I seethed. "You murdered the woman you loved."

"She was compromising the mission."

I pushed my sword forward, the tip easily slicing through his surcoat, piercing the skin beneath it. His face contorted with pain as blood began to ooze from the wound that was begging to grow deeper. "Please, Cal. J-just hear me out."

My hand found his neck again and I slammed his head against the wall hard enough that the impact alone could have ended his life. I wasn't that lucky, of course, and I watched him fall into a daze, the bastard blinking hard, mouth opening and closing. I was feral with rage, my heartbeat like a war drum in my ears.

"Give me one reason I shouldn't slit your throat right now. One fucking reason," I breathed. The Lord didn't move, didn't change his expression. He stayed silent, his eyes on me as if any fear he'd shown was simply gone. "I am your King and you will do as I command."

One of his hands found its way into the pocket of his surcoat. If the fucker thought he was going to kill me, he would soon find he was sorely mistaken.

Instead he raised his hand to reveal a small vial, dark red liquid sloshing around inside — blood.

"Your blood," he sputtered.

I narrowed my eyes, his face unreadable as it began to turn purple. "My *blood*?"

"Kill me, and your blood will be sacrificed to the Darkness Beyond."

I laughed, the sound harsh as I threw my head back. "You're going to sacrifice my blood so I become a Bloodsinger like Umbri? Is that your plan?" The Lord stayed silent, his eyes only narrowing slightly as I held him within inches of his life. "You're fucked if you think I'm letting you out of here to get to Blindbarrow."

"Umbri has a vial of your blood already." Even though he was dying within my grasp, his face melted into a nauseating smirk. "You kill me," he choked, "Umbri pours that entire vial into the flame, and the Belin Cal Myrin you know will be *gone*."

"And how will Umbri know you're dead?"

The smirk deepened. "She's a Bloodsinger. The rules of this realm bend for her. She sees all. I give the command or die and you can say goodbye to the honorable and benevolent King Belin. I give the command or die, and you're a ghost."

Rage, anguish, and confusion twisted like vines around every fiber of my being. I breathed heavily through gritted teeth as I stared him down. "How?"

"You were sixteen." His voice had turned derisive. "The day I took you to the pub in Sidus. You were piss drunk and had a little fall. You remember, right?" His tongue curled around the word like a serpent as the scar on my leg throbbed. "I knew you wouldn't miss a vial or two."

The urge to lunge, to shove my blade through his ribs and to crush his windpipe beneath my palm was so strong that surrendering to it seemed inevitable. Damn the consequences. But it wasn't about me. The second my blood fizzled and sparked in that flame, my soul would forever be controlled by the Darkness Beyond, completely void of anything good, anything compassionate, anything *kind*. The world would suffer.

Autumn Eyes, *Petra*, would suffer.

Hands shaking, I pulled my blade back and released my grip. He straightened and ran a hand across the spot of his blood that I'd spilled on his surcoat, the liquid such a dark shade of crimson that it looked black. I inhaled hard, my mouth set in a hard line as I sheathed my sword and glared.

"I didn't want it to come to this," he murmured, pulling at his cuffs, "but you so quickly lost sight of what's at stake."

"You wanted to marry her," I snarled. "You would have if not for the law."

He scoffed. "There's no such law, Cal."

"*What?*"

"I could have married her if I wanted to. I didn't want to, but I had to keep her content in the meantime. Your emotions are compromising the mission, Cal. Of course, that means the Daughter of Katia's *human* father must die, and soon, because now I need to pursue her *human* mother to make up for your impending...*inadequacies*."

My eyes bored into him, but where there had been fear at the end of my gaze in the past, there was none. Just arrogance.

"You're going to bury your aunt in the Backwoods. No one will think to look for her among the poorest of Eserene's dead."

"I'll do no such thing," I snarled.

Castemont cocked his head, as if in challenge. Daring me. "We'll tell people she returned to Anicole."

"And you think they'll believe that?"

"They will," he continued. "I'm a well-respected member of the Court. Why wouldn't they believe me?"

"I will *not* lay her to rest in the Backwoods."

"The main cemetery is far too conspicuous." He took a step forward, eyeing me. "You wanted anonymity. You'll use it to bury her in the Backwoods."

I lunged. "You *bastard*–"

"Ah," he cut in, shaking the vial of my blood, taunting me with my destruction. He slipped the vial back in the pocket of his surcoat, a vicious smile twisting his features as he surveyed me. The smile deepened. "Bow to me," he whispered.

My brows furrowed as the words entered my brain, almost nonsensical. "Excuse me?"

The smile remained on his face, caustic and mocking. "*Bow to me.*"

Fury greater than anything I'd ever felt climbed up my spine. "You're *mad*."

"I give the command, and you're a ghost," he repeated, patting the pocket that held the power to ruin me.

Where I had been pulsing with resolve just minutes before, I was now drowning in desperation. I clawed at the banks of a bottomless river, frantically looking for anything that could save me from the current that was dragging me under. But there was nothing. Every single bit of any kind of salvation was planted just out of my reach.

Shoulders back, jaw tightened, I had no choice but to lean into a stiff bow.

"Lower."

Every muscle in my body tensed at the command. I lowered myself to my knees, every movement painful. The papers strewn about the room were now the only thing separating my hands from the marble floor.

A low, sinister laugh sounded through the study. "I own you."

Chapter 32

Two Years Ago

I forgot the sound of her voice. There were some days I thought I could conjure up an echo of it. A memory of a memory. But it was never enough.

"You get in, you collect Solise's things, and you get out. You are not to speak to Petra. Do you understand?"

I hated the way he said her name, like he was sullying her just by speaking it. Rage vibrated within me as I nodded at Castemont. I had to beg him to let me do this. I needed to see her, to hear her voice again. The glances from afar were not enough. Castemont's half-assed assurance was not enough. I needed to see with my own eyes she was okay.

The sole reason he wasn't forcing me to kill her now, at this moment, was that he didn't trust me to be alone with her, and a lord being caught at a murder scene wouldn't bode well.

"Do you understand?" he repeated more forcefully.

"I understand."

He stood a little taller and straightened his surcoat. "I've already killed Calomyr. I won't hesitate to kill Belin, too."

My breaths were shallow as I placed the helmet over my head to hide my face. I wore full armor along with it, everything from chainmail to gloves to two swords at each hip and two more across my back. I looked just like Tyrak, just as I'd intended. The only difference was the height. Tyrak was tall, but I was considerably taller. She'd have to notice the height difference.

Saints, I hope she'd notice.

Castemont had forged a letter from Solise's sister saying she needed her to come to Skystead immediately. His original plan was to have her killed — that was usually his plan for everyone with even the smallest chance of interfering with *the plan*. But I'd convinced him to lead her away, instead, and spare her life. I'm not exactly sure why he agreed to it, but I didn't question it.

My palms were slick inside my gloves and my stomach was in knots. I thought that maybe the horses that drew the cart waiting behind us could feel my nervous energy, because they were braying and pawing at the ground. Petra was just behind the thin wooden door. I was finally, *finally* going to be able to see her again.

"In and out," Castemont murmured again, patting his breast pocket to reinforce once again that he had my blood and could erase me in an instant.

He knocked on the door. "Come in!" I heard Solise yell from the inside. Time slowed down as Castemont pushed inside. My eyes wildly scanned the interior of the cottage, looking for those autumn eyes.

I paused in the doorway for a moment, my eyes falling on someone I hadn't been expecting. She was rail-thin, sinking into the rickety armchair. The clothing she wore was swallowing her whole. It looked like the sunlight hadn't touched her skin in years. And though she had brown eyes like Petra, they weren't the middle of autumn. They were the upturned dirt of a gravesite, the decomposed carcass of an animal in the forest. They were dead.

Then she looked at me, giving me a cursory glance before turning away again.

That wasn't Petra. That couldn't be Petra.

"Almost ready?" I heard Castemont ask Solise, but I was frozen, staring at a ghost.

"Just about," Solise replied. "Everything that's coming with me is there by the door."

I could almost feel Castemont's stare on me. Tearing my eyes from Petra, I began gathering Solise's things, just as Castemont had ordered, while disguised as Tyrak. My hands reached for a crate and I carried it out to the waiting cart as quickly as I could. When I returned to gather more of Solise's things, my eyes immediately found Petra again.

I did this to her. I turned her into a shell of who she was. Castemont may have killed Calomyr, and he may be trying to kill the Daughter of Katia, but I killed Petra.

Desperation surged through me. I wanted to pick her up like one of these crates — she couldn't weigh much more — put her on the back of one of the horses waiting outside and take her far, far from here. I wanted to build a house for us in the middle of a meadow of the most beautiful wildflowers she'd ever see, with a slow moving creek running through the middle of it. I wanted to fill that house with our children and teach them how to treat others. I wanted to grow old by her side, surrounded by the family we created for ourselves.

I wanted to give her the life she deserved, even if it turned out that life wasn't with me, even if she lived in that house in the meadow with someone else. It couldn't be with me, anyway. She loved Calomyr. Not Belin Cal Myrin. Calomyr.

Snippets of Castemont's words to Petra and Solise filtered through the noise of my armor-clad movements. He was telling them that he'd arranged an escort for Solise from Eserene to Skystead. That I — *Tyrak* — would transport her to the awaiting escorts at Eserene's city gates. Every time I entered the house I stared, trying to permanently memorize the features that had begun to grow fuzzy in my memory. The way her hair fell over her shoulders, even if that hair was now thinner and those shoulders were sharper. The way her profile looked against the fire that burned low in the hearth.

I took the last crate to the cart, and it took everything in me not to double over and wretch in the street. Castemont slipped out the door and shot me a stern glance. "You're welcome."

"You want to kill the Daughter of Katia?" I spat under my breath from behind the helmet. "You're going to get your wish, Castemont. She's wasting away."

"That's not my doing," he answered nonchalantly.

"If you're going to kill her then do it," I snarled. "Put her out of her Saints damned misery."

He sniffed and wordlessly looked over the cart, as if what I was saying was meaningless to him. "Get ready to go."

My jaw clenched at his order, but I once again had no choice but to obey. I forced myself to climb into the driver's seat of the cart and took up the reins as Castemont settled in next to me, leaning in to whisper in my ear. "Try something stupid, Cal. I implore you." I closed my eyes and listened for the creak of Solise's wooden door, when I knew I'd see Petra for the last time.

Sure enough, the healer slipped out and found her place among her crates and boxes on the back of the cart. Now that the time was here, I couldn't make myself turn back to her. I couldn't willingly look at her knowing it would be the last time I did. I snapped the reins of the horses and they began trudging forward, and the cart lurched as they pulled us away.

Dread rose in me as we neared the corner. This was my last chance to look back at her. I wished I could slay Castemont here and now. It'd be easy with any of the swords strapped to me. Then I'd turn the cart around and steal her away. Solise could come too. I knew that'd make Petra happy. I'd build the healer her own little house in the meadow with enough room for all her herbs and tinctures.

At the last moment, I made myself do it. I turned my head to see her standing in the street outside Solise's cottage, bony arms wrapped around herself. She looked so weak, though I knew she wasn't. I prayed to the Saints then that she'd find her fire soon and use it to incinerate Castemont. She had it in her, dormant and waiting to explode. I just hoped it'd be soon.

I managed nothing more than a quick nod. Had she even seen it? Was there any part of her that thought maybe it was me in here and not Tyrak?

The horses turned the corner, and as much as I wanted to stop them. I couldn't.

I had no choice.

PART III

Petra

FROM THE DEPTHS OF THE DEPTHS
OF A WALLED CITY'S SCUM
'NEATH THE HOLIEST MOON
THE PROMISED WILL COME

A DAUGHTER DIVINE
WITH BLOOD OF OLD CREED
AND THE WORLD WILL FORGET
THAT ON PAIN THE DEMONS FEED

HER BLOODLINE EXPOSED
BY HE WHO EXACTS PAIN
CURSED TO WALK THE REALM
WHEN EVIL COMES AGAIN

Chapter 33

The ram's head mask had fallen from Miles' head when he hit the dirt face down. I was crouched over him, his labored breathing the only sound in the forest as my eyes darted between the arrow in his back and Calomyr — *Belin*. Belin had shot Miles with an arrow.

"Why did you shoot him?" I spat through my teeth, slowly rising.

"Petra." My name fell from his lips as both a command and a plea. He stepped forward, concern on his face. "He had you against a tree. He was hurting you."

Raw anger clawed at the back of my chest. So much time I'd spent longing to look into those eyes again, so many years lost pining for the soul I thought had been the other half of my own.

But all I felt in this moment was pure, icy hatred.

I took a step toward Belin, a barricade between him and Miles. "He was teaching me to fight!" I hit my knees again, my hands landing gently on Miles' back. "Help him." Tears flooded my eyes.

"He had you against a tree," Belin repeated, sputtering. "He was–"

"Fucking *help him*."

The Lieutenant's face was still pressed to the dirt, his fists clenched in pain. "It's okay," I whispered. "You're going to be okay." I pulled his dark hair away from his neck. "You're going to be fine."

Belin kneeled down on the other side of the Lieutenant. "I need to snap the arrow," he told Miles.

The arrow quaked with every breath Miles took. "Do it."

Belin gripped the arrow's shaft as gingerly as he could. "On the count of three. One, two–"

Miles cried out in pain as Belin broke the arrow, leaving just a few inches sticking out from the wound. I blanched at the sound of his agony, desperate to take it away. I hated that I cared about his pain, suddenly longing for the old Miles, for the Miles who hadn't told me of his guilt, of the responsibility he felt toward my fate. It would have been a hell of a lot easier not to care about *that* Miles.

"He needs a healer. Help me turn him to his side," Belin ordered quietly.

"No," Miles moaned.

"The quicker you're up, the quicker we can get you to a healer," Belin answered.

"*No*," he repeated.

"It's going to hurt, but you have to do it," I said quietly, trying to sound as comforting as I could manage.

He took a pained inhale as his hand reached above his head. "Don't."

Realization suddenly hit me. "Miles, forget the mask."

He fumbled blindly in the dirt for the ram's head that was just out of his reach. "Give me the mask," he snarled.

"Why the hell does it matter so much? We need to get you to a healer!"

"He needs to get up," Belin said, his voice now urgent. "Just give him the mask."

"Get up," I demanded furiously.

"Give me the mask."

"Miles! *Get up*!"

Miles suddenly rolled to face Belin, his back to me, distressed breaths heaving through his body as blood poured from the wound and pooled in the dirt.

The Invisible King's stare hit the Lieutenant's face and he froze, eyes narrowing then flying wide. His mouth opened as he sucked in a silent gasp, his head beginning to shake.

"I..." Belin whispered with a choke, his chest rising and falling so quickly that I could tell he wasn't getting enough air. He shot to his feet, his eyes cemented on the wounded man who lay before him.

Still crouched beside Miles, my attention turned to him, my own brow furrowed in confusion. Miles carefully pushed himself to sit as pained grunts escaped a tight jaw, arms resting on bent knees and his head hanging between shoulders that seemed to sag with defeat. I stared at the man, his black hair still curtained across his cheek, his face still obscured.

Belin backed up, his head shaking as he continued to stare. I reached forward, gently tucking Miles' hair behind his ear. He didn't resist me, his face still downcast as I squinted at his profile. "Miles, look at me."

After an excruciating second he turned to face me, eyes as dark and deep as a midnight sky pinning me in place. Every feature was lined with pain, but his gaze was comfortable, almost familiar. I stared at the man, the strong jawline, the slight shadow of scruff smattered across it, the straight nose. He was handsome — more than that, Miles was beautiful. The angry scar peeked out from beneath his chin, his throat working beneath it. My mind scrambled, desperately grabbing for what was familiar about his face, what past life I'd known him in.

Miles' eyes diverted away from me, back to the Invisible King. Belin spun to face us, and that's when I saw it.

The cheekbones, the nose, their eyes — almost identical, except for the color. "Who are you?" I whispered, though I knew the answer already.

Miles' eyes closed tightly as his brow furrowed, bottom lip tight between his teeth as Belin slowly approached, towering over us, his face marked with hurt and confusion. "Tobyas?"

"Hi, Cal."

◆ ◆ ◆

Miles' arrow wound had slowed to a trickle while Belin stared at his brother in disbelief. Just like when he'd worn the mask, I couldn't read the look on Miles' face. So much of his own truth still lay hidden, buried by deception and the workings of an evil far greater than any of us could fathom. But the Lieutenant stayed quiet, letting his brother work through his own thoughts as he endlessly stared.

The Invisible King finally lowered himself to the ground, a gloved hand shakily reaching for the side of his brothers' head, his eyes brimming with disbelief and something else, something warm.

"It's you," he breathed with a quivering smile. Some sort of tension broke then, some unseen glass bottle that shattered into millions of pieces and released years of longing and heartache and sorrow. "How?"

I'd been with Belin's brother this entire time. I'd been with Tobyas, the little boy who'd died. The man who'd been a boy behind the mask, trying to decode the truth that followed him around for years. That's why Miles' touch had been uncomfortably familiar. That's why I could never quite relax.

292

"The cliffs," Miles started, his voice even raspier than normal, "I didn't fall. I was shot, ironically enough, with an arrow."

The cliffs. So what Belin had told me about his brother falling to his death had been true — or at least he thought it was.

"But how did you... *Where* did you–"

"I still don't know who they were. And I didn't know who they were working for until I put the pieces together," he answered quietly. "Kauvras' men. Or..." he stuttered, his face puzzled, "Maybe Castemont's men. They meant to kill me, whoever they were, but when they pulled my body into the rowboat and saw I was still alive, they just...didn't," he explained with a shrug.

Belin's head shook with disbelief, his molten gemstone eyes flashing with questions. "Why didn't you try to find me?" he whispered.

"When I fell, I... I landed on one of the rocks in the harbor." He pointed to the jagged scar that marred his throat. "Jolted me enough that I couldn't remember anything from before the fall. I didn't know who I was or where I'd come from."

"I didn't see a rowboat that day," Belin said, and I could tell the day replayed in his mind over and over.

"There was an inlet that couldn't be seen from the top of the cliffs, I think. It's all a bit fuzzy."

"And you ended up in Taitha?"

He nodded, then rolled his head between his shoulders and took a deep breath. "One of the men brought me to Taitha, yes. He told me my name, put me in an orphanage, and told me my parents died in a fire. For a long time I thought that was the truth. I didn't have memories of it, but I didn't have memories of anything else, either. I figured I'd inhaled too much smoke or hit my head and that's why I couldn't remember anything."

"*Saints,*" I whispered, my eyes shifting between the brothers and their striking similarities.

"I started to remember bits and pieces," he continued. "Just little things, like a random memory of our street in Eserene or the pastry shop we'd visit as kids. I heard there was a newly crowned king in Widoras, King Belin Cal Myrin. The name was familiar, but I didn't know why. And then one day I remembered her, our mother." His eyes were focused somewhere far off, the sorrowful ghost of a smile flashing across his lips before falling away. "And I remembered how she died. It hadn't been a fire at all. Someone had murdered her in front of us." His words were clipped, each syllable painful to hear. "Right?"

Something about the way he asked for confirmation tore a piece from my soul, as if some tiny part of him held onto hope that it wasn't true. That hope, that miniscule crumb that still remained was quickly brushed away.

Belin's brows turned up as he quickly looked away. "That's right."

Miles let a breath loose, nodding slightly, his eyes closing against his brother's words. "When is my birthday?" The question seemingly came out of nowhere, but there was pain in his tone.

Belin's eyes narrowed for a split second. "Two weeks before the first full moon of spring. You...forgot that, too?"

Miles nodded, unable to meet his brother's eyes.

"I should have looked harder for you," Belin whispered, and a part of my heart that had scarred over split again. In that moment, Belin hadn't hurt me, he hadn't lied to me, but rather he was the victim, *he* was the one I felt pain for. I sat with that feeling, didn't try to push it away like I knew I should have.

Miles shook his head. "You couldn't have known. Shit, I didn't even know." He winced in pain as he shifted and let out a long sigh. "I joined Kauvras' army as soon as I was old enough. That's what boys did when they got too old for the orphanage. And I just...went on with my life, sure that there were things I was forgetting but knowing I'd probably never get my answers. I'd considered seeing a Bloodsinger, seeing what they could tell me. In fact, that was the plan when I got back from Eserene."

"You didn't, did you?" Belin asked, concern evident in his words.

"No, I didn't. I didn't have a chance before I met Oh Holy One over here," he jeered, gesturing to me with a smile that was heartbreakingly Calomyr. "Figured since Kauvras could *talk to the Saints*, he might be able to tell me something without a blood sacrifice."

"And did he?" Belin asked.

"Fuck no," he laughed. "He's beyond mad. But the second I was brought before him and saw him up close, saw the color of his eyes… I remembered. I remembered you. Then I saw you in the throne room when you were dragged before Petra and I knew for certain."

Belin took a deep breath, his jaw working. "Does he know?"

"No. The mask stayed on. Like I'd intended it to," he answered. "I wasn't planning on telling you for a while, if at all. There was too much to figure out."

The sorrow on Belin's face quickly morphed into something like fear. "And Castemont? Does he know?"

Miles pursed his lips. "No, but…Castemont…" he murmured, trailing off as if he were testing the name on his tongue. He took a few deep breaths, trying to find the words. "Is he… He was around, wasn't he? He was the one who gave us the wooden swords?"

Belin was silent as he looked at his brother. His eyes flashed to me for a split second, the weight of his stare leaving me breathless. "Yes."

"And he's the one behind all of this." It should have been a question but it wasn't. It was a statement, heavy-laden with sorrow.

Belin nodded, his brows pinched and jaw tense.

Miles returned the nod, his obsidian eyes falling distant again as we sat in the stillness of the forest, a tense silence befalling us.

"You knew who she was?" Miles breathed suddenly, his head tilted toward me. "You knew she was the Daughter of Katia?"

I felt my heartbeat speed up. I wasn't ready to talk about this.

Belin's head dropped low, shame radiating off of him so heavily I swore I could reach out and touch it. "I did."

"Why did you…" Miles' voice had grown sharper, the air between them growing heated. "How could you knowingly lie to her?"

I bit my lip, nervous at the answer that was coming. "Miles, it's–"

"No," he cut in. "Let him answer."

With a clenched jaw, Belin stared at his brother. I froze, convincing myself that if I just stayed still, the conversation wouldn't continue.

"I thought…" Belin started, his voice trailing off, threatening to break.

Miles turned to me, assessing my expression the way he had in the pub, waiting on my word. All traces of brotherhood and love had left the air. My breath caught, my lungs beginning to burn under the pressure of the moment. I didn't know what to do or what to say.

Belin swallowed hard, a ruggedness to his expression that I couldn't place. "There's a lot I need to tell you. Both of you. But we need to get you to a healer."

Chapter 34

Belin had hooked the horn of the ram's head mask through a strap on his saddlebag, the metal bobbing against my ankle with every step, a constant reminder that I'd been with Belin's younger brother since I was taken from the castle in Eserene.

No one said a word for hours as we trekked through the forest on our way back to Taitha. I had so many questions, but my mind couldn't settle on one long enough for me to ask it before it skipped to the next one. Squeezing my eyes shut, I exhaled hard, trying to make sense of how we all found ourselves here.

"Are you all right?" Miles' — no, *Tobyas'* voice was low enough that Belin couldn't hear from where he walked behind us. I sat in front of the Lieutenant in the saddle, and until he'd spoken, the only time I even knew he sat behind me was when I caught a note of his oakmoss scent every so often. He was riding tall despite the arrow wound that I imagined pulsed on his shoulder. A low, unsettled fire smoldered within me, one that I made no attempt to extinguish.

"Absolutely not," I answered, the words dry. Miles' presence behind me had been a tiny reassurance, a small piece of familiarity in the turbulence. How ridiculous that the man I'd met just weeks ago, the man who'd turned me over to my enemy, the man I didn't know the identity of until just hours ago... He was somehow my lifeboat in a storm I'd done nothing to create. "I guess I should call you Tobyas now," I said, cutting my thoughts off before I could spiral any more than I already had.

He shifted uncomfortably behind me. "I still don't know who Tobyas is." Something like regret laced his tone. "Miles is good. Miles is...me."

I nodded, a part of me thankful that this tiny thing hadn't changed. "Miles it is."

"We're going to have to make camp, you know," he whispered quietly. The sun had grown dangerously low, but no one dared to be the one to suggest bedding down for the night. Not when the silence between all of us was so weighted.

I closed my eyes to the truth I was dreading, the awkward stillness that I knew would surround this campsite. Belin and Miles could talk all night, but at some point, I knew Belin would approach me. "I know." I craned my neck forward to look for an upcoming clearing in the trees but saw only dense, endless forest. Miles suddenly flinched behind me. "Are you going to be okay?"

"I've survived worse," he laughed. "Ready?"

"Never."

He cleared his throat. "We'll need to bed down for the night," Miles declared into the quiet forest. The horse came to a stop in the middle of a poorly designated trail, the brush dense and dark around us.

Belin began piling firewood in his arms without a word, kicking aside some brush to make space for a firepit. I threw myself into helping Miles, anything to keep from facing Belin. But still, agitation built in my chest as I helped the Lieutenant lean back against a tree trunk, careful to avoid disturbing the arrow wound. A fine sheen of sweat shimmered against his brow in the final

298

remnants of daylight. Even in his weakened state, he didn't need my help, but I appreciated the distraction, even if it was at Miles' expense. Did that make me a shitty person?

His brother. It was strange, to say the least. Absolutely fucking bizarre, to say the most.

The rhythmic clanking of the logs lulled me into a fragile calm as Belin arranged the firewood. I knew I could blow the calm to pieces at any second, knew that the flames inside me weren't far from igniting. As Belin reached into a pocket in his cloak and pulled out a flint, I laughed involuntarily.

He turned to me, a single brow raised, face otherwise blank. I held a hand out, quickly burrowing within myself to find that heat, and expelled a tiny spark from my hands that landed perfectly at the base of the logs.

Belin flinched, his eyes flying wide as the fire ignited. Miles let out a chuckle and I gave a slight nod before lowering myself to the ground, satisfied enough with myself that I smiled a bit, a part of me thankful that it'd actually worked and I hadn't burned the entire forest down.

But even if I'd leveled this forest into a field of ash and soot, I'd still have been the only one with the power to do so. No man could make the same claim. I was the one with the power, and I needed to make sure I remembered that.

◆ ◆ ◆

Stars peeked through the canopy of trees, and I stared. Just stared. The deep blue night was cloudless, the moon missing only a sliver of her face, the air mild. I let it fill my lungs, willed it to clear my mind of the smoke that had suddenly clouded it. Animals howled and screeched around us, the noises like nothing I'd heard before, not even in the Onyx Pass. But fear never entered my mind — it didn't have any room.

Miles slept just a few feet from me, the fragment of the arrow still jutting from his back as I watched the even rise and fall of his breathing. I begged my own body for sleep but knew it would be an unanswered prayer. There would be no respite from these thoughts. The minutes ticked by, my consciousness never waning. It had to be well past midnight now, but still I closed my eyes and let my mind run rampant.

"Petra," I heard from across the fire.

I knew better than to look. I knew what I'd see if I turned. But like a fucking idiot, I let my head drop to the side, let Belin's features materialize through the low burning flames. The light danced in his eyes like the crystal cave in Eserene, a bright spot among the darkness that cloaked the world. I basked in his stare, reveled in the fact that his eyes were on me. Because even now, even after everything, he was still the most beautiful thing I'd ever seen.

And it made me *angry* that I still saw him in that light, shot ire so deep into my core that it seeped out of my skin, trickled down my back. A thousand words passed between us in the silence, and while I knew my eyes betrayed the hurt that he caused me, his eyes betrayed the guilt that he caused himself.

This was it. It was time. Miles had gotten his answers. It was time I got mine.

I stood suddenly and brushed the dirt and leaves from my body. Without looking back I walked into the forest, knowing I was a far more dangerous monster than anything that could be lurking among the trees. I breathed a quiet sigh of acceptance when I heard the sound of footsteps behind me as I headed deeper and deeper into the trees, away from the fire and into the moonlight.

"Petra," he finally said, and I stopped in my tracks. The forest had gone still, even the wild creatures ceasing their roars and shrieks as if they, too, were settling in for the truth.

I spun to face Belin, his eyes crystalline, his face illuminated just enough by the pearly light to see pain etched into his features. My instincts warred with each other, half of me wanting to scorch him to soot where he stood, the other half needing to reach out and touch him, make sure he was safe and whole. My fists clenched painfully at my sides as the battle raged.

"First, I need you to tell me," I whispered, my fists releasing for only a moment, "was any of it real?"

I held my breath as something flashed across his face. Despite the tears that threatened to fall, my fire hadn't gone out. I didn't stop the burn.

Belin's mouth bobbed open and closed as he wrestled with the question. "Yes," he breathed, a sharp inhale following it.

I closed my eyes at the word, because I knew it was the truth. The fact that it had been real... I think that hurt me more than if it hadn't been, because it meant that a part of him had loved me and still made the choice to hurt me. A part of him loved me and still made the choice to lie to me. I didn't wipe away the tear that rolled down my cheek. I let him see it, watched the anguish it caused him as his eyes followed its trail.

"Since the beginning," he said quietly, "you were my priority. Not Castemont's plan. You."

"Don't," I choked out. "That's not true. Because if it were, I wouldn't be standing here right now. I'd be back in Inkwell with my family, where I want to be." My breaths came in quick heaves now. "I don't know what this *plan* was, but I know that you are one of the reasons I lost everything."

His head shook, despair etched in each of his features. "Before I met you, I agreed to Castemont's plan. Get close enough to kill you. And if I killed you, the realm would be saved."

My heart jumped into my throat, anger rushing through me hard and fast. "You were going to *kill* me?"

"No," he stuttered. "Well, yes, in the beginning, but then I met you and—"

"You were going to kill me," I repeated, my voice low, the flames burning hotter in my chest. I let them smolder to the surface, my hands beginning to glow with embers.

"I thought I was doing the right thing."

All at once, my fire died. There wasn't even smoke to prove that it'd been there at all. It was just gone.

The right thing. Hadn't Miles thought the same thing? Hadn't I thought the same thing? We thought that we were doing what was right, what would bring the most good. Right?

And who was the bigger fool? The one who did the right thing for the wrong reason or the one who did nothing at all?

The battle between hatred and longing, blame and forgiveness continued to tear me apart from the inside as I spun back to face him. "But you *died*. Calomyr died."

He gritted his teeth in frustration, fury setting his eyes ablaze. "I fell in love with you, Petra. That wasn't his plan."

"But how can you say that? How could you be in love with me and do that to me? Why didn't you tell me the truth?" My voice had raised, assaulting the quiet forest.

"It's complicated, I..." He took a step toward me and I instinctively stepped back. "The day after we spent the night in the castle, I told Castemont I was out." I fought a rising blush at the mention of the night we'd spent in the King's Keep, not knowing the whole time we were in *his* quarters. "I'd known from the moment I met you at Cindregala that I wasn't going to be able to kill you. The second you looked up at me... It was that moment I knew that I'd throw myself off the Cliffs of Malarrey if it would make you smile. I knew from *that fucking moment* that I would die for you. I'd die if it meant you would be safe. I'd carry the weight of the world on my shoulders, Petra, if it meant you'd be able to walk tall."

My gaze softened at the truth in his voice, the raw pain that he wasn't trying to hide. "I told him I was done," he continued. "Told him I was going to tell you the truth of it all."

"So he killed Calomyr."

"Yes, he killed Calomyr," he answered.

"Why didn't you..." I trailed off, too many questions fighting to be asked. He was the *King*, why couldn't he have struck Castemont down? Why didn't he just come back? Why didn't he–

"I'll explain everything, I promise. There are things I can't tell you right now."

The words made my anger flare. "Are you serious?"

"I shouldn't even be speaking to you, but I have to. It's worth the risk." I saw his fists clench and relax at his sides. He was telling the truth. Something was stopping him from explaining. "The day Solise left Eserene," he started, his words fast, "Tyrak wasn't the one to help her load her belongings and escort her to the gates."

I squinted my eyes at the sudden change in subject, but let my mind materialize the memory around me. We had been standing in Solise's living room. Castemont had arranged for guards to escort her from Eserene to Skystead to care for her sister. Tyrak... It had been Tyrak. I saw him with my own two eyes. He'd been shuffling in and out, loading boxes and crates onto the cart that waited in the dank Inkwell street. He'd looked back at me while he steered the cart away with Solise on the back. The guard had been in full armor, larger than life with gloves and a helmet that covered his entire head and–

I gasped. "It was you."

"I begged Castemont to let me see you for two years, just to make sure you were okay. He'd tell me you were fine, you were moving on with your life, but I needed to see you." He took a step toward me, and this time I didn't back away, let his familiar smoke and cedar scent permeate my senses for the first time in so long. "You were thin, *so* thin. And so pale." His throat worked as he swallowed hard. "I tried to show you the truth that I couldn't tell you. That's why I left your father's cloak in the cave for you to find. I was praying that it would be enough of a sign to make you question Castemont." He shook his head at the memory, the look on his face almost excruciating to see. "I had to try something. You were wasting away and it was because of me."

My head shook as I stared at him. "You..."

He took a cautious step forward. "I love you. And from the bottom of my heart, I'm sorry. I feel fucking stupid apologizing, because no words come close to expressing how sorry I am. But they're all I have."

My lip quivered and I did my best to keep it still as turmoil churned through every muscle. I wanted to close the distance, wanted so badly to fall into him, be consumed by him. There was a sincerity in his eyes that looked so real, so genuine. But...

"Tell me everything."

He paused, his tongue running across his lips, brows turned up. "I can't yet." I didn't like that answer, and he could tell. My arms crossed as I watched him. His voice grew quiet as he looked down at me. "But it'll make sense one day. I'm sorry, Petra."

I didn't push it. What was the point? How could I know this wasn't another lie? That even *this* wasn't a part of Castemont's master plan? That these *truths* he hinted at were not the cracks that broke Castemont's plans apart, but braces keeping the whole thing together?

I took a silent breath, willing my lungs to expand as if the action could pin my resolve in place and keep it from slipping away. "No."

His face flashed with confusion in the moonlight. "No?"

"No," I repeated, steadying my feet in the dirt, pretending it would give me strength. I clenched my jaw against the tears that once again threatened to surface. "I don't believe you. I can't believe you. I don't accept your apology, and I can't forgive you."

His chest fell with a pained exhale as his mind silently worked over my words. "I understand, but please know–"

"You don't know what it was like," I cut in, my voice sharp and biting. "You don't. Do you know what it did to me when he told me you *died?* Do you know how many nights, no, *years*, I prayed that the Saints would take me too so I could be with you again? You came out of nowhere and changed everything for me, and then you were gone. You don't understand, Belin."

The foreign sound of his name on my tongue struck something within him. I'd never said it out loud before now. He'd been Calomyr. Cal. I watched the name hit, absorb into his skin, rattle

304

around inside him. He opened his mouth for a brief moment, searching for something to say but coming up short. "I want to explain why, but I can't," he repeated. "I can't risk it. I can't risk your safety."

My scoff was loud enough to echo off the trees. "Okay, Belin."

He chewed his lower lip, unspoken words hanging between us, the air turning stale. I squeezed my arms tight across my chest, a feeble attempt to comfort myself. "We need to get back to camp," I murmured, my gaze breaking painfully away from the broken man in front of me as I pushed past him.

"I'll explain as soon as I can," he said to my back as I left him standing there. "I'll do whatever you want me to do to prove that I'm sorry."

I almost faltered in my steps at his words, but I trudged forward. *Don't,* I told myself. *You are a queen. You can't concern yourself with this game. He doesn't deserve your forgiveness. He doesn't deserve a moment more of your time.*

"I don't want your forgiveness," he called after me as if in answer to my thoughts. A tear escaped my eye and rolled to the corner of my mouth, the salty taste of yearning and regret spreading across my tongue. "But I want you to know that you are my reason for every breath. You are my reason to be here, my reason to fight, my reason to keep fighting. Unceasingly you, Petra."

Chapter 35

I awoke to the sound of something like gravel, something jostling and chattering–

"Miles," I breathed, sitting up straight and scrambling away from where I had been curled up on the opposite side of the fire from Belin. Miles' figure was still turned on his side, arms wrapped around himself. The sun had just begun to rise, the forest gilded in pinks and golds that set his black hair alight.

Before I had even reached him I could see that he was shaking, the arrow fragment sticking menacingly from his back. I pulled the hair from his face, his skin slick with sweat as his teeth rattled against each other. "Miles, are you okay?" I didn't even know why I asked. I knew the answer. His breathing was labored, his eyes squeezed shut in agony.

Belin shot up then, his eyes instantly clear and alert as he moved closer and pulled Miles forward. "The wound is infected. He needs a healer *now*."

We propped him up, the sun hitting a face that was gaunt and gray. *No.*

"We're half a day from Taitha," Belin said through gritted teeth as he hoisted his brother atop the awaiting horse. "I just got you back. I'm not going to lose you again."

I stayed silent as I climbed atop the horse in front of Miles, letting him lean against me. He didn't smell like oakmoss anymore — he smelled like death. His weight was no longer reassuring at my back but a rising pressure to save him. *You owe him nothing,* I reminded myself. That was true, but I couldn't let him die. Not like this.

"Just follow the trail. I'll be right behind you," Belin said, handing me the reins and slapping the horse on its flank. The animal broke into a gallop, the air hissing through Miles' teeth with every strike of hoof against dirt.

I kept my eyes ahead, letting hope bloom in my chest like my flames, letting it grow bigger, telling myself that Miles was going to be okay. Then the idea hit me.

"Katia," I whispered to myself. If Miles had heard me, he made no comment. "Katia, I don't know if you're listening." I felt awkward, unsure of what to say. "We need help. I don't know what you can do, but please, do something. *Please.*" I looked into the clear morning sky, no sign of any Saint, Benevolent or Blood. "You can't let him die. We need him. Can you heal him? Is that something you can do?" I spoke into the air, trying to discern if I heard an answer in the hoofbeats or the birdsong. "Or just keep him safe until we can get to a healer. Please, whatever you can do." I didn't know what else *I* could do. "It's me, Petra, by the way. Your daughter," I threw in for good measure. Maybe she didn't know my voice.

"Thanks," Miles whimpered from behind me. His voice was weak, and his weight grew greater against my back with every passing second.

"You're going to be okay."

◆ ◆ ◆

I squinted through the passing trees, hoping with everything in me that Belin knew what he was talking about when he told me to follow this trail. It'd been hours now. Then I saw it — the surface of a pond reflecting the early-afternoon sun, the same pond I'd woken up next to a few days before. It had the same peculiar ripples it did then, too, as if someone had just skipped a stone, though no one was near enough to do so.

"Petra!" I heard Nell scream, and relief flooded through me at the sight of her small figure waiting on the bank of the pond with Whit beside her. I watched their faces scan the newly unmasked Lieutenant as we neared, his slumped figure, the urgency on my face.

"We're here, Miles," I murmured back to the Lieutenant. The heat that radiated from his body was stifling, even through his leathers. I pulled the horse to a stop but stayed mounted, ready to ride into the burning city of Taitha to search for a healer.

A third figure I hadn't noticed rose then, and disbelief flooded my senses as they came into focus.

"*Solise.*"

As soon as Nell and Whit had their hands on Miles, I ran to the healer, my arms folding around her as sobs racked my body. "I'm so sorry," I cried into her thin shoulder, the sound muffled by her robes. "I'm so, so sorry Solise. You were brought to Taitha because of me. You were thrown in the dungeon because of me. It's–"

"Hush, child," she whispered into my ear. "Nothing to apologize for."

Reality rushed back in then and I pulled away, spinning to see Miles propped up on Nell and Whit's shoulders, the Lieutenant's dead weight pulling them down. "Can you help him?"

Solise laid the back of a wrinkled hand against Miles' forehead and nodded, noting his sallow skin and sunken cheeks.

Beads of sweat dripped off him in sheets as Nell and Whit lowered him to the ground, pulling him forward to expose the wound. She reached into her robes and pulled out a small vial before gently grasping his hand, his grip weak as she spoke to him. "You're going to be just fine, dear," she said quietly, the calmness that was Solise washing over me. "Can you tell me what your name is?"

His breathing was choked but he managed to push the words out. "M-Miles Landgrave."

"Okay, Miles Landgrave. Can you tell me where we are?"

"Forest."

She nodded and tipped his head back, emptying the vial down his throat. He sputtered for a moment before all of his features relaxed, the pain melting from his face immediately as Solise turned him to lay on his belly. "Arri root," she gave as a simple explanation. "I'm assuming someone has clean water?" Whit pulled a small canteen from his hip and passed it to the healer. "And I know at least one of you has a flask." Whit and I both looked to Nell, her face flashing with a poor attempt of innocence before she reached to her hip and handed it over with a sigh.

Solise began to work, quickly propping him on his side. How did she know we'd be here? How did she even know to come here? She carefully unbuckled the fasteners and peeled the leathers from Miles' skin, taking extra care around the arrow. The defined lines of muscles were evident even as his entire body was relaxed. There was the scar on his right shoulder from the arrow that had hit him when he plunged from the Cliffs of Malarrey. And there was the tattoo across his left shoulder that I'd seen in the Onyx Pass — two ships sailing past each other, now forever separated by what would be another jagged arrow wound.

Nell stared at Miles and whistled. "You did spend the night at the inn with him, right?"

My eyes flashed to her, mortified. Solise didn't look up from her work but raised a thin brow before reaching into her robes for a roll of bandages. "I didn't *spend the night* with him."

Nell shot me a knowing look then winced as she watched Solise wrench the arrow from Miles' back and quickly press the whiskey-soaked bandage to his skin. After a moment, she pulled it away to reveal a festering wound. I had to turn away to keep the bile from rising in my throat. Nell and Whit both groaned at the sight, and I cringed as I heard Solise uncork the flask again and pour more whiskey into the wound.

She gently lifted the Lieutenant's arm, coiling the bandages around his shoulder. Every move she made was careful, compassionate, and I smiled to myself at the thought that some way, somehow, I had Solise back.

"He's going to have a tough recovery. You got him back here just in time," she murmured. "The arri root will keep him unconscious for a bit and help lower his fever."

Tension I hadn't realized I'd been holding melted away from my shoulders as I felt my heart rate return to some semblance of normal. It seemed like everyone else relaxed a bit, too. "Thank you," I whispered.

Solise's eyes crinkled with a smile as she looked up at me, her hand finding my cheek. "Petra."

I folded her into my arms again, savoring the feel of familiarity. "How in the hell are you here?" I finally asked.

She exhaled a breath I could tell was heavy-laden with unspoken words. Her head shook slightly, as if she didn't know where to start. "Did King Belin find you?"

My chest tightened with what those words meant. "Yes, how did—"

"The dungeons," she cut in. "Castemont didn't think *everything* through, because King Belin and I ended up in cells directly across from one another."

My eyes widened as I stared at the woman. "So you know the truth."

"He told me everything he could tell me."

I lowered myself to the ground to lean against a boulder, my eyes warily on the Lieutenant who slept peacefully in the dirt.

Nell and Whit silently excused themselves as Solise found a spot next to me. A breath left my lungs hard and fast. "You were right about him."

"I was only right that something was *off*."

A humorless laugh escaped my lips. "Just a little off, yeah. But I did find Belin. Or rather, he found me. And his arrow found Miles." She nodded, staring at his limp figure. "Long, long story. He was behind us on foot. I'm not sure how long it'll take him to make it here."

The healer nodded, her eyes scanning the forest before turning back to me. "There are some things you should know." I turned to her expectantly, sure that nothing she could possibly say could shock me. "I believe I do have...*some* soothsaying abilities."

I blinked at her. Maybe she could shock me.

"Compared to my sister, Ingra, it's not much. I get small snippets here and there, whatever the Saints would like to show me. I have no control over what I see." She toed at the dirt beneath her boots absentmindedly. "It had been years since they last sent me a vision, Petra. *Years*." Her voice had taken on an exasperated edge as her eyes searched mine. "After the wedding, when some of Kauvras' men had turned on him and ushered King Belin out of the throne room, they came for me in the dungeon. They brought me to a young family who gave me shelter. But this morning, the Saints spoke to me again."

Had my prayer to Katia been answered? Had she sent Solise a vision? She must have.

The healer's eyes moved beyond me to where Nell and Whit stood on guard, their backs to us as they scanned the forest. "I saw two soldiers, Enella Augen and Sentos Whitley. They had been with you in Aera, yes?"

"Yes."

"I knew I had to get to them." Her face melted into a warm smile. "I had to sneak around through the melee, but I was able to secure a few herbs and tinctures," she motioned to her robes, weighted with the tools of her trade. "We crossed paths as they reentered the city this morning."

I smiled, so grateful to be in her presence again. But then her words sank in, my skin prickling with goosebumps as I recalled her words. "Melee? Still?"

As if on cue, Nell turned to us, the picture of the perfect soldier with a hand resting on the hilt of her sword. "It's bad."

"How bad?"

Nell looked to Solise, something unspoken passing between them.

"Tell me," I urged.

"Alright. I'm just going to say it. Aside from the small legion of soldiers appointed by Kauvras as guards, the residents of Taitha have all been given leechthorn," Nell said quietly, looking away.

My stomach bottomed out, my heart following along with it as my gaze moved between the healer and the soldier. "*No,*" I whispered.

Solise's voice was small as she spoke. "Kauvras' army of Vacants is now thirty thousand strong."

I shot to my feet, my hands tangling in my hair as my eyes squeezed shut. *No no no no no.* Summercut had convinced me to give a merciful, dignified death to ten thousand Vacants, a thought that made the bile rise in my throat and sweat form on my brow. I'd agreed to it, if only for the reason that the innocent people trapped deserved to be free, even if only by death.

But thirty thousand? There was no chance, not even a sliver of a chance. Even if I managed to push the guilt aside, the amount of sheer power it would take me to eliminate thirty thousand barbaric Vacants? It would be almost impossible.

All the conviction I'd built up within myself to take on the role of queen... It was all gone. "I can't do it," I whispered, my hands dropping to my sides. "I cannot do this."

Solise slowly rose, her robes pooling around her feet as she stepped toward me, brows furrowed. "None of that."

"Solise, I *can't*," I sputtered. "Did they tell you the plan?" My voice had grown louder as I pointed to Nell and Whit. "Did they tell you what they want me to do?"

"Yes," she answered quietly.

"And you think I can do it?"

"I think you have to try."

I stared at the woman, my jaw clenched as the breaths came and left my body with building heat.

But alongside the dread was the truth. I knew there was no other way. They knew that. The first step to defeating Castemont was defeating Kauvras. The only way to defeat Kauvras was to take away his strength, which was the Vacants.

And then we'd have to deal with Castemont. Noros.

"Okay," I murmured, defeat rolling through me like seasickness. I pushed it aside. If I had no choice but to do it, then I was going to do it right. "Fine. Let's make a plan."

Distant footsteps sounded and I swung my head toward the noise. Belin emerged from between the trees, his brow pouring sweat and his chest heaving. My stomach flipped at the sight of him, at the way his eyes found mine and scanned me from head to toe, assessing to make sure I was okay. But I shook his gaze from me. I needed it *gone*.

"Thank you, Solise," he panted, his eyes finding Miles' limp figure on the ground. "Thank you for saving my brother."

Solise's head whipped to me, confusion on her face. Nell and Whit went still.

"His name isn't Miles Landgrave," I said quietly. "His name is Tobyas Vic Myrin, and he died thirteen years ago."

Chapter 36

As Miles' eyes slowly fluttered open, Belin explained the identity of the Lieutenant. Solise's face remained stoic and unsurprised, as if Belin finding his brother alive more than a decade after he died wasn't at all shocking. Whit and Nell on the other hand... A minute didn't pass without a gasp.

I thanked the Saints that Miles was lucid enough to be a part of the conversation, and thanked them again when he pushed himself to sit up. "We need to get moving." He reached for a twig and began outlining a map in the dirt, only half-conscious but always the Lieutenant. "This is the shortest route from the edge of the city to the barracks. We'll cross the fewest guard stations," he said, drawing a line across the makeshift map of Taitha. "Kauvras will most likely have guards here, here, and here." He circled the locations, staring hard at the outlines in the dirt. "Those are the three major landmarks we'll need to cross to get to the barracks."

I followed the route he'd drawn out and tried to ignore Belin's intense gaze that had been on me since he realized his brother would be okay. "Are the barracks large enough to hold as many Vacants as Kauvras has now?" I asked.

"No, which means there will most likely be Vacants in regular buildings — homes, shops, anywhere he can put them. But I think it'd be a good idea to start at the barracks since there'll be a large number of them in one area. Easier for you to..." Miles trailed off. I didn't need him to finish the sentence. "We'll enter the city here." He marked a spot between the Taithan castle and the edge of the leechthorn fields. "As soon as we make it to the barracks, it's all yours.

My stomach soured further at the thought of all those people, of who was in those barracks. I tried to push the thoughts away, but they festered like Miles' arrow wound, hot and acrid.

"Petra," Solise said softly when she saw my face. "It's going to be okay."

"My mother," I whispered. A tear slipped from my eye and I didn't bat it away. No one said anything. I blinked the tears back as best I could, my eyes falling once again on the map as I cleared my throat. "And then we go to the castle?"

"By that point, Kauvras will know what's going on. That's your chance to do what you want with him," Miles answered evenly. Belin tensed beside me.

What I wanted with him? What did I want from Kauvras? An apology? An explanation? His life?

Miles looked at me expectantly, in the way I was getting used to. I looked around to see the same look on everyone else's faces, too. I had to ignore Belin's once again, or else I'd lose my nerve. "Alright," I muttered. "Rest up. We move at nightfall."

◆ ◆ ◆

The eeriness of a silent, torch-lit Taitha permeated my bones. The castle loomed overhead, still standing but badly scorched, keeping a wary eye on her empty streets. Houses and shops showed evidence of the violence that had torn through Taitha after the wedding, and bits of broken glass had been hastily swept to the side. Every window in the city, whether shattered or intact, was pitch black.

The soldiers that patrolled the streets were masked, each in full Cabillian armor, each outfitted with a sword at each hip and two more across their backs. I swallowed hard, the nervousness bubbling in my throat impossible to ignore.

Solise and Miles stayed back at the pond, despite the Lieutenant's protests. Belin's hulking figure stood in front of me, peeking out from an alleyway into the streets. I eyed him, trying to keep the bitterness and resentment and longing from intertwining and wrapping around my core. I needed to focus. Nell and Whit waited behind me for the signal.

All at once, Belin gave a quick nod and Nell and Whit sprung forward, their movements lithe and exact as they lunged from behind to split two patrolling soldiers' necks from ear to ear. I cringed, my stomach tightening at the sound of their bodies hitting the cobblestones, their lifeblood splattering. But there was no time to cower.

We clung to shadows as we made our way to the barracks. It almost felt like I was back in Inkwell, doing my best to be a part of the scenery so I could steal jewelry or fabric to sell, hoping to feed my family. Hiding came naturally, and I felt myself sink back into my old ways of being invisible. Back and forth across the streets we moved, patrolling Cabillian soldiers falling left and right as they died, unaware it was their former comrades that ended their lives. Every movement, every swipe of steel against skin injected anguish and dread deeper into my very soul.

I summoned the heat within me, finding it easier this time. It smoldered as I told myself over and over again that I could do this. But something else was happening within me too, like a slow-moving storm forming on the horizon.

Belin turned around and I froze under his gemstone stare. *Dammit.* Even in the throes of misery I was incapacitated by him. I forced myself to break the eye contact. His gaze flashed to Whit and Nell, the three of them exchanging a nod.

My stomach roiled with nausea as I fought against my instincts to run. I would walk in, light the place up, and leave. I didn't want to think about who was in there, didn't want to stick around to hear anyone scream. Then I'd do the same to every building on my way to the castle. Or at least I'd try, and pray to the Saints that my power didn't run out.

I was going to vomit.

All at once we were moving, the four Cabillian soldiers guarding the barracks taken by such surprise that the fight wasn't a fight at all. Four more bodies weighed on my conscience, and my companions stood watch as I pulled open the narrow wooden door of the barracks.

Buckets of clean water lined the front wall. They'd been forced to drink from *buckets*, like fucking dogs. Only a few torches lined the interior of the massive, dusty structure. Thousands and thousands of tiny cots were stacked three-high, their surfaces uneven with leechthorn-crazed inhabitants as far as I could see. The chamber was completely still and completely silent. I heard not a single breath, not a single rustle of bedsheets, only my own heartbeat and the voice in my head.

I took a deep breath, stepping forward as I burrowed into the sorrow that stoked the flames inside me. *A quick death.* That was the mercy these people deserved.

I could do it. I had to do it. *I had to do it.*

Something tugged at me then, some invisible thread tied around a rib. It tightened and yanked me forward. I tried to fight against it, tried to focus on my flames, but instead I found myself walking to the first row of cots, looking down at a small, blonde-haired woman. She looked peaceful as she slept, though I knew that the moment she woke, all traces of peace would dissipate like smoke in the wind.

But still, I let that thread tug me, let my hand reach out to push the hair from the woman's face, only to be greeted with a familiar profile.

My mother. Because of course.

I froze at the sight, staring at the woman who'd raised me. *Now or never, Petra. Give her and all of these people the dignity of a quick death.* I couldn't look anymore, had to separate the memory of her from her ghost that lay before me. I took a step back but I stumbled, the noise of my shuffling feet echoing throughout the cavernous chamber.

My mother shot upright, her stare blank as she turned her head to look at me.

Maybe she'd recognize me. Maybe I could save her. "Ma," I whispered.

Instead, her mouth split with a blood-curdling screech. Every cot across the entire chamber began to stir. My mother threw her legs over the side and stood, her face familiar but plastered with an unfamiliar rage.

No part of her recognized me. No part of my mother remained.

The stranger began to stalk toward me, her movements inhuman and malicious, her jaw hanging open in an unnatural way. She looked like she could tear me apart with ease. When was the last time she had a dose of leechthorn?

"Petra!" I heard Belin yell as he ripped the door open and saw what was happening. "Petra! Now!"

I scrambled back, trying to right myself and conjure up my power as the rest of the Vacants rose from their cots. I couldn't get my feet under me as my mother backed me toward the wall, came closer, too close–

Her hand closed around my wrist, her skin cold and clammy, her grip unnaturally strong. I let myself burn then, a tear fizzling to steam on my cheek as my mother pulled her hand away with a pained screech. "I'm sorry," I whispered as she stumbled back.

318

In no time she lunged for me again, her eyes glassy and crazed as she swiped a hand at me. I did everything I could to muster up my power, to end it right then and there, but only sparks came to the surface as thousands of Vacants closed in on me.

Her nails caught my bare forearm as she screamed, my skin splitting beneath her preternaturally strong strike and her hand coming up bloody. I fell back, crashing into a few of the buckets of water that stood against the front wall.

I scrambled back to my feet and she froze — her movements stopping entirely as her arms dropped to her side. The other Vacants advanced still, faces etched with rage. But my mother remained motionless, blinking hard, her gaze suddenly meeting mine. She raised her hand to her face, my blood gleaming on her fingernails as her eyes went from her hand to me. "Petra," she whispered.

"Ma?"

"Petra, what's happening?"

A single drop of blood fell from her hand to the puddled water on the floor that had sloshed over the sides of the buckets, realization hitting me at the exact time it made impact. I grabbed her by the shoulder and shoved her toward the door, screaming out. "My *blood!*"

Just then a Vacant lunged at me, a gray-haired man with deep set wrinkles. His attempted blow missed me but his wrist collided with the wound on my forearm. Recognition flooded back into his eyes as he blinked, wide-eyed and confused.

Belin's head craned around the door again, his eyes flying wide as he realized what was happening. "Get out! Take Ma with you!" I screamed over the mayhem as I let another Vacant lunge at me. "I have an idea!"

Vacants snapped and swiped and screamed then turned human again as my blood hit their skin and I backed toward the door.

"It's my blood!" I screamed to those who were landing back in their bodies. "My blood is healing you!"

Understanding washed through those who were now human, and they turned to smear my blood on everyone they could reach. I watched, the momentary hope dashed by dread as I remembered there were thousands upon thousands of Vacants. I didn't have enough blood in my body to heal even a fraction of them.

My eyes flashed through the barracks, desperately looking for a solution as my blood began to dry on those I'd managed to touch. I saw the buckets of water and the puddles that had spread around them. If I added my blood to the water, would it be too diluted to heal people on contact? It could work, maybe. But there was still the issue of actually making sure it came into contact with every single Vacant.

The storm I felt within me had grown closer, demanding my attention. What was it? For some reason, my mind flashed back to the pond in the forest where I'd awoken after Oxblood Outpost, where I'd reunited with Solise. The surface had been disturbed, but I couldn't tell why. What if...

I stared at a puddle, willing it to move, to do something, anything as the now-humans shuffled out and more Vacants moved toward me. I burrowed deep within myself, looking for something that was different from my flames. If my flames were fury, then water, or some semblance of it, would be calm. Steadfast.

A deep breath rushed into my lungs. I blocked out the Vacants and their screeches. I blocked out Belin's stare, separated it from where it was stuck to my skin. I was alone in my mind. My thoughts were silent. My fury was nowhere to be found. I was calm.

There. One of the puddles rippled, almost imperceptibly. Maybe it was a trick of the light. Maybe it was the movement of the Vacants. But it was enough for me. I had to try.

I pulled my blade from my hip, bracing myself before running it across my wrist, sprinting to the first bucket and letting the blood flow from my veins. The drops fell across the surface and sank, spreading like crimson ink. All the while, I clung to that miniscule sliver of calm within me that'd made the puddle move.

"Petra!" Belin screamed from the doorway. "What are you–"

"I need help!" I screamed, desperately trying not to lose the bit of calm I was conjuring up. "Take the buckets and throw them over as many people as you can."

Confusion crossed his face, but he listened, grabbing the first bucket and heaving it forward. *Please. Please work.*

He managed to douse maybe a dozen Vacants, each of them pausing then exhaling as they turned human again. It was *working*, but there was only enough water in each bucket to turn the Vacants who were directly in front of us. I ran down the line of buckets, spilling enough blood in each one that the water went red. In the midst of the chaos, I was clinging to the steadfast power that I could feel growing within me. Maybe it was Idros, Saint of Storms, guiding me here. But if it wasn't his doing, I prayed that maybe, just maybe, he could let me borrow his power, if only for a moment. Belin followed behind me, and it was working, but it wouldn't be enough, and I could feel the blood loss begin to set my head spinning.

Calm down. Think, Petra.

Cold sweat began to seep from my pores as I made it to the last bucket, the calm beginning to slip away. "Stop!" I called to Belin. "It has to be quicker!"

Belin stepped back, his eyes wild as he tried to figure out what the hell was going on. I stared at the water in the last bucket, my blood still diffusing through it. I centered myself again, slowed my breathing, and willed the water to move, ripple, slosh over the sides. *Something.*

"Petra," Belin warned, drawing his sword as the Vacants came nearer. I ignored him, sinking deeper and deeper into the solace of my mind.

Please.

Nothing. The last of the clear water went red, my haggard reflection looking back at me. I'd been mistaken. Whatever I thought I found in myself wasn't there at all. I'd wasted time and blood thinking I could save every Vacant.

Belin's eyes were still on me, and I nodded to him in defeat. He sheathed his sword and reached for the last bucket, heaving its contents through the air. I told myself that any Vacant saved was a triumph, forced myself to find peace of mind in that—

The bloody water stopped midair, hovering over the Vacants closest to us. It just...stopped.

Belin's face melted into shock, and so did mine. But I kept centered, my vision focused on the red-tinged water that floated just above their heads. *Holy shit.* I raised a hand, willing the water to rise higher in the air, and it followed.

Who was this? Idros, Saint of Storms? Onera, Saint of Miracles? Frankly, at the moment, I didn't care who it was, because ultimately it was me who was doing this. I raised my other hand, silently commanding the winds to rise along with it, the water beginning to spin and twist as a whirlpool formed in the air above us. Faster and faster, because if what I was thinking was possible, this could actually work.

Blood loss and power exertion were hitting me, but I couldn't stop, not yet. I willed the water on the ground — the water that had already been thrown — to rise, and it obeyed, joining the whirlpool, making it grow and expand, hovering over the crowd of the Vacants that remained in the barracks. The power that rushed through me now felt like a river, cold and clear and serene on the surface with a raging current waiting beneath. Quiet, steadfast power.

I did it. I'd unlocked whatever it was within me. This was a *furious calm.*

Thunder crashed outside, the ground shaking with the noise. It was like a command. I dropped my hands and all at once, tiny droplets of bloody water rained down. Even though my blood had been diluted, the screams and screeches of the Vacants stopped, replaced by a shocked silence. But I didn't have time to revel in the victory as I remembered that there were Vacants throughout the entirety of Taitha, that the Vacants in the barracks were a fraction of what awaited me.

My feet were moving before I knew it as I bolted out the door. The night sky looked like crushed charcoal, angry clouds rolling in from every direction, the moon and stars nowhere to be seen.

"What's going on?" Nell shouted over the raging thunder.

I didn't answer, instead looking straight to the sky, wondering how the hell I was going to accomplish what I was planning to do next. But I didn't have time to think. I pulled my blade once again, running its edge across my other wrist. This cut was deeper, and I flinched at the pain as I watched the blood run down my forearm and drip off my elbow.

"This is what I need to do, isn't it?" I screamed to the clouds.

The city shook with thunder as lightning forked across the sky, and I lifted my arm, sending my blood flowing to the clouds on the wind I commanded. The liquid bubbled and twisted as it rose higher into the sky, the lightheadedness unending as I lost more and more blood. This was *insane*, but it could be just insane enough to work.

As the edges of my vision began to go murky, I let my arm drop. I couldn't hold it up any longer. The clouds swallowed my blood, a low rumble of thunder sounding over the city as the people I'd already healed filed out of the barracks.

The clouds churned angrily, the smell of oncoming rain hitting my nose. *Please let this work.* I nodded my head, and the sky opened up with rain, dropping so heavy that it almost hurt my skin. I just prayed to the Saints that it had been enough.

As if on cue, doors opened on both sides of the street, Vacants bursting out of cottages and townhomes and shops after hearing the commotion outside. I watched as they stumbled back into their bodies, realization hitting them as they stood in the rain, every trace of leechthorn suddenly gone. I knew the same thing was happening on every street in Taitha.

My knees hit the ground. It worked. Somehow, some way, it worked.

With that knowledge, I let the head-spinning exhaustion overcome me, wishing with everything that I'd soon hear the voices of Katia and Rhedros.

Chapter 37

I opened my eyes to blackness. *Yes, exactly where I'd hoped I'd be.*

"Katia? Rhedros?" I pushed the words out through a dry throat.

"We're here," Rhedros answered, his booming voice anxious.

"It's him, isn't it?" I asked frantically. "The Saint of Pain?"

Only silence answered me for a moment. "The Saint of Pain walks among you, yes."

Anger swept into me. "Care to explain, Rhedros? Isn't Noros one of *yours*?"

"It's not as simple as that," Rhedros said. I heard an inhale, the sound echoing through the nothingness. "There's a delicate balance between good and evil. The world can only exist in equilibrium. As long as there is good in the world, there must be evil." I wanted to argue, but he was right. "The bones of benevolence, the things that make up the very core of goodness itself, are evil."

I tried not to scoff at his non-answer. "So it's him? Castemont is Noros?"

There was silence once again before Katia spoke. "The Saint of Pain walks among you."

"What, you won't give me a straight answer, either?" Neither responded. Maybe... "You *can't* give me a straight answer, can you?"

"It's a misconception that we're the ones in control," he explained, seemingly ignoring my question, not a lick of evil in his tone. "Humans, they're the ones in control. We're simply here to mediate, give a nudge if we must, to keep the balance in check."

Katia's voice sounded, the warm, familiar lilt surrounding me. "As long as there are humans, there will be war. There will be pain, and there will be death. But there will also be love," she answered, "and life, and salvation."

I didn't miss the fact that their responses were not answers. "I need you to tell me what's going on," I said, my voice hoarse but laden with authority.

"We're sorry, Petra," Katia answered, her voice breaking. "We tried to protect you from this. We tried to give you a normal life."

"I don't know how much time I have here until I wake up, wherever this place is. I need you to tell me what's going on," I repeated.

Rhedros cleared his throat. "We've been imprisoned," he stated, his tone even and unemotional.

"Imprisoned?" I questioned. "By Noros?"

"The world is going to burn, Petra," Rhedros replied, his voice almost labored. "The forces I preside over are necessary to keep the balance. But the world will burn when they grow too strong, and they have grown far too strong."

A shiver crept through the nothingness, holding me firmly in its grasp. Castemont was responsible for this imbalance. "Where are you now, exactly?"

"Somewhere in space and time, caught between the Saints' realm and your realm. Somewhere in the Darkness Beyond," Rhedros said evenly.

"Petra," I heard a breathy voice say. Belin's voice was getting louder, the blackness around me growing more muted as I began to wake up.

"He put us here. You're the only one who can free us," Katia urged.

I tried to shake my head that seemingly didn't exist. "How can I free you?"

I heard him inhale as if he had to fight to get the words out, the sound echoing through the darkness. "You need to eliminate as much evil as possible, Petra. The Saint of Pain walks among you. Find him."

Eliminate as much evil as possible.

"Petra, love," Belin's voice broke through the darkness like a thunder crack, the nothingness around me dimming as I felt myself regaining consciousness. I railed against it, needing just one more second.

A warm hand cradled my cheek, and I leaned into it involuntarily as I felt my eyes flutter open. Gemstone eyes stared down at me as Belin's face came into focus, the concerned faces of Nell and Whit peering down from behind him. I shook him off, pushing him away, willing myself to separate from Belin and the unwanted comfort he brought me. Hurt flashed on his face as I continued to blink, willing my eyes to adjust.

Solise and Miles were here, and they stood over me as well, the concern on their faces melting into relief as I looked back at them. "Sorry," I murmured to Miles. His skin was still paler than normal, and I could tell he wasn't feeling completely like himself again. "I would have healed you if I knew I could."

"Too little too late," he answered with a smirk.

"Well, you kind of still look like shit." Without thinking, I fumbled for the blade at my hip. "Come here."

"Saints, Petra, you don't have to–"

"Shut up," I interjected, pricking my thumb on the tip of my blade until a bead of blood welled out. I reached for his hand and pressed my blood into his palm. We all watched as the color returned to his cheeks and the dark circles beneath his eyes lightened all at once.

I smiled to myself with pride. *I could heal people.* And I could kill them, too — not a bad combination.

"Thanks," Miles said almost absentmindedly as he drew circles with his wounded shoulder, a look of amazement on his face.

Solise's grin was the validation I didn't know I needed, and I let myself take just a moment to revel in it. A dull murmur, almost like a crowd of people, rang low in my ears, the silvery gray of the earliest morning hours hanging in the sky.

"You saved them all, Petra," Nell whispered then let out a chuckle. "That was by far the most *badass* thing I've ever seen."

I felt myself land in my body once again. We were still just outside the Vacants' barracks. Raindrops dripped from roofs and gutters.

My eyes flashed to Miles, the truth suddenly front and center in my mind. "You were right. It's him. He's the Saint of Pain."

Belin's hand found my shoulder, but I pushed it away, shooting him a warning look that I know everybody saw. "Noros? What do you mean?"

"Castemont..." I knew when I said the words, everything was going to change. "He's really Noros, Saint of Pain."

Silence fell, wide eyes staring at me. "How do you know this?" Whit asked, his tone apprehensive.

"Because I–" I stopped myself. Do I tell them? "I spoke with Katia."

Eyes flew even wider and mouths dropped open. "You *spoke* with Katia?" Nell whispered.

"And Rhedros." I had to tell them, needed help to make sense of all of this. "Because he's... Rhedros is my father."

I let them take the words in, could almost see the words sink into each of their brains from where I sat on the cobblestones. Whit's voice broke the silence. "Oh."

Belin's stare was heavy on me but I couldn't bring myself to meet his gaze, to meet the disbelief I knew would be there.

"I don't know what that means, the fact that he's my father. But we need to free them from the Darkness Beyond, wherever that is." My voice was low as I tried to sort through what I'd heard. "They said in order to do that, we need to eliminate as much evil as possible. If we don't, the world is going to burn."

Solise let out a quiet gasp. "The world is going to *burn?*"

"They told me that Noros, Saint of Pain, walks among us, and I need to find him. That's all I know."

Solise stirred, and Miles' body tensed as let out an apprehensive breath. "The Darkness Beyond," he murmured.

"What is that? Where is that?" I asked.

Belin had tensed, too, his jaw clenched so tight that I listened for the sound of cracking bones. "It's nowhere. It's... I don't know. It's just *beyond*. Beyond this realm."

Shivers ran up my spine at his tone. "That's where they are, and they need me to save them."

Miles shifted where he stood. "So the rest of the prophecy was right?" Everyone turned to him. He looked around to see questioning eyes. "There's a lesser known part of the prophecy. *Her bloodline exposed by he who exacts pain, cursed to walk the realm when evil comes again.*"

All eyes landed on me. "Miles thought that maybe Castemont was Noros, Saint of Pain, considering he knew my true identity, and the fact that he has an affinity for inflicting pain. Now it's confirmed." I swallowed hard, unsure of what exactly this meant as I looked around at the faces staring down at me. "I don't expect anyone to follow me on this quest. I'm going to guess it's a suicide mission."

"I'll follow you," Nell answered immediately. "No question."

"I will, too," Whit added. "Of course I will."

Miles gave a grunt. "I'm in."

"Look at that," Nell crooned. "All Lieutenant Sunshine needed was a little rain."

Miles rolled his eyes. "Yeah, yeah. The Penumbra, or whatever. Cal?"

"I can't think of anything else I'd rather do." I fought the rising blush in my cheeks, the humiliation that came with his words. I felt like everyone was staring at me for the wrong reason.

"I'll help wherever I can, dear," Solise added, a warm smile on her face.

I returned the smile, but it only lasted a moment before I felt the weight of the world pressing in on my chest. "I suppose I'll be needing that army, then."

"Well between all able-bodied men and women of Aera and the Vacants in Taitha," Miles started, "your army is already at least forty-thousand strong."

My eyes narrowed on his. He looked past me and nodded, and that's when I turned. The dull murmur of a crowd had been just that — a crowd, *the* crowd of former Vacants who were human once again, their faces illuminated by torchlight, every one of their eyes on me as their murmuring fell silent.

I pushed myself to my feet, staring at the thousands of people who could fit on this section of the street. "Forty thousand?" I whispered to Nell who had taken up a spot beside me.

"It worked," she answered. "Whatever you did, however you conjured up the ability to move water and command rain... It worked, Petra."

My stomach turned a bit at the thought, but I swallowed it back as tears flooded my eyes, my mind overwhelmed at what this meant.

The silent crowd waited patiently, some of their faces tear streaked and smiling, others stone faced. I caught my mother's eyes in the front of the crowd, her face beaming with quiet pride. Something inside me pushed me forward, a force I was becoming well acquainted with. I didn't have to take Nell's advice and act like I knew what I was doing anymore. I finally knew.

"People of Taitha and beyond," I began, my voice booming, echoing off the buildings that lined the streets. I was only addressing a fraction of those who awaited me, but I knew word would travel quickly. "I am Petra, Daughter of Katia, Keeper of the Benevolent Saints." I took a deep breath, the truth clawing at my throat, begging for escape. "And... I am the Daughter of Rhedros, Keeper of the Blood Saints."

Shocked gasps rang through the crowd as I let my words settle. My mother's eyes widened as she stared at me.

"The Keepers, my parents, have been imprisoned by Noros, Saint of Pain."

Whispers began to rise and so did the feeling of panic rippling from the crowd. I took a deep breath, pushing away the feeling of dread that had found me. I was a queen. There was no room for doubt in me.

"Noros, Saint of Pain walks the realm in a human body. Hear this now, and hear this clearly: Lord Evarius Castemont of Eserene is Noros, Saint of Pain." Cries rang out. I could taste the bitterness of fear hanging in the air above the crowd. "He must die, and it is my responsibility to kill him in order to free Katia and Rhedros. This is crucial, as they are responsible for keeping the balance of good and evil in the world."

Silence fell again as the echoes of my words faded. "In order to do this, I need an army, and I do not ask this lightly. I need an army that is strong and loyal and fierce. One that will stand for me, fight for me, and die for me if called to do so. If not for me, then for the good of the realm." I swallowed hard at the words, knowing that it was impossible to grasp the magnitude of what I asked of them.

Utter silence blanketed the street, thousands of eyes glued to every inch of my skin. "Each of you has been held against your will, captives to leechthorn and soldiers of Kauvras. I will not force you to fight for me. Your days as a captive are over. Each of you is now free to go should you so choose."

I didn't let my stare rest on any one person, terrified that if I stared too long, I'd see every person before me turn away. I took a shaky breath. "But should you choose to stay, I will do everything in my Saints given power to keep you safe. I will do whatever I can to make sure that you return to your families, whole and unharmed. Should you choose to join me, the Daughter of Benevolence and Blood, know that there will never be a cause more noble, a cause more true, or a cause more crucial to the fate of the world. Noros *must* die."

The last echoes of my words died down, the fragile silence returning. Small movements stirred the crowd as a few people filed out, their free will leading them to a life without leechthorn and warfare and pain. I smiled internally at the thought, at the fact that even though they were turning down my plea for help, they had the right to freedom, a right I'd unknowingly never truly had.

The sound of hooves on cobblestone sounded then, and I whirled to see three masked men on horseback emerge from an alleyway, settling to face me in front of the crowd. The man that led the group carried a flag emblazoned with the crest of Cabillia — a gold dragon on jet black fabric. Flames rose in my chest at the sight as one man prodded his horse forward.

"Daughter of Katia," he stated, his voice low and authoritative. "King Kauvras of Cabillia has requested a meeting with you."

Nell stepped forward, hand on the hilt of her sword. "Fat fuckin' chance."

"Your court is welcome to accompany you, and you have his vow that no member of your party will be harmed."

My court? *My court.* The people that stood around me now. I clenched and unclenched my fists as I stepped in front of Nell, shooting her a look to say I had it under control. But did I? Yeah, I did. At least I was going to act like I did. But how could I believe Kauvras' promise to cause us no harm after I just freed his entire army, right under his nose?

I took a deep breath, steadying my feet. "I accept. We'll arrive at nightfall."

Surprise rippled from my companions — my *court*, but I did my best to ignore them.

"Very well," Kauvras' soldier answered with a nod, and the three men turned on their horses and disappeared in the alley-way again.

I turned back to the crowd that awaited me. "Go, be with your families. Shelter will be provided for you should you not be from Taitha, or should you find your home destroyed." Guilt bubbled up inside me. "And prepare for war."

Chapter 38

It had been a whirlwind of people falling to their knees in tears, chanting *Daughter of Katia*. Introductions were made — more commanders and generals and lieutenants, farmers and merchants and more. A group of seamstresses told me they'd sew a dress for me to wear to the meeting with Kauvras, a dress that was fit for the Daughter of the Saints.

I stood in the street with tears in my eyes as I watched Commander Summercut's arms wrap around his wife and daughter. He'd found them. His eye caught mine, and a smile the size of the moon lit his face as he walked toward me with his family.

"Your Majesty, this is Averyn, my wife, and Miri," his voice wavered with tears, "my daughter. Averyn, Miri, this is Petra, Daughter of Katia, the reason I get to see you again."

The two women were teary eyes as they dropped their heads and held closed fists across their chests. "Daughter of Katia."

I couldn't contain my smile. "It's an honor to meet you."

My eyes caught on something in Miri's hand. *My diadem.* I gasped as she held it out.

"I kept it with me, your Majesty. After the Outpost," Summercut explained, his voice soft. "Forgive me for passing it off to Miri. She was fascinated by it."

She placed the diadem in my hands. "I'm fascinated by it, too," I replied with a laugh.

"Thank you," Summercut started, "for finding another solution. I'm glad you didn't listen to me."

I lowered my head, and the look in his eyes was enough to set mine watering. "Go get something to eat," I said. "Enjoy this time with your family."

Summercut bowed and backed away, his wife and daughter absolutely beaming, leaving me a sniveling mess in the street.

"Wipe those tears, your Majesty," Nell quipped as she emerged from the crowd, a sly smile on her face. Whit followed close behind. They stood beside me, looking out on the crowd. "Can you believe it?"

I let out a deep breath. "No, I can't."

"You heard what Kauvras' little dog said back there, right?" Whit jeered. "He called us your *court.*"

I nodded and didn't fight the smile that rose. "He did."

"What do we need to do to make it official, then? Swear our lives to you?" Miles interjected, joining the group with his brother at his side. The smile instantly melted from my face in Belin's presence, the conflicted feelings bubbling up inside me.

I pushed my shoulders back. I could ignore those feelings. I did my best to force a smile. "I think you've all done enough."

It wasn't meant to be sarcastic, but Belin still shifted uncomfortably. I supposed he'd be an asset to my court given his knowledge about Castemont's plan. I told myself that was the only reason he would be any part of my court.

"The Invisible King, a part of another queen's court?" Nell remarked. "Interesting."

"I'll be whatever she needs me to be, whether it be king, sworn sword, or cup bearer."

Nell gave a contented sigh. "Your Majesty," she sketched a bow. "Your court."

"The Penumbra," I smiled.

"Petra," I heard a feeble voice say from behind me, one that was quiet but rose above the dozens that were chattering nearby. I knew who the voice belonged to before I turned toward it, knew who I'd find waiting for me.

"Hi, Ma," I whispered, tears involuntarily flooding my eyes as I stared at the woman, the blonde hair and icy blue eyes, so much like Larka, and so unlike my own. The Penumbra suddenly found better things to do.

I could tell that she'd been wrestling with what to say in this moment as her own eyes filled. I pulled her against me, her body quickly overtaken with sobs. "I didn't know," she choked out between breaths. "I didn't know."

My lungs filled almost uncomfortably before I released the breath and pulled away to stare at her. "I know. But I have questions." She mustered up a soft smile and nodded.

We'd managed to find a small pocket of quiet among the bustling crowd and sank to the ground, our backs against the rough stone façade of a Taithan spice shop. Silence befell us for a moment, the air between us strained and uneasy.

People rushed by, so entrenched in their tasks or their joy or their freedom that they didn't notice us sitting on the side of the street. A woman walked by, clutching her small daughter to her chest as she navigated the crowd. I smiled as she nuzzled her cheek against her daughter's head.

"You're still my mother, you know," I said quietly.

I heard a breath enter her nose sharply as her fingers absentmindedly ran across a hole in the thigh of her tattered brown trousers. "I had no idea," she whispered. "I don't even know *how*, unless..." She trailed off, and I let her gather her thoughts. "I gave birth that night," she began, her voice low and even, as if she were trying to convince herself. "I gave birth to a baby. The same wispy blonde hair as Larka." It sounded as if she were trying to convince herself rather than me. "But I do remember..."

"What?"

"I remember after a few hours, you fell asleep. Larka was asleep upstairs, and so your father and I dozed off. And when we woke up..." Her eyes narrowed, her head shaking as she sorted through memories. "I remember noticing that your hair was darker, much darker than Larka's. Still wispy, but darker than I'd first thought. It was a difficult labor. I figured it must have been the fatigue of childbirth."

"So I was switched at birth." A statement that should have shocked me, but didn't in the slightest.

"I don't know," my Ma answered, her head hanging between her shoulders, her voice so sorrowful that it rang through to my core. "I just don't know."

I leaned back, letting the sun hit my face. "The Bloodsingers told Castemont the Daughter of Katia would be born in Inkwell. Maybe they didn't mean *born*, but *borne*, as in... I was a product of Inkwell."

My mother let out an exasperated breath. "I should have known," she whispered to herself. "But you were my baby." Tears streamed furiously down her cheeks. "I'm sorry. I was never a good mother to you or Larka." Her voice was small, but the words shot through me with a sudden power. I hadn't ever expected to hear the words leave her lips. I hadn't even expected her to be sorry.

My first instinct was to tell her it was okay, to forgive her. But even though I'd come to the conclusion that forgiveness was what made us human, I couldn't forgive her. I sat with that feeling, the foreign, bittersweet taste it left in my mouth. I'd always told myself she'd done her best, but what if the truth was that she hadn't? I was the one who had to provide for us. I was the one who agreed to go through Initiation so she could marry Castemont. It always fell on me.

"Where is he?" she asked then, her tone changing from sorrowful to something hard, something angry. Flames crackled beneath my skin at the thought of Castemont somewhere out there, probably in a tiny village with a bag of leechthorn, a pipe, and a growing army headed to hide behind Eserene's walls.

"He escaped."

Her head shook, fists clenching in the fabric of her trousers, knuckles going white before she let out a heavy breath. "I was so stupid."

Guilt washed through me then. "No," I answered quietly. "You weren't stupid." I took a deep breath, my eyes falling on Belin, his arms crossed and face hard as he spoke with Summercut. "You were in love."

She didn't respond, and the silence settled between us. There was a lot I was angry at her for. She hadn't fulfilled her role as a mother when I needed her most. She'd forced me to make impossible decisions to ensure our survival. She'd turned hollow and despondent and left me no space to grieve. But how could I fault her for it when she wasn't even my real mother?

"You have a court," she murmured suddenly.

The world began to creep back in, and I let it drown out everything else. "I suppose I do." An involuntary laugh escaped my chest, and I saw Belin shift at the sound.

"He didn't die," my mother said, her tone unreadable.

I shook my head, running my tongue across my teeth and sighing. "No, he didn't. He was the Invisible King the whole time. King Belin Cal Myrin." My mother's eyes flew wide. "Roped into Castemont's plan."

Weren't we all?

Belin knew we were talking about him. I could tell by the way he stood — his eyes were on Summercut, but his body was turned just slightly toward us. His head suddenly whirled to me, eyes locking me in place as he approached.

338

My movements were not entirely graceful as I pushed myself to stand and reached down to help my mother up. Solise appeared, coaxing my mother to go with her and catch up on the years that had passed. Belin's shadow swallowed me. I wouldn't feel small. I wouldn't let him affect me.

"What you did was incredible, Petra," he said quietly, head dropped just slightly. His eyes didn't meet mine and I was thankful for that.

I hated these conflicting feelings. Wanting him so fucking desperately but hating him for what he did. At least...I *wanted* to hate him.

Larka would have smacked me in the back of the head if she could hear what I was thinking. "Get your shit together, Petra!" she would have said. "You're going to let him make you feel this way?"

"Thank you," I answered sternly, my shoulders back as if good posture could make me feel better about these fucked up thoughts.

Chapter 39

The first time I entered the Taithan throne room, I erupted into an explosion of fire and wind behind the very doors I now stood before. I'd shattered windows and incinerated guards. I'd heard the voice of Katia, Keeper of the Benevolent Saints, speaking to me and me alone. Hours later I'd marched into the same hall, dressed in a wedding gown, holding a bouquet of fire. Then chaos ensued when an arrow landed in Kauvras' shoulder and the first domino of my command fell into place.

We stood in the antechamber outside the throne room, the members of my court spread protectively in front me. Nell and Whit stood side by side ready to lead us through the doors, their hands on the hilts of the swords they'd been given by one of the Taithan blacksmiths. The blacksmith had outfitted the court in armor so dark it swallowed all the light. He'd even managed to pry the Cabillian crest from their breastplates. There hadn't been time for the blacksmith to forge a new crest, but the message was clear: Kauvras was no longer in control.

Belin stood next to Miles just before me, their hands also on the hilts of their swords, their faces chiseled with formality. The Myrin brothers standing side by side… They were a sight, a formidable force, intimidation pulsing through the air around them. They radiated authority, strength, *death*.

I exhaled the weakness that remained within me, hidden in the fractures of my soul, and inhaled power. I was fire. I was wind. I was the storm. I was the Daughter of Benevolence and Blood.

I made sure none of the guards could hear me when I spoke to my court. "Nothing about Castemont's true identity. I want to get a read on the Rebel King first." My court nodded in understanding, their faces hard set and ready.

Kauvras' echoey voice sounded from inside the throne room. "Bring the lion out."

The guards reached to open the doors, but I pulled my hands back, willing the wind to sweep the doors open as if a hurricane had suddenly blown in. The guards jumped back as the doors crashed against the stone wall, the sound echoing through the antechamber like a fanfare.

Kauvras' eyes went wild at the spectacle as I was led in by my court. Nell's voice cut through the echoes of footsteps. "Presenting the One True Queen of Astran, Petra, Blood of Old Creed, Daughter of Benevolence and Blood."

I kept my shoulders back, letting the power of the titles propel me forward as we neared the Rebel King, perched on his throne of carved stone. Belin's movements were stiff as he stood before his father, but Kauvras' eyes looked past him, locking on me.

Chin high and heart pounding, I beheld the Rebel King.

"My beautiful wife," the man said giddily as his stare roved my body.

"If I remember correctly, there was no kiss to seal the union." I tried to stand a little taller. "I'm nobody's wife."

He sat back leisurely, amusement on his face as he regarded my court, his eyes catching on Belin. "And my son," he said, his voice going softer. "Giving up your own throne so easily to serve another?" I waited for him to notice the resemblance between the brothers, but if he saw it, he made no mention.

Belin's shoulders squared and Miles matched the movement, the two of them an impenetrable wall of muscle and grit. "I'd gladly give up any throne to serve my Queen." Heat flashed through me at his words, my stomach tensing and knees locking. *No, Petra.*

"I see you've trained him well already." His gaze was uncomfortable, something preternatural about the way his eyes moved. "It couldn't have been difficult though, given you look like *that*."

I cocked my head, a bolt of annoyance cleaving through me as I took a step forward. "Are you suggesting that the reason I've found myself in this position is not my divine power, but the way I look?"

Kauvras let out a chuckle, a knowing smile setting his face alight. "Men will do a lot for a great pair of tits."

Steel rang as Belin lurched forward, pulling his sword from its sheath, poised to strike his father. Not even a second passed before the guards on either side of Kauvras found a defensive stance. Tension even greater than before pushed against the walls as the men stared at each other, each daring the other to make a move.

"I serve Petra because she is the rightful ruler of all of Astran," he spat through a tight jaw. "I serve Petra because she is the rightful ruler of the entire realm."

Kauvras looked unbothered as he stared at his son, at the broadsword he had raised in front of him. He gave a curt nod to his guards, the men resheathing their blades and stepping back. Belin's tense figure remained for an extra moment before relaxing, though he dropped his sword to his side, leaving it unsheathed and ready.

"I've heard you've amassed yourself an army," Kauvras cooed after a moment, turning back to me.

"Your army."

342

"Magnificent." His face broke into a smile, something un-hinged and unstable about the expression. "You truly are a queen in your own right."

I furrowed my brows at the man. He didn't seem angry. He didn't seem even the least bit irritated. His face was etched with that same childish wonder it had been since I met him. "You no longer have control of the Vacants," I stated, each member of my court tensing in anticipation of what could come next.

"I heard," he answered nonchalantly, unbothered.

Nell's head turned just slightly, and I knew what expression would greet me if I could see her face. Belin, Miles, and Whit would all have the same look.

"You're not angry?" I asked, trying not to betray the confusion I felt.

Kauvras sat back, a laugh erupting from his throat and echo-ing off the throne room walls. He looked almost sane in this mo-ment. "Angry? I never wanted an army. I even tried to outlaw the use of leechthorn. I simply wanted peace for Cabillia. I wanted to make the world a better place as the Saint of New Beginnings, as Savior of the Realm. The Saints told me it was possible." He crossed an ankle over his knee, his hand propping his chin up like we weren't discussing the fact that I just dismantled his entire military. "It was Castemont's idea. I was just his puppet."

I almost rolled my eyes at the name. Of course it was Caste-mont's idea. "You know his true identity, right?" I asked. I felt everyone in the room freeze, waiting in anticipation for Kauvras' answer.

"I have an inkling." I raised a brow at the Rebel King. "A man can be only so obsessed with the words of a prophecy before the people around him begin to question the meaning behind them."

"And you went along with his plan," I stated, not a question. "You did the bidding of the Saint of Pain."

Kauvras leaned forward, all traces of sanity gone, his eyes once again too wild, his movements too jerky. "I didn't have a choice, sweetheart." The smirk that marked his face was expectant. What was I missing?

Belin's voice sounded from behind me. "A Bloodsinger." He stepped up beside me, his lips pressed into a hard line as he faced Kauvras again. "Castemont took your blood too, didn't he?"

The Rebel King sucked his teeth, the veins in his neck protruding, his eyes falling to his lap where he picked at a loose thread that wasn't there. "Well aren't you perceptive?"

"Unbelievable," Belin whispered. "Un-*fucking*-believeable."

Confusion rocked me, but I kept silent, observing the interaction between father and son. Kauvras' smile was too wide as he stared back at me. "That's what Castemont does. He wants to be ruler of the realm, and he'll do anything to achieve that. The throne of Widoras is only the beginning."

The Saint of Pain as ruler of the entire realm...

Belin's shoulders visibly tensed. "So that's why he tried so hard to get me to the throne. Not because he wanted me to find Petra and kill her, but because he wanted the throne for *himself*. He wanted me to get rid of the only person who had a legitimate claim to the ultimate throne." His words were clipped, almost like they were painful to speak. "Then I'm sure he would've usurped my position. I was a stepping stone."

"We all were," I remarked, my eyes meeting Belin's to see a pain so deep that it looked like a blade had been driven through his heart. Resolve settled within me suddenly, steady and calm. "I'm done."

Everyone in the throne room turned to stare at me. My bones began to grow hot, the energy vibrating through me like the earth was shifting beneath my feet.

"I'm *done*. He's ruined countless lives. No more," I fumed. I knew he needed to die, but now it felt real. My teeth gnashed together at the thought of him sitting in the highest turret of the Eserenian castle, surrounded by the Vacant army he created, the Vacant army he now commanded. "I have in front of me the monumental task of finding and saving my mother and father. He is going to complicate that ten-fold. It has to be now."

Kauvras cocked his head at my words. But he didn't question what I said about Katia and Rhedros like I figured he would. "What are you proposing?"

"I'm going to Eserene. And I'm going to kill him."

Silence fell again as Kauvras surveyed me, his normal look of instability falling away, a flash of something thoughtful showing for a split second. "And how will you get to him?"

"I know my way around the city."

Belin faced me, lips pursed. "You'd be captured at the gates, Petra," he said quietly. "And even if you weren't, there's the matter of actually getting to the castle through his legion of Vacants."

I pushed aside the conflicting feelings that were so fucking strong and considered his words. "Then we march on Eserene," I declared. "We march on Castemont and rip him out at the root."

A laugh echoed through the throne room as Kauvras threw his head back. "You want to march on the walled city?" I didn't answer him, his bellowing laughter filling the throne room, grating against my nerves. "Even with a larger army, victory is almost impossible."

"Then we lay siege," Belin answered, nodding as he turned from his father so that his eyes bored into mine. "If that's what my Queen commands." I felt his words in my very core. *His Queen.*

I nodded in agreement. "We have to try. Life cannot go on as long as Castemont continues his conquest for the realm."

Kauvras cocked a brow. "You mean to sacrifice an entire army to end Castemont's life?"

I stared at the man with Calomyr's eyes. "He won't stop." I stepped forward. "You know better than I do that *he won't stop.* He's the Saint of Pain. You know what's going to happen if we don't eliminate him now." My voice lowered as I stared at the Rebel King, stepping up onto the dais, directly in front of him. "He's going to keep building his own army of Vacants. He's going to work his way across the continent until he makes his way back here. Every single person in this room will fall victim to leechthorn, except for me. And we don't know if the people I've already freed can fall victim to leechthorn again. That is not a question I wish to know the answer to, and that is not a future I have any desire to witness. He is going to impede my true mission of finding and freeing my parents."

"The problem, dear Petra," he started, his tone bordering on patronizing, "is that if Castemont dies, my blood will be sacrificed."

I furrowed my brows. "And why would that be a problem?"

He shifted in his seat, a trace of worry lining his eyes as he sighed. "The woman, no, the *demon* who has my blood has been ordered to sacrifice it to the Blood Saints should Castemont meet his demise."

"I'm not understanding."

Belin stepped up on the dais next to me, his eyes set hard on his father. "Umbri?" he asked. Kauvras gave a curt nod to his son as he seemed to search his face, unease radiating from both men.

"Can somebody please tell me what the fuck is going on?"

"How familiar are you with Bloodsingers?" Belin asked.

My stomach turned at the word. "What are you getting at?"

Belin's eyes flashed from his father to me, creased with concern. He inhaled sharply. "That's the mark of blood magic, right? Pale skin, black hair, bodies like skeletons." He shifted uncomfortably, searching for the words. "It goes beyond that. If you keep sacrificing, keep pushing, the Darkness Beyond will go for your soul. Your morals, your character, anything you value. All gone. Once it's taken your soul, you're out for yourself and yourself only."

Alvar hadn't mentioned anything about this, only about the loss of beauty, as he'd call it. But Alvar hadn't seemed evil, at least not in his interactions with me. "So if she sacrifices your blood, then..."

Belin's chin dipped in a slight nod. "Evil will overtake me completely. And...him, too," he murmured, gesturing to his father, uncomfortable addressing him by any title. "If we want to kill Castemont—"

"We have to retrieve the blood from Umbri, first," I cut in, my eyes closing in frustration.

Belin nodded. "In Blindbarrow."

Kauvras' sapphire eyes stared up at me, and somewhere deep beneath the layers of insanity and madness and craze, I saw it. There was a man trying to claw his way out, buried by delusion. Maybe he'd stood too close to the burning leechthorn one too many times. Maybe the power had gone to his head. Maybe he'd indeed heard the Saints speak to him and went crazy trying to hear them once again.

In that moment, I did something I never thought I'd do. I let the question form behind my lips and didn't fight it as it entered the air between us. "Will you join me?"

Belin's entire body jolted beside me at the question as I stared at Kauvras, the familiar unhinged look rising once again in his features. "Will you be my bride?"

Shit.

I didn't turn to see the expression on Belin's face, didn't turn to see those of my companions. Instead I kept my eyes fixed on the Rebel King, spoke to that tiny sliver of normality peeking through a storm of lunacy. "I will not. I will, however, help you make the world a better place, if that's truly what you wish. You will not have the title of Savior of the Realm, nor will you be the Saint of New Beginnings, but you can be a part of something far greater than yourself, for the good of the realm."

A long moment passed, my heart pounding against my ribs like a damned mallet as I awaited his answer. He was going to decline, or come back with impossible conditions. I could feel it.

"I accept."

The surprise was so profound that I wasn't sure how I didn't fall to the floor at his answer. I managed to keep my composure, simply giving a small nod. "Thank you."

I didn't know if it was a good idea. It could have been the worst mistake I'd ever made, but with Kauvras as an ally... Maybe he could help us. He probably knew more about the inner workings of Castemont's mind than any of us.

Belin returned to his place at Miles' side, hand once again resting on the hilt of his sword, eyes pinned firmly to me. "We can't march the entire army to Blindbarrow before we lead it to Eserene. Castemont had spies everywhere within Eserene's walls. I wouldn't be surprised if he had some in Blindbarrow. They'll send a raven the second you arrive, and that'll give Castemont time to prepare. When the time comes, the army must march straight for Eserene."

"I'd be happy to lead your army to Eserene on your behalf, your Majesty," Whit declared, the formality so unlike his normal amusing self that it took me a moment to realize what he was saying. "I can get them safely through the Onyx Pass."

Nell stepped forward. "I'll help."

I nodded, suppressing a shudder at the thought of the Pass. "Thank you. Anyone who is able and willing to fight, bring them. Leave the elderly, the children, and anyone unable or unwilling. My mother and Solise will stay here in Taitha." I nodded to myself at the half-plan I'd made. "I suppose the rest of us will travel to Blindbarrow."

Miles stepped forward, the Myrin brothers standing like pillars on either side of me. "The smaller the group, the better. If all hell breaks loose and if for some reason you can't fight, you'll need someone there who is able to strike down Umbri. I'll escort you, your Majesty."

"You're not going without me," Belin interjected, raw possessiveness not hidden in his tone. Something carnal rolled up my spine, the feeling quickly spreading to every limb as I fought to tamp it down.

348

Miles surveyed him, and something unspoken passed between the two of them. "Very well," he answered. "The three of us will travel to Blindbarrow for Umbri."

"Then to Eserene for Castemont," I added.

Kauvras smiled, assessing his son where he stood, but his stare finally, *finally* fell on Miles, his smile slipping and eyes narrowing as they flashed back and forth between brothers. "This isn't..."

Miles stepped forward, the picture of a perfect soldier. "Lieutenant Miles Landgrave. Formerly..." He hesitated, the façade of a lieutenant falling away for a split second. "Formerly Tobyas Vic Myrin."

Kauvras' face softened for a moment as he stared at Miles. "Somebody told me Arimara had a son. A second son, apparently." Miles' only answer was a small nod as the man stared at him, his face quickly becoming unreadable once again as he sat back. "You know, your father is the reason she's gone."

Shock rang through each of us as the words echoed off the cold stone walls and settled at our feet. The Myrin brothers were statues, both of them so still that neither appeared to be breathing. "You know who my father is?" Miles asked, his voice not betraying what I knew was brewing inside him.

"I do. But your father has no idea who you are." Kauvras' face morphed into something sinister, a smile forming that was cunning and wicked, not the man who'd agreed to be my ally mere moments ago. "You two do have some similarities."

I saw the muscles twitching in Miles' jaw as he searched for something to say. Belin had gone completely still beside him. "Who is he?"

"I loved her, you know," he murmured, ignoring Miles' question. "And your father is the reason she was taken from me."

The air in the throne room had gone cold and crackling. Belin' nostrils flared. "You left her."

"To protect her," Kauvras snapped, his breath heaving from his chest before a fragile calm settled over him. "I had no idea..."

I watched as his eyes flickered between unhinged madness and sanity, hysteria and rationality. "I didn't know she was pregnant. I didn't think it was possible."

Belin glared, his eyes brimming with raw hostility. "Is that why you had me chained and thrown back in the dungeon when you discovered who I was?"

Kauvras flew to his feet, staring down from the dais. "I had no ch–"

A pained scream pierced the air as the Rebel King dropped to his knees, face twisted in pain as he clawed at the leathers on his chest. He dropped forward onto his hands, his fingers flexing for purchase on the stone floor. Horror rose in my gut as he scratched at the ground, fingernails quickly breaking and going bloody as agonized screams erupted from him.

His guards rushed to his side but he threw his hands out to stop them before clawing at the ground again, the sound of skin grinding against stone audible between his cries.

"What the fuck is going on?" Whit yelled.

Belin closed the gap between them, locking his father's wrists in his hands as Kauvras continued to writhe and scream. "Look at me," he commanded, but still the Rebel King howled. "Look at me!"

His back went straight as an arrow, every muscle in his body contracting, a garbled whisper fighting to leave his mouth. But whatever he was trying to say lodged in his throat. His back arched once again, another scream tearing through him. Back to the ground he fell, squirming as tremors wracked his body. He was going mad once again.

"We'll leave for Blindbarrow now," Miles declared, his eyes stuck to Kauvras.

"No." My head turned to take in each member of my court, four sets of eyes darting back and forth from me to the frenzy I stood before. "We leave for Blindbarrow at dawn. There's something I need to do first."

$\blacklozenge\ \blacklozenge\ \blacklozenge$

I'd been stoking my fire for hours now, letting it crackle and grow. "Stay far back," I commanded the crowd of onlookers standing behind me. Summercut had arranged for masked soldiers to patrol both sides of the fields, ensuring that no one would venture too close to the smoke that would soon hang in the air.

The Rhedrosian Mountains rose high above the fields of leechthorn. I could see the Iron Rise standing taller than the rest of the range, an eerie orange glow radiating from its peak. The sea of violet swayed peacefully in the moonlight, each bloom's poisonous truth hiding behind unassuming petals. How could something so beautiful be the cause of so much torment?

A delicate hand rested on my shoulder, and I turned to see Solise's kind face peering up at me. The corner of her eyes were crinkled beneath upturned brows. "Do you remember what I told you back in Inkwell?"

"You told me a lot of things in Inkwell, Solise." I returned the smile and looked back out on the fields. "A lot of things I should have listened to."

"I'm thinking of one thing in particular. That a stone can be put to the fire and end up burned..."

"But it will not crumble," I finished in a whisper, my eyes falling closed.

"That it can be thrown around by the ocean and smoothed by the waves..."

I took a deep breath. "But it will not crumble."

"And you have not crumbled."

My eyes found hers, kind and empathetic and so familiar. "No, I haven't."

"That's right." She gave a knowing nod. "Now maybe the fire in question is different," she continued, pointing to my hands that hung at my sides, "and maybe the ocean in question is different, too." I narrowed my eyes but realized what she was saying as I followed her gaze to the fields before us — an ocean of leechthorn. "But the sentiment is the same, Petra. You're a war-rior. You've always been a warrior, fire burned and ocean tum-bled."

I let myself smile as a deep breath escaped my lungs. "Fire burned and ocean tumbled."

My fire flared as my hands flew forward and the field of leechthorn began to burn. It caught instantly, the fire spreading quickly, but not quickly enough. I sent a gust of wind pulsing for-ward, pushing the fire further into the field, watching as the smoke began to climb into the air. The firestorm swallowed the last of the unburned leechthorn, and the crowd of people behind me erupted into cheers, growing louder as the flames grew higher toward the night sky.

I turned from the fire and walked back toward the city. With-out looking back, I found that furious calm and raised a hand. The clouds rolled in quickly, dousing the field with a sheet of rain. It snapped and fizzled as the last ember was extinguished.

I couldn't promise the people who believed in me that they'd never be victims again, but I could promise that now, one less threat lay in waiting.

Chapter 40

The Myrin brothers rode ahead of me, side by side on their horses, their voices so low I only made out bits of their conversation as we trekked out of Taitha, headed for the border between Cabillia and Widoras.

"...killed Aunt Berna..."

"...never met Kauvras..."

"...known you were alive..."

Every so often one would turn to the other, the look of surprise evident in their profiles as they sorted through the years they'd spent as different people.

My horse brayed, and I leaned forward to give him a scratch on the neck. "I know you have emotions too," I whispered to him, "but I bet they aren't this complicated."

I wondered if Miles and Belin had broached the subject of Kauvras' words — that Miles' father was the reason for their mother's death. That fact sat heavy in my gut along with everything else I'd yet to consider.

But it meant that Belin had told the truth about the murder of his mother. I supposed he'd told the truth about a lot of things. It didn't do anything to calm my anger though, and my frustration with Belin still raged within me. His voice planted a deep, conflicting ache in my chest.

He was Belin. Not Calomyr. I wanted Calomyr to be real, and I wanted him to come back to me.

Could Calomyr be somewhere within Belin? The dark cloud loomed above me, darkening every thought about him. I fought to keep myself from dwelling on it, but it was hard to ignore the shadow it left. It was even harder to focus on the task in front of me, the reason we were riding for Blindbarrow — to extinguish Castemont's control of two powerful men.

I burrowed within myself, checking on my power, making sure I could still harness it from nothing. There were the flames, waiting patiently for me to summon them. There was the wind, whipping within my ribcage. There was the storm, somehow foreign and familiar all at once.

"Petra," Miles called back to me, snapping me out of my trance. "I need you to tell me how you got involved with Castemont."

◆ ◆ ◆

Miles listened intently as I recounted the way Castemont creeped his way into my life. He asked questions of Belin as he pieced together what had happened with his Aunt Berna, finding a dizzying amount of parallels between the stories. I was a bystander as Belin told Miles what Castemont had done to their Aunt Berna, to the woman who died thinking she was going to see Tobyas once again.

All the while, I made a point *not* to look at Belin, to not talk directly to him. I could feel his eyes on me constantly, and it was a fight to keep from turning to him. I knew I could find comfort in those eyes, maybe even strength, but I resisted. I had to resist.

354

The horses grazed as we set up camp in the middle of the plains that spanned the border of Cabillia and Widoras, the sky a deep indigo, stars speckling the expanse. But it was the moon that was most spectacular — so brilliant that it almost looked like the plains were cast in daylight. I stared, unblinking, my eyes going blurry as I pretended I lay by the waterfront in Eserene, pretended none of this ever happened. It was just me and Larka, no kings complicating our lives, no powers hanging overhead. No Castemont.

I turned on my side away from where Belin and Miles lounged beside the fire, curling in on myself as a strong sense of homesickness rushed in. I'd gone from the lowest of the lowborn, stealing to get by, to an Initiate of the Royal Court getting the shit beaten out of me, to the rightful Queen of all of Astran, maybe even beyond. I wanted to cry. I wanted to scream and stomp my feet and fall in a heap and just *wallow* in it.

I wanted to talk to Calomyr.

The tears flooded my eyes then. He was right behind me, but he wasn't. He was on this journey with me, but he wasn't. I blinked hard, gritting my teeth until the tears dissipated. I needed a distraction, something to keep myself from spiraling. I wouldn't let myself cry tonight.

"Miles," I called, standing from my bedroll and drawing my sword. "I want to train."

He scratched the back of his head. "A bit late for that, no?"

"It's an order from your Queen."

Miles sighed. "Guess I can't argue with that." he quipped, pushing himself to stand. "Alright. Let's train."

◆ ◆ ◆

With each passing night, the Onyx Pass loomed ever closer, ever present on the horizon like a slow moving storm. But it was nothing compared to what brewed in me. I'd been a bitch to Belin. I couldn't deny it. I was apathetic and bitter and avoidant.

And I knew for a fact that it was only because I was trying to defend myself from the hurt he'd caused me, to cope with seeing him here, alive.

He'd been kind. As always. He'd been kind and helpful and considerate, always making sure I'd eaten enough, always making sure I had a comfortable spot to sleep. And I was a fucking bully in return. I hated myself for it, but I had no instructions for navigating how to cope with what had happened, no guidance for forgiving someone whose fictitious death I'd grieved.

"I think we should call it early," Belin declared, pulling his horse to a stop, eyeing the sky as it began to melt into pink and amber. He dismounted, patting his horse on its side before reaching for the saddlebag. "Let's spend the night at the base of the Pass. That's one less night we'll have to spend in it."

"No." I pushed my horse past where he'd stopped, my back to him. "I want to keep going."

"He's right, Petra," Miles answered, and I heard him stop his horse and dismount as well.

Still I advanced, leaving the brothers behind as I kept on for the Pass. "I want to keep going," I repeated, irritation in my voice.

"You can't disagree with an idea just because it's Cal's."

I pulled my horse to a halt, a metaphorical rock slamming into my gut at the accusation he made. I kept my breathing even as the truth hovered above my head, its edges dipping into my field of vision, begging for my attention. My eyes squeezed shut, trying to find some way, *any* way around the fact that Miles' accusation was right, and here it was out in the open.

"How dare you," I spat, sliding from my horse and marching straight to where Miles stood beside Belin. "How dare you accuse me of something so juvenile." *Something so true.*

Belin shifted uncomfortably. "Tobyas, it's–"

"No, Cal," he cut in. "We're all in this mess because of Castemont. You can be angry, Petra. Hell, stay angry for the rest of your life. That's understandable. But you can't be..." He trailed off, the incomplete sentence hanging in the air.

"I can't be what, Miles?" My voice was sharp as I stared up at him, my jaw tight as I waited for him to answer me. His mouth bobbed open as he searched for the word. "Cruel? Resentful? A bitch? Is that what you were going to say?"

"No, it's–"

"Am I not your Queen?" I snarled, my voice eerily calm as I took another step toward him. The horses must have sensed my anger, because they suddenly grew restless.

He bowed his head, a few rogue strands of hair falling loose of their tie and brushing his cheek. "Until the day I die, you will be my Queen."

"Then as your Queen, I am allowed to feel *whatever* the fuck I want about what has happened to me, and I owe neither of you a reason or justification. So if I don't want to accept any of Belin's ideas, I won't." I felt the familiar burn in my hands, steam rising in my throat as I stalked toward Miles, my eyes pinning him where he stood. "If I want to continue into the Pass tonight, I will." Tiny flames began to lick at my palms, and I felt both of their attention glued to the fire that was growing. "And if I want to end both of your lives right here, right now, I'll do so, and I'll do so gladly."

Miles nodded, and my eyes moved to Belin, fury rumbling through me. "I want you to stop, okay? You're not going to receive my forgiveness, and I'm fucking sick of you trying." His face was unreadable as I stepped toward him, resolve coursing through me. "I don't need your explanations. You'll serve me as my sworn sword and nothing else, or I'll take your fucking life. Understand?"

Fear flashed across Miles' face, and I reveled in it, let the feeling of power wash over me. My eyes flicked to Belin, but his expression had changed, quickly dousing my fire in icy water. I could tell exactly what he was thinking as my flames flickered out. It was written on his face, and he made no attempt to conceal it.

"Yes, my Queen." The words were hollow, completely emotionless.

That wasn't Calomyr. It wasn't even Belin.

I spun away, something like shame replacing my fury. My chest felt empty. Clarity rushed back into my brain as I stared at the shadows growing longer on the face of the Onyxian Mountains.

At the core of it all, it wasn't Belin's fault. As desperately as I wanted to blame him, I couldn't. As desperately as I wanted to hate him...

Without turning back, I nodded. "We camp here tonight."

Miles silently placed my bedroll next to me and retreated back to his brother's side where they began to build a fire. I turned back toward them and watched them as they worked alongside each other, their movements as natural as if no time had passed at all. But it quickly became evident that the damage was done. The energy had turned like a sudden squall in the dead of summer. No low rumbles of warning thunder, no smell of oncoming rain. There was no calm before this storm. This was angry, with jagged lightning and a deafening crash out of the clear blue sky, and suddenly I was being rained on.

I'd exploded, and the carnage from my words was worse than any I could have caused with my flames, or my wind, or my storms.

Guilt had been radiating off of Belin since he found us in the forest, almost as if his movements were slowed by the weight of it. But now I felt nothing from him. Not guilt nor anger nor fear. There was just...nothing. He seemed to stand taller, straighter, his movements more defined and rigid as the fire ignited and he began to make camp. It was like he'd shaken me off completely, and I was no longer weighing him down.

It was better this way, right? It *was* better this way. I could focus on retrieving the blood from Umbri then turn all my energy, all my fury on Castemont, then on finding Katia and Rhedros. No more of my time would be spent pining over what had been, what could be. I was a queen now. I had more important things to worry about.

Turning my back to them once again, I fixed my eyes on the highest peak of the Onyxian Mountains, gilded by the last rays of the setting sun.

It was better this way. It was better this way. *It was better this way.*

◆ ◆ ◆

The familiar feeling of being watched prickled across my skin as we entered the Onyx Pass, the air suddenly feeling denser, the towering trees imposing. It was only mid-morning, the terror of nighttime in the Pass still hours and hours away, but I felt the seeds of that terror being sown in my gut. The brothers rode on either side of me, my own guilt growing more acrid on my tongue with every step I took between them.

Creatures rustled in the forest on either side of us, neither brother betraying even a lick of worry as growls and screeches echoed off the trees. The horses were unsettled as the unmistakable sound of an animal being attacked by a beast much larger than itself sounded down the trail, and my stomach turned as its dying howls were interrupted by ripping and shaking and tearing...then silence.

The smell of death suddenly permeated the air, clutching the three of us in its nauseating jaws. The packed soil of the path was disturbed, and it dawned on me that this was it — this was where the beasts of the Onyx Pass had attacked the group of leechthorn-addled prisoners, where I'd somehow killed dozens of feral animals and healed myself from the marks of their claws and teeth and talons. Their mangled bodies rotted just beyond the treeline where I knew clumps of fur and feathers littered the ground and bones lay snapped and craggy.

I recounted that day, but my mind quickly strayed and I didn't stop it. Why the hell had I told Belin to stop trying? Why the hell had I threatened to kill him and Miles? Why the hell was I so angry? I'd ruined the fragile understanding that I'd fostered with Miles. And I didn't know what I wanted with Belin, but what hung between us now made my skin crawl.

Visceral silence trailed us as we made our way deeper and deeper into the Pass. Shadows grew shorter and then longer as the sun rose and sank. All the while, shame was spreading throughout my body, mixing with the rage that still remained and becoming more inescapable as it found every fracture and nook within me.

Moving forward gave part of my mind something to focus on. We were heading to Umbri. This was the first leg of our journey to ultimately free my parents. Those were the concrete facts that pulsed in my head with every footstep. But I knew that every second that passed was one second closer to having to set up camp, and I wouldn't have the distraction of movement to lean on.

It'd be me, Miles and Belin, my mind, and the beasts of Onyx Pass.

◆ ◆ ◆

The fire crackled, sending sparks floating into the air. Each spark rose before its light faded into the black of night, as if they were trying to join the stars that hung above us. Miles was asleep next to the fire. I felt unfamiliar eyes on me, almost as if something had been stalking us as we traversed the Pass. But the beasts that lurked in the trees around us had almost faded into the background, and I found I was no longer afraid of them.

I was afraid of myself.

My eyes fell on Belin, the Invisible King sitting across the fire on the trunk of a tree that had fallen across the path, hunched over his sword as he sharpened it on a stone. It was a heady mix that entered my blood at the sight of him, the need to both atone and punish running parallel down the middle of my soul.

360

My mouth opened and closed as I tried to decide what to do, if I should do anything at all. But before I could make a decision, some distant part of my mind made it for me. "Belin," I breathed.

Only his eyes looked up from his blade, his head still bowed over his work. I fought to keep the breath moving in and out of me as he stared. No signs of Calomyr remained. In fact, he'd detached from the Calomyr altogether — the Calomyr that had loved me, the Calomyr that had been working for my forgiveness. His face was no longer familiar, instead locked in a stern glare of formality and disdain. His eyes... They still sent lightning through me, but the emotionless state of them grounded each strike, snatched them right out of the sky.

He was a stranger.

His jaw locked as he straightened, features impassive. It was like I was an inconvenience, but he was working to keep the feeling hidden. But I couldn't break my stare. Could he tell there were words in my chest that so badly wanted to be spoken? Could he tell what I was thinking right now, that I hated him to his core, but would fall to my knees before him if I let my resolve slip one more inch?

Gemstone eyes dropped then, leaving me cold in the absence of his stare. "You are the rightful Queen," he began, his voice flat, "and I will serve you in my role as your sworn sword. But as you've requested, that's where it ends." His head raised again, the picture of austerity. "There is no longer anything past my duty to you. Everything I do for you is in service to the realm. So if you aren't in need of any assistance, I'll take my leave of you now."

My mouth opened and closed as I tried to pull myself together, tried to understand what he'd just said. I blinked, my eyes beginning to sting from smoke or tears or both. My voice came out in a faint whisper. "Of course."

He nodded, turning back to his sword, and I wondered if he knew he'd driven it straight into my ribs...but I knew I'd been the one to aim it.

Chapter 41

Blindbarrow was desolate, only rubble left behind. We'd tied the horses to a broken fence post and stared down the empty main street of Eserene's closest neighboring village.

"He was here, wasn't he?" Miles asked as the three of us began walking. "Castemont?"

Belin nodded, expressionless. Nobody wanted to breathe life into the question. It hung above us like a hangman's noose, haunting us as it swung in the wind.

Was Umbri even here in Blindbarrow anymore?

The wind whistled through the empty streets, doors and shutters hanging open. Baskets of half-done washing were tipped over in the street, loaves of bread and wagons of fish left to the rats and roaches that were the only living beings left. It was as if life had existed in Blindbarrow one moment, and the next...

I trailed behind the Myrin brothers, both of them silent as they surveyed the devastation. I realized then that Miles had done this, been a part of this in Saints knew how many towns and villages. He'd forced leechthorn on innocent people, stolen their lives from them. I'd been able to return them to their bodies, but what about those who didn't make it? What about those who'd ripped themselves to shreds?

Disdain bubbled up within me. How could he have followed Kauvras' orders — Castemont's orders, actually — so blindly? How could he have been a part of such evil?

Rhedros' words flooded back to my brain. *There's a delicate balance between good and evil. The world can only exist in equilibrium.* By that logic, evil had to have an equal pull against good. So could someone truly *be* evil? Or were they simply acting in the way the world demanded? When the pull is too strong in one direction, is it even possible to act any other way?

My eyes locked on something in the street. At first I thought it was just a piece of cloth, maybe a handkerchief, but something about it drew me closer. It was... I bent down to pick up the ragdoll that lay in the dirt. It was worn and tattered, the loose strings and faded color evidence of a life spent clutched to a child's side. I held the doll in front of me, trying to come to grips with the fact that the child who loved it... They were gone.

Miles suddenly broke away from his brother, running to the other side of the street and folding himself in half as he wretched, one hand on the side of a cottage that bore the scars of a fire that once raged. Belin watched him intently for a moment, trying to make sense of the sight.

I kept my distance from the Invisible King as we approached Miles slowly. His teeth were clamped, eyes squeezed shut as tears trailed down his cheeks and fell to the upturned cobblestones below. He shook his head side to side as if doing so could erase whatever he was seeing in his mind.

"I did this," he pushed out between heaving breaths. I suddenly felt guilt rise within me for the thoughts I'd had, almost like part of me had believed he was following Kauvras' orders for the hell of it. "I did this to people, and it doesn't matter how many you saved, Petra, because there were so many that didn't even make it to Taitha."

Belin's hand rested on his shoulder, silence settling over all of us as Miles choked on regret, his face contorted with pain. I could tell Belin wanted to speak, wanted to say something to make his brother feel better about his actions, but he just stared wordlessly.

Miles straightened suddenly, walking into the street, back turned to us. "This is why she left," he murmured. "Because I was a part of *this*. Because maybe it wasn't that child," he pointed to the ragdoll in my hand, "but it was dozens of others. Hundreds. And their parents and friends and neighbors. I was blind to what I was doing, but she saw it for what it was. That's why she left me, and she was right to do so."

Belin took a step toward his brother, confusion chiseling a crease in his brow. "Who?"

He shook his head, rubbing his jaw as he looked up the street, bottles and shoes and remnants of lives strewn about. "Cielle."

Cielle... He'd mentioned the name before...in Aera. He told me he'd lost the woman he loved, and that her name was Cielle. I saw Belin nod in understanding as he put the pieces together.

Miles spun to us, jaw squared, the hollow look of loss so familiar it hurt. "She told me I could either abandon my post or she'd leave, that she wouldn't stand for me having any part in something like this." His head dropped between his shoulders, the picture of defeat. "It's not even as if I felt like my duty to the crown was more important. I just..." He exhaled hard, black eyes rimmed with red. "I still had no idea who I was then. I felt like this position, leading conquests like this, it anchored me. It *was* me." His eyes fell distant. "I've ended lives by blade and by leechthorn. I've killed hundreds and felt nothing. And I lost her because of it. She went back home."

"Where's home?" Belin asked quietly.

"Coldwater, in the Surging Isles of Tadrana." He could barely get the words out as the floodgates opened and Miles spiraled in front of us. We were watching him unravel, every bit of repressed violence and anger and guilt culminating in this moment.

"I'll go with you," Belin blurted suddenly. "Yeah, I'll go with you to Coldwater. As soon as this is all over. You can find her again. I'll help you."

Miles shook his head, the bitter smell of loss hanging in the air. I watched him try to take control of his emotions, his face as neutral as he could manage. "I don't intend to see the other side of this battle."

Belin stepped forward. "Tobyas, I–"

"Tobyas is dead, Cal. He's dead. Tobyas wouldn't have done this."

No one spoke, his words sinking in slowly, my heart aching as the meaning resounded through me.

A sudden clatter intruded upon the silence, my heart jumping in my chest as the three of us spun toward the noise. Belin's eyes narrowed as he surveyed the street, but everything was perfectly still. "Who's there?" he called, voice low with authority.

A figure stepped out from behind a shop, tall and slim beneath a billowing cloak. They lowered their hood and raised their palms, as if they were trying to seem less threatening. I stared as recognition sparked in my brain, and before I knew it, I'd dropped the ragdoll and I was running, *sprinting* toward the man in the cloak.

It was Ludovicus.

Rage overtook me as I lunged for him, my hand promptly finding his throat as he fell to his knees in the Blindbarrow street. A war cry built in me as heat erupted in my chest, Rhedros' fury entering my body and taking control as I wrenched Ludovicus' face to mine.

I didn't know how he was here or why, but *finally*, I would get a tiny sliver of sweet revenge.

But my scream died and my flames banked as I stared at him, into the eyes that had so mercilessly looked upon me in the Es-erenian throne room. Because they were no longer depthless and empty; they were still dark as oil but somehow dimensional, somehow...human. The features that had been so sharp and menacing had softened, suddenly looking more man than monster. His skin was no longer translucent but a light olive tone, a deep flush rose to his cheeks that was quickly going purple beneath my grip. Hair fell around his face, and it was no longer raven black but a deep chocolate that looked like it could melt in the sunlight.

My grip loosened slightly as I wondered if I'd been mistaken, questioning whether this was Ludovicus at all.

"Kill me," he choked out under my grip, and though his voice was garbled, I could tell it was no longer the slithering hiss it had been. "Daughter of Katia, I'm begging you to kill me. I deserve to die by your hand."

I breathed through clenched teeth as I stared into his eyes, a plea and a prayer in the obsidian depths that now stared back at me. "I don't understand," I whispered, swallowing hard, my brows furrowed.

"I'm sorry," he sputtered. "I'm sorry I hurt you."

Hot, angry tears blurred my vision and I did my best to blink them away. "*How?*"

"C–" he stammered. "Castemont."

I let him go, shoving him to the ground as I stepped back, watching him cough and sputter in the dirt. A scorched handprint marred his throat, and the smell of burning skin bit at my nose. "Explain yourself," I commanded.

He did his best to straighten, remaining on one knee, a fist across his chest. I fought the urge to spit, to tell him he didn't deserve to breathe the same air that I breathed, didn't deserve to swear fealty, didn't deserve–

My blood went frozen in my veins as I realized what he meant. It hadn't been Ludovicus, it had been...

Castemont.

Bile surged up my throat as I stared, my lungs fighting for air under the crushing weight of the truth. "The Bloodsinger," I whispered. "Castemont had your blood too...and he actually used it."

Ludovicus' eyes closed, his lips pursed with the turmoil that I could tell ran through every part of him. "I'm so sorry."

No, it didn't make sense. But it did. It made perfect sense.

"It's been years," he breathed, his voice deep and even, sending chills up my spine for a a very different reason than it had before. "He had me trapped for years, hurting the young women of Eserene through Initiation. Every time he sacrificed to the Darkness Beyond, it was with my blood. Not only did he use it to influence the actions of others, he also used it to influence *me*, and he made me commit the most abhorrent acts."

His head remained bowed as I stared with wide eyes. "I..." Words escaped me as I tried to wrap my mind around what he was telling me.

"Kill me," he repeated, his eyes finding mine. "I want you to kill me for hurting you." His head dropped, the curtain of deep brown hair falling in front of his face.

"He hurt you?" Belin murmured from beside me. His voice was a deadly calm, but beneath the surface I could tell that a turbulent torrent raged.

I narrowed my eyes on Belin, my anger toward him momentarily outweighing my anger toward Ludovicus. "You don't recognize him? This is the monster that led *your* kingdom's Initiation."

Belin stared, his jaw hard set. "The King wasn't privy to the rites of Initiation."

My head swung to him, disbelief pulsing through me. Castemont was so fucking meticulous, so fucking conniving that he even managed to keep the King from knowing what occurred within the walls of his own castle.

"Yes," I breathed, looking back to the man kneeling on the ground, begging for death. "He hurt me."

Belin was moving, snatching Ludovicus by the collar of his cloak and dragging him off his feet, the Invisible King towering over the quivering figure that had brought me to my knees, broken my bones, punctured my skin.

"Please," Ludovicus sputtered, "I–"

Belin's fist landed square across his cheek, Ludovicus' head flying painfully to the side with a heave. He hardly had time to recoil before Belin's fist made contact again, blow after blow after blow landing heavy on his cheeks and chin and nose. Blood began to spatter and still he unleashed, ravaging the man who'd tormented me.

He was going to kill him.

I took a deep breath, reminding myself that he was only doing this because I was his Queen. He was only doing this because it was his duty. *There is no longer anything past my duty to you.* "Belin," I called, stepping toward them. He showed no sign of slowing down, beating Ludovicus bloody. "Belin!"

He paused, his face feral as he glared at Ludovicus, whose head rolled back and forth between his shoulders. If he hadn't been conscious before, he definitely wasn't after Belin pitched him to the ground, his head bouncing off the dirt with a hollow *thud.*

Belin's eyes landed on me for a split second, and he was there. That was Calomyr looking at me. But the mask quickly dropped, the rugged soldier that was Belin Cal Myrin showing his true face once again. "He'll die for what he did to you," he panted, teeth gritted. "Either by your hand or mine. He'll die for it."

It's because you're his Queen. Nothing else.

I nodded and watched as all traces of Calomyr vanished once again. I forced myself to turn back to Ludovicus. "He'll die." I surveyed the limp figure on the ground. "But not today. He may have information we can use."

Belin's nostrils flared as he nodded and turned away, marching up the street, shoulders heaving with a palpable rage I could almost taste. I turned to Miles, his face glued to Ludovicus' profile against the dirt. "Tie him up, will you?" I asked quietly, wincing. "Before your brother snaps again and kills him."

368

I trailed after Belin, trying to match his stride to walk along-side him. His eyes were trained forward, no sign that he even re-alized I was here. "Thank you," I said quietly, and he stopped sud-denly. He turned back to Ludovicus, staring as Miles tore strips of cloth from a discarded quilt and restrained his unconscious body.

"Don't thank me." Flat words with no warmth behind them. "It's my duty as your sworn sword."

I nodded, unable to look him in the eyes. "I know, but still, thank you."

His jaw flexed. "It's my duty as your sworn sword," he re-peated, his voice empty. Silence swelled between us as we watched Miles. It was uncomfortable, the energy between us dead and decaying, repelling me like a water droplet on a feather. "Umbri's shop is two streets up," he said suddenly. I swallowed, centering my mind on the task ahead. "Let me address her."

I cocked a brow in challenge. "Do you think I'm incapable of handling a Bloodsinger?"

"No, my Queen." Cold, cold formality. "I don't know what kind of forces she's employed. She could have cast something over the vials already. You do not put yourself in danger."

My lips pursed as I considered his words. I nodded, surveying Miles as he walked toward us, Ludovicus' restrained body slumped against a building. "Okay. You address her."

"You, wait outside," he commanded Miles. "In case we aren't actually alone in Blindbarrow after all. And to keep Umbri from feeling cornered and doing something stupid."

Miles nodded, his body here but his mind obviously some-where far away. I narrowed my eyes at him, trying to read his face, but Belin was moving, and us along with him.

Chapter 42

The smell of incense and burning metal greeted us as we silently slid through the open door of the unmarked building. It looked similar to Alvar's shop in Aera with doorways and candles, but there was something disconcerting here that I hadn't felt at the Empty Mirror. I couldn't place it, but it rattled in the back of my head, slight but undeniable. A stack of crates and boxes lined the front wall. She was here, but she was preparing to leave.

My eye caught on the back wall, a massive, dark, wooden bureau seemingly watching over the whole room. It felt like it had its own pull of gravity as I approached it, my stomach suddenly unsettled as I reached for one of its cabinets.

Blood. Dozens and dozens of vials of blood.

"Belin..."

"May I be of assistance?"

Belin and I whirled to see a figure standing in one of the doorways, the tell tale skeletal form of a Bloodsinger silhouetted in smoke. She stepped forward, her features coming into focus as the candlelight hit her face. My stomach instantly bottomed out, anxiety rushing through every one of my veins at the sight of her. Alvar had looked like Ludovicus and the rest of the Board of Blood, but there'd been an air about him that was much less threatening — kind, almost.

If something beyond evil existed, it was in the form of this woman.

"Ah," she hissed, a sinister smile twisting her face. "King Belin Cal Myrin." She turned her face to me, her gaze crawling over my skin. "And I know you, Daughter of Benevolence and Blood."

Shit.

"You have something of mine," Belin stated evenly, authority coursing from him with each measured breath. I could tell he was fighting to keep his eyes from wandering to the bureau, where both his destruction and salvation waited.

The Bloodsinger smirked, one brow raised. "Do I?"

"Hand over the vials. Mine and Kauvras'. Now."

A spindly finger ran a long, pointed fingernail over her translucent cheek, the look on her face maddeningly sardonic as she glanced to the bureau, then reached into the pocket of her trousers, producing two small vials. "Are these what you're looking for?" She shook them around, Belin's eyes following the liquid inside. "Why?"

"I am King of Widoras," Belin answered. "You'll do as I command or I'll see you hang. Hand them over. *Now.*"

Umbri yawned, placing the vials back in her pocket. "If you'll excuse me, I must be on my way to Eserene."

Anger began to rise in my throat, the familiar burn following it. She knew my identity, knew what I was capable of. And still she decided to play this fucking game.

"We know who he is," I snarled. Belin tensed next to me as he felt my energy darken. "We know Castemont's true identity."

Her eyes widened in mock surprise. "Do you now?"

"Give us the vials, or I'll burn this place to the fucking ground," I seethed.

Umbri threw her head back and cackled, the sound filling the room before she quieted and an eerie silence creeped in.

I didn't wait for permission — didn't need it. I lunged for Umbri. Belin began moving too, blocking the exit and drawing his sword. But as soon as I reached her, she vanished, thin air in place of where she'd been standing.

"How do you know these are the vials you seek?" I spun to see her standing on the other side of the room, the vials in her raised hand.

No. I was tired. I wouldn't play her game any longer. I let my fire flare, my palms splitting open with embers as I shot a hand out, a pillar of fire headed straight to the Bloodsinger, but it seemingly extinguished as again she vanished, materializing on the other side of the room. Those angular features turned up in a teasing grin.

Belin had been right. This was *dark*. This wasn't Rhedros, or any of the Blood Saints for that matter. This was beyond even Noros' evil. This was something different, something truly sinister.

Umbri vanished and reappeared over and over, and I watched as Belin slowly worked his way closer and closer to the bureau. Finally, *finally* he managed to reach it, Umbri's taunting laugh suddenly cut short as she realized what was happening. With a battle cry he heaved the bureau forward, the sound of wood crashing and glass shattering like a symphony in my ears. A pool of blood spread quickly as the vials broke.

A skeletal arm closed across my chest, the unmistakable smell of death clinging to my senses. Umbri held both vials in one hand and ran them slowly over the skin of my neck, a long fingernail tapping against the glass as the goosebumps raised over my skin.

Belin's sword flew out in front of him, pointed directly at her throat. When he spoke, his voice was low, a bone-chilling calmness behind it. "Unhand her."

Umbri snickered in my ear, a slithering whisper following it. "So close. Yet not close enough." I railed against the Bloodsinger behind me, her preternatural strength taking me by surprise as I let my fire build, let my skin heat as the flames grew beneath it. She let out a pained hiss, jumping back as the two vials in her hands fell and shattered on the ground.

Relief only flooded me for a brief moment as I looked at her face to see a perverse smile, contradictory to the fact that we'd just shattered Castemont's control on Belin and Kauvras — and countless others.

She reached into the pocket of her trousers once again, producing one more vial. "Compliments of my brothers who oversaw your Initiation."

Panic crawled up my spine, goosebumps raising across my skin as I realized. She had my blood, too.

The prospect of being a Bloodsinger didn't scare me. But being a Bloodsinger, one as far gone as Umbri and Ludovicus and the Board of Blood, *and* having access to the powers that ran through my veins...

Pure severity pulsed from Belin as his sword hovered inches from Umbri's throat. The Bloodsinger was suddenly gone once again, nowhere to be seen.

"Come find me."

"*No,*" I heard Belin breathe as he took off toward one of the wooden doors at the back of the room. I followed him through the threshold only to be swallowed by a darkness thick as oil. The door slammed shut behind us, echoing through like a cavern.

I conjured up a small flame in my palm, squinting through the empty room, looking for any sign of the Bloodsinger.

"*Hostinhah vel az agyun.*" She'd appeared in the corner, chanting in a language I'd never heard.

"No!" Belin bellowed, charging her, sword drawn, but Umbri disappeared again, turning up on the other side of the room. Belin was frantic in his movements as he sprinted from corner to corner in pursuit of the Bloodsinger. I was trying to build the fire within me, but my attention was being pulled in too many directions.

"*Ki ah vebenzna ve nomisenz ki ful,*" she continued, holding the vial of my blood higher in the air. I spun in circles, the tiny flame in my hand the only light in the room, trying to keep track of her as she disappeared and reappeared over and over and over, chanting, chanting, chanting.

She materialized before me, the look in her eyes mocking me as she stared. Belin approached silently from behind, blade poised to strike.

"I won't be a Bloodsinger today," I snarled, not cowering from a stare that would surely haunt my nightmares.

Umbri laughed, that nerve-grating cackle. "You were never going to be a Bloodsinger."

Belin's eyes met mine for a split second before the wall behind me was suddenly alight, white candles lined up on the ground, a single black candle on an altar in the middle.

Unbridled terror split across Belin's face as Umbri threw the vial across the room, the glass shattering on the black brick wall behind the candles, droplets of my blood spattering and sizzling as they fell into the flames. Before I could blink, Belin had grabbed the Bloodsinger from behind and dragged his blade across her throat. She writhed on the floor, smiling while blood shot from her neck in nauseating spurts. With a final choked cackle, she stilled, her face still upturned in a mocking grin.

Despair rushed through my body as I whirled around to the sight of my blood dripping down the wall. Belin was beside me then, sword clattering to the ground, his hands on the sides of my face as he desperately searched my eyes.

I didn't have the mental space to process what was happening. "What did she mean I was never going to be a Bloodsinger?"

Belin's mouth was open, his head shaking as he looked around the room, at the blood that now dripped down the side of the black candle. "I don't know."

His hands dropped from my cheeks and he straightened, retrieving his sword and resheathing it. I let myself relax a bit, but something wasn't right. A part of me felt hollow, a part of me missing that I'd never realized was there. I flexed my hands at my sides, rolled my head between my shoulders, searching for the missing piece that had left a gaping hole, but *what*? What was gone?

I had fury, but no heat. Rage, but no fire. Calm, but no storm.

"My powers are gone."

Chapter 43

"How did that happen?" Miles rode between Belin and me, a beaten, bloody, and unconscious Ludovicus draped across his horse behind him in the saddle.

I was only half listening as Belin explained to Miles what he'd explained to me three times already. Umbri had cursed the vial of blood, probably because she'd foreseen we were coming. She knew that the worst punishment she could inflict upon me would be to leave me living and breathing but unable to use the powers the Saints had given me.

The other half of my mind was trying to find some sign of *something* within me to prove him wrong. I searched every corner of my mind twice, hoping with everything in me that I'd find some residual heat, some spark to tell me that all hope was not lost. But there was nothing. No flames, no wind, no rain. Not even ash to prove I'd had powers to begin with.

I trudged through the reeds in my mind, searching for some sign that Katia and Rhedros were still able to hear me. I didn't know how to find them, didn't know if they could still see me or hear me. But that nagging emptiness that I'd felt when I realized my powers were gone... I knew it was more than just my powers.

They were gone, too. I was useless.

We were two days from Eserene. Two days from laying siege to the walled city. Two days from finding Castemont and trying to... What, kill him with my bare hands?

And we were two days from reuniting with Whit, Nell, and my entire army, when I'd have to tell them that I no longer held the power that made them follow me in the first place.

I thought about postponing. Could you do that? Postpone a battle? But even if I did, what would I be waiting for? A bigger army? There was no one left on Astran after the conquests of Kauvras and Castemont. Would I be waiting for my powers to return? I had no idea how that would even be possible. I hadn't the slightest clue how to go about trying to restore them. I let my head drop back, surrendering to hopelessness.

"You can't tell them," Miles said suddenly, breaking my brain away from its spiral as if he was witnessing it firsthand. He leaned forward to look at me, his midnight eyes piercing in their intensity. "You can't tell them your powers are gone."

I raised a brow. "You want me to lie to my army? You want me to tell them that yes, I'll be able to conjure fire and water from thin air and heal them with my blood? Knowing I can't do either of those?"

"Do you know what it'll do to morale if you tell them the truth?" He was the Lieutenant now, his mind sharp and focused on the logistics of the battle ahead. "They're not going to run into a losing battle if they know that's what it is."

"You can't tell them," Belin suddenly cut in. I saw the surprise on Miles' face at the fact that Belin was addressing me outside his direct duties. This was the most he'd spoken to me in days. "People need hope. That's what keeps them going. That's what keeps them fighting battles they'll never win."

"With that logic, why are any battles fought at all?" I muttered, staring up into the trees that swayed above us.

"Every battle that's ever happened has had a winning side and a losing side," Belin didn't look at me as he spoke, his eyes trained on the trail ahead. "But each side has something in common... Hope. Hope is what powers every battle. The hope that they'll be the ones to prevail, that their efforts will prove triumphant. And that goes for those fought on the battlefield and those fought here," he pointed a finger to his forehead, "and here," and a finger over his heart. "You always have hope you'll be on the winning side."

I tried not to think too much into the meaning of his words, tried to keep the focus on the battle. But fuck if he wasn't right.

"They've all witnessed your power," Miles said. "Don't give them any reason to believe it's gone."

◆ ◆ ◆

Another night in the Pass — one of the last. Perhaps one of the last nights we'd ever spend alive. The air was awkward. No one had addressed Miles' outburst about Cielle in Blindbarrow. No one had addressed the intensity with which Belin beat Ludovicus, who was still restrained and now propped against a tree, barely conscious and struggling to stay that way.

And no one addressed the fact that we were crusading into a battle we'd lose horribly.

Belin had turned over, his back to the fire, his breathing deep and even as he slept. I tried not to stare but found it impossible to look away. The longing had crept in, longing for what had been, what could have been.

If we'd met under different circumstances, would he still have loved me? If it had been chance rather than grand design, would he still have looked at me as if the stars rose and fell for me? Acid rose in my throat as I turned away, the despair of the what-ifs sweeping through me.

378

"You'll be okay." Miles stared at me from across the fire, as if he'd read my thoughts.

My eyes closed, smoke pouring into my lungs as I took a deep breath. It wasn't the same smoke that Calomyr had smelled of. This was acrid and stinging, taunting me as it billowed from the firepit. *Remember me? Remember when you could command flames?*

"You won't stop missing him," Miles said quietly. "But you'll be okay one day."

I dropped my head back, not wanting to be vulnerable in front of him. But I was unable to fight it off. "He didn't even exist."

His gaze was lost in the flames. "How can you mourn someone who never existed?"

"That's a good question," I answered. "Yet here I am, doing just that."

He reached into his rucksack and bit into a piece of dried venison. "I've looked for her in every woman I've met, you know." I blinked as I realized he was talking about Cielle. "You'll do the same thing one day. Compare every man to him."

I covered my eyes with my hands, the truth too unbearable to face. "And have you found her?"

"No. I've found bits and pieces of her. I even see some pieces of her in you," he added quietly. "A lot of her, actually."

I stared at him, surprise evident on my face. "Really?"

"Yeah, not the good pieces, though," he jeered with a snicker.

I rolled my eyes. "Gee, thanks."

The smile melted away from his face until his features looked gaunt in the flickering shadows of the firelight. "I see her everywhere."

"Tell me about her."

A corner of his mouth lifted. "Really?"

"Yes. Distract me from everything. I want to know all about her."

"It isn't some great love story, if that's what you're hoping for."

"Tell it anyway."

There it was again, turning the squeals of sows and bartering voices into an orchestra worthy of a king. A laugh that ceased the world's turning for a split second. I wasn't angry anymore, not after hearing that laugh. A flash of blonde hair was swallowed by the crowd, and I followed. What was I doing? I was a new soldier, unranked, without two silvers to rub together. But I didn't stop. Instead, I dodged people to keep her in my field of view as she bobbed and weaved through the market square.

She was with a friend, a sister perhaps, each with a basket hanging from the crook of an elbow. A horse and cart passed in front of me and she was gone, taken by the crowd once again. Damn. What the hell was I supposed to do now?

I turned back and resigned myself to the fact that I'd lost her. Who wasn't to say her laugh was the only beautiful thing about her? Who wasn't to say I'd've had a chance with her anyway?

"Pardon me, soldier," a small, teasing voice sounded as a tall blonde woman stepped around me. She whispered something to her friend and laughed, my veins singing with the music of it once again.

"Hey," I called after her without thinking. The two women turned to me and her eyes met mine, piercing blue — the color I imagined the ocean would be when the sun shone on it. I couldn't have told you what her friend looked like in that moment. I couldn't even have told you what day of the week it was. I was captured in the light of her stare. It was all I could see. No feeling I'd ever had in my life came anywhere close to this. I didn't even have a name for it. All I knew was it made me want to leave my life behind and spend the rest of my days living in her gaze.

She raised a brow as I stared. I could feel my mouth hanging open like an idiot, but there was nothing I could do. "Yes, soldier?"

"Just..." I stammered. "Hello."

She smiled with closed lips, something mischievous and sly about it, like she was delighting in watching me flounder. "Hello."

A hand closed around her arm. It was her friend dragging her away. She obliged, but her head stayed turned toward me for an extra second, eyes narrowed as she watched me watch her. And then she was gone.

"I made sure to be at the market the next day," Miles said, absentmindedly toeing the dirt. "She wasn't there, of course. She wasn't there the next day, or the next day either. I was buying fruit and bread I didn't need and damn sure couldn't afford."

"Didn't you say you were a new soldier then?"

"I was."

"So...shouldn't you have had training sessions to attend?"

He let a slight smile turn up his lips. "I did. Ran a lot of extra laps in those days. Scrubbed a lot of floors. Missed a lot of meals. It was worth it, though, because I saw her again."

"Following me, soldier?" I turned from the cart of honey apples I'd visited four times this week, and there she was, cloak hanging over pronounced collarbones, those eyes the color of the ocean on a sunny day. She peered out from behind a thick fringe of lashes, as if they could hide her from my stare.

"Following you?" I stuttered. "No, I–"

"He's bought honey apples from me four times this week," the small, stout woman behind the cart chimed in. "No one needs that many honey apples. Of course he's following you."

My teeth gnashed together and my eyes widened in embarrassment as I shot daggers at the woman. I turned back to the ocean before me, giving her what I knew was the most sheepish smile she'd ever seen. "I'm sorry, miss." I shuffled past her, trying to hide the shame in my face, but she caught me by the arm.

"I was hoping I'd find you here. What's your name?"

I froze. What was my name? I scrounged every corner of my mind for the only piece of information in this life I was obligated to know. "Miles Landgrave."

"Hello, Miles Landgrave. I'm Cielle Andyr."

I smiled at the lightness of his tone, something I'd never heard from Miles before. He told me about how he'd taken her to a crest in the Rhedrosian Mountains where they could look out on the city at night. He told me she always dreamed of learning to play the harp. He told me she asked him a lot of questions about being a soldier, and if he liked it, and how he felt about Kauvras' conquest. She was from Coldwater, somewhere across the Widow's Sea in a place called the Surging Isles, and had traveled with her brother to Taitha. He'd been born with his ankles twisted like vines on a tree trunk, and they'd heard there was a blacksmith in Taitha who could make braces to help him walk on his own.

But it didn't take long for his voice to lower, the momentary joy on his face turning to grief. I could almost taste his heartache hanging in the air as he told me about how she left.

"She never liked the idea of Kauvras' conquest. She'd made that clear from the beginning. I didn't like it either, but it was my job. There was nothing I could do to stop it." Miles stated, sounding defeated.

"You can take a stand, Miles! You can leave! You don't have to do what he says!"

"I do have to do what he says. I can't abandon my post, and I sure as hell can't abandon my men."

Her face had flushed with anger, her hands waving as she spoke. "You're going to continue murdering people for him because he told you to?"

"I'm not murdering anyone."

"You're taking their lives away from them. That's murder." She shifted on her feet, her blue eyes on fire as she stared me down. "You leave Kauvras or I leave you. Those are your choices. You're not stupid, so I suggest you make the smart choice."

"I was stupid. So fucking stupid, Petra, to choose Kauvras over her." His agony hung between us, almost tangible. "But at the end of the day, there was a truth to it all that was much harder to face." Black eyes met mine, and in them was a sorrow so deep, so profound that I felt his grief in every one of my bones. "I didn't

382

choose Kauvras over her. I chose *myself* over her." He nodded, his eyes finding the fire as he spoke. Despair was etched into every one of his features as his truth fell from his lips. "And not because I value myself more than I did her. Hell, to this day, I'd die for her. I chose myself because it was easy."

I watched him, his eyes staring at me but seeing her. "Abandoning my duty was the hard thing to do, even if it was the right thing to do. It was much easier to let her leave, blame it all on her. And I did. I blamed her for a long time. I blamed her for leaving, I blamed her for ruining my life, I blamed her for the fact that I was unhappy."

He slowed his breathing, trying to recover from the turmoil he'd caused himself by telling me this story. I could tell by the way his scar flexed over his neck that he was fighting back words. "What?" I asked.

His tongue ran across his lips, as if he were measuring what he was about to say. "I know you're my Queen and this may cross a boundary, so forgive me for intruding." He took a deep breath. "It might be hard to understand the reasons behind Cal's actions. It sure as hell would be hard to forgive him. It's easy to withdraw from him completely. I don't blame you for wanting to do that." He inhaled again, blinking the smoke from his eyes. "But don't let the easy way out keep you from your happiness."

I was silent, breaking my stare from him as something foreign washed over me. I shook my head, furrowing my brows, trying to find a rebuttal to his words, but there was nothing. Nothing but the stark naked truth looming uncomfortably over me.

"Choose yourself over Cal if you want to. But it seems to me that by choosing Cal, you'd be choosing yourself, too."

Chapter 44

It'd been a long, long day on horseback as we traversed the trail through the Pass. Every part of me ached, but I welcomed the pain. It distracted me from a truth I'd yet to face. Ludovicus had regained full consciousness but had stayed silent. I caught him glancing at Miles more than once, as if he was afraid that Miles would finish what Cal started.

I'd left Miles and Belin sleeping beside the fire and trudged my way across the leaf-strewn ground, barely illuminated by the moon that was just beginning to rise. I knew better than to venture off the trail, especially after sunset, but the sound of a stream called to me, and I was desperate to get the grime of the Pass off my skin. I had to remind myself to fear the monsters that I knew tracked me with glassy eyes. I no longer had any power against them aside from the sword at my hip.

Somewhere on the bank of this very stream, I'd saved Miles from dying a gory death at the wrong end of a bonehog's tusks. That's where he'd figured out the leechthorn hadn't affected me.

I squeezed my eyes shut at the thought, at how little I'd known about myself then, about how little I still knew.

The stream was frigid, the breath leaving my lungs as I dipped under the surface, my bare skin rising with goosebumps as I stood again and waded back to the shore. I took my time dressing, savoring the feeling of solitude, even as the animals in the forest around me screeched and cawed. This was what I needed — to feel clean, at least in one way.

"What the hell are you doing?" I jumped as a familiar voice barked from behind me. Belin approached me from the treeline, his face hard with anger. Those were his first words to me all day, and they hung in the air between us like smoke.

I shrugged, wringing my hair between my hands, trying to keep my composure under his gaze. "Bathing."

He continued marching toward me, and each step was so hard, so intentional that I swore I could feel them reverberate through the earth. "Why the fuck would you leave the path?"

I scoffed, my wet hair falling over my shoulder as I crossed my arms in a defensive stance. "I can take care of myself."

"You know it drives me mad, right?" he blurted.

Miles' words rang through my head. *Choose yourself over Cal if you want to.* Yes, I did want to. A conversation like this was useless to both of us. I sighed, preparing for the bullshit that I knew was about to unfold. "What drives you mad? My silence? My attitude?"

"Your blatant disregard for your own life."

My eyes narrowed, trying to make sense of his words.

"When I shot the arrow at Tobyas in the forest, you threw yourself over him without even considering an arrow could be coming for you next. You charged at Umbri, putting yourself in danger when I *specifically* asked you not to. Now you wander off the trail through the Onyx Pass to bathe, naked as the day you were born."

I raised a brow. Had he seen me bathing in the stream? I swallowed hard, looking him up and down, acting like I was composed. "So?"

"I see it in your eyes, Petra. You'd burn yourself to dust if no one stopped you, even without your powers. You're giving up." The words were seething, scorching in their intensity.

"How the hell could you say that? I solved your little Umbri problem, did I not? I'm going to try to kill Castemont, even without my powers. How is that giving up?"

"You're giving up on yourself."

"How–"

"Because you've made no attempt to understand the reasons behind my actions," he snapped. "And that's not you."

My brows shot up, complete disbelief plastered on my face. "That's not *me*?" I fumed.

"No, that's not you!" he yelled back.

I inhaled a sharp breath, uncertain what he was getting at. I pushed Miles' words from my mind, but they came back swinging as a persistent echo, over and over again. *Choose yourself over Cal if you want to.* I would do just that, thank you very much. I didn't give a fuck if it was the *easy way*.

"What do you want me to say? What are you looking for, Belin?" I snapped. "An apology?"

"Fuck an apology," he shouted back. He let out an exasperated breath and turned away, pacing as he rubbed his jaw.

"What the fuck do you want then?"

He whirled to me. "Dammit Petra! I want you to understand!" he roared. Raw fury radiated from behind his eyes, the sapphire and emerald alight, as if wildfire raged within him. "You think I don't wish I was him?" he growled. "You think I don't wish I was Calomyr? I've wished every day for the past four years that Belin didn't exist. I *want* to be Calomyr. He had everything I couldn't." His chest rose and fell as he stared at me, the muscles in his jaw twitching. "Don't forgive me, Petra," he breathed through his teeth, the flames within him now crawling up my spine where

386

mine no longer did. "That's fine. I don't need you to. But you *should* understand, better than anyone in this Saints forsaken realm, that I was doing what I thought I had to do."

My nostrils flared, fists clenching and releasing at my side. The truth scratched at the deepest parts of me. He was right. I didn't want him to be right — *Saints*, I didn't want him to be right. I wanted him to be my enemy. I needed him to be the villain. Because moving past what he did to me, moving past the hurt and the betrayal, choosing Cal...

What kind of person did that make me?

Fury and mercy battled within me as I glared at him. "I don't care." I spat the lie in his face, my resolve teetering dangerously close to slipping and tumbling headfirst into him. My teeth ground against each other as his stare threatened to set me on fire, the same damned way it always had.

"You do care," he answered, taking a step toward me, the movement forceful. My heart hammered in my chest as if he was lightning incarnate and I was a summer storm. "And I know that because I hear the way you talk to Tobyas."

"I haven't forgiven him either."

"But you understand *why* he turned you over to Kauvras." His words were clipped, coming from a place of anger. He took another step toward me, close enough now that I could reach out and touch him. "If you didn't, you'd treat him the same way you treat me. Like fucking trash."

I didn't back away from him, instead I steadied my feet on the riverbank. For a split second, I thought my flames were returning. But these weren't holy flames, no. These flames burned for him, and he could see it. They were bitter and resentful and all-consuming, but at the heart of the fire, buried deep beneath the embers, there was something reminiscent of need that I was fighting to ignore.

"Then explain it to me, Belin," I ordered. "Castemont doesn't have your blood anymore. His control over you is gone. So explain it."

The glass vial of his blood had broken, and so had the flood-gates on his explanation. He was no longer bound to Castemont's will, so he told me. He told me *everything*, every bloody detail of Castemont's vision of the Daughter of Katia burning the world. Every gut-wrenching facet of Castemont's plan, and how and why he'd agreed to it, and how the fear of transforming into a Bloodsinger and hurting me was enough for Castemont to control him. How he had no doubt that Castemont was in fact Noros, Saint of Pain.

"I would have done it for the good of the realm and lived with myself after the fact. But it was *you*," he seethed, a finger pointed hard, landing just below my throat. Chills rippled from the touch, my entire body going still in its wake. "If it had been *anyone* else, Petra, I would have ended their life for the good of the realm. But it was *you* who had to be the Daughter of Katia. It was *you* who I was ordered to kill. And it was you..." he panted, out of breath. "It was you who I loved."

Loved. The word pierced my chest and twisted the knife. It watched me writhe in agony, sputtering and bloody. It pushed me to the dirt, kicked me in the ribs, laughed as I fought and pleaded. I was spiraling, cursing myself for betraying the steadfast resolve I was trying to portray. And it made me angry — it made me so fucking angry that he'd *loved* me. *Past tense.*

Cold rage overtook me as I swiped for the finger still pointed at my chest, but he caught my wrist in his grip. I gasped, his expression malicious and impassioned and *enraged* as he stared down at me. That smoke and cedar scent wrapped around me, a dense fog obscuring my will to resist.

"Let me go," I ordered, my voice firm.

He pulled me toward him, my wrist still firmly in his grasp at his side, our chests heaving against each other. My back arched of its own volition, my body so tightly pressed to his that his heartbeat resounded through me. "Do you really want me to?" His voice was a growl, low and feral. A different kind of heat shot through me now, radiated from every inch of my skin as the anger ravaged my body, his eyes darting back and forth between mine.

"Let me go," I repeated, but my voice was a Saints damned whimper. The beasts of the Onyx Pass howled around us, a chorus of everything right and wrong about this moment.

His gemstone eyes softened then, his brows raising as he held my stare, desperation suddenly replacing the fury that had marred his features. But still his grip tightened on my wrist while his other hand found my face, his palm resting softly against my cheek.

I fought to keep my eyes from fluttering shut, fought like hell to keep myself from melting into his touch. I couldn't give in to him. *I had to choose myself.*

"Tell me to go again," he whispered. "Tell me again that you want me to stop trying. I will, Petra. We'll go back to silence between us. I'll be your sworn sword and nothing else." He inhaled a shaky breath. "Tell me to go. But you have to understand."

My very soul trembled within me as he stared down at me. His eyes followed his thumb as he dragged it across my bottom lip, the taste of anger and longing like saltwater on my tongue.

"Then make me understand, Cal."

I stopped fighting myself the moment he crashed into me, the force so great that I was sure the earth shuddered beneath us as his mouth collided with mine. Agony was evident in each of his movements, his need quickly settling into every part of me. Calloused hands ran frantically over my body, his fingertips tracing the invisible scars he'd left.

He pulled away suddenly, holding my face in his hands as he searched my eyes so fervently that had my heart stopped in my chest, I would have faded away knowing that I'd borne witness to need in its rawest form. The center of my soul was laid bare for him to see, and he drank it in like rainfall in the desert.

My body surrendered fully to the man who was supposed to be my enemy, the man whose dagger had been at my back countless times. My mind surrendered to the man who'd done what he believed to be right, the man who only acted on his duty to protect the realm he served. And my soul surrendered to the man who never was, the man I'd mourned.

And there was peace in me as I realized I no longer had to mourn him because he was here. The man he was and wasn't and would one day be, he was *here*.

Miles had been right. In choosing Cal, I was choosing myself.

He gripped my hair, wrenching my head back to claim my exposed throat with his tongue. A moan escaped my lips and he tensed at the sound, a hand running down my thigh and hiking it to his hip, the feel of his arousal pressing hard against me. He groaned into my neck, pulling my hips closer, closer, *closer*. I wrapped myself around him, his hands roving every inch of me with a hunger that permeated my core. And I knew that I'd let him consume me, let him destroy me if that's what he desired.

His mouth broke away from mine, our foreheads still pressed together, our bodies hopelessly tangled. "Petra."

I reached for the fasteners on the front of his leathers, fumbling to loosen them. One hand landed on mine, making quick work of the buckles and straps as his other arm clutched me to him. The leather fell to the ground as I clawed at the tunic beneath, dragging it over his head, relishing the feel of the planes of his chest under my hands. He was here. He was here and he was alive.

Then I saw it — his left arm was covered in tattooed flames from wrist to shoulder. I ran my hand up and down his arm, marveling at the ink I'd never seen before. "This is new," I whispered.

I felt his eyes on me as I stared at his arm. "You had your fire all along, even if you hadn't found it yet," he murmured. "I wasn't going to let Castemont extinguish it, even if he managed to kill you." The backs of my eyes pricked with tears. "I wanted to keep your flames with me." I looked at him, his eyes brimming with truth. "I wanted to keep you with me." He looked down to his other arm. "Looks like I'll need to add storm clouds now, too."

Words failed me. The words simply did not exist to describe the feeling that washed over me. He let my feet hit the sandy riverbank, his eyes holding my stare as he reached for the ties at my collar, pulling and tugging at the cords that kept us apart. Frustration lined his face for a split second before he gripped the cloth in both hands and tore, the sound of ripping fabric echoing through the forest as my tunic fluttered to the ground.

His stare was merciless, more animal than man as he beheld me, the rising moonlight illuminating my skin like spun silver. His hands reached greedily for me again, our bodies falling together like no time had passed, like we were exactly where we were supposed to be. I shivered as his mouth traveled from my lips to my neck, ravenous in his pursuit to make me catch fire, heat pooling between my legs as his tongue continued down my body. Every nerve in my body sang as his fingers found their way to the waistband of my trousers.

Insatiable and eager, he worked the fabric from my body, tossing my trousers to the side before he gripped my chin with a force that made the breath catch in my throat. He let go only long enough to finish undressing himself, his eyes never leaving mine. But I broke his stare to look over his body, at the skin that I'd dreamt of so many times, at the part of me that he'd tattooed on his skin and the muscles that rippled beneath it, at the length of him, tempting and rigid. He was the most beautiful thing I'd ever seen.

We were each both predator and prey, aggressor and victim. I wrapped my legs around him once again as he so easily lifted me from where I stood, my feet hooking behind his back. Molten, turbulent eyes stayed on me as he reached between us, guiding himself around the slickness that so impatiently awaited him.

"I want to understand," I whispered, taking a sharp breath in. "Please, make me understand."

He thrust into me where we stood, my core seizing with pleasure at the feel of something so familiar, something *so fucking right*. Birds flew from the trees as we found each other again, screams and groans and howls and wingbeats rippling through the forest like a symphony that had only ever played in a distant dream. His lips were demanding against mine, the feel of him thrusting in and out sending me into a state of ecstasy as he pushed me closer and closer to the edge.

My feet hit the ground, my body going cold in his absence only for a moment as he laid back and pulled me toward him, prying my knees apart as I lowered myself to straddle his hips on the bank of the stream. Inch by beautiful inch, I let him in, the breath leaving my lungs as I slowly rocked back and forth. Strong palms squeezed at my hips before one hand worked its way between my legs, playing me like a damned fiddle, his gaze locked so intently on mine that the Saints themselves couldn't have torn us apart.

Until yesterday, I'd been able to heal my wounds from teeth and steel. I'd been able to heal my gashes and breaks and bruises. But every movement he made deeper and deeper within me healed a part of me that I was never able to. Every pulse of his body against mine was a jagged piece of my shattered heart finding its way back to where it belonged. His every breath returned life to the dead and damaged parts of me.

It was a good thing my powers were gone, because had I had them, I would have burned the forest to the fucking ground.

My head dropped back, release thundering through me like a herd of kelpies rising from the depths. His hands squeezed harder as I grinded against him, suddenly reaching for my face and pulling me to him while the last of my climax roiled through me.

"I'm sorry," he breathed into me. I pulled back far enough to stare at him. My mind had melted into nothing but pure ecstasy, but I gave him a nod as I finally admitted it to myself.

I understood. I couldn't forgive, at least not yet, and I'd never forget. But I understood.

As if it were a silent command, he unleashed, fingers flexing against my back as he pounded into me beneath the canopy of trees and stars. My eyes rolled back as he once again pushed me toward that brilliant summit. Moving beneath me, I watched his eyes close as he fell over the edge, legions of fury and yearning and anguish releasing in this pinnacle moment between us. The thought of it alone was enough to send me careening over with him, his groans resounding through me as I fell. The forest could have burst into flames around us and I'd never notice. We were the only two beings to exist in the world.

Chest to heaving chest, his arms wrapped around me, holding me firmly to him, a gratified sigh leaving him as a hand tangled in my hair.

"Can I ask you something?" I whispered. Something snarled nearby, but neither of us flinched, too lost in each other to notice.

"Anything."

"Do you still love me?" I couldn't look him in the eye. I felt stupid asking. But he pulled me to face him, his thumb dancing gently over my chin.

"I knew I was going to fall in love with you the day I met you by the harbor," he started. "And I was right. I never stopped, Petra. Until the oceans rise so high that they drown the sky above us, until the last star is swallowed by the tide, my soul is yours." My breath caught in my throat at his words, at the way his mouth curved around each one. "When the Saints call on me, I'll be sure to fall at their feet and beg forgiveness for the sins I've committed against you. And if they decide to punish me for those sins, Petra, I'll take every blow, every strike, and I'll take them gladly. I'd suffer an eternity of the Saints' retribution if that's the cost of this moment." He let out a deep breath. "Yes, I still love you. I don't think I could ever stop. It's always been you, and it'll always be you. Unceasingly you, Petra."

Tears threatened to spill from my eyes. I couldn't believe we were here, couldn't believe that this moment was actually happening, but I finally managed a whisper. "I love you."

Side by side, we walked back to our campsite on the path, Cal's tunic hanging from my shoulders. I thought Miles was asleep until he opened one eye, taking in the scene in front of him, one corner of his mouth turning up in a smile.

He knew I'd chosen myself.

Chapter 45

"There's not much we change in the way of strategy." Cal stared at the ground, another makeshift map drawn in the dirt, this one of Eserene and the land just outside its walls.

"The Cabillian army has trebuchets stored in Taitha," Miles said. "I say we approach here and use them to hammer the city wall as hard as we can."

I stayed silent, knowing my skills were not suited to military strategy. We'd set up camp at the southern end of the Onyx Pass, the plains that bordered Eserene before us and the forest of the Onyxian Mountains at our backs. I had to keep my hands from shaking when I thought of Nell, Whit, and the rest of my army. They'd be arriving tonight, and the battle would commence to-morrow.

My nerves were ragged thinking about it — knowing deep in my gut what the outcome would be. I finally let myself find comfort in Cal's presence, and I'd been glued to his side since last night. His arm was looped around me constantly, as if he were trying to make up for lost time. This tiny slice of happiness in the face of certain death was enough to keep me standing. I couldn't forgive him, not yet. But I understood.

But that happiness was dampened just a bit every time I caught Miles' stare, because there was sorrow somewhere in his dark eyes. It was veiled behind the focus and vigor of a lieutenant preparing for battle, but it was always there. I knew he was thinking of Cielle, seeing me make the choice he hadn't. I wanted to ask more about her, but I didn't know what to say.

All the while, the words he spoke in Blindbarrow haunted me. He didn't intend to survive the battle.

"The second the wall falls, we charge. Full force," he stated. I blinked, trying to separate myself from my mind. "We'll lead them in and find Castemont. Petra, you'll be in the back."

Surprise shot through me. "The back?" I asked. "Absolutely not."

Miles flexed his jaw. "You don't have your powers. Fewer people will notice that if you're bringing up the rear."

I steadied my feet in the ground. "I'm leading an entire army to their death in an attempt to kill one man. I will not do so from *the back*." I leaned down to pick up a stick and promptly stuck it at the front of the scribbles that represented my army. "I'll be right here at the front. With you two. I'll be the one to kill Castemont."

"I don't–"

"What if I asked you two to stay toward the back?" I cut in.

Miles looked to his brother. "We wouldn't." Cal shook his head.

"Then you understand why I won't, either."

Cal inhaled, shaking his head. "They're going to see that you don't have powers."

"Then I'll carry a torch to make it look like I can command flames," I offered. I knew it wasn't a good idea, but I wasn't going to entertain the idea of sending a single person through the city walls before me. If I was asking people to charge into what could be their death, I would be leading them in. "This is not a negotiation. This is an order from your Queen."

"Going to pull rank, now, are you?" Miles jabbed, but there was a sternness to his voice.

"Absolutely."

The brothers exchanged a glance before Cal looked down at me. "I'd really rather you stay toward the back."

I cocked a brow, staring back as intensely as he stared at me. "And I'd really rather not have to do this at all, but here we are. There is nothing you can say that will make me abandon those who believe in me."

His eyes stayed on me for a moment longer, and I could tell he was considering pushing back again. But he nodded silently, his gaze turning hollow as he looked back to the map.

Miles' black eyes lingered on my face. They were a brand on my skin, painful and persistent. "So, trebuchets here? Near the city gates?" I asked, pointing to their designated spot in the dirt, trying to move the conversation away from me.

"Yes," Miles answered, his focus returning to the map. "Mounted cavalry here. Archers here. And the infantry here."

I couldn't let my eyes land on any one spot for too long. "Okay."

"All that's left to do is wait for the troops to arrive and pray to the Saints that this works." Miles' eyes hadn't left the map. Worry creased his brow and he bit the inside of his cheek.

"Miles, one more training session before tomorrow," I ordered. "I want to work on my swing."

"Absolutely. We can start now."

"Not yet. I have one more thing I have to do." I turned toward the hunched figure that sat bound to a tree trunk.

◆ ◆ ◆

"You're going to tell me everything," I demanded, staring down at Ludovicus' hunched form. "From the beginning."

He opened his mouth to speak but hesitated. "I'm not even sure where to start." It was hard to look at him. He looked so different than when I'd seen him knocked unconscious by Kauvras' men and hauled away from the Eserenian throne room. One cheek was still swollen from Cal's unleashing. His lips were split and bruises shadowed the creases beneath his eyes. He looked fucking awful. "I suppose I'll start with Castemont. It all seems to start and end with Castemont, doesn't it?"

His voice was strangely melodic. It may have even been pleasant had it not been coming from a man who'd almost murdered me. I tried to reconcile that the man in front of me was not that man, not technically. *Somehow.*

"My family was a prominent family back in Nesan. The capital city of Araqina, the Holy City, to be exact. That's where I hail from originally, though I haven't returned since I was just twenty years of age. That's when I traveled to Taitha to further my studies in the art of weaponry. My father accompanied me on the journey." He ran his tongue across his lips, measuring his words. "Castemont's father was the official spice merchant of King Divos of Cabillia. That was not a position of much honor, but he used his father's proximity to the King to make sure he was always in the right place at the right time. Even though he was young, Castemont always knew the right people. He ended up in my family's employ, tending to the horses, mostly, and stitching my wounds when my training got the better of me. But he and I were close in age and quickly became friends. I didn't have many as a foreigner in Taitha, so his friendship was most welcome." I saw familiar regret flash across his face as his eyes scanned the trees. He leaned back, the picture of defeat. I let myself revel in it, just for a moment. "He came to me one day with a plan to ensure the survival of the realm."

Ludovicus told a story almost identical to Cal's. Castemont had popped up, seemingly by chance, here and there, and that's how he'd earned a spot working for Ludovicus' family. He brought him to see the Bloodsinger all the way in Blindbarrow and convinced him that it was in his power to save the realm from the *tyrannical* Daughter of Katia.

"You hadn't even been born yet," he murmured, the pain in his eyes so pronounced that it almost made me hurt, too. But I caught myself, reminded by those ink-black eyes what he'd done to me.

"Go on."

"Castemont convinced me to move to Eserene, where the prophecy stated the Daughter of Katia would be born. He'd thought up the idea of Initiation, and he was going to propose it to King Umfray in order to rid the castle of its past follies. Then he'd find a way to get the Daughter of Katia to the castle to test her healing powers."

"I thought he wanted me dead."

"He did. He said he had multiple plans in place to ensure you'd be *dealt with*. I told him I'd only go to Eserene on the condition that I could finish my studies first. I had just two years left. But he didn't want to wait." He drummed his fingers across his knee, the dirt like crescent moons beneath his fingernails. "We had a bit of a falling out, one that resulted in Castemont leaving for Eserene on his own. And then the changes started."

His eyes met mine, and I couldn't do anything to break the stare. It was almost as if he saw through to my soul, to the very essence of what made me who I was. "It was my hands first. I noticed that they seemed to be bony where they hadn't been before. One day, one of my fingers snapped as I was pulling back a bowstring. I was doing nothing violent, nothing forceful, and it just snapped." His hands laced together in his lap, his arms shifting uncomfortably beneath their restraints. "And then the fingernails. I'd cut them short only for them to grow back within days, sharp as the blade I'd cut them with. I didn't know what was happening. But I truly didn't think much of it at the time.

"Eventually my skin began to lighten and pale, and it was then that my father took notice. I walked into our home one morning after retrieving a repaired sword from the blacksmith, and my father grabbed me by the throat and demanded I stop seeking favors with blood magic." His stare broke away then, falling on the campsite, his gaze lost in the flames that licked toward the sky. "I told him I wasn't, of course. But he didn't believe me. He told me if he found out I'd seen a Bloodsinger again, I'd be exiled from the family.

"But the changes kept coming. I was able to hide the thinning limbs under tunics and trousers, and my hair was already dark enough that when it went jet black, he didn't notice. But when my voice began to change..."

His expression was mournful when his eyes met mine, and this time I had to look away. Feelings of empathy were beginning to form in my chest, and I wasn't ready to face them yet.

"He made good on his promise and threw me out. For the time he remained in Taitha, he kept our home guarded, and the guards were instructed to keep me out by whatever means necessary. It was always force. I'd tried to come talk to my father and explain that I didn't know what was happening to me. That resulted in a black eye and bloody nose. Then, I tried to retrieve some of my belongings, and that resulted in multiple shattered ribs. Within a week, my father returned to Araqina and the house was abandoned. I wrote letters, dozens and dozens of letters to my mother and sisters back home, but they all went unanswered.

"The entire time, I was transforming into the monster you know me as. I didn't know why at the time, but now I do, but it doesn't make remembering my actions any less painful. Castemont had secured my blood somehow, most likely one of the times that he was all too eager to stitch me up. And little by little he was sacrificing me to the Darkness Beyond, using my blood, my lifeforce to further his plan."

My entire body had gone cold, my limbs numb as I stood in place over Ludovicus' battered form.

"I remember the first time I realized that my soul was under attack. A month after my father left, I was walking through a market square in Taitha, past a textile merchant with fabrics stacked in a cart. And I just…tipped the cart. I walked up to the man, looked him in his eyes, then tipped his cart and let his fabrics fall in the dirt. I had no idea what possessed me to do it at the time. It felt awful, like something evil was growing inside me alongside my actual self."

He swallowed hard, closing his eyes and letting his head fall back against the tree trunk. "It only got worse from there. He not only sacrificed my blood, but he used those sacrifices to make me do things… Horrible, wretched, unforgivable things. Even before he concocted the idea of the Board of Blood and appointed me as its head, he made me do things that no man would ever be able to atone for, not just to strangers, but to people I'd grown to love. I've stolen, I've maimed, and I've killed." Hands trembling, he wrung his fingers together, the muscles in his jaw working under olive skin. "But do you want to know the worst part?"

I couldn't answer, couldn't find an affirming word in the agony of my thoughts. I only managed to blink beneath furrowed brows.

He inhaled, the air shaky as it left his lungs. "I was there the whole time. Through every wrong, every wound I caused, every murder I committed, I was there, stuck in my body behind the darkness that had possessed me. I had no way to control what I was doing, and no way out." Those now-human eyes stared up at me, his gaze intense. "I was there. And I was powerless to stop it. I'm sorry."

All I could do was breathe in and out, frozen in this moment in time. How many people could wrong me against their will? How was I supposed to accept the fact that I was surrounded by people who'd hurt me even though it hadn't been by their own will?

It was maddening, this convoluted, hair-thin line between wanting so desperately the revenge I deserved, but being forced to accept that I may not get it. Those who'd wronged me… They didn't deserve to face their consequences any more than I did.

My teeth gnashed together as tears began to prickle the back of my eyes. I blinked furiously, a question burning a hole in my tongue. "How are you...yourself again?"

"Your blood, Petra. It healed me." His lips upturned into a smile, an actual smile, not a wicked or sinister grin. His eyes crinkled, his cheeks rose. "When you saved the Vacants, I'd been among them. I'd managed to avoid being given leechthorn by acting like I was already addicted. It wasn't hard considering a Bloodsinger's affinity for violence. When the rain fell and I stumbled out of a cobbler's shop, I was me again." His shoulders rose and fell with a silent laugh. "I was back in control of my body and my thoughts. I wanted to approach you in Taitha, but I was afraid, so I followed you through the Pass."

He was lying. He was telling a lie and I'd caught him in it. Here was my evidence that though he may not look the same, evil still lurked within him. "You came into contact with my blood in the Eserenian throne room. You *drank* my blood. Now you're going to tell me that it suddenly healed you in Taitha when it hadn't before?"

"You hadn't yet come into your power in Eserene."

Shit. He *wasn't* lying.

His mouth thinned as he surveyed my face. "I was retrieved from my cell the morning of your wedding to Kauvras. I was brought to sit among the crowd." My eyes widened. He'd been there that day? "Even bound to Castemont's will, the part of me that was left could see the fear on your face. It was hidden by the sheer will to survive, but it was there. I could feel the tug of the blood sacrifice on me as I moved, and as always, I had no control. The soldier seated in front of me had a bow slung across his back, and in one swift motion, it was in my grip, an arrow pointed straight for you where you stood at the altar.

"But at the last second," his eyes narrowed, turning almost wistful, "I was able to adjust, to shift my view ever so slightly, somehow. *Me,* not the body that Castemont controlled. I was able

402

to peek through the darkness just enough, for one tiny moment of control. So I released, and hit my target. Kauvras."

My stomach bottomed out at his words and it was all I could do not to fall to the ground in shock. "You?"

"Through all of this, Petra, Castemont said over and over that by no means could we let you secure an army. He said that if you managed to secure an army, his mission would be at stake because you'd have the protection of not only your powers, but also legions of soldiers who'd die for you. I knew that by killing Kauvras, you'd have a shot at taking over his army. But I didn't kill him, and you still managed to do it."

"Why wouldn't Castemont kill me himself? He had more than his fair share of chances."

"He couldn't. I don't know why. He just told me he couldn't be the one to do it."

"And your *brothers*?"

He shook his head. "I don't know who they were. Castemont assembled the Board with no explanation."

My face betrayed a million different shades of confusion and anger and hurt, and I made no attempt to hide it. Cal must have been watching from the campsite because suddenly he was there, Miles close behind. "I'm here. What do you need?" Cal asked with a hand on my back, voice low in my ear as his eyes shot daggers at Ludovicus.

Remorse hung dense in the air like fog. I couldn't help but breathe it in, feel it resonate within me. I could tell Cal to kill him and he would do so gladly. I could tell Cal all of the terrible things he did to me, tell him to make Ludovicus confess to the other atrocities he'd committed but hadn't specified. But I didn't, because he hadn't been the one to commit them. Not really.

An act he did commit, however, was giving me a chance to escape from Taitha and assemble an army in the process.

"He shot the arrow at Kauvras."

Ludovicus had been the catalyst behind everything that had happened since that day. Ludovicus was the reason I hadn't sealed my marriage to Kauvras. Ludovicus was the reason I had an army.

"Kill me, your Majesty," he said quietly, repeating the same request he'd made in Blindbarrow, his eyes still locked on me. "I can confess my sins a thousand times and never feel clean. I have no wish to live with myself a moment longer."

Miles shifted where he stood, and though Cal still stared down at Ludovicus with vitriol, I knew he, too, was conflicted.

I squared my shoulders, willing my mind to go quiet. I only wished to consider this moment, this single moment of realization and redemption. Killing Ludovicus, taking his life with my bare hands would heal the wound he'd ripped through me. But it would leave a new one in its place, a wound that I'd never be able to heal, even if my powers were one day restored.

"If you wish to die," I said through a tight jaw, "you can give your life for me tomorrow in the battle to take Castemont's life."

His eyes closed for a moment but opened again, clear and intentional. "With honor, your Majesty."

I nodded, backing away and turning toward the campsite. "Untie him," I called without looking behind me, knowing one of the Myrin brothers would see to the task. "But the moment he tries anything, kill him."

Chapter 46

Eserene's walls were just a speck on the horizon across the plains. But I felt their pull, could almost hear Castemont's laugh echoing from behind them.

The smile on Nell's face as she descended the final hill of the Onyx Pass alongside Whit burst through me, knowing I would soon strike it from her the moment I told her my powers were gone. Summercut rode just behind them, a banner rippling through the air above him, held just as tall and proud as he sat. It was a deep red, the color of freshly spilled blood, with a half-sun, half-moon emblem stitched in glittering gold. Below the moon was a snake, and above the sun flew a driva, the entire sight exuding a fearsome power.

My crest.

And behind the banner came the army, dozens of men and women cresting the hill every second, some on foot, some on horseback. My smile faded as I watched them inch closer and closer, my mind nagging on the fact that each soldier that marched toward me was a life I was indirectly going to take. Each soldier that marched toward me was blood on my hands. I did my best to look like everything was fine, like everything was going according to plan. But on the inside I was floundering, and I knew Cal and Miles were also floundering internally where they stood beside me.

"All the old soldiers at the pub always tell stories about the *night before the battle*," Nell called as she approached, giving a satisfied sigh. "Never thought I'd get to be a part of one."

I forged another smile. "What do they say?"

"That half the soldiers live like it's their last night alive. And the other half pray like it's their last night alive." She dismounted, folding me in a hug and giving me another beaming smile.

Whit let out a laugh as he landed on the ground. "I can guess which party you'll be a part of."

"The latter are probably the ones doing the right thing. But the former have more fun. Feasting, fighting, and fucking, they say."

"I'm in," Whit chimed then turned to Cal. "But before that, I believe I have something of yours." He reached to where I realized he had a second sword sheathed at his hip, handing the blade to the Invisible King.

Those gemstone eyes widened as he wrapped his hand around its worn filigree grip, the rubies inlaid beneath the guard glinting in the light. "I thought it was gone forever. Where did you get this?" he asked in disbelief.

"It was in Castemont's quarters back in Taitha," he answered with a shrug. "Figured we'd take a little look around, see if we could find anything embarrassing. No such luck, but we did find that."

My heartrate quickened, thinking about my dagger that Miles handed over to Castemont. "You didn't happen to find a dagger, did you?"

Whit shook his head. "No dagger. Just the sword."

I tried not to let the disappointment sink in as Cal offered a hand to Whit. "Thank you," he said with a smile so genuine, I couldn't help but mirror it. But Whit grabbed his hand and pulled him into a hug, one of those hearty hugs between men where they slap each others' backs and laugh the whole time.

"Enough of the love fest. Come on, Whit," Nell chided, yanking him away to set up camp with the other arriving soldiers.

"Your Majesty," Commander Summercut said with a bow as he approached, staking the crimson banner in the ground. "I had the seamstresses in Taitha sew your banner. I hope you're satisfied with the design."

It billowed against the blue sky, the gold-stitched symbols of Katia and Rhedros reminding me that was all I had of them — symbols. I wouldn't have them to lean on tomorrow.

I mustered up a nod and smile. "It's perfect. Thank you."

"I'd like to review the strategies for the battle with the other leaders. We brought tents for you and your court, as well."

I nodded, thankful for the thought behind his gestures. "Thank you, Commander."

He raised a hand, a mess of soldiers jumping into action to erect the tents where Nell and Whit directed them. Soldiers continued to file down the Pass, my stomach churning with each one that arrived.

"I need to speak with you," I murmured to Summercut, leaning in slightly. I stared at the distant walls of Eserene rising in the hazy distance. "As soon as the first tent is up."

◆ ◆ ◆

"They're just gone?" Nell breathed, shock in her words.

I nodded, fighting to keep my face straight, the sound of the crowd of soldiers outside the tent a constant reminder of my fucking inadequacy. "I have no powers. Not even residual power. Nothing. I'm so, so sorry."

Summercut's face was grave, his cheeks sucked in as he thought, staring at the map of Eserene that had been sprawled across the table in front of us. "No apology necessary. But it's going to take some manipulation to make it look like you still have powers."

"We tried to convince her to stay toward the back of the charge," Miles said flatly.

"I can't do it. I understand why I should, but I can't." My eyes traveled through the tent. "I'll be in the front, leading the charge. I'm not going to cower in the back."

"It's not cowering, your Majesty," Summercut answered cautiously. "The soldiers can't know that your powers are gone."

"She offered to *carry a torch*," Miles scoffed.

My mind grappled for something, anything, when an idea hit me. "We'll tell them I'm saving my strength for when I come face-to-face with Castemont. They have to know my well of power is not unlimited. I need to conserve it."

Cal's gemstone stare was on me, I could feel it. Summercut pursed his lips in thought. "You really want to lead the charge?"

"I have to."

"It'll be easier for you to make it to Castemont if you're in the back," Summercut explained. "The frontlines will weaken Castemont's forces and give you more room to run."

I shook my head. "I know my way through the city. I know it sounds crazy, but this is what I need to do."

He nodded, running his tongue across his lips as he thought, looking to Miles and Cal. "Okay. We'll make it work." His finger hit the map, at a point on the wall just west of the city gates. "Trebuchets hit here, yes?" He placed a tiny wooden trebuchet on the map, behind the cavalry and footsoldier figurines. "Castemont will no doubt be stationed in the castle, and this is the closest point to his anticipated location. His army is most likely no larger than ten thousand strong, but they're Vacants, so even their weakest soldier is more powerful than our strongest soldier. They also have the advantage of the walls." He looked to me, his

408

expression lined with severity. "We must breach the wall and keep the battle inside the city. It'll be easier for us to overpower them in the narrow streets."

"Wait," I cut in, walking to the other side of the table, zeroing in on Inkwell. "We want to hit the weakest part of the wall, right? That's our best chance of bringing it down quickly. If the wall has a weak point, it'll be the portion surrounding Inkwell."

Cal looked to Summercut. "She's right. And the streets are narrower, which could give us an advantage as not too many of his Vacants will be able to get through. Easier for the frontlines to manage."

I slid the figurines from one side of the map to the other, arranging them outside Inkwell's walls, letting my eyes trace the path I'd take to Castemont.

"Her Majesty, the Queen. A war strategist," Miles quipped.

"But it's as far from the castle as you can be," Summercut responded, his eyes trailing from where my finger lay to where the castle sat. "There's no clear path."

"I know the way," I stated firmly. "I can get there."

Cal's entire body tensed next to me. He didn't want me on the frontlines. He didn't want me parading through Inkwell then the rest of the city to get to Castemont. If he had his way, I'd be on another continent, as far from the battle as I could be. I understood that. I didn't want him there either.

What choice did we have?

Summercut's face was apprehensive, his war-weathered eyes leery. "It is absolutely imperative that you keep Castemont's forces within the city walls. And keep the impact zone narrow. If too much of the wall falls, it'll be easier for them to push us back."

I nodded, feeling as good about the plan as I could. "Everyone knows where they're supposed to be tomorrow at sunrise?" I asked, my eyes flicking over the map again.

"Aye."

"Then everyone is free to go. You can spend tonight living or praying."

The tent emptied of everyone but me and Cal, my eyes still on the map, and his eyes still on my face. He reached a hand out, tipping my chin to look at him. "What will you be doing tonight? Living or praying?"

"Both."

Chapter 47

"Thank you for being here." I tried to sound as convincingly cheerful as I possibly could as I made my way through the camp of soldiers, introducing and shaking hands and thanking, thanking, thanking. The same sight greeted me over and over — bent knee, fist over chest, "Daughter of Katia." Cal and Nell trailed behind me. They were an odd looking duo, their height difference so substantial that it felt like people stared just as long at them as they did at me.

Whispers followed each step I took, the sounds of *she'll burn them all* and *you should ask to see her powers*. I was sick to my stomach.

The energy in the camp was oscillating between frenzied and solemn. Some people played cards and threw dice. Some passed bottles and flasks and exchanged drunken laughs. Some tents billowed and shook though there was no breeze. And someone strummed a lute in the mess of it all.

Others sat quietly, hunched over the Book of Saints. Some held each other close. I wondered if they held loved ones or strangers, trying to find comfort where they could.

But every single person, every single soldier, whether they were laughing or weeping, said some variation of the same thing. "I will die for you with honor."

I swallowed hard, trying to make it look like my insides weren't screaming out in desperation. "Daughter of Katia," I heard from behind me, and I turned to give a now habitual nod in the direction of the voice. But my heart stopped in my chest when I saw who it came from.

"Elin." Larka's dearest friend. I hadn't seen her since a few weeks after Larka's death, when my days blurred together and my mind was constantly telling me I'd be better off taking my own life.

She'd told me I should have been the one to die in the explosion, and I'd agreed with her. Part of me still did. No, all of me still did. She'd said Larka was perfect, and she'd been right about that, too. I remembered that moment vividly — the freezing ground we sat upon on the waterfront with only our cloaks to separate us from the ice, the all-consuming pain that slashed through my chest and straight to my soul, the violent resentment that coursed from her body and caught me in a vice.

She rose, her expression unreadable at first as she stared back at me. Large brown eyes were guarded and weary over cheeks that were not as full as they had been. Her chocolate hair was longer now, much longer, braided into a plait that fell to her low back.

"I heard the rumors that it was you," she breathed, taking in Cal and Nell who stood guard beside me, Katia's diadem atop my head. "I knew I wouldn't believe it until I saw it."

I had to keep myself from shifting awkwardly under her gaze. "Well, here I am."

"Here you are." She opened her mouth to speak but hesitated. I thought I saw her lip tremble for a split second before she finally spoke. "I'm sorry, your Majesty, for what I said–"

I cut her off, my palm raising to stop her. "There's no need to apologize, Elin. Truly, there isn't."

"No, there is. I wasn't kind to you. Her death..." Her inhale was shaky, and I recognized the pain on her face. I'd seen it on so many people. Too many people. "It ruined me."

The emptiness behind her eyes was jarring, a hollowness that I knew would always remain with her to some degree. "I understand."

"I loved her."

"I know you did, and–"

"No," she said, stepping forward, her fists clenched at her sides. "I loved her." Her shoulders shook with a sob that she fought back. "And she loved me."

Realization washed through me. *She loved me.* My brain went silent as a piece of my heart that I didn't even know existed split apart, the edges sharp as shattered glass. It slashed a new wound in my chest, this one for Elin. My hand flew to my mouth as I watched a single tear trail down her cheek. My voice was a muffled whisper. "Why wouldn't she tell me?"

"She wanted to," Elin answered, her mouth quivering. "She was going to tell you at Cindregala. She was waiting for you to meet someone first, because she felt like she could never let herself be happy unless you were, too. You were always her main concern. And she was watching, you know, when you met him." Elin nodded to Cal behind me. She mustered up a weak smile. In all this mess, in all the hurt I'd witnessed in my life, in all the heartbreak that I'd suffered, her smile was the most excruciating, most distressing sight I'd ever seen.

I turned away, fighting the instinct to double over, anything to combat the hollowness that ripped a canyon through me. Cal was at my side, a hand on my back as he looked down at me. He was silent, simply there if I needed him. And I did. Saints, I did.

The back of my hand was pressed so hard to my mouth that I was sure it'd leave a bruise, but it was all I could do to keep the agony from boiling over, because I knew what Elin was going to say next.

"She saw him offer his hand, and she saw you look up at him. She looked at me and said that you were going to fall in love with him. That you didn't know it yet, but he was the one sent to you by the Saints. And she saw the same look in his eyes, too, when he saw you. So she said yes, that was the day she was going to tell you that she and I...were in love. She was waiting until we met up later that night at the waterfront to tell you that we were going to move across the sea to Zidderune, where our love wouldn't have been looked upon as...unfavorably as it would have in Eserene."

Every part of me hurt, every bone ached at my naivety. I'd missed the signs, all of them right in front of my face. I wished Larka had told me, was sick that she felt like she couldn't. It had all been for my sake.

But that'd been Larka. I'd spent so much time breaking up the fights she'd started, dodging sideways glances from strangers at her words, and trying to come up with rebuttals that were half as witty as hers, that I must have been blinded to the person at the core of it all. She'd been a hot-headed, foul-mouthed spitfire, but she'd loved me in a way I could never be loved by anyone else.

"So I take it back," Elin bleated, standing a bit straighter, blinking hard to rid her eyes of the flood of tears. "It shouldn't have been you that died that day. It *couldn't* have been you that died that day. And not because you're some prophecy waiting to be fulfilled, but because Larka would've never let that happen. It had to be her."

I closed the distance between us and folded her into my arms, clinging so tightly to this last piece of my sister I had no idea had remained. "I'm sorry she was taken from you, Elin." I was a mess, but she held me, too. I think we were holding each other together in that moment, and that without each other, we would have shattered completely. "I'm so sorry."

"She wasn't taken from me," she whispered, pulling back to look at me. "Not fully. I'll always have her with me." Her lip trembled again. "And so will you."

Elin backed away, wiping the tears from her cheeks as she lowered herself to the ground once again. "Tomorrow," she started, crossing a fist over her chest, "I will die for you, and for Larka, with honor, if only to be with her again."

Chapter 48

A pallet was laid in my tent, and the table was covered with food. Roast pig and rabbit stew and sliced potatoes, biscuits and pastries and the most beautiful looking cake I'd ever seen. I tried to decline both luxuries more than a few times. How could I accept these comforts? But Nell informed me that every soldier would have a bedroll to sleep on, a tent to sleep under, and a hot meal to eat, and insisted I accept. I did so, begrudgingly. The moment I hit the pallet, I was so happy I did.

And the wine... It made me forget, just for a moment, where we were and what was about to happen. It made me forget my exchange with Elin, the realization that still rang through me. Just for a moment, it was me and Cal, eating a meal in candlelight. There was no battle to come. There was no harried past. There was no Castemont. There was just us, together.

I placed my goblet of wine on the table, suddenly feeling much more sober than I wanted to.

"What are you thinking about?" he asked suddenly.

"I'm thinking…" I trailed off, convincing myself to admit to the thing that had been nagging at me. "I'm afraid to die tomorrow."

"You're not going to die tomorrow," Cal cut in, his voice stern.

"Cal."

He reached across the table, his thumb finding my chin and lifting it toward his face. "Powers or no powers, you are the rightful queen of the realm. Powers or no powers, you are the Daughter of Katia and Rhedros, the Daughter of Benevolence and Blood. That is power in and of itself."

I inhaled. "You could die, too. You could be hurt, and I'm not going to be able to heal you."

His mouth turned up in a close-lipped smile, gemstone eyes crinkling at the corners. "I accepted death a long time ago. And if I'm going to go anyway, this seems like a good cause to die for." He leaned forward, tucking a strand of hair behind my ear. The sudden brush of his fingers sent shockwaves to my core.

Defeat crept in at the thought of the man at the center of it all. My mind zeroed in on him, everything else going quiet. "When I go, I have to take Castemont with me." I stood from the table and moved to sit on the pallet, elbows on my knees as I cradled my face in my hands, kneading at my temples in a feeble attempt to rid my head of the ache it'd been carrying since Blindbarrow.

"Whatever happens," Belin whispered, lowering himself to sit next to me, thumb stroking across my cheek, "I'll be right there with you."

A breath whooshed out of me as my back hit the pallet and I squeezed my eyes shut. Cal's hand found my knee. "Can I ask you something?"

My eyes opened, assessing his face, but it was unreadable. "Okay."

"Back in Taitha, after you saved the Vacants, you said you'd spoken with Katia and Rhedros. Have you spoken with them since?"

I swallowed hard, dreading the answer I had to give him. I managed only a weak whisper, afraid that if I heard myself speak the words, my shortcomings would stop my heart where I laid. "Not since I lost my powers."

"Have you tried?"

I pursed my lips and nodded. I had tried to find them, but I had no idea how. I searched for them in my dreams at night, trying to figure out how I could get to the Darkness Beyond. I forced myself to meet Cal's gemstone stare. There was the sympathy and warmth I'd been craving, but beneath that, I saw fear. Cold, rigid fear.

"Can you try now?"

The question caught me off guard. "You want me to pray," I responded. It wasn't a question.

"You said you were going to both live and pray tonight. Maybe you can't hear them. But maybe they can hear you."

My heart quickened at the prospect. What would I say? *Please help us win the battle tomorrow?* That seemed pointless. But Cal's expression was so genuine, so intense, so hopeful... How could I deny him?

We dropped to our knees at the edge of the pallet, lowering our heads, folding our hands at our chins and closing our eyes. "Hello," I said weakly.

Cal laughed, dropping his hands in his lap and turning to look at me. "*Hello?* That's how you start a prayer?"

"I mean, I've never *really* prayed before. In my mind, sure. And I sort of prayed when Miles' arrow wound was infected. But not like this."

His eyes were full of amusement. "Your parents are the Keepers of the Saints and you've never prayed before?"

"Have you prayed to *your* parents?" I asked.

He smirked. "My mother was a baker, and it turns out my absent father is an *allegedly* impotent lunatic." I rolled my eyes as he let out another laugh. "So no, I haven't prayed to my parents. But I've prayed to yours."

The air in the tent suddenly turned somber as Cal faced forward again, lowering his head. I cleared my throat, unsure of what to say. It felt silly speaking into the silence. I peeked at Cal beside me to see his face was etched in concentration. Despite his joking, he was clinging to this, waiting on my next words.

He'd told me that every battle fought was powered by hope. This, right here, was his hope.

I was his hope.

Deep breath in. "It's me, Petra," I spoke into the empty tent. "I can't hear you anymore, but I'm hoping you can hear me. I'm asking that you help us tomorrow, from wherever you are in the Darkness Beyond. I'm asking that you do whatever you can to help me end the tyranny of the Saint of Pain, because it won't stop as long as he lives and breathes. Wherever you are, whatever you can do. Just...*please*."

I exhaled, letting my hands drop. "To our Saints, we pray," Cal murmured.

"To our Saints, we pray."

He stood, offering me a hand and pulling me to him. "We've prayed." He gently pressed his lips to mine, his finger under my chin. "It's time we live."

The kiss deepened. I made sure to note the feeling, the taste. His movements were slow and intentional as his tongue began to dance across mine. Hands tangled in hair as I pulled him closer to me, reveling in the glow that built between us.

I was going to die tomorrow. That, I knew for certain. But Cal was right. It was time — the last time — I lived. At the end of the day, I didn't need my flames or wind or rain or anything holy or divine to live. I needed *this*, holy and divine in its own way.

I greedily clawed at the cords of his tunic, but he reached for my wrists, my eyes flying wide in surprise. "I'm going to take my time with you," he breathed.

"No, I need you *now*." I was impatient, and he could tell.

"That's too bad," he taunted, a smirk on his face as he watched me try to escape his grip, tongue running over his teeth. "If this is to be my last night alive, I have a few dying wishes that I think you could grant."

I wrenched my wrists back again, but within seconds he'd pinned me to the bed, arms over my head. Shock pulsed through me, along with something else, something darker. Every nerve stood alert at the intoxicating look with which he stared at me. Maybe it was the wine, or maybe it was my certain death that hung over me, but I decided I could play this game.

He released me and backed away only to stare down at me, a thumb on his chin as he feigned deep thought. "Huh. Something isn't quite right here."

I furrowed my brows, my eyes scanning the room trying to figure out what the hell he was talking about. "What?"

"You're still clothed." His eyes were on fire, melting me from the inside as he knelt before the pallet, a hand running up my thigh to my hip, teasing over my ribs. "How can I solve that?"

I was panting already, slick with want as his finger drew circles over my belly, my thin tunic the only thing keeping his skin from mine. "Take them off," I breathed.

He cocked his head. "I feel like there's a better solution." His breath was hot on my neck as he leaned in, tongue running from my throat to my ear. I let my hands grapple across his shoulders as goosebumps covered my body. "You take them off."

My hands paused, a smile coming to my face as he stood and pulled me to him. He fell back to the pallet, expectantly waiting, his lower lip between his teeth.

"Undress for me. My first dying wish."

420

My face reddened, but I obeyed. I was going to die, so I wanted to live. My eyes stayed on him as I untied the cords at my neck, letting them hang loose as he watched. "Like this?"

"Just like that," he growled.

The collar of my tunic fell open, my shoulders and collarbones exposed and glowing orange in the light of the candles. He stared so intently that I knew I was the only thing in his world right now. *Me.* I pulled the fabric over my head and watched as he took me in.

His words were a whisper now. "Just like that." His trousers began to strain as I slowly ran my fingers down my bare chest, teasing him, before I found my waistband. I could see the want on his face, feel it pulse through the air like it was alive as I rolled my trousers down my legs. Completely exposed to him, I stood and let him stare.

"There's another problem," he murmured. I blanched, once again wondering what could be wrong. "You're not writhing under my tongue." *Fuck.* Heat began to pulse wickedly between my legs. "My next dying wish," he breathed, standing and pushing me to the pallet, "is to taste you again."

Pulling me to where he kneeled on the floor, he pried my legs open. I gasped at the suddenness of it, but shyness got the better of me, and I tried to slam my knees together on instinct.

"Hide if you want to," he whispered, trailing his mouth up the outside of my thigh. "I won't push you. But you spread before me? I've never seen anything more beautiful in my fucking life."

Shit. I let my knees drop open at his words, all apprehension melting from my body as his tongue made contact. He wanted me to writhe, and I had no choice but to obey. A moan escaped my mouth and the noise made him burrow deeper, move his tongue against me faster as his arms hooked around my thighs.

Every part of me was on fire, every nerve burning as his fingers began to tease me. He pulled away, staring me down while he closed his mouth around his finger and thumb, then ran them up my belly. They pinched around my nipple, and I couldn't take it, couldn't take the agonizing pleasure. I was coming apart beneath him, and still he worked me with his fingers and tongue, still he pushed me closer and closer.

"Cal, I–"

"Not yet," he murmured, pulling away completely. "I want to savor this."

I opened my mouth to protest, but he shot up, working his clothes off slowly enough that it drove me mad. The contours of his body in the flickering candlelight were...

He leaned over me, but I put a hand up and threw his words back at him. "I want to savor this." The air changed completely, from want to need. I stood, letting my hands run across his chest, his belly, his hips, letting his smoke and cedar scent cloud my senses. The tips of my fingers trailed up his tattooed arms, relishing the feeling. My eyes caught his, and the look on his face was nothing I'd ever seen before. It was denial and acceptance. It was grief and joy. It was love and longing and regret, and everything in between. It was *hope.*

"I'm sorry, Petra," he whispered, running the back of his fingers against my cheek.

The weight of the world upon my shoulders had grown far too great for me to carry. But there was one thing I could rid myself of, one thing I was ready to let go. One thing that I didn't want to carry into battle tomorrow. For him. For me.

"I forgive you."

He was completely still at first, eyes searching mine as if he were waiting for me to take it back. I didn't. He realized that my words were real, that I'd actually spoken them, and his head tipped back, his throat working as I stood before him. When he looked down at me again, I couldn't tell if it was the candlelight reflecting in his eyes, or if there were tears.

With his hands at my hips, he pulled me down over him. Outside the tent, the world prepared to fall apart around us. But in here, there was nothing but Cal and me, spending our last night on this earth *living.*

422

The feeling of fullness was mind-numbing as he sheathed himself in me, gemstone eyes piercing straight through to my soul, looking at me like the sun rose and set with me. But he was holding something back. I could tell that there was something he was trying to control. But I clawed at him, pulled him closer, willing him to release what I knew he was holding onto.

I willed him to forgive himself.

The groan he let out ricocheted through my body as he moved within me. I watched his eyes change as he broke through that fragile control he'd cast over himself. I don't know if he saw something in my stare as I ground against him, but he turned absolutely feral, nails digging into my hips. Marking me. *Claiming me.*

All at once he sprung forward, holding me to him as he flipped me to my back, his face wound up in a savage snarl. I was his and he was mine, and he made sure I felt that in every corner of my body. His hand wrapped around my wrists, pinning them over my head. He must have seen the shock in my face at the aggression behind the move, because his mouth turned up in a wicked smile.

I wrenched my wrists back, but he held steady. "Do I need to restrain you, my Queen?"

My eyes flew wide at his words. I could play this game. "I don't know, do you?"

His eyes narrowed for a moment before he pulled back, reaching for the belt he'd strewn on the floor of the tent. His eyes didn't leave mine as he bound my wrists above my head.

I was completely at his mercy, and my body knew it. I began to unravel as he hooked one of my legs over his shoulder and entered me again. Whatever look crossed my face made him move faster, harder, deeper. I felt his eyes watching me as I moved closer to climax, our heaving breaths falling in sync with each other. I had no control as my legs began to quiver, and a sinful smile returned to his face. "My last dying wish, Petra," he breathed, fighting against his own rising pleasure to keep his voice even, "is to make you come."

And once again, I obeyed. *Saints*, I obeyed him. The breath caught in my throat as release thundered through my body. He roared as he came with me, sounds ripping from his throat like a wild animal. He may have called my name so loud the whole encampment heard it, but I was so wrapped up in what he was doing to me that I wouldn't have known or cared.

Stars swirled through my vision as though I was falling through the night sky as he collapsed beside me, pulling me to his chest, pressing his lips to my hair. For a moment we just breathed together, reveling in the afterglow.

I raised my wrists, still bound by his leather belt. "Care to release me?" I laughed.

"I'd rather not," he teased, "but if you insist." He loosened the belt and slid it from my wrists, his hands immediately moving over the red marks it left behind, his thumbs rubbing slowly back and forth. "We've lived and we've prayed," he breathed. "Now what?"

"We could always live again," I answered, looking up to see the smile I'd heard in his voice.

He stared down at me, eyes vibrant with lust. "That was always the plan." One side of his mouth quirked up in that smile I loved so damned much, the dimple on his cheek making me smile, too. He pushed a strand of hair behind my ear, and I winced as reality creeped back in. I grappled for a hold on my emotions. "I don't know what tomorrow will bring," I said, "but I'm glad we get to be here together."

He ran a hand down my back, leaving goosebumps in its wake. "I am, too. I just wish…" he trailed off.

"You wish we had more time?"

A heavy breath escaped his lips. "Yeah."

The regret ran deep as I thought of the time I spent being so bitter. "I'm sorry I wasted so much of it being angry at you."

His thumb found my chin, pulling me to look at him. "Don't you dare apologize for that. You could have taken all the time in the world and still chosen not to forgive me and I would understand. You could take back your forgiveness and I would understand. I don't fault you in the slightest for being angry at me."

My lips were a hard line as I nodded. "Do you think we would have met if Castemont hadn't been around?"

He ran his tongue across his lips. "I can't say I have an answer to that." A small smile quirked one corner of his mouth, his dimple showing for just a split second. "But that's at least one thing he was good for."

I smiled back at him, reveling in his gemstone stare if only for a moment. But the darkness crept in again, unwavering in its persistence. "What if I can't do it?" I fought to steady my breathing at the thought that had been nagging me incessantly for days. "What if I can't kill Castemont?"

"You will," he answered. "I have no doubt."

"I appreciate the faith you have in me. I really do," I answered, turning back to him, "but you have to be realistic. There's a very real chance I won't make it to the castle. There's a very real chance that Castemont's reign, *Noros'* reign, won't end tomorrow."

He was silent for a moment, his thumb running lazily across my shoulder. "Realistically, yes. That's a possibility. But I know you. You're going to charge in with everything you have and fight your way to that castle. You're going in there with your powers and you're not going to accept defeat."

"I don't have them, Cal," I whispered, still unable to face the truth, and it sounded like he hadn't been able to either. "I don't have my powers."

"When I was... When *Calomyr* was dead, I used to pray that you'd find your powers. I knew they were there, even if they were dormant. And just like then, your powers are here now, Petra, whether you can use them or not. I see them in your eyes, in the way you move, in the way you speak, the same way I did when I was Calomyr."

I knew I needed to push the self-doubt away, that I was going to end up sabotaging myself. I was going to be charging into battle tomorrow. I *needed* to be confident. But I couldn't push the feeling away any longer, and it was going to swallow me.

"Look at me," Cal said, tipping my chin to look at him as if he could feel the doubt that coursed through every part of me. "You *are* fire. You are wind, and you are the storm. You are death, and you're coming for Castemont. He knows it. Why else would he be hiding behind the city walls?"

I took a deep breath, letting his stare anchor me. He *was* hiding, wasn't he? Castemont… He was scared. I nodded at Cal, clinging to that thought.

"There's a very real possibility that Castemont lives through tomorrow," he said, his gaze hard on me. "But you know what? The possibility of him falling is just as real."

My lungs expanded as I tried to take in as much air as I could. The uncertainty was inescapable. "It isn't fair," I whispered.

"No, it isn't." He planted a kiss on my forehead, squeezing me to him. "But such is life, Petra."

Chapter 49

We would wait until midday to strike. A fog had descended in the early morning hours, so heavy that Eserene's walls were invisible behind it. That was no good for an army made up of mostly inexperienced soldiers.

The atmosphere was sober. There was no more living. Everybody prayed. And that was absolutely terrifying, considering they all believed I had my powers.

"I was told to come see you?" I called as I ducked into the blacksmith's tent, Cal trailing behind me. I didn't recognize the man who stood waiting, but he was the epitome of a blacksmith, with arms the size of tree trunks and soot beneath his fingernails, maybe ten years older than my father would've been. He gave a gruff smile beneath an unruly mustache and bent to one knee, fist across his chest. Of course, he didn't have his forge, but there were weapons and armor propped all across the tent.

"For ye, yer Majesty." He raised his hand to a set of black armor on a form, shoulder plates made of gold scales, my crest emblazoned on the breastplate. Atop the form sat the traditional helmet that went with Cabillian armor, but he'd fashioned razor sharp golden fangs to the visor.

"I didn't have time to make ye a whole new set, so I worked wi' some o' the old Cabillian armor I had. I hope ye find it acceptable, yer Majesty."

I blinked at the metal that swallowed all the light around it, the sun and moon that both glinted in the hazy gray light. My fingers ran across the scales at the shoulders, the teeth on the helmet.

I hadn't even considered armor. To be truthful, I hadn't even considered what people wore to a battle. I probably should've, but my mind had been preoccupied with, well, everything else.

It was perfect.

"What is your name, sir?" I asked, unable to tear my eyes from his work.

"Pavo, yer Majesty."

"And where do you hail from?"

He nodded toward the door to his tent. "Eserene, yer Majesty. Found me'self in Taitha after..."

I smiled at him. "Thank you, Pavo, for this kindness. It's beautiful work."

"Ye're welcome, yer Majesty." I could tell by the way he wrung his hands that he had something else to say. "If I may," he said apprehensively, waiting for the nod I gave him, "I know Castemont." My stomach bottomed out, and I felt Cal tense beside me. "He frequented my shop when he first moved to Eserene. Never got a good feeling from 'im."

Cal looked at me. I kept my eyes forward on Pavo.

"If it please you, when you find 'im..." He turned to one of the many racks of blades, pulling a broadsword and laying it across his palms. "Will ye use this?" The entire weapon was almost as dark as the armor, except for a sun and moon inlaid just below

428

the guard and a serpent winding around the hilt, all in gold. My eyes traveled up the blade, and I gasped.

THE MERCY OF KATIA was engraved in the steel. I reached forward, flipping it in his hands to see *THE FURY OF RHEDROS* on the other side. The same inscription on the dagger that had been left for me before Initiation, the dagger that Miles had handed over to Castemont.

"The inscription..." I whispered, my eyes stuck on the words.

"A man came into my shop a few years back. Asked for a dagger wi' the same inscription. I always remembered the saying, and thought it'd be a good blessin' for yer efforts today, yer Majesty."

"Who was the man?" I asked, my eyes wide.

He flinched at the sudden severity of my tone. "I'm sorry, yer Majesty, don't remember much about 'im. Just the inscription."

"Do you remember anything? Anything at all?"

"I think 'e had dark hair," he answered apprehensively. "Maybe."

"That's the dagger you told me about?" Cal asked. His stare was glued to the blade with the same inscription, brows furrowed.

I nodded in response, trying to think of *who* would've had the dagger forged.

Heavy hoofbeats suddenly sounded outside. A gallop — and they weren't slowing. "Your Majesty!" someone called. "Your Majesty!"

I walked out of the tent into the foggy air to see Tomkin approaching on horseback, throwing himself from the steed before it even stopped. "Your Majesty," he panted. "A raven sent from the scouts at the wall. Castemont's army of Vacants is gathered at the city gates and are preparing to meet you outside of Eserene's walls. There are tens of thousands of them."

My eyes flew wide. *Tens of thousands? How?* "The city gates," I whispered. My mind struggled to connect what was supposed to happen to what was happening now. "The battle needs to take place within the city walls if we want any shot at winning." I took a deep breath, trying to steady myself.

Summercut's horse galloped in at breakneck speed. "Do you have new orders, your Majesty?"

Adjust, Petra, adjust. "Send a legion of soldiers to barricade the city gates," I commanded Summercut. "Ready the rest of the forces now. We're marching on the eastern wall."

It was time.

Chapter 50

"Each of you chose to be here, to fight for me. To fight for *good*."

I rode up and down the frontlines as we waited at the edge of the eastern wall of Eserene. I tried to sit straight on my horse, pushing against everything that tried to weigh me down. I didn't have Katia or Rhedros to guide me today. I had to do this on my own, and though I was terrified to my core, I wasn't going to let any member of my army see it.

I was fire. I was wind. I was the storm. I was the Daughter of Benevolence and Blood, and I was going to eliminate the Saint of Pain or die in pursuit.

"I have not a single desire other than to promise you that we will triumph. I cannot make that promise. I cannot promise you that Castemont will fall. I cannot promise that good will reign supreme. And I cannot promise that you will live to see tomorrow."

My heart thundered in my ribcage at the truths I told and the lies that were to come. The armor Pavo had fashioned me was surprisingly light, but I still felt like a fucking boulder was dragging me under the surface.

"But I can promise that I will be with you, fighting alongside you, for you, for the good of the realm. I can promise that I will drain myself of every dreg of my power, every flame, every ember in the pursuit of Castemont's life." I swallowed hard, the lie burning on its way out of my mouth. "I can promise you that should we fall, I will fall with you. And I am honored, I am so honored to do so."

That was not a lie.

"They'll sing songs of this day. Your sacrifice and your glory will live on long after you're buried in the dirt. *You* are the force that protects the weak from the opportunistic. *You* are the force that protects the realm from a darkness that is more sinister than anything imaginable. When the time comes for your life to end, whether it be today or decades from now, you can die knowing that you fought for what was right."

I stared out at the thousands of people, every one of them armed to the teeth and ready to die should that be their fate. Kauvras was out there somewhere. Ludovicus was out there somewhere. Farmers and shopkeepers, cobblers and stonemasons, tailors and peddlers. Mothers and fathers. The oppressed, the beaten down, and the abused. They were all here because they believed in me.

From the deepest pits of my soul, I let out a cry that echoed off the Onyxian Mountains that loomed above us. "For the good of the realm!"

"For the good of the realm!" my army answered.

I turned to my court, my Penumbra, my *friends* as they waited patiently for me. Miles' face was stoic, but there was palpable fear behind it. Nell and Whit sat side by side, swords in hand, their horses pawing at the dirt. Summercut looked ready as I'd ever seen anyone. And Cal's eyes were alight, his mouth set in a smile. And although it was small, it beamed with admiration. I took a deep breath, and nodded to him.

432

He kicked his horse's sides, cantering down the frontlines, addressing the army. My heart skipped at the sight of him commanding my army, the strong, formidable Invisible King. My king. "Trebuchets! At the ready!"

Those who manned the trebuchets screamed. "Aye!"

This was it.

"Archers! At the ready!"

"Aye!"

It was happening.

"Cavalry! At the ready!"

"Aye!"

Everything to lose, and everything to gain.

"Infantry! At the ready!"

"Aye!"

"Soldiers of good, believers, and all those who fight on behalf of what is good and what is right!" Cal's voice boomed, commanding the attention of every single soldier. "At the ready!"

"Aye!"

"Trebuchets! Ready…aim…SHIELDS!"

Flaming arrows rained down from above, spearing soldiers throughout the lines who hadn't raised their shields in time. Heads poked over the top of the wall, almost as if the Vacants were tallying up their kills.

My voice bellowed out of me. "FIRE!"

A dozen trebuchets creaked as their arms slung forward, hurling flaming rocks at the Eserenian wall. They landed with a deafening crack, the wall rumbling with the impact.

The trebuchets launched again, stones tumbling to the ground as the wall began to weaken where it'd been hit. Another round of flaming arrows fell like hail, and it seemed like almost everyone raised their shields this time. But those who were hit, their dying screams rattled through me.

This was just the beginning.

Again and again the trebuchets launched, the wall crumbling little by little, the cavalry and infantry holding nervously in dreaded anticipation.

"Shields!"

Arrows.

Launch.

Crash.

"Petra!" Cal called, stationing his horse next to mine. "This next launch is going to be it. Are you ready?"

I leaned over, catching his helmeted cheek with my palm. "The bastard's going to die."

"That's my girl," he growled, a feral smile marking his lips.

My eyes scanned the top of the wall for any sign of an onslaught of arrows. "I'm sorry it's ending like this."

He smiled. "Don't be. I'd follow you to Hell and back."

"I led you to Hell, but I don't think I'll be leading you back."

He shrugged, staring out over the waiting soldiers. "Doesn't matter. I'm proud of you, Petra. I'm so fucking proud of you, of the woman you are, of the leader you've become. A fucking *queen*. I'm proud that I even get to walk this realm the same time you do."

"In the midst of the oncoming storm, I smiled. "You know what? I'm proud of myself, too."

He lowered his head with a fist across his chest. "Daughter of Katia, Queen of Astran, love of my life."

But I had no time to respond before the trebuchets launched and a narrow portion of the wall collapsed, the Vacants that were still atop it careening through the air.

"*Charge!*"

My beloved Inkwell opened before me as I charged headfirst to my fate, Cal at my side and the Penumbra at my back. Though the army that followed me bellowed and screamed from the depths of their souls, the only sound I heard was my own heartbeat.

Vacants rushed from all directions as we clashed with Castemont's frontlines, my sword swinging as if it acted on its own, one goal in mind: get to Castemont. The melee was all-consuming as I cut down Vacant after bloodthirsty Vacant. The army pushed forward, through the wall. *We had to be within the city walls.*

In the chaos of it all I was struck by the fact that Miles' had actually trained me to do this, and he trained me well — kill, kill, *kill.* Kill every being that stood in between me and Castemont, that stood in between me and *good.* But every chest I pierced, every limb I caught, every head I severed killed a piece of me that knew I could have saved them. Now they were going to be our ruin. Castemont's Vacants were pouring into the streets of Inkwell, so numerous they were almost on top of each other.

This was where I was meant to be. On my way to rip Castemont out at the root once and for all.

The breath was quickly stolen from my lungs by the sight of what was happening in front of me. My soldiers fell by the dozen, limbs torn from bodies by Vacants.

The air split with the boom of cannonfire from the harbor where dozens of ships were stationed, their sails rippling canvas in the wind, like they had on the day of Cindregala. *Ships?* Cannonballs fell from the sky, the screams of their victims indiscernible in the twisted symphony of death and destruction that played around us.

No.

I knew this outcome was possible. Probable. I knew that we were outnumbered, sickeningly so. From where I sat on horseback, I had the perfect vantage point to witness the downfall of every person who believed in me. But I couldn't stop to mourn. I needed to *get to the castle.*

I found Cal in the crowd, swinging his sword on horseback like it was an extension of his arm, his teeth gritted, blood spattered across his face already. Saints, if I weren't in the middle of saving the realm, I would have stopped to take in the sight. Summercut, Whit, and Nell weren't far behind, each of them skillfully cutting through flesh and bone. Where was Miles?

Cal ran his blade across the throat of a charging Vacant before he caught my stare. Even in the maelstrom that surrounded us, his mouth quirked up in that familiar way, the dimples dipping in his cheeks.

The smile fell away as he reached into his boot and threw a dagger in my direction, the blade barely missing my head and sinking into the chest of a Vacant that lunged for me from behind. He nudged his mount forward until he was alongside me, but I was suddenly knocked from my horse by another mounted soldier.

"Petra!"

The air escaped my lungs in a painful *whoosh* as I was pushed deeper into the battle. My ears still rang with the impact of the fall, and I furiously searched for Cal, but he was gone. Something about being on the ground was so much more raw, so much more grisly, and bile rose in my throat as I assumed position, my arms heaving my sword through muscle and bone.

My eyes were on Copper Street — the street I'd lived on in Inkwell. If I could get there, I could take the back alleys to the castle. Buildings began to catch fire around me. A splatter of blood hit my face from someone, somewhere.

The sound of stone on stone was unmistakable. It seemed like the battle paused for a split second to watch the hole in the city wall grow larger, wider as more of it fell. *No.* The Vacants were endless, streaming in from every direction as they pushed my army back.

I could hear the panic rise, the frantic shouts of people who realized they were fucked.

How the hell did he have such a large army? He'd only had small villages to raid with leechthorn. Summercut said Castemont would've only been able to scrape together ten thousand *at most.* This was... Something was wrong here.

Just get to the castle.

Hope was a distant friend as I made it to Copper Street to see that it, too, was shoulder-to-shoulder with Vacants. I ducked into an alley and breathed a tiny sigh of relief as I found some space to move, only a few Vacants using the narrow passage. Darting around the corners I knew so well and dodging swiping limbs, I think my mind blacked out. I coasted through the motions. Swing. Kill. Repeat.

But my consciousness returned as I was suddenly pushed against a crumbling brick building, a preternaturally strong grip on my throat, my sword knocked from my hand. I stared into the eyes of the Vacant who held me, a man who looked only a few years older than me. But those eyes... They weren't empty. There was something churning within them. It was almost like smoke billowed behind them, a swirling pool of falling ash. Something I'd never seen before.

Fight! I reached for his wrist, my vision beginning to go spotty, the number of Vacants funneling through the familiar Inkwell alley increasing. But then he smiled — a sinister, foreboding smile. This wasn't right, this wasn't a normal Vacant, and he was seconds from killing me–

His head hit the cobblestones, Miles' sword sailing through the Vacant's flesh like butter.

Chapter 51

Miles was covered in blood, panting in all his battleborn glory. "You alright?" he asked, instantly moving.

I trailed behind him. "Yes. Thank you."

"I'm getting you to that fucking castle. This has to end."

The alley spit us out onto the waterfront, cannonballs sailing overhead, Inkwell burning behind me while every inch of it crawled with Vacants. And still they flooded all the space around us, running from the direction of the castle to Inkwell.

"How the fuck are there so many of them?!" I screamed to Miles. He shook his head, moving again, cutting through as many as he could as we ran parallel to the water. The castle towered above, and I could almost feel Castemont's eyes on me. *I'm coming for you.*

I spun in place to bring my sword down across a charging Vacant's back. "Impressive," Miles shouted, his own sword sailing through the air to end another Vacant's life. "Who trained you?"

"Shut the fuck up, Miles!" I yelled. Motherfucker wanted to make jokes now?

"Get down!" He tackled me to the ground just in time for a cannonball to crash behind us.

I didn't have time to thank him before we'd scrambled to our feet and were moving again. There were so many Vacants, I had no time to take a breath between kills. Noros was here, and he was showing us the full span of his power. This was not going to end well.

My eyes caught on the harbor then as the deep blue waters began to churn unnaturally, tossing Castemont's ships side to side as if they were nothing but wooden toys in a puddle. The chaos of battle continued in spite of what was happening at the water's edge, even as the sky darkened and thunder cracked out of nowhere. The waves grew larger, some ships threatening to capsize.

It was like they materialized from nothing, a herd of wild horses emerging from the water just beyond the harbor, their hooves carrying them over the angry waves.

I blinked hard. I was hallucinating. I'd hit my head when I'd fallen from my mount and my mind was playing a twisted trick on me as it grappled with the death it was soon to meet. But Miles' steps had also faltered, his swings growing uncoordinated as his eyes saw the same thing mine did.

The herd charged on, closer and closer to the ships that bobbed in the harbor, lightning branching through the sky as thunder split the air. Stallions of saltwater and salvation.

Kelpies.

My feet moved of their own volition as I found a building with a staircase, Miles following close behind. My legs pumped faster than I'd ever known them to as I climbed the steps, desperate for a better view. The harbor was its own battlefield.

The screams that surrounded us morphed into something different then — they were no longer screams of pain and war and death. They were screams of *terror*. Fissures suddenly forked across the ground, cobblestones falling into chasms that split and widened. Soldiers and Vacants alike jumped back, scrambling away from the growing rifts. Just as quickly as the kelpies had emerged, so came the women made of stone and rock with strings of cobwebs for hair, their mouths falling open to let out ear-piercing screams.

Soulhags.

They clambered for the Vacants, their fingers of stone tearing through flesh as easily as a blade as they dismembered Vacant after Vacant. Ships in the harbor began to tip, their hulls splitting apart, the *crack* resounding through the city as the kelpies surrounded them, Vacants falling into the harbor like sand in an hourglass.

Miles stammered on the step below me. "Did you... *How?*"

"I..." Words escaped me as I watched. Hope spread through me then as I realized we may actually have a fucking chance.

But for every soulhag and kelpie there were ten Vacants, just as bloodthirsty and twice as feral. The energy that rippled from Miles began to turn as we watched my soldiers fall, wiped out by the dozen.

My eyes caught him from where I stood at the top of the staircase — Cal, *my Calomyr*, face slick with the blood of all he'd slain, his stare fixed on me from atop his horse on the waterfront, the battle raging all around him like wildfire.

His brow had been split, but his mouth turned up in a close-lipped smile. It was a smile of truth, a smile of acceptance. He nodded, reality slamming into me as if a cannonball struck me where I stood, cracking every one of my ribs to pieces.

Because *it wasn't enough*. The army, the kelpies, the soulhags. They weren't enough. The path from here to the castle was somehow a torrent of Vacants that I'd never get through. I'd built myself up so much in my head, acted like I knew what I was doing, that I thought maybe I had a chance. But it wasn't enough. I wasn't enough. I was going to die here today, and Castemont would reign on.

I nodded at Cal, and he was gone — once again swallowed by the battle.

440

"Daughter of Katia!" someone screamed from the ground level. "Daughter of Katia, please!" My eyes caught on a woman, her hands clutched to her stomach, blood pouring from around her grip as she stared, wide-eyed and frantic. "Please, heal me!"

My blood went cold as a Vacant swiped across her throat. I flinched, fighting the bile back as the blood spilled from her neck to the cobblestones.

"Daughter of Katia!" I heard again. And again. And again. A small group of soldiers had spotted me where I stood. They waved their blades through the air, trying to catch my attention. "Your Majesty! Use your powers!"

I blanched. It was all I could do to stare, completely helpless as they were cut down one by one.

"Hey." Miles nudged me, and I turned to see black eyes, pensive and proud. "Daughter of Katia," he breathed. "It's been an honor."

"I forgive you," I blurted.

His eyes widened momentarily as the words hung between us. I wanted to say something, *anything*, but I found myself speechless as he stared at me. "Thank you," he murmured, and I almost didn't hear it over the sound of warfare. "Maybe I'll see her again in another life, right? If I'm lucky."

I couldn't look at him as the meaning of his words sank in. Cielle was out there in the world somewhere, and she had no idea that she'd be the only thing on his mind as he took his last breath. I stared out at the people calling for the Daughter of Katia, begging me to heal them, pleading for me to use my powers, but I thought maybe it was Miles who was in Noros' grip. The pain in his voice was unbearable.

"Absolutely, Miles. You will see her again."

He almost seemed relieved for a moment as his lips parted in a beaming smile, pride once again washing over all of his features as he looked out over the battle then back to me. "Go down swinging."

I would.

Miles had taken the first step down the stairs when a noise began pulsing low and heavy. The battle came to a dead halt as the ground began to vibrate beneath our feet. The soldiers stopped, the Vacants stopped, the soulhags and kelpies just...stopped. Blades froze in midair, archers dropped their bows. Even the dying ceased their screaming. Utter silence descended over streets that had become a battlefield, cobblestones slick with crimson. My head swung around to the north wall, trying to discern the source of the sound that shook all of Eserene.

I was cast in shadow only for a split second as it crested the wall, wings half as wide as the castle was tall. Four more followed, soaring above the city with leathery wings. I shook my head, because this was impossible. This was utterly impossible.

"Drivas," I whispered.

I didn't know if it was blood or tears that I swiped from my cheek, but the sob broke from me then as I stared, each driva massive and terrifying, each covered in opaline black scales, each with a maw that hung open to reveal rows upon rows of glistening teeth as long as a broadsword. The city was swallowed by their menacing shadows, dirt stirred up with every wingbeat.

"Fucking *drivas*," Miles murmured from beside me, his voice thick with disbelief.

Every bone in my body shook as the largest driva's jaw opened further and angry red flames exploded from its throat to where the Vacants poured down the streets. Any of their dying screams were muffled out completely by the sound that came straight from the depths of a nightmare.

Miles pointed to the sky, identifying each one. "Rixa, Obitus, Gehenna, Ventus..." His finger hovered in the air, pointing to the largest driva as it incinerated everything in its path. "It's her. Adorex."

A sound broke through the terror then, the sound of Miles' laugh landing in my ears like the sweetest music as I watched each of the five legendary monsters reduce Castemont's forces to ash. Nell and Whit were suddenly there, somehow, both of them

442

erupting into shouts of victory. My broadsword clattered to the steps.

Adorex's serpentine neck snapped toward me at the sound of steel on stone, and even as the beast soared a hundred feet above, her eyes unmistakably locked on mine. I stood, dwarfed by this myth that wasn't supposed to exist as she watched me. Her wing-beats slowed so she hovered in place, intently staring at me with glassy, pale blue eyes.

Without thinking, I pointed to the highest tower of the castle, where I knew Castemont watched over the battle like a reaper.

The driva blinked once, some kind of knowing in her gaze before she turned in midair. Mighty, massive wings pounded hard, eyes set on the tower as she gained altitude. As if they were of a single mind, the four other drivas moved in the same direction, the mass of beasts converging on the place where I knew Castemont waited.

This moment... I relished the feeling, the anticipation, the knowledge that the fucking bastard was staring out the window of the stone tower, panic seeping into his muscles as he realized he was going to die, and he was going to die in an *inferno*. Screams of both terror and triumph sounded around me as the drivas surrounded the tower, their heads cocked back, their jaws wide and dripping.

Waiting.

My voice was a whisper, but they heard it loud and clear. "Now."

The roars that ripped from their throats were beyond deafening, every district of Eserene quaking and rumbling and burning as each of the five drivas unleashed fury unparalleled.

The flames kept coming, the sandstone castle quickly turning black in the heat of the fire, whole sections of it beginning to disintegrate and crumble. I held my breath as the tower began to teeter. And as the drivas let their flames die, the castle crumbled to the ground in a heap of smoking rubble, the Saint of Pain along with it.

Chapter 52

The castle that once stood was replaced by a column of billowing black smoke.

No ships remained in the harbor, and I watched as a wave rose and crashed over the herd of kelpies. When it calmed, the herd was gone, returning to lurk in the deep. The soulhags climbed back into the rifts they'd opened in the ground, the massive canyons cracking shut behind them.

Five pairs of wings slowed their beating until each landed on the ground, their talons scraping across ashy debris while their nostrils flared and huffed. Adorex clawed at the stone, her icy eyes locked on me. I descended the staircase, watching her as she watched me, my breath heaving in and out as I tried to come to terms with what just happened.

With a single hand raised, I approached her, disbelief the only thing propelling me forward. She lowered her serpentine neck, her head just feet from the ground. A low growl rumbled in her throat as she pushed her snout forward, teeth gleaming where they jutted from her maw. The fear was undeniable, but I gently laid my hand against the scales above her nose, breath huffing from her flaring nostrils as she stared at me. She was a myth, a fearsome legend that never existed, yet here she was.

I let out a deep breath before she pulled away, great wings beginning to move and lift her off the ground. The other drivas followed, their massive forms soaring over the city. Adorex slowed her wings once again and landed atop the north wall. Massive talons scraped against stone as she tipped her head to the sky and erupted into a roar so thunderous that I swore the Onyxian Mountains trembled where they stood. The other drivas joined in where they hovered, letting out roars that I knew could be heard throughout the realms and the Darkness Beyond. The most beautiful noise I'd ever heard.

Adorex took off then, massive and terrifying and beautiful, the other four beasts following behind her, leaving Eserene smoldering in their wake.

Smoke and disbelief hung in the air, a fragile silence descending as the skies cleared and the sun shone again. Even my own heartbeat quieted in my ears as I stood in awe of the castle I'd stared up at my entire life, now reduced to nothing but embers and ashes.

Another roar started, but this one was much less menacing. It was quiet at first, slowly growing louder as cheers rippled through the streets, sweeping each and every survivor in its wake as the feeling of victory set in. Noros, Saint of Pain, was dead. Castemont was *dead*.

I wanted to see him. My feet moved of their own accord as I took off for the pile of rubble, each step purposeful as it carried me toward what remained of the man who'd pulled the strings of every destructive force in my life.

"Petra!" It was Cal, emerging from the cheering crowd, his footsteps quickly catching up to mine as I climbed over debris.

"I have to see," I answered, my eyes intent on the pile of rubble. "I have to see for myself."

He said nothing, simply following behind me as I carefully stepped through the wreckage, ascending the mountain of ash.

An eerie smoke clung to the stones in a way that was almost unnatural — it wasn't stirred up by my footfalls, didn't dissipate or float off like it should have. It was different than the smoke that floated into the air... It was thicker, almost opaque. I narrowed my eyes but kept moving, determined to make it to the top, determined to find what remained of the man who had so thoroughly ruined–

As if someone had simply summoned it, the smoke began to move up the pile. "Petra," I heard Cal call from behind me, his voice apprehensive as his footsteps halted.

"What the hell are you doing?" Miles' voice sounded nearby.

I ignored them both, climbing further, higher, closer. The smoke had grown thicker, still clinging to the rubble but traveling upward, a sour feeling settling low in my gut at the unnatural sight. Angry clouds rolled across the sky then, the sun blotted out within seconds, casting the city in a supernatural darkness.

"This isn't right," I whispered to myself. Something was happening.

Thunder cracked so loud my brain rattled in my skull, the smoke amassing in a swirling cloud at the top of the charred stones.

I blinked as I took in the scene before me. A charred body lifted from the rubble like a ghost, hands and feet burned away, features indiscernible as it rose through the air. Smoke surrounded it, obscuring it from view for a split second before revealing Castemont's figure, completely unburned.

Only it wasn't Castemont as I'd known him. It was like his figure was made purely of shadow and that unnatural smoke. I could tell it was him, but he was only swirling gray and black.

My jaw clenched as I swallowed against the panicked nausea that rose in my throat. I was shocked into silence.

He cocked an antagonistic brow. "Hello, Petra. I'd like to re-introduce myself."

My teeth ground together in furious disbelief. "Noros," I seethed.

The Saint of Pain threw his head back and cackled, smoke swirling around him. "Noros?" He lifted his arms, more smoke rising around him. "I'm afraid you're mistaken, dear." Crackling blue flames ignited beneath him, blue flames I recognized from some distant nightmare…

Realization hit me like a fist to the gut, the air leaving my lungs just as quickly.

The Vacant who'd almost killed me, his eyes — that same swirling mass of shadow and smoke. And there were so many Vacants, *too* many Vacants…

Because they weren't Vacants at all. They weren't even human. They were demons of the Occulti, created and commanded by their demon lord.

"Malosym."

A wry smile broke across his face as the blue flames grew, the smoky figure rising higher into the air as thunder roared over the city, the smoke around him growing darker and thicker.

"Mother*fucker*," I snarled, lunging for his figure with no plan, only rage.

"Petra!" I heard Cal and Miles scream in unison, starting toward me.

Malosym threw out a bolt of blue flame, lightning crackling around it. Cal managed to duck just enough that it only grazed the side of his head, but–

"Miles!" I screamed in terror, watching the bolt knock him backward into the rubble. Cal cried out for his brother at the sight of his chest split open, the edges of the massive wound charred and smoking. "*No!*"

I started toward Miles, but I was knocked back as a pillar of black smoke and blue flames shot to the sky, the noise straight from the depths of Hell as Malosym's figure was swallowed whole.

He was gone.

Something glinted in his place. I knew I should go to Miles, but the draw was undeniable. I knew Cal was probably calling me back. But I was unable to hear anything as I realized it was a dagger. *My dagger.*

I snatched it from the rubble, turning it over in my hand to realize the inscription on the blade was gone.

"Petra!" Cal yelled again.

I whirled to where he kneeled over Miles, but a cloud of smoke materialized around me and the ground cracked open beneath me. I was sucked into a chasm, falling, spiraling, grappling for anything as I screamed at the top of my lungs, confusion and fear and–

Nothing. I stopped. I didn't hit the ground. I'd just stopped, and there seemed to be solid ground beneath my feet, but no impact. Darkness closed in around me. I looked down and saw no body, tried to flex my hands but they weren't there.

"Hello?" I shouted, my voice breaking with terror, because I knew exactly where I was.

Malosym's voice slithered into my ear, a hiss as he said, "Welcome to the Darkness Beyond."

Thank you for reading!
Reviews are extremely helpful for authors. Thank you for
taking the time to support me and my work.

COMING SOON
Untitled Novella: Miles Landgrave's Story
Untitled: Book 3 of the Benevolence & Blood Series
Untitled Prequel: The Birth of Benevolence & Blood

ACKNOWLEDGEMENTS

To my OG beta readers this time around, Samantha Guidry, Matrasa Connolly, Amber Peterson, Kristi Cole, Brigitte McGuirk, Taylor Moon, Renée Godinez, Vesta Nicol, Patsy Brown, and my TSoS betas who stuck around in the Facebook group — Holy shit. I can't believe you all hung in there through this past year. I am beyond thankful for every single bit of feedback you gave me. You all know TBoB's beta process was a lot different than the beta process for TSoS. I gave you guys a MUCH rougher draft this time than I did last time, and still you all ate it up. So thank you from the bottom of my heart. I love when I get to tell my author friends about my beta team, because I truly feel I have the one around.

To the beta readers I enlisted to read the almost-final product, thank you for swooping in to save the day. Emily Firth, Shelby Rossiter, and Alexandra Moyer, you guys gave me so much reassurance that the story was working, and I can't thank you enough for all the hype.

To the person who answered my character naming poll with the name Malosym — you said Malosim would look better with a *y* and damn were you right. You didn't leave your Instagram handle, so if you're reading this and it was you, let me know so I can thank you properly in the next book. Until then, thank you, you sweet nameless badass.

To Ivy at Beautiful Book Covers, you once again slayed. You are one of the reasons this series has become as popular as it has, because yes, people do judge a book by its cover, and the judges give this one a perfect 10. You are so incredibly talented, and I'll never be able to thank you enough for using that talent to make me the book covers of my dreams.

To my street team, you guys are some of my favorite people. I feel so blessed to have you all in my corner, constantly hyping me up and pushing me to keep going. I'll never get over the fact that there are people who like my work enough that they want to be on my street team. Shit's wild. I love you all.

To the Bitches group chat — Jennifer Rogers, Ashley Garner, Jessica Pettry, Chelsea (almost Hunzinger!!!) Fredrickson, and Maddie Neumann, what a fucking hot mess we are. I love us so much. Thank you for keeping me laughing with the most unhinged TikToks. I'm so happy my son gets the best feral aunties/cousins because of you guys. And to Cody Rogers, Alex Garner, and James Cook, what a treat it is to be one of ya gals. Forever thankful for each and every one of you.

Special thanks to Ashley Garner, the event assistant who gives me bombastic side eye when I give away stuff for free, the boba tea-bringer and plot-hole sounding board. Thanks for running around at events and waiting in line to get me the stuff I want. But I'm not going to stop giving away stuff for free.

To Lauren Peel, the friend I miss so much, I love you!!! I need a bullshit session, a classic Lauren Lauren mess-around STAT. Thank you for always including me in the tea when it's still piping hot.

To Bianca Bongiorno, the freaking mastermind behind my logo and branding, one of my very best friends in the entire world, and the absolute kindest soul you could ever meet. I can't even express how happy I am to still call you a friend after all these years. So much has changed over the last few years but we haven't. So happy we met in a Publix on a hot July day. Love love love you, and Jess too.

To Claire Hawley (soon-to-be-Harmon), it's freaking go-time. Commence Operation Harmon Wedding. All aboard the Key West Hot Mess Express, conductor: me. Choo choo bitch. I'm so so so excited to celebrate you, and I'm so happy that we're still friends. Good ol' college roommates, they'll always getcha.

To all my amazing friends, whether they be school friends or bookish friends or mom friends or anything in between, thank you for being there for me.

To Dr. Christy Moore, I love you, I miss you, and I'm proud of you. So much has changed since this time last year, but what hasn't is my love for you and all you do. I'm so happy to know you and honored to have been a part of your journey. I'm a better person because I met you. We've laughed until we cried and cried until we laughed, and I know that's not ending anytime soon. You are a badass, an amazing doctor, and an even better friend. I love you forever!

To Lauren Cox, my right hand gal, thank you for always reassuring me that it's okay to ask for help. I'm so happy I met you through this process. I will be asking you to dress me in the near future, fair warning.

God dammit. I knew the second I started writing this book that I was going to have to write the acknowledgement to the wloe group chat, Anna Guinta and Julia Kon. I don't think that our friendship is healthy for multiple reasons — it is built upon a foundation of bullying each other, we literally talk all day every single day, and we've all said things that can absolutely not be repeated. But, like I said in the TSoS acknowledgements, we will be friends forever. See you both in Hell. Also a shout out to Devlin for drinking Anna's wine, a shout out to Justin for finally taking down the blue painter's tape, and a shout out to Max for saying the F-word a lot.

To my mother-in-law, Ann, when I say this book wouldn't exist without you, I mean this book would absolutely not exist without you. The hours and hours you've spent babysitting so I could hole up in the man cave and write or edit... You truly are the reason this book is out (so I hope my use of the F-word and other questionable topics doesn't embarrass you too much). You are the absolute best mother-in-law and friend I could ask for, and I'm so incredibly lucky to have you.

To my mom, Little Debbie, Classic Deb, the encouragement and the laughs are the fuel behind this book. You've believed in every single thing I've ever done. I could tell you I'm going to become a deep-sea fishing boat captain and you'd be waiting on the dock the next morning with your sunscreen and giant hat. You are the reason I've never shied away from a goal. Thanks for all the time spent helping me prep for events (stuffing and labeling 689 teabags was not for the weak) and the late nights and early mornings helping me finish whatever random project I decided to take on. I swear on my life that Petra's mom is not inspired by you.

To my siblings, Steve, Lexi, and Paige, I am so so so freaking excited to be reunited again sometime soon. Maybe we can convince Steve to play bulldog like the old days. Don't ever forget to stop or I'll start, and I really mean it. I love you all.

To Keely Maldonado, my literal soul sister, my lifeline, I can't even explain how happy I am to know you. You never fail to make me laugh, and you've given my family the ultimate gift. You are a huge reason why this book is finished and out in the world. I will never ever ever be able to repay you. Thanks for being you.

A shout out to the Hyperemesis Education and Research Foundation for helping me through the absolute hardest time in my life. For those that don't know, I suffered from hyperemesis gravidarum during my pregnancy, an extreme type of pregnancy sickness involving incessant nausea and vomiting. It started just a few days after TSoS was released and it lasted all the way until I gave birth. It was a surreal feeling to be so incredibly happy to be having a baby but wildly depressed because of this sickness. The HER Foundation was the reason I knew what to ask my doctor in order to get the help I needed. I'm a bit scarred from the whole ordeal but so proud to be among a group of warriors who experienced HG. I wouldn't wish it on my worst enemy (maybe Castemont). If you're interested in learning more, check out hyperemesis.org.

To Joyce Fernandez, officially ReJoyce Literary Editing Co., dude. Where do I even start? You were one of the first people I told I was pregnant, and you watched me go through the darkest time in my life. You never failed to be a cheerleader or a shoulder to cry on, and you didn't leave even when I completely isolated myself. You always told me I'd come out of it, and you were right. And we're BACK! When I say you did all the things, I mean you did all. the. things. I gave you a massive pile of stinky coal and you polished it into a freaking diamond. It was so incredible to be in the rhythm again and watch you grow as an editor. You have a true talent for this and I'm so excited to see where it takes you. You've become one of my closest friends, and I wouldn't trade it for the world. I cannot WAIT for Apollycon!!!

To Steven... You are quite literally the reason I survived this past year, always making sure I was fed and hydrated so our little boy could grow. You wiped every tear, held me up when I couldn't stand, and gave me the strength to keep going. They say a baby's first year is hard on a marriage, but I've only fallen more in love with you. Watching you become a dad has been the greatest joy of my life. Seeing you with Everett... I am the luckiest girl in the entire world. You work harder than anyone I know, all to give me everything I've always dreamed of. I'm so proud of the life we've built and are still building together, with Everett, Sadie, and Sport. Thank you for always making me laugh with Nick and Schmidt quotes (twenty-noine), always being there when I need you, and always bringing me my towel when I forget to hang it up by the bathtub. Love you to Gallifrey and back.

And finally, to Everett — I would do it all again in a heartbeat, without question. You are the love of our lives, and watching you grow and learn has been the most indescribable feeling. Your smile is the absolute best thing in the world, and I can't wait to see who you become (but don't grow up too fast). I promise I will never take a single moment for granted. You are so incredibly loved and will be forever.

Lauren M. Leasure is the author of The Benevolence & Blood Series. She's an avid fantasy reader and a lover of all things mystical and magical.

A Maine native, she moved around quite a bit growing up but is now content to call Florida home.

When she's not writing, she's thinking about writing, baking sourdough bread, and spending time with her husband, Steven, their son, Everett, and their dogs, Sadie and Sport.

www.ingramcontent.com/pod-product-compliance
Lightning Source LLC
Chambersburg PA
CBHW031952150726
47990CB00005B/1675